THE
INHERITANCE

BOOKS BY SAMANTHA HAYES

The Reunion

Tell Me A Secret

The Liar's Wife

Date Night

The Happy Couple

Single Mother

The Trapped Wife

The Ex-Husband

The Engagement

THE
INHERITANCE

SAMANTHA HAYES

bookouture

Published by Bookouture in 2023

An imprint of Storyfire Ltd.
Carmelite House
50 Victoria Embankment
London EC4Y 0DZ

www.bookouture.com

ISBN: 978-1-83790-689-5
eBook ISBN: 978-1-83790-688-8

For my dear son, Ben – my shining light
'Love you forever'

PROLOGUE

The rain shrouded the loch, almost as if the weather knew a body was being recovered, that the poor visibility would provide dignity, privacy, a veil for the onlookers – shielding them from the grim scene. The misty, grey air pulsed neon blue from the ambulance and police car lights, the first responders having arrived within twenty minutes of the emergency call. Radio static crackled around them as an officer reported to base.

Mountain rescue on scene... at least one deceased... recovery in progress...

Three emergency vehicles were parked at angles in the parking area where, a few days ago, the family had unpacked supplies for an afternoon of fun. And indeed, they'd all enjoyed the shores of Loch Muir many times over the years, when the children were small, right up until now with children of their own.

Except one of those children from decades ago had never got to paddle in the icy water or sit astride an inflatable dolphin or peck at ham sandwiches on a tartan rug, grinning up at the sun like their siblings had. Not that anyone knew this.

Until now.

The loch, the scenery, the mists that came down like a cloak over the hills had a way of keeping secrets, of burying the past.

The group clung on to each other, shivering, waiting, watching as the tragic scene unfolded. Someone was crying – a soft whimper, a face covered. Another was agitated, pacing – their erratic movements showing their anger, frustration, disbelief.

How had their family holiday turned into this horror? How had none of them seen this coming? Like the storms that lurked behind the mountains – one moment cascades of sun lighting up the heathered moors, the next shards of lightning stabbing at the drenched hills – life had turned on a dime.

Their sobs and cries and silent guilt went unnoticed by the tireless crew, who put their own lives in danger to retrieve the body. A rescue worker trudged past the group, a grim look on his face as he carried a white trainer and a blood-soaked jacket, each sealed inside a clear plastic bag.

Only when the stretcher – with its scarlet nylon covering concealing the horrors within – was finally lowered down the rocks, its contents bound in place with black webbing, did the chilling reality hit them.

One of them was dead.

And one of them was a killer.

PART I

ONE

KATE

A week earlier

Kate looked out of the top-floor window of the lodge, a pile of fresh towels in her arms. 'I see car headlights!' she trilled, calling out to anyone who might be listening. 'They'll be here any minute.'

She squinted through the darkness, waiting for the cones of light to reappear through the trees to make sure she hadn't imagined it. A flickering beacon in the blackness surrounding the lodge. *There* – it had to be them. Very few cars came this far into the forest, especially on a rainy evening. While it was still August, just, the weather had been mixed since they'd arrived on Wednesday a couple of days ago. The air hung humid and heavy, thick with drizzle and midges – so much so that it was hard to tell raindrop from insect. But that hadn't mattered as Kate had been busy with her mother sorting out the bedrooms, preparing for everyone's arrival. Ten whole days together. The whole family. *Almost.*

'Be a bloody miracle if there isn't a murder, all of us lot

together,' her husband, Adrian, had said on the long drive up from the Midlands.

Kate knew that while there wouldn't be an *actual* murder, there was still truth in what he'd said. When her mother had planned the family gathering only a month ago, she'd been insistent that they all come, but as yet, no one had dared ask why. Kate couldn't help wondering who would be most likely to kill who. Briefly, she was reminded of the dangers of mixing cleaning chemicals, the way you might inadvertently make a kind of bomb. The Hunter family felt like a similar concoction.

Kate placed the towels on the end of the double bed. The lodge hadn't been used for over a year and all the bedding had smelt slightly damp when they'd arrived, so she'd done what seemed like a gazillion loads of washing, freshening everything up. She and her mother had cleaned the entire place, stocking the fridge and freezer with plenty of food, while Adrian had driven the twenty miles or so to Ayr and brought back a carload of alcohol. She wanted this break to be perfect for everyone. God knows, after everything that had happened this year, they all needed it.

She went downstairs to the living area, casting her eyes around. A cluster of candles flickered on the mantelpiece and, while it wasn't cold enough to light the actual fire, they made the space seem cosy and inviting. Mia, Kate's daughter, sat on one of the two large sofas, her legs curled under her and her eyes skimming her Kindle. That was Mia – nose always in a book. Her twin brother, Finn, was the opposite and likely in his room FaceTiming a mate back home, chatting about whether he'd missed any action from their beloved football team. Though so far, he'd been frustrated because 4G was patchy around here and the Wi-Fi speed was dragging at best. Her eighteen-year-old twins were perfect clichés, she knew that – they could be straight out of an American high school movie.

White-blond hair, top marks at school, and not a bad bone in their bodies. She loved them dearly.

And then there was Adrian. Yes. Of *course* Adrian. She banished her thoughts. Right there and then. No place for them. Nope. She'd been trying so hard lately to not feel less than a whole, as if she wasn't enough for him.

Or he wasn't enough for her.

In the kitchen area at the other end of the lodge, Kate's mother, Connie, was at the stove, stirring something in a big pot. Rich gravy smells permeated the air – almost visible, thick and brown, spiralling up from the pan.

'I know it's getting late, but they'll be hungry after their journey,' Connie said. 'We all know Theo eats for England.'

Kate slid an arm around her mother's slim waist, not recalling any instances of Theo overeating. It was hard to imagine – the boy was a wisp and didn't seem to have changed much since he was fourteen when they'd first met him. She'd only encountered him a handful of times since her sister, Darby, had got together with Theo's dad, Travis, three years ago, and her overriding memory of the teen was of him skulking around like a hand-drawn stick character that had somehow prised itself off the paper.

'Smells delicious,' Kate said, resting her head on her mother's shoulder. 'But you're not to be chief cook and washer-upper the whole time, OK? There are enough of us to take turns. You need a break more than any of us.'

Connie smiled up at her eldest daughter. 'And you,' she said, sweeping a strand of grey hair from her face. They both knew how easy it was to fall into the role of carer – satisfying everyone else's needs before even thinking about their own. It was a hard habit to break.

'Oh, I think that's them!' Hearing the crunch of tyres on gravel, Kate turned and went to the window, pulling back the thick plum and navy tartan curtains. While the soft furnishings weren't exactly bang on trend, the lodge had a certain vintage vibe about it now, having been decorated by her parents when her father, Ray, had inherited the place in the late seventies. He'd dubbed it Hunters' Castle – though it was far from grand. Remote-log-cabin-in-the-woods-that-was-a-squash-for-everyone was a far more fitting description of Kirk View Lodge. Since the Hunter girls – Kate, Darby and Bea – had grown up, their parents had encouraged them all to make good use of the lochside retreat whenever they could and, indeed, Kate, Adrian and the twins had spent many a relaxing summer or New Year up here. Just not lately.

Since their father's death in May, three months ago, Kate had gently hinted to her mother that perhaps it was time to sell the lodge or maybe rent it out through Airbnb. It was expensive to maintain and upkeep, not to mention the worry of having it sitting empty for many months of the year. But Connie wouldn't hear of it. 'Your father's blood and sweat are in the very fabric of it,' she'd insisted. 'I'm not selling it or having strangers stay, final answer.'

'Darby's here!' Kate sang out, letting the curtains fall closed again.

Mia looked up from her Kindle, a slight frown creeping across her face. She snapped the cover closed and straightened her legs, sitting upright as if she was bracing herself for something. 'It'll be fine...' Kate mouthed at her as she headed for the lodge door, but the look she got from Mia in return reignited the knot of concern in her stomach that she'd been trying to convince herself meant nothing.

As she opened the front door, a gust of wind sent a lash of rain across the threshold. Kate shoved her feet into a pair of old green Crocs and ventured outside into the darkness, pulling up the hood on her sweatshirt and clamping her arms around her body. The ground felt soft and springy underfoot from all the pine needles that fell every year.

'Darbs!' she called out, shielding her face from the drizzle. 'You're here!'

'Katie!' A female figure emerged from the passenger seat and Darby, Kate's slightly younger sister, peeled herself out, arching her back. Then her face broke into a broad grin, her straight white teeth and sparkling eyes seeming to light up the forest.

Kate ran up and flung herself at her sister. 'God, it's so good to see you,' she said over her shoulder, holding her tight. 'How was your journey?' Then she held her at arm's length and drank her in. They'd not seen each other since their father's funeral, and even then she'd noticed she'd lost weight, how quiet she'd been – especially when they'd said their goodbyes that evening. But even more seemed to have dropped off her in the intervening months. Two dark halos sat beneath Darby's eyes – perhaps just smudged mascara or exhaustion from the long drive – and her usually long, dark hair had been chopped into a layered jaw-length cut with a messy fringe that gave her an almost androgynous appearance. Her usual staple of jeans, trainers and a faded, capped-sleeve black T-shirt added to the effect.

'Tiring and endless,' Darby said, beaming out another grin. 'Just getting out of London took ages.' Kate relaxed a little when she saw her smile. The Darby she knew was still there. Just a little... concealed. A little *less*. 'Not to mention the number of times we had to keep stopping for Charlie.'

As Darby opened the rear door of the car, Kate spotted Charlie's soft blond hair stuck to his forehead as he lolled to one side, asleep in his car seat. Her heart warmed to see her two-year-old nephew coming round from his snooze. She couldn't wait to take him down to the loch for a paddle, show him how to use a fishing net, perhaps go out on a little boat if they could find a life jacket small enough for him.

Then her eyes darted to the driver's side of the car, where a tall figure emerged from the shadows. She heard a deep groan as the man stretched out, turning to face her over the roof. Their eyes locked for a moment, until the drizzle caused Kate to blink, but there were no smiles exchanged, no warm greetings or stepping into each other's arms for a welcome hug.

'Hello, Kate,' he said flatly, before opening the other rear door of the car, holding it wide.

'Travis,' Kate replied, giving him a nod. Her eyes darted to the final passenger as he wormed out of the car, the hood of his black sweatshirt virtually obscuring his face. A tall, wiry figure stood there. 'And hello, Theo,' Kate said to Travis's seventeen-year-old son. Every time she saw him, she reminded herself that he wasn't Darby's son, not their flesh and blood. *Thank God.* 'Come in before you all get drenched. Adrian will fetch your bags.'

Darby shielded Charlie's head as she ran to the lodge door, while Travis and Theo sauntered up behind, not seeming to care if they got soaked. Inside, Connie greeted everyone in the usual flap of hugs and exclamations of excitement with Kate's black Labrador, Scout, running circles around them, thumping his tail against their legs. Except this time, the reunion was overlaid with a sense of sadness and grief.

Because one of them wasn't here. The Hunter clan was a man down.

'Hey, Travis mate,' Kate heard Adrian say as he joined them, aware of her husband and Darby's partner doing that blokey thing of not-quite-handshake and not-quite-hug. Back-slapping and hand-gripping. A bit awkward.

And then Adrian turned to Darby, who suddenly thrust Charlie at Kate to hold. The toddler smelt of biscuits and sleep as he nuzzled her neck and writhed on her hip. Kate watched the two of them. Just as she had at the funeral. The hug between her husband and sister was brief – briefer than a regular hug, one could argue. But she noticed the way Adrian's fingers curled around Darby's shoulder blade angled beneath her T-shirt, their faces close. And she didn't miss the flare of their eyes syncing as they pulled away, rejoining the clamour of their arrival as the twins gathered around to say hello. *Yes*, Kate thought as she made cooing noises at Charlie, *I'll just keep watching and let's see.*

TWO

CONNIE

Hunters' Castle feels alive again, Connie thought with an inner smile as she submerged herself in the happy, noisy swamp of her family. It would be even more of a squash when Bea arrived, but oh, how she'd waited for this moment to come, after everything. And how she'd braced herself for the unbearable void that would sit, darkly, at the centre of them all – though she knew he'd still somehow command a larger presence than anyone physically present simply because he was always on her mind.

As she'd said in her eulogy at the funeral, a ray had indeed gone out of all their lives. *Her* Ray – the man, the husband, the father, the grandad. She'd never imagined a time when she'd have to exist without him – or even be able to. But here she was, within the safety of her family, doing just that.

But another shadow loomed over her, too – the reason she'd invited everyone in the first place. Though whether she'd find the courage to tell her daughters about their father's will was another matter. It was constantly playing on her mind – how to break the news to them. Not to mention the hurt and anger that would follow. There would be questions – *so* many questions –

and answering them truthfully would take all her courage, leading her down a path she never thought she'd have to tread.

But the time for honesty had finally come. She hated lying to her daughters, and they had a right to know the truth about the past.

'Oh my, Charlie,' Connie crooned. 'What *has* Mummy been feeding you? You've grown so big.' She tickled her grandson under the chin, making the toddler shy away.

'He loves all food, it would seem,' Darby said, wrangling her son back from Kate. Connie watched her girls. *Two* of her girls. Her youngest daughter wouldn't be here for another day or so. *Whenever I can get away, Ma,* she'd sung out on the phone the other night. Little Bea... the last of her trio. She closed her eyes for a moment, like she always did when she thought of her daughters. Her reasons for living. For *staying*.

'Right, come in properly, you lot. Let's not stand in the doorway all night. Make yourselves right at home.'

Connie ushered everyone towards the living area with its two L-shaped sofas angled around the fireplace.

'Who's for a drink?' Connie fielded the requests fired back at her, trying to memorise them. It felt strange, playing both host and hostess. While the wider family had often used the lodge over the years in varying combinations, when they'd all been here together, it had been her and Ray, side by side, orchestrating the ballet of their gatherings. Between them, they'd put on a good show. *A fine act,* she'd always thought.

'I'll help, Mum,' Kate said, taking her arm and giving it a squeeze as they retreated to the kitchen.

'The place feels alive again,' Connie said quietly as they counted out cups and glasses. She looked up at her eldest daughter, waiting for a reaction, waiting for her to acknowledge the same pain as she had in the knot of her heart. It was beating to an unknown rhythm, an unfamiliar tune.

'It does,' Kate replied, glancing over. The little smile she added told Connie that she felt the void too but didn't want to mention it. Not now. Perhaps not ever. These ten days were meant to be about rebuilding, restoring, making good in the fallout from losing Ray. And Connie would do anything to protect that outcome – especially once she'd sat her daughters down and broken the news.

Together, they carried two trays of drinks and snacks over to the living area, where everyone was sitting and chatting, the layers of sound seeming to warm the interior. 'Right, you wanted red wine, Darby, and Theo, this is for you.' Theo leant across and silently took the Peroni. No one said a word about him only being seventeen. The Hunters weren't like that and believed nothing in moderation would kill you. *Except for Bea*, Connie thought fondly as she passed a cup of tea to Mia and another beer to Finn. Bea would have asked for an organic matcha tea or freshly pressed exotic juice of some kind.

'What are you laughing at, Mum?' Darby said, shoving up so Connie could sit down.

'Just you lot,' she said warmly. 'Being here.' Then she coughed, noticing what had caught in her throat. Smoke. 'Oh, you don't need to bother with that, Travis,' she said to his back as she spotted him kneeling in front of the fireplace, a band of flesh showing above his jeans. Connie's eyes lingered for a moment. 'I can put the heating on if anyone's cold.'

Travis twisted around, eyes flicking at his audience as he pushed back his thick black hair. It seemed that everyone always held their breath when he was about to speak.

'My fault for shivering,' Darby chimed. 'I'm not used to the chilly evening air up here.'

'Shall I light it or not?' came Travis's voice, heavy with his south London accent.

'Oh, go on, then, why not,' Connie replied, taking her own glass of wine off the tray. There was no need for a stand-off – not like there once would have been. She drew in a long sip of her drink, hoping that would distract her from saying anything else, such as how Ray never allowed the fires to be lit before the first of September, that it was his way of heralding in the autumn. A tradition. *Ray's way*. Instead, she sighed the thought from her mind and smiled, clasping her fingers around her glass.

Travis and Darby had been together nearly three years now, having met when Darby was thirty-five. Connie had never aired her thoughts about her daughter's choice of man, of course she hadn't, but there was something about him that... that *grated*. As yet, she'd been unable to name the feelings he stirred inside her, but they were the polar opposite of the way she felt about Kate's husband, Adrian, for instance. Whereas his intentions were always for the benefit of others, she didn't get that feeling from Travis, as though he was always trying to prove his worth – knowing he wasn't quite good enough for a Hunter girl, that he didn't match up to the memory of Chris, Darby's first husband. And God, don't get her started on how all that must have rubbed off on Theo, Travis's son from his previous relationship. Because something had bloody well turned the boy sour.

But these were all silent thoughts. Little observations she'd filed away over the few years she'd known the Walsh men. Or man and *boy*, she thought. Despite being seventeen, Theo was far from an adult and always seemed – what was the word she was looking for? *Pasty*. Yes, that's it. As if he was only half cooked. Raw.

'So, what's the plan, Stan?' Darby said, wiping dribble from Charlie's chin.

'Dinner won't be long. I know it's getting late, but I figured you'd all be hungry,' Connie said.

Travis turned again. 'We ate on the motorway,' he said, wafting another plume of smoke as it billowed from the fire. Connie could tell him he was doing it all wrong, explain about the quirky draw of the chimney, but she didn't. The peace needed to be kept for as long as possible.

'I meant what's the plan for the days ahead, Mum, but that sounds great. I'm starving.' Darby eyed Travis, a little scowl crossing her brow. Then Connie felt the warmth of Darby's touch on her arm – a gentle stroke that told her *He doesn't mean to sound gruff, Mum...*

'Here, open this vent, mate. It'll help the airflow,' Adrian said, weaving between everyone's feet to get to the woodburner.

Travis stared up at him from the floor and Connie observed – noticed the jut of his stubbled jaw, the way he pulled back his shoulders, his big hands clasped together. The pause before he spoke, as if he was fighting to contain something.

'Right, thanks for the tip. Spot the townie, eh?'

The two men laughed together, chinking bottles, making Connie show a smile as her shoulders relaxed a little. Adrian had a way with everyone, and she felt that he was the closest to filling the void Ray had left behind. Not a perfect fit, of course, but someone she could rely on to help take some of the load. *To help defuse a situation*, she told herself. Because God knows, with what she'd gathered them all here to announce, she knew there would soon be one.

THREE

DARBY

'Can you hear it?' Darby whispered. The room was dark, though the thin chink of light at the top of the blackout curtains told her that it was morning. Charlie had woken her from a shallow, restless slumber several times in the night, causing what, she convinced herself, was plain old exhaustion. Nothing else. Nothing untoward or linked to the growing sense that her mother had invited them all here for a reason. Her son lay in the travel cot next to their bed, emitting sweet snuffles every few seconds.

'Hear what?' Travis whispered back. Though his whisper was more of a low growl.

'A corncrake. Listen.'

For a few seconds, Travis and Darby lay perfectly still side by side, each of them focused on the sound of nothing.

'There,' Darby said quietly.

'Sounds like a rusty hinge to me,' Travis replied, suddenly turning on his side.

'Shh, it's really rare. Listen...'

But the bed creaking and Travis's noisy breathing, as well as him tossing the duvet about as he shoved out a long, hairy leg, blocked out the call of the bird. Growing up, her father had taught Darby what to listen for, explained about all the different birds in the area, told her how far they'd travelled to spend the summer in Scotland.

'What, you mean it's flown all the way from Africa?' she'd asked as a spellbound little girl, shaky binoculars pushed against her eyes in the rickety hide her father had made from fallen branches, twigs, bracken and moss.

'Yes, Africa. Incredible.' Her dad had laughed, pulling her close for a hug. 'Your grandma used to say that the call of the corncrake meant the grim reaper was coming to take someone, that the birds were warning of his approach.'

Darby hadn't known what the grim reaper was back then but had thought it sounded scary. She'd watched as her father opened the wax paper-wrapped packets of sandwiches her mum had made for them, and they'd shared them in the moss-scented hide, discussing what route the bird would have taken to get here from Africa, and how many flaps its wings would have had to make. A trillion and fifty-nine was Darby's best guess. *And a half*, her father had added with a wink. Then, later, back at the lodge, they'd sketched all the birds they'd spotted that day, cutting them out and sticking them to the fridge for everyone to see. Kate had watched on, silent and staring, as she'd sat alone with her book.

'I miss him so much,' Darby said now, her face close to Travis's. 'Dad.'

'I know you do,' he replied, laying a hand on her hip. 'I know.'

As the bird rasped out its call again, Darby couldn't help wondering if it was a warning that the grim reaper was on his way again – and who he was coming to take.

. . .

'Mum, what on earth time did you get up?' Darby asked, guilt powering through her as she approached her mother, who was standing at the stove, three pans on the go and the salty, fatty smell of bacon filling the air. Connie was dressed in a pair of soft navy trousers and a matching fleece, though she still seemed to make casual clothes seem elegant – the simple jewellery she wore, her grey hair styled in an updo, a light touch of make-up.

'Early enough to catch the sunrise by the loch,' Connie admitted. 'Coffee's in the pot.'

Darby kissed her mother's cheek and poured herself a mug, cupping it with hands covered by the long sleeves of her sweater. She'd already deposited Charlie on the floor in the sitting room with a tub of plastic bricks and a rusk to amuse him.

When the front door opened, Darby looked up. It was Kate coming back with Scout the dog lumbering in after her, his coat beaded with water and burrs caught in his tail.

'No, Scout! *Out!*' she scolded with a roll of her eyes.

Scout halted in his tracks and his head drooped. Then he turned and looked up at Kate with the faintest of wags in his thick tail. Kate grabbed the old towel that hung on the back of the door and beckoned for him to follow her outside, which he did, obedient as ever. Darby had once joked that she wouldn't be surprised if one day that dog opened his mouth and joined in the conversation.

A few moments later, Kate returned with a dry dog with clean paws. 'Smells amazing, you guys,' she said, opening the cutlery drawer and gathering a fistful of knives and forks for the table.

'All Mum's doing,' Darby said, noticing how Kate hesitated briefly – a barely perceptible pause in her path towards the old pine table that they'd all sat around for countless mealtimes. 'Charlie had me up in the night,' she found herself explaining.

What was it that always made her feel slightly... *less* than Kate, especially in the presence of their mother? That she had to justify why breakfast was not a joint effort and that their mother had done it alone. That she'd, seemingly, slept in. Even though she hadn't. This feeling – guilt, perhaps – had always been there, right back to when they were girls, with Kate blending seamlessly with Connie's running of the household as though she was another limb attached to their mother.

Darby, on the other hand, had made herself scarce as a youngster, and could either be found in her room or out on her bike, or down at the stable yard in the village helping with the horses. And if she wasn't doing that, she was out on the land helping her father. That was when they all lived in the farmhouse in rural Lancashire – Foxhills Farm, the place where the Hunter girls had grown up. Her parents had relocated to Preston about a year ago – a small bungalow right on the edge of the city. It was where her father had died. He'd hated it there, and Darby had wondered if it was partly responsible for his demise – as if he simply hadn't wanted to exist away from the farm, from everything that was familiar. Foxhills had been his childhood home, too, and the old place had kept his heart beating.

'Oh, you must be exhausted, darling,' her mother said to Darby, glancing up from the hob where she was cracking eggs into another pan.

And there it was – words that would set the cement that held the invisible wall between her and her sister in place. Darby would never be Kate, and Kate never Darby, and their mother had always inadvertently highlighted their differences. Kate – the stoic, the people-pleaser, the practical one who just got on with things and never complained even though inwardly she'd knot herself up with anxiety. Darby – the dreamer, the fantasist, the wild and unruly one. *The less-than.* And then there was Bea. Her parents must have finally got it right because that's where they'd stopped. Third time lucky.

'I'm OK,' Darby said, grabbing ketchup from the fridge and

plonking it on the table. For some reason, Kate eyed her suspiciously. 'Charlie was restless all night. Probably overtired from the journey and all the excitement.' Darby smiled at her sister just as she heard someone coming down the stairs, appearing in the doorway that led from the back hallway.

'Morning, all,' Adrian said, his eyes casting around to see who was up.

His eyes didn't linger on Darby, though, and Darby's eyes didn't linger on him. She made sure of that, quickly rejoining her mother in the kitchen area. She pulled open the dishwasher to empty it. But it had already been done. *Damn.*

'Morning, Adrian,' Connie said, sliding a pile of bacon rashers into a lidded ceramic pot before putting it in the oven to keep warm. 'Sleep well?' She slipped off the oven mitts.

'Log-like.' He stared at Kate, a confused look in his eyes. 'I thought you'd taken Scout for a walk, love. I literally just saw you from the upstairs window heading down the drive.'

'No, no, I've not long come back from a walk.' Kate pulled a puzzled face and shrugged.

Adrian strode over to the window, staring out as he stretched his shoulders and ruffled his hair – hair that was neither brown nor blond and, depending on the light, sometimes even had a soft auburn tint to it. But in all honesty, it was mainly grey. 'That's odd,' he said, turning around and stretching again. 'I swear it was you heading off.'

Darby couldn't help noticing his exposed stomach above the waistband of his khaki-green shorts where his T-shirt rose up as he loosened his shoulders. She forced herself to look away.

'As I said, it wasn't me. And no one else has been out,' Kate said, going up to her husband and hooking her thumbs in his belt loops. 'Are the twins up?' She kissed his neck and Adrian draped his arms around her. Darby looked away, her heart thumping. There must be something she could load into the

empty dishwasher. Keep herself busy. Appear useful. Not have
to look at them.

Fifteen minutes later and everyone was sitting around the long
table, serving up eggs, bacon, mushrooms and grilled tomatoes.
Everyone except Theo, that was. He'd not yet emerged. There
was coffee and juice and milk and fruit, and countless rounds of
toast. Arms passed and reached, and laughter and chatter
competed with the clatter of cutlery. But all Darby focused on
was the empty space at the head of the table, where her father
should have been sitting, watching on. The place mat he always
insisted on using was still there – the one with two stags on a
bracken-clad hillside with a thunderous Scottish sky above. The
last one remaining from a set her parents had been given as a
wedding gift.

'When's Bea arriving?' Kate asked. Darby bent down to
pick up the plastic spoon that Charlie had chucked under his
highchair for the third time.

'In time for dinner tonight,' Connie replied, buttering some
toast. 'One of us should meet her at the station,' she added. 'Her
train gets in around six.'

'Pass the eggs, would you?' Travis said to Darby as she
resurfaced with the spoon. She reached across the table, but
Adrian was already stretching for the dish himself, causing their
fingers to lock on the ceramic lid.

The clattering and chatter suddenly faded as Darby felt the
warmth of his skin against hers. She let out an inaudible gasp.
And there was no helping the look she gave him – it was invol-
untary. As was his in return. She blinked. He blinked. She drew
in a sharp breath, noticing the rise of his chest beneath his pale-
blue T-shirt, the one he wore most often with some slogan or
other printed on the front.

'Sorry, sorry,' she heard someone say. It was her. She'd said it. Her hand whipped away, and the noise of the room returned as Adrian passed over the dish. Darby felt the burn of Travis's stare as he took it, slowly lifting the lid and sliding out a fried egg with the spatula. But the heat of Kate's stare was greater, scalding Darby's conscience.

'So, what's first, then?' Adrian said in an overly loud voice. 'Anyone fancy joining me on a hike across the moor to Tulloch? The weather's set fine today so we may as well make the most of it. There's a pub in the village. We could get some lunch.'

There was a beat of silence until Travis replied, 'Sure. I'll come with you.'

'And... and me too,' Darby added. She really wasn't sure that it was a good idea – the two men going off alone.

FOUR

BEA

Bea wasn't sure if she would tell everyone what had happened between her and Louis just yet. Or about her new job at the gallery (she hadn't technically been offered the position, but she'd felt hopeful after the interview). Or that she'd sold her beloved car, the one her father had given her, because she was skint. Or that she'd moved out of Louis's flat in north London last week and she was now officially homeless – or, rather, she was sofa-surfing between tolerant friends. And she certainly wasn't about to mention the terrible thing that had happened. *Terrible things* weren't for other people to know about. Especially if any of those other people happened to be members of her family.

The train rattled through the countryside, one parched field blending into the next. Occasionally they passed through woodland or a small town, stations flashing past. And once or twice they stopped at a city, more passengers filling the already crowded train. When the trolley rattled down the aisle, Bea bought a cup of milky tea and a Snickers bar. She'd never admit the chocolate to anyone. God, no. And probably not the milky tea, either. Instead, she'd grumble, if anyone asked, that there'd been no healthy drinks or snacks on board. She smiled to herself as she unwrapped the chocolate, her teeth sinking into the glorious sweetness. She washed it down with the tea, and somehow the combination of the two things satisfied her more than anything else had recently.

Bea caught sight of her reflection in the window against the countryside backdrop. In her ears, Black Sabbath's 'Paranoid' was playing loudly, an oddly appropriate accompaniment to the scenery speeding past. She wondered if this was anything like one of those near-death experiences she'd heard about – everything flashing before your eyes. She contemplated what her final visions might look like, and what her personal soundtrack would be. She figured the intense beat of heavy metal wasn't far off, though she was less than enamoured with the prospect of what she'd achieved in her thirty-two years so far, seeing as all she really had to show for herself right now was a half-empty paper cup and a nearly finished chocolate bar. Plus whatever she'd lugged along in her suitcase.

Another bite of the Snickers and she realised that she'd not yet done anything memorable enough for a decent showreel in her final moments if she suddenly dropped dead. Then she was thinking about dying – how that would happen if it wasn't through old age. Would it be a horrible accident, or a disease whipping through her, dissolving her organs, or perhaps something unbearable would drive her to take her own life? Or maybe she'd be a murder victim and die at the hands of an evil criminal. Then her thoughts swerved onto her friend from school, how his parents had found him hanging in their garage. Then, for some unfathomable reason, she sent a text to Louis telling him she still loved him. Which led her to make a note to bring him back some Scottish shortbread – she figured he'd like that; wondered if it might help – though she wasn't sure hand-delivering it to him would be a good idea, or appropriate under the circumstances, and subsequently she imagined what her mother was making for dinner, what the others had been up to all day.

It was how her mind worked. Fast. Chaotic.

As the train rattled on, her brain hopped, skipped and jumped from one random thought to another. And of course, it wasn't just her thoughts that spiralled out of conscious reach. Life did, too. Bea careered from one good idea to the next, though it usually transpired that none were *good* as such. Like the time she decided to become a teaching assistant. She thought she liked kids, but after a term on the job, she didn't – not other people's kids, anyway. Too many bodily fluids, too much noise, and someone always *needed* something – whether that was the toilet, food, comfort or a nose wiping. The tour guide idea was reasonable, she'd thought, but they'd let her go after she'd lost an entire coach party and had ended up, alone, in a museum marvelling at the sculptures on display. Waitress, barmaid, admin clerk, carer and retail assistant filled up her CV, but she wasn't cut out for any of them, either. She wished she was more like Kate. Or Darby. They had their shit together. The train sped onwards.

Bea suddenly jerked awake, for once thankful that her overwrought brain never fully let go – always one ear open, keeping her mind alight. It was her stop. 'Excuse me... sorry,' she said, scrabbling for her handbag – a charity shop find with a faulty clasp – from under the table, the contents of which had spilt out onto the floor. Stuffing her things back in, she stood up and squeezed past the passenger next to her – a middle-aged woman engrossed in a novel. Nearly forgetting, she reached back to retrieve her faded old denim jacket, the one she'd had since forever, and scuttled down the carriage towards the doors. Thank God she'd woken up in time. Well done, brain.

It was only when she was on the platform, putting on her jacket as the train pulled away, that she realised she'd left her suitcase on board.

Bea didn't swear or cry or stamp her foot. She was used to things like this happening. And she was also used to not telling anyone. She dropped down onto a bench on the platform.

'Hi, Mum,' she said, when her mother answered after just two rings. 'Yes, yes, it's me. I've got a new phone and number. Long story. I'm at the station. I'm early, I know!' It was true. She'd got a different train and had forgotten to text the details. 'OK, that's fine,' she replied when Connie told her the others had all gone out on a hike. 'I'll go into town and amuse myself. I can always get a taxi.' Though she wondered how she'd pay for it, given she only had about eight pounds in her account.

She hung up after arranging to meet Adrian outside the station later in the afternoon. She looked at the time – she still had a few hours to kill. Her mother had offered to come and fetch her, but Bea sensed the nervousness in her voice, knowing she didn't feel confident driving the ancient Land Rover too far these days.

Walking to the exit barrier, she figured she ought to pass the time buying some clothes and essential toiletries. And maybe a lipstick. It'd all have to go on her credit card, even though it was likely maxed out. But even just one change of clothes would be useful, or some spare underwear. Darby and Kate would have stuff she could borrow.

At the barrier, when she felt in her pockets, then checked her purse and every compartment of her handbag, she realised her ticket was in the side pouch of her suitcase. Bea thanked her lucky stars that the attendant was friendly and took pity on her. He even gave her a phone number to call for lost luggage at the train's destination in Glasgow. Yes, she'd do that. And she'd get her stuff back. It would all be fine.

Dumfries town centre was only a short walk from the station, and Bea headed straight to a discount store that sold packs of pants for a fiver. 'Better than nothing,' she said to the cashier, holding up the plastic packet of pastel-coloured knickers. He nodded vaguely and scanned them, while Bea held her breath as the transaction went through.

In the street, she checked the time again. 'It's going backwards, I swear,' she muttered to herself as she went into a small café and ordered a mint tea – slightly more Bea-like, she thought as she sat at a sticky laminated table feeling nauseous, probably from the chocolate and milky tea she'd had on the train.

What would Dad do? she typed into Notes on her phone. Then some bullet points:

- Give me a hug.
- Tell me not to worry.
- Say *They're only stupid clothes.*
- Say *It was only a stupid job/flat/car/boyfriend.*
- Give me some money.
- Have a quiet word with Adrian to phone some of his pals to see if they can get me a job.
- Give me more money.
- Give me another hug...

She sipped her tea, unable to think of any more points. But what she'd typed was already enough to make her feel better. More hopeful, as if she hadn't quite yet fucked up her life completely, and there were still more chances waiting for her. Every day felt as though she was playing darts blindfolded. If she threw enough arrows, sooner or later she'd hit the bullseye. Wouldn't she?

How she wished he was here now, her father. That he

hadn't died. She couldn't stand to think of his last moments, alone, afraid, not having a chance to say goodbye to the four women in his life. 'Keep buzzing, little Bea,' he'd say. 'And one day, before you know it, life will feel right. It'll fit you like your favourite sweater.'

But that, sadly, was in her lost suitcase.

FIVE

KATE

In the end, it was the two couples – Kate and Adrian, Darby and Travis – plus Finn, who went on the hike. A manageable ten miles, five each way, to blow away the cobwebs. And Kate wanted to try out her new walking boots, having worn them in for short stints over the last couple of weeks. Adrian had bought them for her birthday. A practical present for a practical wife.

Before they left, she caught sight of herself in the mirror by the door, not liking that her thoughts coincided with an image of herself that did, indeed, make her look... *practical*. Or maybe it was *useful, sensible, homely...* Kate wasn't too sure, which in itself was a concern. And she'd always felt as though a piece of her was missing, as if she wasn't quite a whole person. Not enough to do a decent job of anything. She wondered how far she'd have to go to surprise the others, what it would take to shock people. There was no doubt that something was stirring inside her – an unfamiliar feeling of discontent that kept bubbling up to the surface. But what scared her most was what would happen if the feelings spilt right over.

'C'mon, Scout,' she called out, waving the dog's lead. 'Show us how it's done.' She clipped it onto his collar. 'You sure you won't join us, Mia?'

Her daughter was, as expected, sitting curled on the sofa looking content with her Kindle and a mug of tea. Cosy socks poked out from beneath a knitted throw as she reclined on the cushions. Summer in the Scottish lodge wasn't the same as summer further south in England. She'd insisted they all packed knitwear.

See? *Practical.*

'I'm just getting to a good bit,' Mia said, waving her Kindle at the group. 'Take some pics and show me later.'

Kate didn't begrudge her not joining in. The twins had had an intense couple of years studying for A levels, culminating in their final exams this summer. They deserved a good rest, though Finn staying indoors with a book wasn't a likely option. She knew he'd come along for the exercise, guessing he'd have already done an hour's worth of press-ups and squats in his room. 'Nan's here to keep you company.'

'And Theo and Charlie,' Darby added flatly as she zipped up her orange windcheater, flicking a glance at Kate.

Kate nodded, though wasn't sure how Darby could relax knowing Travis's seventeen-year-old was in charge of her toddler. She certainly wouldn't. Charlie was at an age where he was into everything. If there was a marble to choke on or a staircase to throw himself down, Charlie would do it. But at least her mum and Mia would be around to keep an eye open.

'What's *that* face for?' Darby hissed at Kate, giving her a shove.

Kate didn't reply. Darby knew how she felt about Theo. *Troublemaker*, that's what she'd once dared to tell Darby soon after she'd got the measure of Travis and his son, baffled as to why her sister would want to be a stepmother to someone so disagreeable... so *selfish*. And especially so soon after what had happened to Chris – though she suspected that's *why* she'd got together with Travis in the first place. Grief had consumed her, led her to make irrational choices. But Darby still continued to brush off Theo's behaviour as normal teenage pranks. Kate wasn't sure that stealing a motorbike or smoking weed fell into that category. Nor any of the other similarly questionable things she'd later discovered the boy had done.

Half an hour later and the terrain turned hilly. They were finally out of the thick forest that engulfed the lodge, nestling between the mountainside and the edge of the loch. The land was owned by the Klintoch Estate with a network of footpaths criss-crossing the brown, bracken-strewn landscape. The sky was part brilliant azure and part steel grey – whether it would rain or not was anyone's guess up here, and the weather could change in minutes, but they'd come prepared. Well, most of them had. Rocky outcrops provided an occasional resting spot when the incline made each step feel as if it was one forward and two back, or somewhere to remove a stone from a boot, as Kate was now doing.

'Wait up, guys,' Darby called ahead. The two men and Finn halted, their figures bent forward against the hill – Adrian's taller frame clad in his bright blue cagoule and Travis, slightly shorter and stockier, dressed in an impractical black fleece. If it rained, he'd get soaked.

'There's definitely something in there,' Kate said, banging out her boot against the rock. 'It's been driving me mad this last mile or so.'

'Everything drives you mad, Katie,' Darby said, and she only didn't get a wallop because of her jokey tone. But the message was still clear, and it cut deep. Lately, Kate *had* been on edge, but she could hardly tell Darby why. 'Check your sock.'

Sure enough, Kate plucked a small piece of grit from the

weave of her thick walking sock, holding it up as if she'd struck gold. 'It felt like a boulder,' she said, tossing it into the scrubby grass. And when Kate glanced sideways at her sister as they set off again, she wondered if the feeling in the pit of her belly she'd had these last few months – the jelly-like sense that she was losing hold of something – some*one* – was similar to the stone. That her concern felt way greater than the actual cause.

The fire was always lit at the Forester's Arms – rain or shine. A holiday at the lodge wasn't the same without a brisk walk and a pint, plus one of their famous ham hock and cheese lunches. And they did a cracking roast on a Sunday, which they'd all no doubt be back for en masse another day. The pub had been run by the same family since she, Darby and Bea were kids. The clientele never seemed to change, with locals, who Kate remembered as ancient even back then, still frequenting the place now.

'This one?' Adrian said, spotting a big enough table in the window beside the fire.

'Perfect,' Kate said, unzipping her jacket. 'Finn… come here, your back is covered in burrs.'

She reached over to pull off the little sticky seeds from her son's coat, but he shied away, shrugging off his windcheater as he continued his chat with Travis. They'd been talking non-stop on the walk up – or rather, Travis had been talking at Finn. She'd tried to overhear the conversation, but Darby had kept interrupting, regaling her with stories of how hard it was to get reliable staff at the little café she owned, or ideas for a new autumn menu.

She bent down to unclip Scout's lead – she knew he'd just slump at her feet under the table, recovering for the trek home – but when she stood up, everyone had shuffled into place around the table. The only spot left was a low stool with torn velvet, the padding poking out of the split. For a moment, Kate thought it looked like cut skin that needed stitching. Flesh slashed by a knife.

She shook her head. These thoughts were getting ridiculous. *Dangerous*, even, she told herself, dropping down onto the seat, about six inches lower than everyone else, as she tried to tune into what Adrian was saying. He was at the head of the table the other end, with Darby right beside him. Their hands were only an inch or two apart on the tabletop. She imagined their knees brushing together underneath. Kate bristled inside, forcing the lid down on her feelings.

'Right, what's everyone drinking?' Adrian said, suddenly standing. 'Finn, mate, want to give me a hand at the bar?'

But Finn wasn't paying attention – he was still talking to Travis – so Darby got up and squeezed out from the window seat. 'I'll come,' she said, placing a hand on Adrian's arm.

'Just a Diet Coke,' Kate heard herself saying after the other two had decided what they wanted. Her eyes were glued to her sister's hand, her fingers settled on Adrian's forearm as if... as if they *belonged* there. She didn't allow herself to stare as the pair headed to the bar, although she desperately wanted to – to watch how close they stood, how they looked at each other, if they shared secret smiles. Instead, she heard Adrian's voice greeting Mick, the bartender, making chit-chat, and Darby's shrill tones harmonising with him.

'Just chatting finances with young Finn here,' Travis said, causing Kate's ears to prick up at the change in his tone. She looked up.

'Sorry?'

'Talking bitcoin,' he said, tapping his phone screen. 'Reckon Finn's got a good grasp already.'

'Bitcoin?' Kate said, bemused and uninterested. Knowing her son, he wouldn't have been that enamoured with it either, but she assumed he was being polite and probably now wishing he'd stayed at the lodge.

'He should get his savings into crypto quick smart,' Travis went on. 'Something like that could set you up for life.'

'I'm not sure that's a good idea,' Kate remarked. Both Finn and Mia had healthy savings accounts, into which she and Adrian had paid an amount each month since they were born. And they'd had Saturday or holiday jobs over the last couple of years, which had added to the pot, plus any cash gifts for birthdays. They had quite a stash between them. 'Sounds like a good way to blow all your savings, if you ask me.'

'No, Mum, it sounds pretty sick, actually.' Finn swept his finger across his phone screen. 'Is this the app you mean, Travis?'

'Yep, that's the one I use,' he said. 'You and Theo should chat about it. He's far more knowledgeable than me. What with bitcoin and gaming, his face is hardly out of a screen.' Travis laughed, as if this was a quality to be admired.

Kate thought about this, reminded of herself and her sisters at a similar age. Perhaps it was because they were girls and a different generation, but their weekends had been a hectic orchestra of various activities – friends coming over, dancing and music lessons, parties to go to, plus Darby and Bea often helped their father on the farm. Though Connie had always made a point of corralling Kate in the kitchen, teaching her how to bake and sew, or the two of them would go out on a bike ride – all of which she'd enjoyed. But sometimes she'd wished she could have joined her father and sisters, instead of being excluded as she often was. It had made her feel different from the others – a feeling that persisted even now.

As Adrian and Darby returned and set down the drinks, Kate was struck by a thought. Each of her sisters had had their passions at various stages of life – and still had – but what had *she* had to keep her world turning?

Nothing that she could think of. And apart from the twins, there was nothing now either. It scared her. The hole inside her felt bigger than herself. Just like the stone in her boot.

SIX

THEO

Theo reckoned he could kill someone. As he pondered the possibility, adrenaline fizzed in his belly, like his insides were preparing to unleash the *thing* that had been burning inside him for a long while now.

He sat on the sofa, staring at his little half-brother, who was playing on the floor in front of him. How the kid hadn't hurled all those wooden bricks at Mia, sitting on the other sofa looking smug, was beyond him. *He* would have done. One after the other, pelting her shin bones with the coloured wooden blocks. He smiled to himself. Imagining it was almost as good as doing it. They were all the same, these girls, and she'd no doubt turn out just like his mother – untrustworthy and intent on hurting him.

He put down his phone and slid onto the floor beside Charlie. From the corner of his eye, he noticed Mia glance up from her Kindle. It seemed like she'd been reading the whole time since they'd arrived last night, probably immersed in some stupid teenage romance with ponies and girls with filtered pouts and big tits and tiny waists fawning over hot guys like Finn. Guys who were nothing like him. Theo was used to living in the shadows and being ignored, though he vowed that, one day, the whole world would sit up and take notice. Then everyone would be sorry.

'Want to make a tower, Charlie?'

Charlie looked up at his big brother, the kid not aware that they had different mothers – Theo's mother having buggered off one day without so much as a backward glance or a peck on the cheek.

That had hurt. Still did.

He and his dad had muddled along somehow, each trapped inside their own pain. His dad had coped by casually dating a string of unsuitable girlfriends, who'd all despised Theo, then a couple of years later, he'd got together with Darby. Big mistake, Theo reckoned. She'd no doubt pull a similar stunt to his mother in time, hurting them all over again, and he'd end up having to pick up the pieces with his dad, stop him sinking into the bottle again, losing his HGV licence, losing his shit.

Charlie babbled up at Theo. He had the same almost-black eyes as him – eyes that no one could fathom – but apart from that, they didn't look much like each other. Charlie with his blond curls, oddly unlike either of his parents, and rosebud lips and chubby arms, and Theo – skinny as a broom handle with a sweep of black hair that covered half his face.

'Dat!' Charlie said. 'Yeaaahh.'

Mia looked up from her Kindle and smiled. Theo stared at her. Felt his lip twitch into a sort of snarl.

'Let's start with these ones. The big bricks go at the bottom,' he said to his little brother, wishing Mia would piss off upstairs.

'Dat!' Charlie said again. 'Dat bwick.'

'Go on then, put that down. But it won't be very stable.'

Charlie slammed the small yellow block down, clapping, before he grabbed another couple of random sizes, placing them on top, slightly askew.

'Don't think he's quite got the principles of basic architecture yet,' Mia said with a laugh, unfurling her legs from under the soft beige throw. Theo hated the way his eyes automatically flicked up and down their length – bare, slim, smooth legs ending in shorts at one end and fluffy socks at the other. What was she bloody smirking at?

'He's two. Of course he hasn't.' She was clearly thick as well.

'Duh, jokes,' she replied in a silly voice.

To Theo's horror, Mia slid down off the sofa and joined them on the rug. As she crossed her legs beside them, he smelt her body wash or shampoo. It was sweet and sickly, and he didn't want it up his nose.

'You want to put this one on now, Charlie?' she cooed, handing him another brick. 'Get it straight if you can.'

'Dat one, Mimi...' Charlie said, clapping his hands when the brick stayed in place. 'Do nuvva one!'

'Here you go, poppet,' Mia said, leaning forward and handing him another. Her baggy grey sweat top drowned her upper body, while her denim shorts were almost invisible, they were so tiny. 'Yay, go Charlie. This tower will be as tall as you are soon!'

'Yeh...' Charlie mouthed beneath a runny nose. 'Me big. Big towwa.'

'His speech is really coming on, isn't it?' Mia said, turning to Theo.

Wait, she's a fucking child development expert now, is she? Jesus effing Christ.

'Yeah,' Theo replied, placing a brick on the tower.

Charlie immediately took it off. 'Nooo!' he squealed, scowling at his big brother. 'Mimi do it.' He handed his cousin the brick, making Mia laugh.

'Oh, Charlie, you funny little thing. We'll do it together, yeah?'

Theo got up and went to the kitchen. He'd had enough of

playing with bricks. He pulled open the fridge and stared inside, not knowing if he was hungry or thirsty. There was a ton of food in there, but nothing that he actually wanted to eat. In the fridge door, there were a few bottles of beer, so he grabbed one and popped the top off with an opener he found in the drawer.

'I'm going upstairs for a bit. You OK to watch him?' Theo asked Mia as he passed through the living area.

'Oh... how long will you be? I was going to have a bath before the others get back.'

Theo smirked. 'A while,' he replied, heading for the stairs. 'I'm going to have bath.' He winked at her and continued up, hearing her mutter something as he went. In the bathroom, he turned the hot tap on full, but didn't put the bath plug in. Instead, he went and lay on his bed, grateful that Finn, who he was sharing a room with, was out of the way. He waited for all the hot water to run out while he fired up his laptop. He could use some advice from the forum.

Th3ology: Help bruhs! How to get rid of a girl?

And then he typed as fast as he could.

SEVEN

CONNIE

Connie decided to leave them to it – Mia, Theo and Charlie. Things seemed peaceful enough. While she didn't think Theo was particularly trustworthy, she had no such concerns about Mia. Responsibility flowed through her veins, and she was used to babysitting to earn a bit of money. Besides, the others would be back early afternoon. Their hike wasn't a long one. And Connie needed to get out.

She got into the old Land Rover, closing her eyes for a moment before she started up the rattling diesel engine. Driving it never got any easier, she thought, heading off down the bumpy drive towards the lane, even after all these years. But her anxiety was soothed by the sight of the moors, the forest, the mountains – the stunning scenery still taking her breath away as she rounded every corner.

All apart from *one* particular bend in the road.

Connie gripped the steering wheel tightly as she forced herself to keep her eyes fixed straight ahead, refusing to allow the flashbacks to spin through her mind as she approached *that* spot. Where it happened. Where everything changed.

A few minutes later, she slowed down, entering Glengalloch village. It was a small but thriving community, with an influx of newcomers over the last decade buying up the crofts and cottages and turning them into holiday homes or permanent residences to escape the rat race – though the core of Glengalloch still remained as it had always been, with locals forming its beating heart. There was a parking space outside the little shop, so she pulled straight into it, turning off the Land Rover's engine. She wondered how much life the old vehicle had left in it but she couldn't risk parting with it. Not after everything.

'Margie, hello!' Connie said as she went into the store. She could open and close that door a hundred times and still not tire of the little tinkle it made. There was comfort to be had by the familiar things, the things that reminded her of when she and Ray would pop in for a loaf and the paper on a Sunday morning, gripping their children's hands, buying them an ice cream in the summer – watching as they peered down into the magical freezer cabinet with its sliding lid – or treating them to a packet of hot chocolate powder in the colder months. She shuddered. Had the past all been a fleeting dream?

Or a nightmare, said the voice inside her head.

'All your clan up now, Con?'

'They will be when Bea gets here later,' Connie replied. 'A rare treat.'

'And how are you doing, you know, since...' Margie trailed off. Their friendship was a close one, formed over many years that had been punctuated by absences when they were back at Foxhills. But out of all the people she knew, both back home and locally, Margie understood what she was going through the most. She'd lost her own husband five years ago.

'Trying my best,' Connie replied. 'Having family around helps. I don't know what I'll do when they all go back. I'm planning to stay on a bit longer.'

'Aye, it's all you can do, Con. One foot in front of the other.'

The two women's eyes connected until Connie nodded, blinking away the tears.

'Now, what did I come in for?' *Nothing*, Connie told herself. *Nothing apart from company, familiarity, connection, an escape.* 'Apples. Yes, we're out of apples.' She went to the fruit display and picked out six red Braeburns, putting them in a paper bag. Then she perused the tins, racked up on the old-fashioned shelves – the same shelves that she and Ray had bought things from countless times.

'Best stock up,' Ray would say. 'Weather's closing in.' She loved that about her late husband – always thinking ahead, planning, staying in control and staving off a disaster. And God knows, he'd been good at that in the past. The pantry at the lodge had always been stuffed full of provisions, the small barn filled with sacks of potatoes, carrots and oatmeal, and the log store piled up with seasoned wood.

She couldn't help wondering how he'd handle the impending disaster if he were here – how he'd ready them all for the nuclear-sized hole she was about to blow in her daughters' lives. The irony being it was all because of him.

Connie placed a few unnecessary provisions on the counter, including several large bags of corn chips and crackers. She'd noticed Theo staring into the food cupboard, closing the door with a sigh he didn't think she'd heard. 'I'll take these, Margie,' she said. 'And... and a small bottle of the Klintoch whisky,' she said quietly, pointing behind the counter at the range of locally produced spirit. 'Helps me sleep.'

'Aye, no need to explain.' Margie scanned the bottle, glancing up. 'When I have my wee bedtime tipple later, I'll be raising my glass to you, Con.' She smiled kindly, bagging the groceries.

'Widows unite,' Connie replied with a plaintive sigh. She paid and left the shop, relishing the little tinkle again, and got into the Land Rover, driving it the short distance back towards the lodge. But instead of turning off onto the lane that led to the lodge's drive, she headed down the hill towards Loch Muir instead.

She parked the old vehicle in the gravelled area facing out across the water and switched off the engine. It was her favourite thinking spot.

The late morning sun fanned a wedge of light across the gentle ripples, and some of the trees surrounding the loch – although it was still technically summer – were showing hints of their colour to come over the next couple of months. Auburn, ochre, coffee and gold – the extraordinarily hot July and August having caught them out, causing them to give up and succumb to autumn early.

'Oh, Ray…' Connie said in a breathy, wistful voice. She reached into the bag of shopping and took out the bottle of Klintoch, cracking the screw cap with her slender fingers.

She put the bottle to her lips and let a dribble of whisky slip into her mouth and down her throat. She closed her eyes, relishing the burning sensation as she drank – slowly at first, but then more greedily.

It's been a while, she thought, wiping her lips on her sleeve, *since I've needed it as much.*

Perhaps it was everyone being together again and what it all meant that had brought about her desire to drink. She wasn't about to down the whole bottle but had needed something to quell the rising feelings. The aftershocks from the contents of her late husband's will were still reverberating through her, the disbelief as she'd sat in the solicitor's office several months ago still haunting her at night. Imagining her daughters' reactions to the legacy Ray had left behind was enough to drive anyone to drink. And it wasn't just about the money.

Or perhaps it's for old times' sake, she wondered, gazing out over the loch again, watching as a small white power boat cut a line across the water. *For what might have been.*

'A storm's brewing,' she whispered, twisting the cap back on the bottle as she noticed the gunmetal-grey clouds gathering in the west. And then she saw the lone figure standing at the edge of the loch, casting a line out into the water – his shoulders broad, his stance square as he waited patiently for a bite. But just like that he was gone again, a figment from the past. It felt like she'd never even known him.

Snapping herself out of the looming self-pity that threatened, Connie started up the Land Rover – which took several attempts as the noisy engine finally rattled to life – and drove back to the lodge before the alcohol had a chance to blur her thoughts. Which, after all, was exactly what she wanted.

EIGHT

BEA

'Bea!' Her mother's voice was shrill, though it wavered slightly in that way she'd noticed when women got older. The cracks of age showing. 'Bea, darling, you're *here!*'

Connie pulled off her rubber gloves and embraced her, pulling her against her bony frame. Bea noticed she felt a little frailer since the last time they'd hugged – more breakable. Though she and her sisters had never seen her as anything but robust, it now seemed as if their mother had been forced to take on their father's strength after he passed away. An unexpected inheritance.

'I know, I *know!*' Bea replied, her tone matching her mother's. 'Bloody incredible I actually made it.' She laughed, holding her mother at arm's length. 'It's so good to see you, Mum.' The last time had been at the funeral. In fact, that had been the last time she'd seen any of her family – well, actual *blood* relatives. She shuddered briefly. It wasn't that she hadn't wanted to spend time with them, just that she usually forgot to call them or didn't know how to make it happen, what with most of them living in different parts of the country.

'Did Adrian fetch you from the station? I thought they were still out on their hike.'

'No, no... I got a lift instead. It's fine.' Bea wafted her hand about, knowing there would be questions.

'Who with?' Her mother turned to the kettle and took two mugs from the cupboard.

'Just a man. A guy.'

Her mother turned. 'Do you know him?'

'No.' Bea laughed, slipping off her denim jacket. 'But it's fine. He was fine. Just a guy I met in a café. He was heading up this way from Dumfries. Turned out he lives around here, so it was on his way home.'

Her mother scowled, deepening the furrows on her forehead, though there weren't many in the first place. An eraser would fix them, Bea often thought. Just a gentle smudge here and there and her mother's face would be young again – the woman she remembered from her childhood. Her cheekbones were still high, her lips fuller than those of most women her age, and her shoulders sat square and elegant beneath her sweater. Her mum still had it – beautified by her years, rather than ravaged by them.

'You got a lift from a *stranger*?' Connie placed the mugs on the worktop. Hand on the kettle.

'He's not a stranger now, is he? And I'm still alive. Fret ye not, Mama Bear.' A little squeeze around her mother's waist seemed to appease her. 'I'm not a baby, Mum.'

At this, Connie laughed. 'You'll always be the baby, Bea.' She closed her eyes for a second, but then they both whipped their heads around at the noise – laughing, boots coming off... chit-chat and the bark of a dog. Bea skipped to the opening that joined the kitchen to the living area, leaning forward as her arms spanned its width, holding on.

'I'm here!' Bea sang out. But no one turned, no one saw her in their haste to get in from the rain. Scout shook, his body spraying water and mud everywhere as he rippled from head to tail. Then he looked up at Bea and let out another bark – one that alerted Kate.

'Oh, Scout, no... Let me get your towel and...' She trailed off. 'Bea! Oh my God, you're *here*.' She beamed at her younger sister, kicking off her boots and meeting her for a hug.

Then Bea received more hellos and hugs than she could cope with as everyone crowded around her. Scout circled their huddle, barking and wagging his tail, thumping it against their legs. When the melee – which is what it felt like to Bea – dispersed, Travis was left standing a few feet away, his dark hair wet and stuck to his head. One arm twitched upwards, making Bea think he was going to shake her hand or, worse, hug her too, but he quickly shoved his hand in his back pocket and gave her a tight smile. 'Hello, Bea.'

'Hi, Travis,' she replied, without looking him in the eye. She couldn't face that.

'How are things, little sis?' Darby asked, but then her eyes were darting around the living room, her smile replaced by a frown. 'Mum, where's Charlie?'

Bea couldn't imagine what it must feel like to be so responsible for another life, to have to constantly monitor their whereabouts and well-being, never taking your eye off the ball. She was barely able to watch out for herself, so the thought of keeping someone else out of danger, fed, warm and happy seemed impossible.

But before their mother had a chance to reply, Mia appeared at the bottom of the stairs with Charlie wedged on her hip as he tried to poke a Duplo brick in her mouth. 'He's right here, aren't you, Charlie-warlie? Such a good little boy.' Mia nuzzled his neck and gave him a kiss on his chubby cheek.

'Down!' he squeaked, writhing in Mia's arms. She lowered him to the floor, and he ran over to Darby, hurling his arms around his mum's knees.

'Don't worry, Darbs, he's been fine. We've been making a den under the bedsheets. Waiting for Theo to finish his bath.'

'Theo... a *bath*?' Travis scoffed, grabbing Charlie and hoisting him onto his shoulders. 'That'll be a first. Can barely get the boy in the shower these days.' Charlie writhed and squirmed, tugging on a handful of Travis's hair.

Bea noticed Mia's eyes flash first from Travis then across to Darby. A slight flicker of her eyebrows told Bea there was more to this than met the eye. She'd bet her lost luggage that the little weasel only went into the bathroom so Mia couldn't. He'd done something similar at their father's wake – grabbed the last vegetarian sausage roll just as she was about to take it, even though he usually ate meat like a caveman.

'I'm so *glad* to have you all here,' Connie suddenly interjected, stepping between them all. Her hands were clasped at her chest and her eyebrows pulled together in a frown that signalled she was about to tell them something important. But instead, she looked at each of her daughters in turn with whatever it was stuck firmly between her lips. 'Last time we were all together was so sad... so unbelievably painful. Even though I feel your father's spirit here with us, this also feels like a new era, the next chapter for the Hunter girls.' She held her arms wide and beckoned the three of them close, pulling her daughters against her. 'One where we have to learn to survive without him... and, well, learn to live with... with everything that's thrown at us going forward.' She cleared her throat.

Definitely something on her mind, Bea thought, though she was more preoccupied with what was on hers.

'Oh, Mum,' Darby said, joining in the hug. 'I feel Dad's presence, too.'

'Yeah,' Kate added – the first to pull away. 'Time together is just what we all need.'

Bea felt it was her turn to say something. Something meaningful and sentimental. But, oddly, her usually overwrought mind contained only one thought at that moment. And her brain conspired with her mouth to spit it out, even though she'd made a pact with herself that she absolutely wouldn't say a word.

'I'm pregnant.'

NINE

KATE

Kate's first thought was tea. Tea fixed everything – a trait she'd inherited from her mother. Her second thought was alcohol. That fixed things better in the short term. She stared at her little sister. Suddenly, she seemed so much *more* little. Was this news good or bad? She was never sure with Bea.

'Bea?' she said, sliding her hand onto her sister's arm. 'You're *pregnant*? How... how does Louis feel about it?' Then she checked herself, sensing the creep of a blush rising up her cheeks. 'God, I'm so sorry... I mean – *congratulations*! That's amazing news. I'm so happy for you!'

Bea smiled up at her, and instantly Kate saw in her eyes that it wasn't amazing news at all. In fact, what she saw was pure terror – as well as realising that Bea probably hadn't meant to say anything about her pregnancy at all. But in her usual haphazard way, she'd been unable to help herself.

'Louis doesn't know yet,' Bea finally said, dropping down onto the sofa. Scout plonked his chin on her knee, as if he knew she needed comfort. Dogs were intuitive like that.

Kate sat down beside her, perching on the edge of the old sofa, trying to block out the noise around her – the others all declaring their delight, slight shock, but general happiness that there was to be another baby in the family. Connie knelt on the rug in front of Bea, joining in the huddle. She put a hand on her daughter's knee.

'You should tell him,' Kate said softly, glancing at her mother. 'Don't you think?'

'I know, I *know*...'

'But?' Connie said.

Kate tried to make eye contact with her sister, but Bea wasn't having it. Her gaze was fixed firmly on her lap as her fingers toyed with the frayed fabric in a slash on the thigh of her jeans. Something was wrong – she just wasn't sure what yet.

'I haven't known long myself,' Bea replied quietly. 'And the time... it hasn't been right to tell him yet.'

'Is Louis still joining us?' Connie asked. 'You could tell him when he's here.'

Bea shook her head. 'He's not coming now.'

'How far gone are you, darling?'

Bea shrugged.

'Oh, my little honey Bea...' Kate pulled her in for a hug. 'It'll be OK. You'll see.' She felt Bea sniff and quiver against her shoulder as they huddled together, blocking out the celebratory noises around them. Suddenly, someone shoved a glass of fizz between them.

'Not for you, of course, Bea,' a man's voice said. When Kate looked up, it was Travis. She took the glass, not really wanting it, but then not wanting the inevitable squabble if she refused either. She knew what Travis was like. Forceful.

'To Bea and Louis,' Darby sang out, standing beside the fireplace.

'Thanks, Darbs,' Bea said, managing a smile. Then she pulled herself away from Kate's arms and ran out of the room, heading for the downstairs toilet.

· · ·

Once the commotion about Bea's news had settled down and all
the excited yet predictable questions about due dates, names,
sex, and breast versus bottle had been asked – none of which
Bea was able or willing to answer – Kate wasn't sure what to
focus on: her sister's announcement or keeping watch on Adrian
and Darby. She'd been doing both, badly, for the last couple of
hours. Since they'd arrived home from the walk earlier, contact
between her sister and her husband had been minimal. She was
imagining it, surely. And now with the news that Bea was pregnant, Bea needed her support. Kate didn't want to be distracted
by the impossible, the unimaginable thought that something
untoward was going on between her husband and Darby.

Untoward, she thought to herself as she rolled the dice.
Jesus Christ, was that how she saw a potential affair? Like a
niggle on a 'to-do' list? She wanted to feel angry, incensed,
betrayed and vengeful, but until she had concrete proof of
anything, none of those feelings would materialise. It wasn't
Kate's way. But then neither was it Darby's way to betray her.
Nor Adrian's. He was her *husband*, for God's sake.

Kate wasn't naive enough, however, to blindly believe that
these things didn't happen, even in the happiest of marriages.
Sure, they'd had a few challenging patches in their two decades
together, but they'd worked through them. They were solid. But
still... intuition was tapping her on the shoulder. And it had all
started at their father's funeral back in May.

'What were you talking to Darby about?' Kate had asked
Adrian at the wake, keeping her voice low. She'd seen the pair
standing close, her husband's hand on Darby's waist. Then her
eyes had flicked down to the crisp white collar of his shirt – to
the small make-up stain that she knew wasn't hers.

'Nothing,' Adrian had replied, shrugging. He hadn't made
eye contact with her; rather, he'd distracted himself with a sandwich, another drink, loosening his tie.

'You've been outside for ages. I came looking for you but couldn't find you. Then just now I saw you through the window with Darby and you were—'

'Kate, stop, OK?' He'd glared at her. 'You don't know what you're talking about. Leave it.'

But Kate hadn't left it. She'd questioned him again when they'd got home and, instead of reassuring her, her husband's reaction had only worsened her fears.

'I saw you with your hands cupped around her *face*,' Kate had almost screamed at him. 'What am I *supposed* to think?'

'It's not like that, and you know it,' Adrian had shot back. 'Like I said, you don't understand. Just drop it.'

'Are you having an affair with my sister?' There. It was out. And his answer – or rather *non*-answer – had only served to fuel her paranoia. Because in response, he'd simply told her she was mad, before shaking his head and walking away.

'Lu-*cky!*' a deep voice rang out. Adrian. His thigh was pressed against hers as they sat on the sofa, with Kate leaning forward to move the little metal car that represented her in the game. 'Ah... Chance. Go on, love, take a card,' he said keenly.

She'd never known Adrian get so worked up about a game of Monopoly. 'Get out of jail free,' she read out. *Useful*, she thought, wishing she could have one in real life. 'Your turn, Travis.' She passed the dice to him.

'Bloody hell, typical,' he said, landing on Adrian's Mayfair house.

'Cough up, mate!' Adrian replied, rubbing his hands together.

'I'll have to mortgage something,' Travis replied, shaking his head. Then he got up and grabbed a log from the basket, hurling it into the fire. Sparks rained upwards and a couple of embers shot out of the fire. He stood there, watching them glow brightly on the rug.

'Quick, stamp them out,' Bea said and, being the nearest, she leapt up and did just that, with Travis's foot landing hard on hers as he did as he was told.

Kate saw the grimace on her little sister's face, noticed how she refused to react, blinking away the pain. And no apology from Travis, either. There was something *off* about that man, though she couldn't quite pin it down.

'Right, is it my turn?' Connie rolled the dice and moved her little dog forward. 'Ahh, King's Cross Station. I'll buy it!' Kate watched as her mother paid for and added the card to her collection just as there was a sharp knock on the front door. Scout hauled himself up from his fireside spot, barking deeply, though without much vigour. He'd probably lick an intruder to death.

Kate looked at her husband in the hope he might get up to answer it, but he was engrossed with whatever Darby was saying to him across the board, so she got up to do it herself. In the hallway, she pulled back the curtain and unlocked the door, opening it. While it was still just light outside, the sky was overcast and murky, the rain still falling, with the thick forest around them adding to the gloominess.

'Hello,' Kate said to the man standing there. She didn't recognise him, and guessed he was in his mid-thirties. He was tall and dressed in jeans, an army-style camouflage jacket and heavy work boots, with a decent head of light-auburn hair. His beard was neatly clipped. But it was his intense blue eyes that unnerved Kate the most, threw her off balance. Somehow familiar, yet she had no idea who he was.

'So sorry to disturb you,' he said in what Kate believed to be the kindest voice she'd ever heard. A blend of thick Yorkshire and Scottish, as if he'd been raised in the former but perhaps lived locally now. 'I found this in my car. I believe it belongs to a young lady here.' The man held out a credit card, and Kate noticed his hands – strong and capable, as though he was used to manual work. 'I gave her a lift up from town earlier.'

'Oh...' Kate replied, the penny dropping. 'That's so kind of you.' She took the card and read the name on it. Beatrice Hunter. 'Typical,' she added, rolling her eyes. 'Bea loses everything. Do you want to come in? She can thank you herself.'

'Oh, no... don't worry. I don't want to disturb you.' The man's sharp eyes flicked behind her to where the others were sitting by the fire.

'You wouldn't be. In fact' – Kate leant forward and spoke in a quiet voice – 'you'd be doing me a favour. We're playing Monopoly and my husband has turned into a monster. Any reason to stall the game is a bonus. Feel free to knock the board over if you like.' Kate opened the door wider and ushered him in. The man stomped on the doormat a few times and followed her through to the living area. 'Hey, guys, this is...' She turned and looked at him.

'Cameron,' he said, scanning all the faces.

'Bea, Cameron found your credit card.' Kate held it out to her sister across the coffee table where the game was spread out. 'You left it in his car when he gave you a lift earlier.' But Bea sat motionless, staring up at the man behind Kate. 'Bea?'

'Oh, sorry... yes, yes of course,' Bea suddenly said, reanimating. She leapt up and leant over, taking the card from her sister, but not before she'd tripped on Travis's foot, which was sticking out, and she'd crashed forward, her hands coming up to save herself and landing on the edge of the board, sending the Monopoly game flying to the floor.

Travis gave a slow clap.

'Sorry, sorry, sorry,' Bea said, her voice wavering as she righted herself. She didn't seem to know what to do first – take the card from Kate or clear up the mess. So, instead, she just stood there, blushing, staring at Cameron as Kate reached over and slipped the card into her jeans pocket.

Kate turned to the visitor, winking. 'She saved you a job.'

'Would you like a drink, Cameron?' Connie offered. 'And thank you for giving Bea a lift earlier. Are you local?' She stood up and approached Cameron, a slight frown catching her brow as she started up at him, making Kate wonder if she recognised something about him, too.

'I am indeed a local now,' Cameron replied, his face relaxing into a warm smile. He seemed amused by the goings-on in the lodge. His being from the area perhaps explained her mother's expression. They'd possibly seen him about. 'Since my father moved back, I've been spending more time at his place. His mobility isn't so great these days and there's only me to take care of him, so I decided to move here too.'

Kate's mind filled in the blanks of his story – an only child, his mother perhaps having passed away, his father needing his help, Cameron giving up his home and career elsewhere to come and care for him. As she raced ahead with his make-believe life story, she even imagined him holed up in another lodge by the loch writing a scary novel or shaping sculptures to sell in London. There was a brooding sense of creativity about him.

'Here you go,' Connie said, passing him a glass. 'It's what we're all having.'

'Aye, just the one, then,' Cameron replied, raising the shot of whisky before taking a sip. 'It was a coincidence that I should have stumbled across you in town, Bea,' he said as he sat down in a big armchair, leaning his forearms on his knees. Warmth radiated from his face – fine lines around his eyes that he was barely old enough to have, and an easy smile that revealed straight white teeth. 'My father has mentioned the Hunter family several times in the past. Ray Hunter, especially.'

Kate flashed a look at her mother.

'Is Ray not here tonight?' Cameron asked, glancing around the group.

A mocking voice suddenly cut through the air from the other side of the room, shattering the moment of awkwardness. *Theo.* Kate whipped her head around, not even realising he'd left the game.

The teen was standing in the doorway, dressed entirely in black, his greasy jet hair covering half his face as he spoke, seeming to enjoy the attention.

'Nah, the old bastard's dead,' he crowed, followed by a laugh.

TEN

THEO

To be fair, Ray *had* once described himself an old bastard, so Theo's announcement wasn't entirely unfounded. And he was certainly dead. He'd seen the coffin. Been to the funeral. Therefore he reckoned the shocked faces glaring at him from the group were a bit harsh as he was only saying it like it was.

But Theo couldn't deny that he relished the way they all stared at him, almost as if he'd had a hand in Ray's death himself. He'd only met the old boy a handful of times and, as far as he could make out, he was indeed a grumpy sod – though there'd been a more intriguing side to him, as if he'd been hiding something that had forced him to put up a tough outer shell, turning him into the self-proclaimed old bastard.

And for that reason, he'd liked him. *Related* to him, even.

Theo laughed inwardly as he strode through to the kitchen, ignoring all the stares. Beer time. He'd be fucked if he was playing that stupid Monopoly game any longer. He pulled open the fridge, remembering when his dad and Darby had dragged him along to visit Ray and Connie nearly three years ago at their previous home in Lancashire – a run-down farm. It was the first time he'd met the old couple, and he'd been grateful that Ray had ushered him from the floral living room where he'd been drowning in fairy cakes and oestrogen, leading him outside to the garage – well, more of a falling-down barn, really – to show him the old engine he was rebuilding.

'My pride and joy,' Ray had said, and Theo understood. Not his wife, not his three daughters or grandchildren. Just a hunk of oily, rusty metal. 'Giving her a new lease life.' If nothing else had come of that afternoon, Theo now knew how to grind out the cylinders of a 1974 Ford Escort.

Ray, spanner in hand as he'd leant over the disassembled engine, had got talking about family, the importance of it, as though he was trying to teach Theo a thing or two about life. 'I got lucky with Connie. She's an angel to put up with an old bastard like me. We all have our faults, son. Like this engine.' He'd passed Theo the spanner and showed him which nuts to loosen. 'You got a girlfriend, lad?'

Theo had laughed. 'Nah, not likely,' he'd replied, deciding not to mention his crush. As far as he was concerned, girls were a different species, and nothing would change his mind on that. After his mother had walked out on him and his dad without a backward glance, plus the incessant mocking from the girls at school, he'd turned his back on them. It was safer that way.

But there was something else about those few hours of tinkering with Ray that had stuck with him – the freezing air numbing their fingers, the reek of car oil in their nostrils, the tinny radio playing songs he didn't recognise in the background. The garage was a messy Aladdin's cave of tools, mechanical parts, bits of rusting bodywork, greasy old rags, plus a legless and filthy ancient sofa over one side beside a gas fire that didn't seem to emit any heat whatsoever. It was something Ray had said.

'I always wanted a son, lad,' the old man had blurted out, looking up from his work. There was a wistful look in his eyes as he stared at him. For a terrible moment, Theo wondered if Ray was going to hug him, but the couple of feet remained between them. 'Don't get me wrong, though, I love my two daughters dearly.'

Harsh, was Theo's first thought, but he'd kept quiet about the old man's mistake, not correcting him. He'd wondered if this was how dementia started.

But above all, Ray's comment had made him feel *wanted*, as if he had a purpose in life. That being someone's son was important, rather than an annoyance to be dealt with. Or *abandoned*.

'So, you see this bit here?' Ray had continued, holding up a chunk of metal. 'This is the cylinder. Look at all the pitting.' He didn't mention anything else about a son that afternoon, but sensed that Ray's words had come from a place deep inside him. A place that was shielded by the armour he'd built around himself over the years. The place no one ever saw. Except him. He'd just been given a glimpse.

Theo had peered closely at the pockmarks on the metal, reminded of the skin on his cheeks until he'd got those antibiotics.

'This is the part we need to make smooth again.'

'So, like, you're going to get rid of all the rust and marks on the entire engine?' Theo stared at the racing-green carcass of the car. He had to admit, as old bangers went, it was pretty cool with its fog lamps and orange racing stripes.

'Indeed,' Ray had replied.

'Why not just get a new engine?'

'Because then it wouldn't be original, would it?' Ray had replied, spitting on the piston head and wiping it with a rag. More dints showed up. 'It would be pretending to be something it's not.'

Theo had thought about this a lot, and now, as he returned to the living room with his beer, squaring up to the glares he was still getting for what he'd just said, he wondered if *he'd* been pretending for most of his life, that it was *him* who wasn't being his true and authentic self, whatever that was – and, like the engine, he was pockmarked and broken.

———

The next morning, Theo was out of bed before everyone else. The adults had all got a bit tipsy last night. But not Theo. He didn't see the point. A beer or two – fine. But getting shitfaced in company only ever led to trouble, to saying things you didn't mean. In any case, being awake early gave him some alone time. He sat beside the warm, glowing embers of the fire, the air filled with the fragrant tang of woodsmoke from last night as he drank a coffee and checked the men's advice forum on his laptop to see what replies he'd had.

None.

Then, when he heard the stirrings of the others getting up, it was time to make his exit. He snapped his computer closed and stuffed his feet into his trainers. He was going for a walk.

He had no idea where he was going, but Google Maps showed him the route to the nearby village, Glengalloch, only a mile or so away. Theo had never been one for getting his steps in or going to the gym. What was the point? Nah, he was just out walking to avoid eating breakfast with a bunch of people he didn't really like.

He trudged down the lane, shrouded in semi-shadow by the tall pine trees either side, even though the sky was already brilliant blue above the forest. Occasionally a flare of sun caught his eyes, making him slip on his wraparound shades.

Down the hill to his left was the route to the loch, and straight ahead at the small intersection was more forest, which eventually led to the open moor and the pub where the others had been yesterday. He knew this because he'd tracked his dad's new work phone – not that Travis knew he had tabs on him. When the haulage company had presented him with the latest iPhone, his dad had let him have a play about with it and sort him out with a few apps. He'd given him the password, which also allowed him to track the phone on his own iPhone when he was away in Europe. Idiot. The reception had been patchy here in Scotland but, bit by bit, the blue dot representing his father had caught up with their location yesterday. He'd probably connected to the Wi-Fi in the pub.

Eventually, feeling more breathless than he was used to from the steep incline, Theo reached Glengalloch. First impressions didn't take any more of his breath away. A run-down farm sat on the outskirts of the village, followed by a terrace of white-washed cottages with doorways that looked only just high enough for a child to use. Then there was a row of concrete-fronted council houses with neat pots of geraniums and heather out front, and a couple of bigger stone properties as he approached the village centre, and then a pub – the Stag and Pheasant, a real spit and sawdust-looking place – set opposite a village green with a memorial at its centre. He spotted a sign for a doctor's surgery, and on the other side of the green was the village store. He headed over and went in, thankful it was open at this early hour. The bell on the door tinkled as he went inside.

'Mornin', duck,' came a voice.

Theo looked over. A woman, about the same age as Connie, stood behind the counter. She wasn't slim and elegant like he had to admit Connie was – rather, this woman was stockier, with her exposed forearms padded with muscle, fat and crêpey skin. Her wispy grey hair was packed up in a tight bun, and the backs of her hands were mapped with blue veins and freckles. She was taking tins from a box and pricing them up with a sticker gun.

'Morning,' Theo said, approaching the counter. The shutter covering the cigarettes had been left open, and his eyes scanned what they'd got. 'Twenty Bensons, please.'

The woman stopped what she was doing and thrust her hands on her hips. 'Ach, what is it with you young 'uns?' Her accent was thick and undeniably local, and Theo had to tune into it to understand her.

'Eh?'

'Wi' the smoking, boy? Why you wannae do that to yourself?' She shook her head.

'Not really thought about it,' Theo said, shrugging. Shopkeepers never usually spoke to him, not in Deptford, anyway. The woman turned and pulled down a pack of cigarettes and ran them through the till. Only then did she think to ask for his ID.

Theo pretended to check his wallet and then the back pockets of his jeans, as well as the inside of his camo jacket. He pulled a face and rolled his eyes. 'Damn... I left it back at the lodge.' Even if he had any ID, he wasn't about to show the old bat he was seventeen and be refused his fags.

'Aye, and my name's Mary Poppins,' the woman said, pulling back her head so that her neck rolled under her chin.

'No, really. You can ask Connie, if you like.'

The woman's face lit up. 'Oh, you're Connie's wee lad?'

Theo nodded. 'Step-grandson,' he replied, forcing a smile. 'She asked me to get some milk and eggs, too,' he added. 'For breakfast. I could walk back again for my ID, I guess... but then we'll be late.' For what, he had no idea, but his lie seemed to be softening the woman's features, so much so that she went off to fetch a dozen eggs and a large carton of milk. She popped them into a bag along with a pack of cigarettes, and held out the card machine, allowing him to tap through the transaction. *Yes!*

'So how long are you up for?' she asked. 'I'm Margie, by the way. Connie and I go way back. Know everything there is to know about each other.' She laughed and her chest bounced as she followed up with a cough. 'And I believe you about the ID.'

Theo stared at her, one eye twitching involuntarily. He had

to be nice. *Fake* nice. 'We're staying about ten days or so,' he said, not really knowing. 'It's beautiful around here.' *Desolate and boring,* he thought.

'Aye, we're lucky to live in such a place. Connie and I both lost our husbands. We've been through a lot together.'

'You knew Ray, then?' Theo couldn't resist. Seeing the old boy's stuff in the lodge – his fishing equipment, his binoculars and birdwatching books, his coat and boots on the rack in the hall... it was so weird to think that the flesh and blood person who used those items was now nothing more than ash.

'Of course, lad,' Margie said, fielding another cough into her plump elbow crease. 'Such a loss, him going so sudden.' She shook her head, a wistful look in her eyes.

Theo nodded. He hadn't bothered to ask anyone exactly how the old man had died.

'Heart attack,' Margie said as if she'd read his mind. 'And he weren't even that old. Early seventies is no age for a fit man like him.'

'That's really crap.'

'Didnae surprise me, though,' she said, the neck rolls appearing again. She leant forward on the counter as if her legs were tiring of her weight. 'I don't know, I'm not one for gossip, lad, but I'm surprised he lasted that long, you know, with the weight of it all pressing down on him. Enough to give anyone a heart attack.'

There was a look in her eyes that defied even the coolest of cats not to ask. Theo bit. 'Weight of what?'

Margie shook her head, loosening several wiry strands of black-grey hair from her bun. 'Ach, don't mind me and my tongue. It was all a long time ago and not my business any more.' Margie grabbed another tin to label. 'But you cannae help thinking about these things, why bad stuff happens. What do they call it now?'

Theo shook his head and frowned, confused.

'What goes around comes around kind of thing. Help me out, lad...'

'You mean karma?' Theo suggested, grabbing the bag ready to leave. He needed a fag.

'Aye, lad, that's it. Karma. Ray Hunter got a good dose of that.'

ELEVEN

DARBY

It was getting harder and harder to keep it a secret. Darby was certain Kate had noticed that something was going on between her and Adrian. She could just tell. Sisters *knew*. It had been the same when they were growing up – nothing was sacred or private in the Hunter family, least of all between the three siblings. They say twins have a kind of psychic ability, but she'd often wondered if the three of them were somehow triplets, albeit years apart.

She felt dreadful about what was going on, but how could she explain it to Kate? No, there was no option but for her and Adrian to keep things quiet between them, though they both admitted that it was getting harder and harder as time went by. Neither had ever expected this to happen.

'Hey, you...' Adrian said to her, after everyone had eaten breakfast and the plates had been cleared away. It was only her remaining in the living room – Kate having taken Charlie to play outside – and the others were either showering or getting ready for the day. Travis had gone out searching for Theo, who'd been absent for breakfast and, worryingly, his bed had been empty when Finn had woken.

Darby turned at the sound of Adrian's voice and the warmth of his hand on her shoulder, her solitude disturbed. Instinct was to shrug away in case Kate suddenly came back inside, but she held still for a moment. They both felt it, were unsure what to do.

'Hi,' she said, looking up at him. At well over six foot, Adrian towered over them all – even Travis. Darby closed her eyes briefly, breathing in as his pine-scented body wash flooded her nostrils. His proximity wasn't helping matters, and her nerves were on fire. This was wrong. *So* wrong.

'I can't do this any more,' she admitted, surprising even herself. 'We have to tell—'

Adrian put a finger over his lips. 'No,' he said, kindly but firmly. 'Not yet. We've already talked about that. No good will come of it.'

Darby turned and walked off, continuing to the kitchen where she'd been heading. She flicked on the kettle, her back turned to him, thinking, *thinking* of the best thing to say. But there was nothing left to voice between them. It had all been said. Snatched moments alone – hard to engineer given the distance between their houses – deleted WhatsApp messages and guarded phone calls at work were going to be their downfall. Yet the burden of their secret fuelled things between them, as if by knowing what was going on – what had *already* gone on – gave them reason to continue.

'Ray's death is still too recent to drop another bombshell on the family,' Adrian said.

'Then what *do* you suggest?' Darby replied in a harsher tone than she'd intended, swinging round to face him. 'That we continue as we are, as if there isn't this... this *thing* between us?' She didn't even know what to call it, and 'thing' hardly did it justice. Two people inextricably bonded, their secret dragging along between them. Let it out and who knew what kinds of hell would break loose. And it wouldn't affect Kate alone. The

ripples – no, *tidal waves* – would rip through the family. Kate
and Adrian's twins, Connie, Bea, Travis, Theo, Charlie... the
shockwaves would be far-reaching.

'Nothing. I suggest we do absolutely nothing.' Adrian tried
to take hold of Darby's hands, but she whipped them away,
busying herself making a hot drink, and one for him, too.

'Is that your executive decision? You just want to carry on
like this, being clandestine, forevermore?' Darby shook her
head, refusing to let the welling tears spill down her cheek. She
didn't want Kate asking questions when she came back inside.
Out of guilt, she grabbed another mug for her sister.

'Where are you going?' Adrian asked, when Darby slid a
mug towards him and gathered up the other two, heading off.

'To see Kate,' she said in such a way that Adrian knew not to
follow her.

Kate and Charlie weren't in the vicinity of the lodge. The
scrubby parking area directly outside the front veranda led not
to a manicured garden, rather to the edges of the forest that
surrounded the lodge. The air was thick and oxygen-rich this
deep into the forest, though the midges were everywhere –
waterside or not. Darby was about to call out, knowing that
Charlie was totally safe in Kate's care, guessing that she'd probably taken him on a 'bear hunt' through the trees or something
similar, but she stopped herself. She didn't want to break the
tranquillity. Placing Kate's tea on the low wall at the edge of the
veranda, she smiled at the memory as it came to her, taking her
own tea and ambling a few paces down the track that led to the
narrow lane beyond.

'We're all going on a bear hunt...' echoed through the forest
as she remembered her father leading the way when they were
kids and had spent long, lazy summers up here. She, Kate and
Bea would follow him, breathless with excitement as they set off

on their adventure. They each had a little backpack for their lunch – Kate's was blue, Bea's was pink (of *course*) – and her little sister had ridden on their father's shoulders most of the way. Darby's pack was black, to match the rest of her outfit. Even from a young age, she'd never been into girly stuff.

'Did you hear that?' their father had said, stopping suddenly. He crouched low, gripping on to Bea's legs as they wrapped around his neck as she sat on his shoulders. Darby and Kate had followed suit and ducked down low, their breathing and thumping hearts the only thing to be heard. 'A bear...' he'd whispered.

'Yes, yes, I heard it,' Kate whispered back. Her face was a portrait of wonder, highlighted with fear. 'Is it close?'

'Very,' their father had replied. 'Just over there.' He pointed deep into the woods where the dappled sunlight gave way to darkness.

Darby had stood up then, her legs cramping. She'd pulled a packet of gum from her pocket and popped a piece in her mouth. Kate was the eldest and should know better – so why was she being sucked in? Surely this charade was for little Bea, rather than them? She rolled her eyes at Kate's attempt to go along with their father, to suck up to him as she always did, desperate to win his attention.

'Will the bear hurt us?' Bea had asked, leaning down and speaking softly in her father's ear. Darby noticed the anxiety on her little sister's face – the way her rosebud pout quivered, and her fingers curled into their father's slightly greying hair.

'*Noo*, my sweet girl,' he'd crooned up at her. 'She's a mama bear and is looking for food for her young cubs. And besides, she doesn't know we're here.'

Young Darby had mulled this over as they'd walked deeper into the woods. She'd wanted to go out on the boat today – the sun had finally come out after days of rain – not tramp through the gloomy forest looking for make-believe bears. 'So does that mean that if you can't see something, it won't hurt you, Dad?' she'd asked.

Their father had stopped in his tracks and, when he swung around, she saw the complete opposite of what he'd actually said written all over his face. 'Spot on, Darbs. Spot on.'

'Hi, Theo,' Darby said now, taking a sip of her tea. The boy was coming up the track alone, the sound of his footsteps snapping her from her memories. 'Have you seen Kate and Charlie, by any chance?'

Theo stopped abruptly and stared at her. 'I saw Kate a few moments ago – at least I think it was her. She was alone, though.'

'*Alone?* Where did you see her?' Darby's heart skipped a couple of beats.

'In the woods as I was walking back from Glengalloch just now. I called out, but she... well, she kind of ignored me and ran off into the trees. I figured she wanted to be by herself.' Theo shrugged.

Darby frowned, staring at him. 'Are you sure it was her?'

'Yeah, pretty sure. Black cap, dark hoodie and jeans. I recognised her face and ponytail.'

'But she's supposed to be looking after Charlie... oh God...' Darby hugged her arms around her body, staring out into the dark forest surrounding them, imagining Charlie lost and alone. 'Where have you been, anyway? Your dad's worried. He's out looking for you.'

'Just to the shop in Glengalloch,' he said, holding up the bag. 'Got milk and eggs.' He grinned.

In the three years Darby had known him, he'd never once done anything thoughtful – especially if it involved spending his own money. 'That's very kind of you,' she said, peering down the drive and scanning the forest again.

'I met the woman in the shop.'

'Margie?'

Theo nodded.

'Did you tell her you were staying here?'

'Yeah. She knows Connie.'

'That woman knows everybody.' And every*thing*, she thought, though concentrating on anything other than Charlie's whereabouts was impossible right now. 'Did... did she say anything else?'

'Yeah, actually. She mentioned your dad, Ray.'

'I know she was very upset by his death,' Darby said. 'She lost her own husband a while back. God... Kate, where *are* you?' She pulled her phone from her pocket and dialled her sister's number, but it went straight to voicemail.

Theo made a strange noise in his throat. 'She didn't sound *that* sad,' he continued after Darby had hung up. 'She was on about karma or something. That your father had got what was coming to him. What did she mean by that?'

'I really don't know,' Darby replied, distracted. 'She's a right old gossip, is Margie.' And now she had plenty to gossip about, Darby thought, because Margie had been the one to catch her and Adrian in a tight embrace as she came out of the toilets in the pub yesterday. They'd been whispering to each other in the corridor – a snatched private moment interrupted.

'She knows... I *swear* she knows something,' Darby had said to Adrian after they were alone again. But she hadn't had a chance to explain further because someone else had come out of the gents' toilets, so they'd quickly pulled away from each other, going separately back into the pub lounge to join the others.

'Oh thank *God*... Kate's back,' Darby suddenly said as she spotted her sister tramping up the drive, although panic set in again when she saw she was indeed alone. 'Kate, where the hell is Charlie?' she called out, her eyes frantically scanning around. 'Is he OK?' Darby charged up to her, grabbing her by the shoulders. 'Where *is* he? Theo saw you in the forest by yourself. What have you done with him?'

'*What?*' Kate looked taken aback, shrugging out of Darby's grip. 'What's got into you? Calm down, for heaven's sake. Charlie's right here with me.' She turned to reveal Charlie toddling along close behind her.

Darby let out a huge sigh as her heart hammered in her chest, holding open her arms as her little son came waddling up to her. If nothing else, the brief shock had provided a distraction from awkward questions, and Theo was now tramping back up to the lodge, glancing at her over his shoulder.

'Went bear hunt, Mummy,' Charlie sang out, his cheeks rosy and a string of dribble on his chin.

'Did you, darling?' Darby said, scooping him up in her shaking arms. He smelt of pine forest and excitement. 'Did you find a bear?'

Charlie nodded vigorously. 'A big scary one.'

Darby kissed her son on the cheek and stared at Kate – her eyes narrowing as she noticed her cream sweatshirt, her pale-grey tracksuit pants. She frowned, praying that her sister hadn't got a glimpse of the big scary bear, too. Because, like their father had said all those years ago, what she didn't see couldn't hurt her.

TWELVE

CONNIE

Connie jumped at the sight of the hand in front of her. It was holding out two wet socks.

'Thought you might want some help,' Theo said, dangling the items.

'A matching pair,' Connie replied, catching her breath. He'd caught her deep in thought – a moment alone to work out exactly when and how she was going to sit her three daughters down and tell them the reason she'd invited them all here in the first place. It wasn't so much about missing opportunities to get them alone; it was more wondering how she'd deal with the fallout afterwards.

Ray had been clever, she thought, with the way he'd left things in his will. A final blow to her, having to pick up the pieces of her family – because that's what it would be in once she'd said the words. There'd be no taking them back. As Ray knew full well when he'd written his will, each of their daughters would be left with one burning question: *Why?*

Connie stared up at the sky. The treetops swayed in the breeze that had picked up this morning, even though it was much stiller down at ground level. But the washing would dry, nonetheless.

'Thanks, Theo.' She took the socks and pinned them to the line, grateful that the boy was saving her aching back as he handed her a T-shirt, though it seemed most out of character for him. Theo's helpful actions reeked of ulterior motive.

'Didn't have you down as the domestic type,' Connie said after she'd removed a peg from between her lips. She glanced at him sideways. The boy returned a sly look.

'Bet there's a lot you don't know about me.'

'Tell me something, then. Something that would surprise me.'

Theo thought for a moment. 'I know how to grind out the cylinders of a 1970s Ford Escort,' he said, reaching into the basket of wet washing. Connie didn't like the way he leered at her, as though he was baiting her somehow. When she remained silent, he continued. 'Ray showed me. Taught me a lot about engines.'

'He certainly loved his old bangers,' Connie replied, making sure her smile was a pleasant one. 'He'd bore anyone who'd listen half-witless,' she added, remembering how he'd not spoken for three days when his beloved cars had been sent to auction several weeks before they'd sold Foxhills. No room for them at the bungalow.

'I wasn't bored by it,' Theo said, handing over a couple of tea towels. 'In fact, I mended the lawnmower back home because of what Ray taught me. Not that we have much grass in south London, but Dad likes to keep it neat.'

Connie imagined Theo and Travis living in Darby's house. It hadn't taken long for them to move in. It was a small Victorian terrace that Darby and Chris had scrimped and saved the deposit for. When they'd first bought it, it was all worn carpet and greasy cooking smells, but between them, they'd soon decorated and made it a home.

And then Chris had died.

Since Travis and his son had got their feet under the table – far too soon after losing Chris, by her reckoning – Connie hadn't been invited down. It was as if Darby now had another life that Connie wasn't a part of. The handful of times mother and daughter had met up, it was either on neutral territory or at Foxhills before she and Ray had sold it.

Darby's excuse for her infrequent visits was distance, which was plausible at least, though moving to the bungalow, which was a little closer, hadn't made much of a difference. In hindsight, Connie wished they'd never left the farm. It had been the start of Ray's demise. That's what she told herself, anyway.

'And I like taking photographs,' Theo went on. 'There, I bet you didn't know that about me, did you?' A pair of black boxer shorts were suddenly dangling in front of Connie's face as Theo held them up. She pegged them on the line.

'No, no I didn't,' she replied, glancing across at him.

'Have you got any old pictures, you know, like of family?'

Connie raised her eyebrows, not because she wasn't sure if there were any photos here at the lodge – there were hundreds of them in a suitcase under her bed – but rather because she was deciding if she wanted to show them to him. Theo wasn't a member of the Hunter family, not really, and having him pick through old pictures, not knowing the history behind them, might feel like an invasion.

'Sure,' she found herself saying against her better judgement, dropping a pair of Mia's knickers on the ground. Before she could retrieve them, Theo lunged down and grabbed them, staring at them for too long as far as Connie was concerned. She tried to take them, but he held on to them until the silky fabric stretched between them.

'I'd like to see them,' Theo said, allowing the pants to ping from his fingers as he finally let go.

. . .

The local weather forecast showed the gusty squalls would drop this afternoon so it was decided that a trip to the loch would be best saved for then. Connie said she'd head to the village shortly to pick up some fresh bread for sandwiches, and Kate offered to make salads and pack up the picnic basket. She enlisted Bea and Mia to help, while Adrian collared Finn to find the fold-up chairs with him in the shed.

Before long, Connie heard a hose running and, as she lugged the case of photographs downstairs, she caught sight of Finn and his father through the window as they washed down the chairs and inflatables, with Adrian dodging the jet of water as Finn aimed it at his dad.

'God, those things haven't seen daylight in a long time,' Connie commented as she smiled at the blow-up dolphins and lilos. 'There's a paddle board out there somewhere too.'

'Sick,' Theo replied, which, from hearing Finn and Mia say similar, Connie knew was a positive thing.

'Right, here you go, young man. They really need sorting out, but you'll find all sorts in here.' Connie plonked the case on the coffee table, which creaked under the weight as she unzipped it. For a moment, she couldn't move at the sight of them all. There were a few albums in there but also dozens of envelopes, tatty and worn, with many hundreds of photographs stuffed inside. Ray had been meticulous about photographing and documenting the time they'd all spent up here at Kirk View, but not so at much organising the pictures. They'd rarely looked at them over the years – maybe once or twice – but mostly they'd just gathered dust under the bed.

Connie's heart skittered at the thought of what seeing them might do to her – give her a warm feeling and make her grateful for her family, or send her into the depths of darkness by reminding her of things that felt as if they'd happened to someone else?

Theo dived straight in, pulling out a white envelope that

had yellowed around the edges. 'Is this my stepmum?' he asked, showing a rare grin. Connie sat down next to the boy, peering at a picture of a young Darby astride a grey pony.

'Yes, yes, it is.' She laughed. Darby's long, skinny legs hung down almost to the pony's fetlocks and a wide-brimmed hat covered her head as she squinted in the sun. Connie remembered nagging Ray time and time again to make her wear a proper riding hat, but his comeback was always the same. *My girls are horsewomen...* He'd always emphasised the '*my*'.

She wiped a finger under her eye, hoping Theo hadn't noticed. There'd been no point in arguing. Ray always got his own way. *Ray's way...* she thought, wondering who, exactly, she'd been back then – what kind of woman she was to tolerate his demands, his moods, his unpredictable temper. Long gone was the woman who did as she was told, the meek person who put up and shut up. Connie shuddered. The process of change in her hadn't been something she could pinpoint to an exact moment. It had just happened, like the elbows of a favourite sweater wearing away.

'She looks like a boy in this one,' Theo said, holding out a photograph of Darby and Kate. They were standing at the edge of the loch dressed in shorts and T-shirts. Where Kate's long hair hung down over her shoulders in pigtails with bows at the ends, she remembered Darby had taken the scissors at the end of the summer term and lopped chunks of her hair off. Connie had been left with no option but to take her to the hairdresser's to have it neatened into a short crop and, sure enough, for a time, everyone thought she was a boy. Darby had loved it, and it had somehow cemented her relationship with her father even more, inadvertently highlighting the unspoken gap that existed between Kate and Ray.

'Who's this?' Theo asked, holding out a photograph of a man sitting in a camping chair at the edge of the loch, his back to the camera. The photographer was a good distance away, as if they hadn't wanted to be spotted.

'Hard to tell,' Connie said, knowing there was no chance Theo would suspect she was lying – that *she'd* taken the picture and knew exactly who the man was. She'd guessed he'd be out fishing that day and had engineered the walk, taking several discreet snaps of him as she and Ray had ambled along – Ray oblivious as to who the man beneath the fishing hat was from a distance, assuming Connie was simply taking pictures of the scenery. As she stared at the photograph, Connie could almost smell the smoke from his cigarette, twisting in a vertical plume from his hand. Feel his fingers on her face, her neck. She'd just wanted something of him to keep.

'Is this Ray when he was younger?' Theo asked, sliding out another picture.

'It is,' Connie replied. 'Handsome, eh?' And it was true. Ray had never been anything but a head-turner in his younger days, and Connie only ever had eyes for him. Until she didn't. 'Look at those muscles,' she said, stroking Ray's forearms in the photo. 'They come from carting bales and hefting sheep for shearing,' she said with a wistful sigh.

Theo shoved his hand deep into the piles of photos and pulled out another packet. Inside were pictures of a much younger Connie holding a baby. She instantly knew who it was from the crocheted shawl with green edges that the little mite was wrapped in.

'Oh, my,' Connie said, smiling. 'Just look at us – me and Kate. She's so tiny.' She put her thumb and forefinger at the edge of the picture, forcing back the tears, but Theo kept a firm hold of it. He looked up at her. 'She was only about two months old.'

'Babies all look the same to me,' Theo remarked. 'Bald and drooly.'

Connie found another laugh, even though inside she was

curling up. Seeing these pictures was hard, but it was also a good chance to remind herself of the reason she'd invited everyone up here. With what she had to tell her three daughters about Ray's will, it meant that *everything* would have to come out – not just that one of them had been disinherited. It was time for total honesty.

'I don't think that's true at all,' Connie said, thinking back. 'Babies have their own little characters and quirks. I crocheted that blanket myself,' she added, remembering how initially, she'd only made one in that style – something to do to pass the endless days of pregnancy.

For the next half an hour, the pair flicked through more pictures as Theo asked questions. Connie saw a side to him that, so far, he'd kept hidden. She couldn't work out if this new, sensitive part of the boy was genuine interest or if he had another motive – something to do with his father, perhaps. In their case, she reckoned the apple had fallen directly under the tree.

'Is this Chris?' Theo asked, holding up a picture of Darby and a man.

'Oh...' Connie wasn't sure if it was appropriate for him to see these, but then thought that if she hid them away, she was erasing part of her daughter's past. 'Yes, that's Chris, Darby's first husband.'

'Why did he die?'

Connie swallowed. She assumed that Darby would have told Travis the full story, but she wasn't sure how much Theo knew about the circumstances. 'An... an accident, I'm afraid.'

Theo didn't react. Just stared at her, making Connie realise he didn't know much at all.

'How come?'

'How come he had an accident?' Connie asked, knowing full well what he meant. She just wanted an extra second to think how to make it sound more palatable. *Murder* seemed so dreadful. 'No one really knows.' She put the photo back into the packet, but Theo took it straight out again.

'What kind of accident was it?'

'An unexpected one,' Connie replied, almost relieved that she was interrupted by a loud scream from outside.

THIRTEEN

BEA

Bea dropped her phone on her bed and sat up, listening. From the window, she couldn't quite see around the back of the house to where the piercing scream had come from. A quick glance at the top bunk told her that Mia wasn't there, though she'd been in the room shortly after breakfast.

She thrust her feet into her battered trainers, and grabbed her old mohair cardigan off the chair, slinging it on with one shoulder exposed as the baggy garment settled lopsidedly.

'Mum, where are you?' she called out as she ran down the stairs. 'What's going on?' she said to a gawping Theo as he sat alone in the living room, a suitcase of photographs in front of him.

Theo shrugged.

Bea continued on and dashed out of the back door, tripping on the step as her left trainer flapped off her foot, scanning the scrubby area for where the scream could have come from. Colourful inflatables were strewn over the ground with a hose spewing out water as it lay coiled around the toys. She went to the tap on the back wall of the house and turned it off.

And that's when she saw them, all crowded around the

rickety old garden shed that her father had erected years before she was born. It was nothing special, with a moss-covered roof sitting over wooden walls, about ten feet square, but that little hut had been so many things when they were growing up. A playhouse, a fairy castle, a spaceship, an ocean liner, a time machine... then just a plain old shed once again for storing bikes, dinghies, deckchairs and other outdoor detritus when she and her sisters proclaimed themselves too old for fantasy worlds.

'What's going on?' she called out, going over. Connie was at the rear of the huddle squashed in the doorway, straining to see inside. Bea put a hand on her mother's back, making her startle. 'Mum?'

Connie turned. 'I heard a scream,' she said. 'I thought it was you.'

Bea shook her head, seeing Adrian's shadow outlined inside the shed. He was crouching down. Then Mia came rushing out, her hand covering her mouth. She clung on to her grandmother. 'Are you OK?' Bea asked, but Mia didn't speak, her mouth hidden behind her fingers.

Then she heard Travis's voice. 'It's nothing, just a fox or something.' He emerged from the shed, rolling his eyes. Bea slid past her mother, easing her way inside. The shed was dark and smelt musty, just as she remembered. 'What's going on?' she asked her brother-in-law.

Adrian stood up and turned. 'Mia was looking for stuff to take to the beach. I told her that old bat and ball set was in here somewhere. She freaked out and screamed when she found this.'

Bea glanced down to the corner of the shed where Adrian was pointing. At first, all she saw in the darkness was the petrol strimmer propped against the wall and a large plastic bucket that they used to gather pine cones in – to spray silver and gold for Christmas decorations. With her foot, she slid a pair of old wellington boots out of the way – her father's boots – and then she spotted the mangy, rotting carcass on the floor.

'Ew, yuk,' she said, recoiling. 'Nasty.' But still, Bea couldn't take her eyes off it. 'What do you think it is?'

'*Was*,' Adrian corrected. 'I think Travis was right. A fox, I'd say, going by the colour of its fur. What's left of it.'

'Poor thing. Imagine just lying down in a corner and dying.' Bea gasped at the sound of her own words, praying that her mother hadn't heard. When she turned to peer out of the door, she was thankful to see that Connie had taken Mia away from the shed and was comforting her. It was exactly how Connie had found her father a few months ago. Dead in a corner, as if he'd known the end was coming and he'd crawled away to let it happen in peace. Her mum had described him as foetal. Bea couldn't imagine what it must have felt like, to see him lying on the floor of their bungalow – their once strong and vibrant father curled up and lifeless.

'Well, I'd better clear it up,' Adrian said, reaching for a pair of old gardening gloves lying on the potting shelf. Bea watched as he scooped up the rotting remains, most of which appeared to have been devoured by maggots. Then it was her turn to scream.

At the sound of her shrill voice, Adrian dropped the pile of bones and fur. Bea shook, her arms clamped around her, her eyes bulging, and then she burst into fits of hysterical laughter. 'Oh, how awful,' she exclaimed. 'It's Kate's old baby blanket,' she said, pointing down at what the fox had chosen to die on. 'Mum must have kept it. It's all covered in dried... *blood*,' she added, watching on as Adrian scooped the whole lot up, blanket included, and dropped it into the plastic tub.

'Just fox blood,' he said. 'I'll put it all in the incinerator.'

. . .

Despite the earlier stiff breeze, the surface of the loch was now flat calm. The forecast had been right. Bea drew in a deep breath as they made their way down to the water – each of them carrying an item from the back of the Land Rover. The icebox bumped against her leg as she lugged it to the beach area, despite her mother having protested.

'You shouldn't be carrying that in your condition,' Connie had said when they unloaded all the stuff.

'I'm not ill, Mum,' Bea had retorted, shying away as Adrian tried to grab the icebox from her. 'I can manage.'

'X marks the spot!' she sang out a moment later, shielding her brow from the sun as she turned to the others following her. As kids, she, Darby and Kate had always raced each other to be first, to choose the best place to sit, even though it was the same little patch most times. Adrian put the picnic hamper down and unfolded several of the chairs he had clamped under his other arm. Then Travis did the same, dumping a few inflatables and the paddle board beside them. Her mother arrived next, the windbreak tucked under her arm.

Ten minutes later and the afternoon's camp had been set up. The adults sat in the folding chairs, each with a drink in hand, while the three teens stripped off down to their swimwear (Theo keeping his T-shirt on), and grabbed an inflatable each. Mia picked up Charlie and tiptoed over the rough shingle and grit, taking him down to the water's edge, while Finn and Theo had a moment's stand-off over who took the paddle board. In the end, Theo stood down and sauntered over to where the inflatable dolphin lay on its side, blown up by Adrian. Finn reached for the long paddle and strode down to the water with Theo following on behind.

Bea shielded her brow and watched her nephew launch the paddle board onto the water, a proud feeling surging inside her.

'How's the sickness now?' Kate asked in a whisper as she leant closer.

'Better since I had that dry toast earlier,' Bea replied, sipping on her bottle of water. 'And...' She lowered her voice, not wanting the others to hear in case they thought she was silly. 'I've got this feeling already that it's a boy.'

'Might be twins,' Kate whispered back, winking when Bea's expression changed to one of shock.

'Oh God, I'd never cope!' She laughed. 'But if it is, then I hope they turn out just like Finn and Mia.' *Confident and capable*, she thought. *Quite the opposite of me.*

Bea turned back to the loch, watching as Finn stepped onto the board without even a wobble, giving a quick look back as he paddled. She smiled to herself, giving him a little wave. *That's if I keep it – or them*, she thought, placing a hand on her flat stomach.

'Looks like Theo's enjoying himself,' Connie said, pointing as the boy sat astride the blue and white dolphin, his feet clearly still touching the bottom of the loch. 'Takes me back to when you lot were little,' she added, looking at her three daughters in turn. 'I can hardly believe that I'll soon have another grandchild,' she said with a fond smile directed at Bea.

'Except we were about ten when we played with inflatables,' Bea said, not meaning it to sound like a put-down, but instantly realising it did. And, sure enough, Travis bit.

'What the hell do you mean by *that*?' Travis's face reflected the looming grey clouds on the horizon, perhaps heralding a storm later.

Bea stared at him, felt her fingertips press into the tight muscle wall of her stomach. Suddenly, in her mind, she saw herself reaching deep into her abdomen and plucking out the tiny foetus and throwing it at him. She shook her head to rid herself of the horrid thought.

'Nothing...' she whispered. 'Sorry.'

But inside, she knew she wasn't.

FOURTEEN

KATE

Kate knew she had to say something – *any*thing. It was just what she did in situations like this – placate people. Often, she wondered what would happen if she didn't step in, smooth things over, chuck water on the smouldering fire – how it would feel to step back and watch the outcome without interfering. But familiar habits won out – it was what she'd done as a child during her parents' volcanic rows, after all, and the only time her father had paid her much attention.

'Bea, you know that's not true,' Kate said in a soothing voice. 'We'd play with those beach toys well into our late teens. God, we loved them.' She reached into the icebox. 'Another beer, Travis?' She handed one to Adrian, too, though only because she didn't want her pacifying of Travis to seem too obvious.

Since their father's funeral, she'd watched Adrian's drinking creep up. No, not creep – *rocket*. She didn't understand why, though wondered if it had something to do with his sudden interest in Darby. But it wasn't like him at all. He'd been fond of Ray and had dealt with his passing better than any of them. He'd taken care of arrangements, comforted her and the twins, as well as the wider family. He'd gathered photographs and helped write the obituary, as well as discussing with Connie what she wanted to say at the funeral, and he'd even sorted caterers for the wake. Connie had been so grateful for his practical help as well as the emotional support. Any grieving Adrian had done was private and personal, and he'd remained entirely in control.

Until the day of the funeral. The wake, to be precise.

Since then, behind closed doors, Kate had watched him virtually pour alcohol down his neck. A wife doesn't miss these things. And he'd become unusually secretive with his phone, even taking it into the bathroom with him. She watched as he popped the top off the beer bottle, taking a long, grateful swig.

'Look how far out Finn has gone,' Connie piped up. She stood and put a hand up to her brow. 'Is he safe?' She turned to Adrian.

'Perfectly,' he replied, wiping his mouth on the back of his hand. 'He's a strong swimmer.'

'So's Theo,' Travis chipped in. Theo was only a few feet out from the shore, his feet still able to reach the bottom as he bobbed about in the shallows on the dolphin. Mia was close by him with Charlie, holding his hands above his head as he paddled, lifting one foot and then the other as if he was trying to avoid the water.

'Finn's been captain of the swim squad for the last two years,' Adrian said, knocking back another long swig of beer.

'Theo is head of his year at school. Did you know?' Travis aimed his remark at Adrian. 'Top marks in all his classes, too.'

Kate – and everyone there – knew this wasn't true. Darby had alluded to Theo being excluded from his previous school and now had to travel twice the distance to the only place that would accept him.

'Want to come for a walk with me, Kate?' Darby stood abruptly, and Kate followed her lead down to the water's edge – a slow amble over the shingle they'd sifted through for treasure when they were kids. 'Couldn't listen to their stupid stand-off any longer,' Darby whispered, slipping her arm through the crook of Kate's elbow. Kate laughed.

'What is it with those two?' Was this the opportunity she needed, to ask Darby about her and Adrian? Kate shuddered. Once the words were out, she couldn't take them back.

'Some stupid male pride thing, I think. No idea why Trav lied like that.'

'Adrian's no better,' Kate said. 'He didn't need to brag about Finn.' They reached the water and said a quick hello to Mia and Charlie – Charlie now giggling as the cool water lapped at his ankles – and continued east along the shore. The loch stretched as far as they could see to the horizon with forested banks flanking either side, though if they'd walked in the opposite direction, they'd have been met by a steep bank of dangerous rocks not far from where they were sitting. They knew from childhood boat trips with their father that each inlet provided a secret bay or a fishing hut or a private dock at a lochside home – or simply an empty little shore to explore.

'How are things, anyway, with you two?' Kate didn't look at her sister as their feet crunched along the shore. Kate in her thick-soled flip-flops and Darby, as usual, in trainers. 'You and Travis.'

'Fine,' Darby replied. 'Travis is busy with work. He's been away a lot.'

'Yeah, I'd heard about the shortage of drivers.'

'He's steady with this new company, but they've been sending him to Europe much more. They pay and perks are good, but he kind of goes... well, off-grid when he's there.'

'He doesn't phone you?' Kate tried to imagine life on the road as a long-distance HGV driver. Sleeping in his cab, rocking up at different truck stops or lay-bys each night. Washing in public showers. Adrian's soft white-collar job – a production manager in the car industry – seemed a world away. And likewise, her part-time job as a doctor's receptionist. They were content enough in their respective jobs, she supposed, but Kate suddenly felt boring and flat, as though any potential character or interesting quirks had long since been ironed out of her when, as a child, she'd learnt it was best to be almost invisible. To *placate*.

'No, he doesn't call or text,' Darby answered. 'It's always been like that. I think he was just used to it from before we got together, but... well, it's a bit triggering for me, to be honest.'

Kate understood. Chris's death, less than a year before she'd met Travis, had come as such a shock to them all – and the police had pretty much closed the case now, unless new evidence came to light. All they were sure of was that he'd died from drowning after a blow to the head, though the cause of that injury was still unknown. They'd suspected from the start that foul play was possible but, equally, an accident couldn't be ruled out either given there were rocks and deep water nearby.

As the officer in charge had told Darby, he'd never known a case with so little evidence. Barely any leads. Chris's body had been found face down in a river by a dog walker three days after he'd disappeared. No drugs or alcohol in his system, no evidence of a struggle, and his mobile phone turned off. With only the gash on his skull to go by, the coroner was unable to rule conclusively from the pathologist's report if it was an accident or if the injury was inflicted by someone else.

Prior to his body being discovered, Darby had tried contacting him over and over – calling, texting, searching for him locally – and his non-response, the fact of not knowing, was almost more painful than learning that he'd been found dead nearly a hundred miles from home. There had been no reason for him to be in that location. When she'd learnt the news, she was devastated, but at least it had given her a point from which to move forward, one slow step at a time. It was those three days of silence, of non-communication, that were hardest to bear. And so out of character for Chris.

'I can imagine Travis's silence is very triggering for you,' Kate said in a voice that made her response sound unintentionally loaded. *If you hadn't shacked up with someone so thoughtless...* But more than anything, she wanted to ask Darby about Adrian and what the hell was going on between them.

'I'd forgotten how beautiful it is up here,' Darby said. 'I don't think we appreciated it as kids, not truly.'

'I agree,' Kate replied, distracted. She glanced back up at the little camp they'd set up on the shore, wondering if the two men had eaten all the food yet. Or killed each other.

'It's wild, isn't it? Like, nature truly is in control. The mountains, the fast-flowing rivers, the deep loch, the weather – one minute sunny, the next you could be shrouded in fog or a storm.'

Kate wondered where this was going. 'Nothing like our safe lives back home.'

'*Your* safe life in the Midlands, you mean.' Darby laughed and poked Kate in the side. 'Jokes.'

But Kate knew there was truth in this statement, and the thought of it bit into her more than she let on. She hated that everyone viewed her as dull and boring, not a risk taker, always erring on the side of caution. When had her heart last pounded from exhilaration or excitement because of what *she'd* chosen to do on a whim, rather than having something foisted on her and simply going along with it for fear of upsetting anyone?

Never, that was when.

'You and Adrian were in deep discussion in the pub on our walk the other day,' Kate said. 'In the corridor by the loos.' Her heart pounded at the thought of it. She only knew this because Margie and her mouth had come over to their table and told her before she'd headed back to the shop. She'd been up to the Forester's Arms to deliver some pies to the kitchen and had used the toilets before she'd left. 'What were you both talking about?'

'What were we talking about?' Darby repeated.

Kate remained silent, continuing to put one foot in front of the other as they walked around the loch. Waiting for her answer.

'I don't recall,' Darby finally said. 'Can't have been very important.' She let out a laugh and shrugged.

'You two seem quite... close these days.' *What am I doing?* Kate screamed in her head, aware that giving any indication she suspected an affair would instantly make them shut down and be more careful. Without evidence, she couldn't do a damn thing. But like when Darby was trying to get hold of Chris in those frantic few days before his body was found, the not knowing was killing her.

'Adrian's a good 'un, Kate. You're lucky, you realise that?' Darby looked across at her, smiling. 'He's a keeper.'

Then why don't I seem to be keeping him? Kate wondered, giving Darby's arm a tight squeeze.

FIFTEEN

THEO

First thing Theo did when they got back to the lodge was to check the forum for replies. He reckoned he'd managed to hide his embarrassment earlier when Finn had to swim out to rescue him after he'd got stranded on the paddle board when he'd finally got a turn. But God, the *shame*. And Finn had been so good-natured about it after the stupid oar had broken. He hadn't expected that.

'Don't worry, the paddle was old,' Finn had said, panting as he'd trodden water, grabbing hold of the rope attached to the board. He'd front-crawled out to where Theo was stranded. 'Hang on, mate, and I'll tow you back in.' Finn had shaken out his wet hair and smiled up at him from the water, their eyes connecting for a moment as Theo shivered in his trunks, clinging on to the paddle board for dear life. Truth be known, he'd been terrified of falling in. His swimming was more akin to flailing than anything resembling an actual stroke. He couldn't remember anyone ever being that kind to him before – and it felt... *unsettling*.

Finn had given him a pat on the shoulder when they reached dry land and handed him a towel. 'You OK?' he'd asked, and Theo had nodded, his teeth chattering and his lips blue.

Sitting on his bunk now, Theo opened his laptop and logged in to the advice forum, still shivering even though he'd dried off and put on warm clothes. Downstairs, he heard everyone else coming inside, unpacking the car.

'Yesss,' he whispered when he saw the notifications alert next to his profile name. Four replies. With a shaking hand, he viewed his thread. He needed this plan to work.

> *Th3ology*: Help bruhs! How to get rid of a girl? This girl is severely pissing me off. She's like here staring at me all the time and in the way of things. Need to get rid of her once and for all. Ideas?
>
> *BingDog*: Just ignore her. Don't waste time thinking of her, Also fill out ur profile more so u don't get booted.
>
> *Rappadory98*: hard agree wit Bing, ignore. or film her in the shower then post it. she'll soon back off *smiley emoji*
>
> *HardcoreCrypt – Admin*: Dude, do as Bing suggests and fill profile info if you want more replies. This community is based on trust and members are rightly wary of newcomers. Post in the 'Intros' section so we know a bit about you, and you'll get more responses.
>
> *MrMan435*: Do what u gotta do bruh. Just kill her, that'll wipe the smug smile off her face innit *laughing emoji*

Theo read the replies several times, his eyes narrowing as he felt his body start to shiver again. 'Christ,' he whispered, glancing at the door. 'They're pretty... *harsh*.' And not at all helpful either, he thought. He hadn't expected that level of anger. Maybe it was his fault, and he should have phrased his original post a bit differently or, he considered, perhaps he was asking on the wrong forum. Though even if he never had the courage to do any of the things that had been suggested –

murdering someone seemed extreme, after all – just having other people listen to his frustration had helped a bit.

Dressed in his staple of black jeans and a faded T-shirt, Theo headed downstairs – feeling unusually confident as he walked past the others, who were gathered in the living room drinking tea or more alcohol and making a hell of a din with their pointless conversation.

He slipped outside, unnoticed, like a shadow passing through the room. One of the few benefits of mostly being ignored in life. On the way outside, he bumped into Finn, still dressed in his swim shorts with a towel roped over his shoulders. Fleetingly, as they were wedged in the doorway together, Theo wondered what it would feel like to pull him closer, to press the sturdiness of his broad chest against his skinny one. But then he was imagining tightening the towel around the other boy's neck, watching as his eyes bulged and the veins at his temples turned blue until they popped. He snapped back to reality when he felt a hand slide down his arm.

'Have you warmed up a bit now?' Finn asked, looking him in the eye. He was up on the step, whereas Theo had just stepped down, making him seem much shorter.

'Yeah... thanks,' Theo replied, feeling his cheeks redden. The small smile on Finn's face made him wonder if he'd read his thoughts – and he wasn't sure which one was worse: pulling him close or strangling him.

Finn nodded and patted his arm again. 'Cool,' he said and continued inside.

Theo went out onto the veranda. He wasn't sure where he was going yet, but he'd got his cigarettes in his pocket, and he needed to get out. It was claustrophobic as hell in there.

Round the back of the lodge, Theo smelt smoke. Not cigarette smoke, rather something smouldering. Looking around, he caught sight of a metal dustbin incinerator with grey-black twists coming out of the chimney. Someone was burning something – and not very well, judging by the acrid smell. He grabbed a stick and prised up the lid. Inside, he saw leaves, twigs and other green garden waste, but on top was a rotting dead animal – perhaps a hare or a fox, he reckoned – and underneath it was… wait… what *was* that? He pushed the hot lid completely off so that it fell to the ground and then dug about inside the metal bin with the stick, poking the dead animal aside. There was a grubby knitted thing beneath it, which he hooked out with the stick and held up, shaking it so the embers fell off the cloth.

A blanket, he thought, coughing as he noticed the pale-green scalloped edging. His mind raced when he saw the bloody patches on it – old blood that had turned a yellowy-brown from age. 'It's that blanket from the photograph, I swear,' he muttered to himself, remembering the suitcase of pictures. The photo with Connie holding the baby, he recalled.

Theo wrinkled his nose. He detested babies. Charlie was only just becoming reasonable to have around, but mainly, all he'd done so far in life was steal his dad's time when he'd needed him the most.

And as for his mother… his *birth* mother. He shuddered. How dare she creep into his thoughts! Was it seeing the blanket that had done it, and the picture of Connie with that baby, being a proper mother? Did this bit of crocheted wool represent everything that was missing in his life, everything that had *betrayed* him over the years?

He was intrigued by the bloodstain on it, wondering how it had got there. He stared down at the dead fox carcass, much of it eaten away by maggots. It could be from that, he supposed, but still, he plucked the blanket off the end of the stick and put the lid back on the incinerator, stirring it up a bit first to burn the fox, before hiding the baby shawl behind a loose slat under a corner of the wooden veranda. It would do for now, until he'd had time to think about what he could do with it.

Suddenly, he heard a noise in the forest – twigs cracking underfoot, someone stifling a cough as though the acrid smoke had blown in their direction.

'Who's there?' Theo called out, turning and scanning the trees surrounding him. He squinted, trying to pick out a human shape, or even a face in the darkness of the woods. 'Hello?' He held his breath for a moment.

Nothing. No sounds or sign of anyone there.

'Hello there!' the voice behind him rang out, making Theo startle.

'*Jesus...*' he said, exhaling loudly as his racing heart caught up with his eyes.

'You all back from the loch now?' A man was standing there – the one who'd brought Bea's credit card round the other night. Theo stared at him vacantly. 'I'm Cameron, remember?' the man said, approaching him and extending his hand. 'We didn't meet properly before.'

Theo took his hand and allowed a slanted smile to form. 'Y'alright,' he said, snapping his hand away. He scuffed his feet about, staring at the ground.

'My father was sorry to hear about Ray when I told him and sends his condolences. He asked me to bring this up for Connie.'

Theo eyed the box that Cameron was holding out. He didn't recognise the name of the whisky printed on it. 'Sure, I'll give it to her.'

'Is Connie here?'

'She's busy inside with the others,' Theo replied. He just wanted him to piss off so he could be alone again. 'I'll take it for you.' He reached out his hand, but Cameron held on to the box.

'Cam!' A voice suddenly rang out from the lodge door. They both turned and saw Bea standing there in nothing but a

T-shirt that just reached down to her thighs with a borrowed swimsuit underneath. Her bare feet padded across the decking until she stepped down onto the ground, tiptoeing her way over to Cameron.

'Hi, Bea,' Cameron said. Theo noticed how his eyes swept up and down her. 'Have you had a good day?'

'Lovely, thanks. It's so good to be up here again. Oh, and excuse my new "look".' She wiggled her fingers in quote marks. 'This is what happens when you leave your suitcase on the train. It's Finn's T-shirt.'

'That's bad luck,' he replied. 'Do you know where your luggage ended up?'

'Lost property in Glasgow,' Bea said, rolling her eyes. Theo felt he might as well not have been there, the way they were focused on each other. But he was used to that.

'I could drive you up there to fetch it if you like. No trouble.'

'I wouldn't want to put you out,' Bea replied, swaying from one foot to another.

'Really, it's fine. I'd like to. Tomorrow, perhaps? Dad's got carers coming in for the day, so I won't be needed.'

Theo's ears pricked up. Carers? What was wrong with him? he wondered. And for someone who knew Connie well enough to send an expensive-looking bottle of whisky to her, how come he didn't already know about Ray's death? It was over three months ago now.

'Thanks, that's really kind,' Bea replied. 'I'll make sure to wear some clothes.' Then she giggled and ducked back inside.

Someone needs teaching a lesson, Theo thought, reminded of the forum replies as he finally prised the whisky from Cameron's grip.

'I'll make sure Connie gets this,' he said, skulking off behind the lodge without saying another word.

SIXTEEN

DARBY

'These snatched moments are killing me,' Adrian whispered as he briefly pulled Darby against him. She stood, head against his chest, listening to the beat of his heart. The rhythm was the same as hers – the lub-dub of fear, anxiety and apprehension. But mostly it was drumming out of love. They would break so many hearts by continuing to be secretive, and yet hearts would also be broken if they were honest.

'Me too,' Darby whispered. She'd gone out for a walk about fifteen minutes after Adrian had left the lodge to go and fill the Land Rover with diesel for Connie – just enough time for it not to appear suspicious. Connie had mentioned it was getting low on fuel and, while Adrian would normally just fill up for her when they were next out, Darby took the hint that it was a signal for their next private meet. And she was right. Knowing the forest surrounding the lodge like the back of her hand, she'd climbed up the steep hill behind the lodge and met him on the lane that led to Glengalloch, where the nearest petrol station was located. She'd managed to get some bars of reception at the top of the incline and dropped him a pin with her precise location.

'Did you delete my message?' she asked. She felt the nod of Adrian's head.

'Of course.' He sighed and held her at arm's length as they stood in the gateway at the lay-by.

'I'm certain Kate suspects something's going on,' she said. 'When we went for a walk at the loch earlier, she asked what you and I were discussing in the pub corridor at the Forester's. Bloody Margie must have told her.'

'What did you say?'

'I was vague. She hinted that we seemed "quite close these days", to use her words. I just brushed that off too and told her she was lucky to have a decent man like you.'

'Oh, the irony,' Adrian growled, though Darby wasn't sure what he meant. He shook his head, staring over her shoulder at the surrounding scenery. From up here, the loch glittered below them in the patchy sun. The storm clouds were still gathering, rolling in from the west like a menacing shroud.

'But you *are* decent, Ade. Like, we're trying to protect her. We're trying to protect them *all*.'

'And what if we can't? What if they find out? It was a close call at the funeral, if you remember.'

Darby did remember, as though it was yesterday. She'd promised herself that day would mark the beginning of moving on from the grief of losing her father. There'd been enough loss in her life the last few years and she needed to look to the future now. She'd never actually considered that one day her dad might die. Stupid, of course, but he'd always been there – a stern but solid pillar at the centre of her life. There would always be a Dad-shaped hole in her heart, but the significance of his funeral and subsequent wake, the sharing of memories and stories and fondness for him had been unexpectedly over-shadowed – she and Adrian plunged into the murky waters of deceit. Now they were left carrying their secret with nowhere for it to go.

'I'm still not sure what to make of it all,' Adrian said, his eyes fixed on the horizon. Darby followed his gaze. The side of the tallest mountain to the west of the loch was daubed mauve, as though an artist had washed over the land with watercolour paint. 'It's not our fault this happened to us.'

'Me neither. Kate just wouldn't understand or accept it. Her world would be smashed apart if she knew. Nothing in the family would ever be the same again.'

'But the longer we keep things under wraps, the worse the fallout when she does find out.'

'*When* she finds out?' Darby closed her eyes, refusing to imagine the scenario. 'We're sisters... we've never had secrets, let alone one as big as this. The three of us... we're the Hunter girls... you don't understand. There's a bond between us that can't be broken.' She let out a sob. 'And yet here I am breaking it. I'm the traitor among us.'

'You're not a traitor, Darbs. You're keeping quiet to protect her.'

'What if we're *not* protecting her, though? We're taking away her free choice. Currently, she doesn't have any say in the matter. I know she's suspicious, senses something. And it won't be long before the others do, too.'

Suddenly, an approaching vehicle rumbled over the brow of the hill. Before they could react, the driver's face was right beside them as the car slowed and stopped. Swiftly, the pair pulled apart.

'Hello, you two!' he called out through his open window. 'Lovely day for a walk. Going to be stormy later, though.' He pointed at the churning sky in the distance. Then his eyes flicked to the parked Land Rover.

'Hi, Cameron,' Darby forced out.

'I'm on my way to get fuel for Connie,' Adrian said, glancing at the Land Rover. 'Came across my sis-in-law out for a walk and asked if she needed a lift in case it rained. We were just admiring the scenery.'

'Stunning, isn't it?' To Darby's horror, Cameron switched off the engine and got out. He leant on the open car door, gazing around him. 'You know, I'd forgotten just how much I love it up here. My father moved down south many years ago after his accident. That was where I was born. We came up here once or twice when I was growing up, but my mother was never keen on living up here.' Cameron laughed, a twinkle in his piercing blue eyes. 'She said my dad somehow got lost when he was here, as though he transformed into someone else entirely. She said she didn't recognise the Scottish version of him.'

'So does your mother live up here now, too?' Adrian asked.

'No,' Cameron replied. 'She divorced him years ago. They were only married a short time. Truth was, I think he turned into someone else a bit too much for her liking.' Despite the serious revelation, Cameron's eyes remained lightly creased from his smile.

'Oh, I'm sorry to hear that.'

'Don't be,' Cameron replied. 'My mum's much younger than him and I don't think she fully realised what she was taking on when they married. I was just a kid when they split, but even then, I knew that my father is... well, he's a lot – a lot for anyone to cope with, however much they love him.'

Darby tried to hide her frown, wondering what he meant. She heard Adrian and Cameron's conversation raining around her, but she just wanted to leave, get out, escape. Where to, she had no idea, but she didn't want to go back to the lodge and face Kate's stares and suspicions, and she didn't want to go home to London either. Right now, she didn't want to be anywhere.

'Don't you think, Darby?'

'Sorry?' She snapped back to reality.

'Don't you think that Cameron and his father should come

over for dinner one evening so we can get to know our new neighbours?'

'Sure, yes. Of course.' Darby smiled, wondering what the others would make of this. 'There's always room around the Hunter table,' she added in the style of her mother's hospitality.

'How about tonight, then?' Adrian said. 'I'll pick up some meat from the farm shop in Glengalloch while I'm getting fuel. They're open for a couple of hours on a Sunday afternoon.' He glanced at his watch. 'And we've got some decent wine in. Say, about half past seven?'

Darby glanced at her phone. That was only a couple of hours away.

'We have to eat anyway,' Adrian said, nudging her, when Cameron was slow replying. 'And that chicken in the fridge won't be big enough for everyone.'

'Thanks,' Cameron finally replied. 'That's very kind. My father doesn't get out much these days. Consider it a date.'

Adrian reached out and patted Cameron's shoulder, with Darby watching on as Cameron got back in his car, driving off down the hill with a couple of quick toots on the horn.

'What the *actual*?' Darby hissed. She covered her face, almost buckling at the knees. 'Do you really think that was a good idea? Don't we have enough going on without having to socialise with virtual strangers all night? And what will Mum say? I think she's tired from being at the loch all afternoon.'

Adrian took hold of Darby's shoulders. 'She won't mind at all. You know how much she loves hosting, and perhaps Cameron's father will have some good memories to share about Ray. They obviously knew each other back in the day. And it'll take the heat off *us*, at least for an evening.'

Darby took a deep breath. 'Yeah, you're right. I'm sorry.' She stared at the ground as Adrian fished in his pocket for the Land Rover keys. 'I'll head back now. I'll say I went out for some fresh air and bumped into you, then Cameron pulled over. He'll let it slip later that he saw us both, so we need a cover story.'

'Fine,' Adrian said, pulling her close again. He planted a quick kiss on the top of her head, making Darby screw up her eyes. She couldn't do this any more. She had to tell Kate. She had to confess the truth. She just didn't know when or how. 'See you later,' Adrian said, getting back in the Land Rover and driving off while Darby watched him disappear out of sight, which, she thought as she turned to walk back to the lodge, is exactly what she wished she could do.

SEVENTEEN

CONNIE

'You did *what?*' Connie stared at Darby.

Company was the last thing she wanted tonight of all nights – the effort and chit-chat she'd have to make. Besides, she'd been planning on taking her daughters aside after dinner and having a quiet talk with them, finally breaking the news about what she'd learnt from Ray's solicitor a month ago. It was weighing down on her so heavily, she could hardly breathe.

'I'm sorry, Mum.' Darby bit a fingernail and, as she used to when she was a child, Connie gently batted her daughter's hand from her mouth. 'It was Adrian's fault... when I... bumped into him on my walk.' She cleared her throat. 'He made the invite, and it would have seemed rude if I'd then objected.'

'You could have tried, at least. Said we had other plans, or something. I... I haven't prepared anything or tidied up or... or even washed my hair.'

'Your hair looks fine, Mum,' came a voice from the kitchen entrance. Kate came in and tweaked a grey lock of her mother's loose bun. 'Did I hear right... we have visitors later?'

'You did indeed,' Connie said with a sigh, patting the neat pile of folded washing on the kitchen table. 'And thanks for bringing this in, love,' she said to Kate, giving her a smile. 'Looks like more rain later.'

Kate stared at the laundry. 'It wasn't me,' she said, shrugging. 'But I'm glad it's dry because I want my navy hoodie for tomorrow.' She looked through the stack, then carefully went through it a second time. 'It was in the wash, wasn't it, Mum?'

'Yes, I definitely remember pegging it out,' Connie replied. 'It must be there somewhere.'

'Well, it's not,' Kate said. Connie peered out of the window to see if it had been left on the line, but there was no sign of it.

'Don't blame me,' Darby said. 'I didn't bring the washing in either. In fact, it was already inside when we got back from the loch.'

'That's odd,' Connie said, glancing at her. Then she looked through the laundry again. 'I swear there was some of Mia's underwear hanging out on the line, but that's not here either.'

In fact, Connie could clearly see that the stack of clean washing was far less than the amount she'd hung out earlier. But for now, she shrugged it off – there were more important things to think about. Like how she was going to get through an evening of socialising that she really didn't want.

'Who's coming tonight anyway?' Kate asked.

'Cameron and his father,' Darby piped up in an overly cheerful voice. It was clear to Connie that she was hoping her fake enthusiasm might provide a distraction and take the heat off whatever was going on between her and Adrian. Connie wasn't blind; she'd observed *things* between Darby and Adrian lately – and if she'd noticed it, then Kate surely would have as well. 'Adrian's just popped to the farm shop to get supplies,' Darby continued. 'I bumped into him when I was out on my walk.'

Connie heard Kate's sudden intake of breath, saw her eyes grow wide.

She knows, too.

'Oh... right, I see,' Kate said, staring at Darby for a beat. 'Mum, have you met Cameron's father before?' she continued, managing to keep her cool. 'From what Cameron has said, he seemed to know Dad.'

Connie shook her head. 'No. He's probably one of your dad's old friends from the pub. I guess we'll know all about him by the end of the night.' Her expression was a weary one, but she was now resigned to the visitors. 'Take the washing upstairs and then come and help me get this place tidied up, will you, Kate?' She noticed how Darby's shoulders relaxed, how her daughter knew that once she'd slipped into coping-and-getting-on-with-it mode, then the invite was an accepted outcome. She would press on without complaint, as she always had.

'Of course, Mum,' Kate said, picking up the pile of laundry. But as she did so, several items slid off the top of the pile, revealing a tiny, pale-pink babygrow tucked between a couple of T-shirts. It was the size a newborn would wear. Kate suddenly let out a gasp, dropping the laundry back on the table. 'Oh my God... what the *hell*...?'

Connie stared at the item, completely unable to speak or move for a moment. Finally, she reached out and picked up the soft baby suit, hardly daring to blink or breathe when she saw it. She shook her head, forcing out a fake laugh.

'Maybe it was one of Charlie's from when he was a baby, and somehow it got put in the washing basket,' she said, aware she sounded unconvincing.

But Connie knew it wasn't Charlie's, and by the looks on their faces, Darby and Kate knew it wasn't his either. And there was no reason that Connie could think of to explain away the dried blood and mud smeared down the front of it.

The table was set. Eleven places plus Charlie's highchair. Adrian had returned earlier with a huge leg of lamb from the farm shop, which, going by the size of it, meant they'd be eating later than usual. The joint was in the oven, rubbed with oil and sea salt, and Connie had pressed little sprigs of rosemary and cloves of garlic into its flesh. Darby and Kate were in charge of vegetables, while Adrian was sorting drinks, and Travis and Theo were bringing in a stack of firewood and getting a blaze going. With the looming storm, Connie thought a fire was warranted, despite her and Ray's September tradition.

It seemed things were changing, had *already* changed – and Ray wasn't here to protest otherwise. It unnerved her, she couldn't deny that. He'd always been in control, and she was used to obeying. He'd cleared up. He'd made things right again. He'd buried the past and reset their future.

Ray's way.

But now, since his death... it seemed as though there were rumblings stirring beneath the ground. Fingers reaching up through the dirt. The truth working its way out. And she didn't like it. It made her feel vulnerable. Scared.

Connie stared at the bottle of whisky on the kitchen counter in its decorative, gold-embossed box. She was tempted to open it, have a couple of shots to calm her nerves. She knew it was expensive – Ray had enjoyed it in the past. But what she didn't know was why Cameron's father had sent it up with his son.

There was a sharp rap at the door, making Connie jump. She didn't need a drink, not of whisky, anyway. A few sips of wine later to ease the awkwardness of meeting new people and that would be that.

Adrian beat her to the front door. 'Hello, welcome,' she heard him say. Connie whipped off her apron, fluffed up her hair and rolled her lips together to ensure the lipstick she'd applied was smooth.

It was the feet coming inside that she saw first – limp, one of them twisted the wrong way, a tartan slipper on each. Then the wheels – small ones at the front followed by larger ones as Cameron bumped the wheelchair over the threshold. A blanket was draped over the man's knees – again tartan – and, as he was pushed inside, Connie noticed that his upper body was very different to his wasted and skinny lower limbs.

Her mouth suddenly went dry as she gripped on to the doorframe, feeling light-headed. Her eyes grew wide, and her heart pounded as she stared at him. *Surely not...*

The man, early seventies, appeared a picture of health and clean living – thick grey hair pulled back in a band, a broad chest beneath his black T-shirt, his muscular arms filling out the short sleeves. His skin was mottled and tanned and, while he had the expected lines of an older man on his face, he didn't appear old as such.

Connie stepped forward, her hand over her mouth, trying to convince herself that it wasn't him.

'Hello, Cameron, lovely to see you again,' someone said.

As the man drew closer, Connie breathed in, allowing her mind to catch up with her senses. Musk, sandalwood, the scent of the forest... she'd never known the name of what he wore, but it located the memories stored in the box at the back of her mind as if they'd been put there yesterday.

She stared at the man in the wheelchair. And he stared at her.

Say nothing...

'Thanks so much for inviting us,' Cameron replied, pushing his father inside so Adrian could close the door. It wasn't raining yet, but the smell of the impending storm followed them in. 'Everyone, this is Fraser, my dad.'

And there it was.

Fraser.

After all this time, he was in her house, just feet away from her.

Connie closed her eyes. She didn't need them open anyway.

She knew exactly who he was, what he looked like, what he felt like, what made him happy, angry, sad, scared.

'Hi, Fraser, hi, Cameron...' The voices rang out around her as her family gathered in the entranceway to greet their guests.

'Looks like you just beat the storm...'

'Welcome to the lodge...'

'Madhouse,' someone else said, laughing.

'Nice to meet you...'

'Come in... do you want a drink?'

'Let me take your coats...'

'Please, come through...'

Connie stood motionless, her closed eyes blocking it all out. She knew Fraser was looking directly at her – she could feel the heat of his stare – neither of them saying a word as the melee swelled around them.

But soon, she would look at him. Oh yes, right in the eye. She would hold his gaze and absorb it, read his mind, try to figure out why he was here, how he could *possibly* be here, and what it was that he wanted. Because Connie knew there was no way in the world this chance meeting was an accident. There'd been enough of those. It wasn't even fate. It went way deeper than that, far beyond anything the universe had constructed.

'Mum, are you OK?' Connie felt a hand on her arm. She opened her eyes. It was Kate. Beyond her, the hallway was now clear. Everyone had gone through to the living area, where Adrian was pouring drinks.

'Yes, yes, I'm fine. Sorry. I was just mentally checking I'd prepared everything. Mint sauce... that's what I need to put on the table.'

Kate nodded in a way that showed her she was unconvinced.

In the kitchen, Connie dolloped spoonfuls of sauce into a little china dish – a dish that Ray had found at a local market years ago. 'For my pheasant collection,' he'd stated with a smile, running his finger over the design and handing across the five pounds it had cost.

'Mum, your hands are shaking. Are you sure you're feeling OK?'

'Chipper, love. Why don't you go and get a drink with the others? It's all under control in here.' Connie handed over the dish for Kate to put on the table. When she'd gone, she released a heavy sigh, covering her face with shaking hands.

Adrian carved. He stood at the head of the table – the place where Ray had always sat – sharpening the long carving knife in slow sweeps up and down the steel. Despite the general chatter growing louder the more wine everyone drank, Connie felt cautious and on edge. She never thought she'd see Fraser again and, even though she'd played out the scenario a thousand times in her head, imagining what it would be like, how she'd handle it, nothing could have prepared her for the feelings rampaging through her now.

'Cam's going to drive me to get my suitcase from Glasgow tomorrow,' Bea announced. *Cam*, Connie thought. Familiar already. Fingers of the past getting a grip on the present. 'So you'll all be pleased to hear that I won't have to keep borrowing stuff.'

'You won't fit into any of your clothes soon enough,' Darby said. Her subsequent look told Connie that she wasn't sure if she should have mentioned anything to do with Bea's pregnancy in front of strangers. *Except one of them isn't a stranger.*

'Why not?' Fraser hadn't said much since he'd arrived and when he did speak, his words were sparse. His voice had changed little since she'd last seen him. Deep and powerful, yet with the softer and kind edge she remembered, too. And the Scottish lilt was still present.

'I'm pregnant,' Bea replied, unflinching. In contrast, Bea

never held back with what she had to say, blurting out whatever came to mind. 'And I left my luggage on the train. I'd forget my head if it wasn't screwed on.'

'That's debateable,' Darby joked, leaning sideways to give her sister a friendly nudge.

'A baby,' Fraser said, as though there was an alternative to what Bea might birth.

Connie forced herself to look up from where she'd been picking at the hem of her napkin – the ones she put out on special occasions. As she'd expected, Fraser was staring directly at her from his position down the other end of the table. His eyes... they were the same, though narrowed to slits as he held his stare. She remembered the looks he'd given her back then, as if she had no choice but to sink into their icy blue depths, shocked by how quickly she'd become used to their temperature. Not freezing, but warm – a heat like she'd never known.

'A granny again,' she forced herself to say, trying to keep everything light. She didn't want it all spilling out here, not like this, not with Fraser and everyone else to witness it. 'My fourth grandchild,' she added, wishing she'd found the courage to talk to her daughters already.

'You have a step-grandson, too, remember?' came Travis's voice nearby. Right on cue, Theo traipsed towards the table, plonking himself down next to his father.

'Of course, of course,' Connie said brightly. The fuse was short enough as it was. 'Thanks for bringing in all the wood,' she said, looking at Travis and Theo in turn. 'Great fire.'

'That was always Ray's job, I remember,' Fraser commented. More words than he usually wasted. 'And it was mine too, until...' He looked down at his legs. 'But I'm a useless old man now.' Another look at Connie.

And that was when they heard the first clap of thunder.

EIGHTEEN

BEA

After having stared at it for a several minutes, Bea cut into her lamb. She'd accepted the plate from Adrian without thinking, but now, as the tender, perfectly cooked flesh oozed pink juice, she found herself salivating. She popped in a mouthful of meat and closed her eyes. *God, that's delicious.*

'Thought you were vegan,' came the predictable comment. From Theo. Of *course* Theo. Like father, like son.

Bea patted her stomach. 'Eating for two now. I want to do right by my baby.'

'You're keeping it, then?' Not Theo this time. It took Bea a moment to realise where the terrible question had come from and, when she did locate the voice, her knife clattered to the floor, getting gravy on her jeans. *Darby's* jeans.

'Of *course* I am,' Bea replied to Travis, red-faced when she emerged from under the table. She glared at him. Whether it was true or not was none of his business.

'What a question!' Darby interjected, giving Travis a sharp nudge with her elbow. 'Sorry, Bea. I don't think he quite meant it in that way.'

'You never know these days,' Travis continued. 'With women. They say one thing but mean another.'

'What's *that* supposed to mean?' Bea half rose from her chair but swiftly turned what was intended as an aggressive action into reaching for the mint sauce. Her hand was shaking as she dolloped some on her plate.

'I'm guessing by the accent that you're originally from Scotland, Fraser?' Kate asked, causing a welcome diversion. Bea simmered inside, flicking occasional glances at Travis. How *dare* he? She'd never liked him. There was something off about him, and him and his son moving into Darby's house so soon after Chris's death had rankled her no end. Especially as it meant there was no room to stay with her sister after Louis had kicked her out. *I hate him*, she thought to herself as she cut another piece of lamb, putting it in her mouth.

If only Darby hadn't asked her to babysit that night, her life would be very different now...

The lamb didn't taste quite so tender this time.

'Yes, I am,' was Fraser's minimal reply to Kate.

'Do you have other family in the area – or Scottish ancestors, perhaps?' Kate went on. *God, someone help her out*, Bea thought. She didn't trust herself to be civil to anyone right now, so she kept quiet.

'Yes again,' Fraser said. In his wheelchair, he was lower than the others seated around the table but had refused Cameron's offer of helping him onto a dining chair or using cushions to raise him up.

'Chris was researching our family tree before he...' Kate continued, though she quickly trailed off, glancing over at Darby.

Not like Kate, Bea thought as she chewed, eyeing the group. *To put her foot in it.* That was usually left up to Travis or Theo.

'It's OK, Kate,' Darby said in solidarity. 'It's fine to talk about him.' She smiled across at Travis, as though she'd previously cleared the mention of her dead husband with him but was still checking. 'He was my late husband,' she added for Fraser's benefit.

'Chris was kind of obsessed with the Hunter family tree.' Kate didn't look up when she spoke. She cut potatoes, sawed into her lamb, pushed carrots about her plate, and kept her head down. 'He found out loads of interesting stuff.'

'Such as?' Fraser asked, suddenly seeming interested.

'A whole string of relatives we never knew existed,' Kate went on. 'Distant cousins and suchlike. All over the country. Darby, if you know his password to the website, you should carry it on. We're not from Scotland originally but it turns out we have ancestors here going way back.'

'What about more recent ones?' Fraser asked, laying down his knife and fork.

Bea looked at her mother. She swore Connie had made a whimpering sound.

'Yeah, I think it threw up a few names. Can you recall any, Darbs?'

Darby shook her head, also keeping her head down.

'Someone at school found out they were adopted through one of those ancestry sites,' Mia piped up. The twins had mainly been quiet so far, with Finn more intent on devouring his food. 'He did a DNA test and went looking for his biological mother, and it caused loads of fuss. His parents split up over it. It was really sad.'

'Lies,' Fraser said to Mia, leaning forward across the table. Mia recoiled. 'You see, that's what they do to families.' He drew a line across his neck with his finger, and Bea noticed he was staring at Connie when he did it. Whatever was going on with those two, she had no idea, but she didn't like the atmosphere.

Bea jumped as the sky suddenly lit up from a flash of lightning, immediately followed by the loudest clap of thunder yet. Rain pelted against the side of the lodge.

Connie stood up. 'I... I think I left the bathroom window open. I'm just going up to check.' She put her napkin on the table and left the room, Bea's eyes tracking her. A moment later, unnoticed because the others were engrossed in discussing family trees, she followed her mother upstairs. She found her sitting on the edge of the bath.

'Mum?' Bea glanced at the windowsill. It was dry and the window was firmly shut. 'Are you OK?' Connie had her head in her hands, her bony spine bent into a curve beneath her blouse.

Connie glanced up, attempting a smile. She was crying.

'Oh, Mum...' Bea sat down next to her, putting an arm round her shoulder. 'Do you feel ill?'

Connie shook her head. 'No.'

'Then what is it? This isn't like you.'

Connie wafted a hand about. 'I'm just tired, love. Nothing to worry about. An afternoon at the loch and all this cooking, it's worn me out. I'm not getting any younger.'

'If you're sure,' Bea said as her mother stood and made a gesture of checking the window again.

Back at the table, the others were nearing the end of their main course. It seemed the topic of conversation was still on family trees and, as Bea and her mother sat down again, she heard the mention of a graveyard. Fraser finally seemed to be opening up, and he held a glass of red wine as he spoke.

'Most of my family is in Canonbie churchyard, further east from here. Their graves are all in a wee huddle.'

'Dad took me there once when I was younger,' Cameron said. 'Can't decide if I found it macabre or interesting.'

'But there's one grave that's puzzled me over the years,' Fraser continued, taking a long glug of wine as he stared at Connie. 'I havenae a clue where one of my closest relatives is buried.' Another long draw on his glass, emptying it. 'And it makes me very sad indeed.'

'Right, shall I clear the plates?' Connie said, clattering her knife and fork together. She hadn't finished. Neither had Bea, but for some reason, she didn't feel like eating any more. All this talk of death and graves... the slices of flesh in front of her... It reminded her why she'd become vegan in the first place, even if she was a really bad vegan sometimes.

Dessert came from the freezer – a hastily reheated apple pie with ice cream. After that, with everyone grumbling how full they were, they squeezed into the living area to get comfortable. Fraser remained in his wheelchair – Cameron positioning him beside the fire – and the others squashed onto the sofas with mugs of tea and coffee. Bea noticed Theo exit before they'd even sat down, his feet thumping up the stairs as more thunder rumbled overhead, and Mia pulled a big cushion from the sofa and sat on the floor at her father's feet.

Adrian stroked his daughter's hair and, for a moment, Bea wished her father was here to do the same to her. Deciding to leave the last space on the sofa for her mother, she opted for the floor too, wanting to sit close to the fire. Her face was level with Fraser's legs and feet, and, at close range, she noticed the skin on his shins between the hem of his tracksuit bottoms and his socks.

It was... scarred, discoloured and hairless, and his ankles were as thin as wrists. She stifled a gasp. Fraser's left foot was bent inwards, and his other foot, while less twisted, seemed limp, his slipper about to fall off. She wondered if he'd had an accident or developed an illness. She recalled him talking about fetching logs, so she presumed he hadn't always been a wheelchair user.

'And Finn is captain of the swim team and hopes to lead the rugby next term. Don't you, Finn?' Adrian continued the conversation, looking over at his son, who was engrossed in his phone, but he humoured his dad with a grin and a nod.

'Sport was never my bag,' Cameron piped up. He was squashed in between Kate and Connie, looking uncomfortable in a thick sweater and scarf that he'd kept on since his arrival. 'I was more into films and music.'

Bea wished she'd bagged the spot next to him, wished it was *her* shoulder and thigh rubbing against his. Perhaps it was the hormones talking, but she fancied him like mad. Or maybe it was the way Louis had yelled at her to get out when she'd announced that the baby wasn't his... She'd never felt so vulnerable and alone.

'But you don't *understand*...' she'd begged, pulling on Louis's sleeve as she'd followed him around the flat. But even as she was pleading for him to listen, to hear her out so she could explain everything, he was stuffing her belongings into bin bags and hurling them out of the second-floor window. Sure, she could have blurted out how her pregnancy had happened but, for once, the words were lodged in her throat and she'd just stood there, watching him get rid of all trace of her, the tears rolling down her cheeks.

'So what do you do for a living, Cameron?' Connie asked, looking across at him. Her mother had been quiet ever since she and Bea had come back downstairs from the bathroom, and Bea knew it was something more than tiredness bothering her.

'Wait, let me guess,' Travis butted in. 'You're a university lecturer. Geology, I reckon.' He clapped his hands together, reckoning he'd got it right.

Cameron grinned and bowed his head. 'No.' He laughed. 'Nothing like that. I'm a vicar.'

NINETEEN

KATE

'Are you going to tell me what's going on?' Kate stared into the mirror above the washbasin later that night, grateful her mother had given them the only bedroom that had an adjoining shower room. It was tiny and they barely both fitted in it as she took her make-up off and Adrian cleaned his teeth.

Adrian glanced up from leaning over the basin, his lips ringed with white foam. He was frowning.

'Between you and Darby,' Kate added in case he hadn't caught her drift.

Adrian rinsed his mouth and spat out, wiping his face on a towel. He was inches away from her, and she smelt his minty breath.

'What on earth are you talking about?' Adrian was deadpan, giving nothing away. But Kate had witnessed it... whatever *it* was. That thing between them. There was no denying it, and she refused to ignore her gut instinct. Besides, Darby had admitted earlier to conveniently bumping into Adrian when she was out on her walk, having decided to randomly take one only a short time after he'd gone out to refuel the Land Rover. Hardly a coincidence.

'I mean, what is it between you and Darby, all the touching and whispers and looks and secret liaisons? Don't think I haven't noticed, Ade. If there's something going on that you know I wouldn't like, then for God's sake tell me.'

Adrian laughed and sighed at the same time, reaching out and giving Kate a squeeze around the middle. 'Whatever you think you've seen, you're imagining it, love,' he said, planting a kiss on her neck. Then he went into the bedroom and pulled off his T-shirt, standing there in his boxers.

Kate saw his reflection behind her in the mirror. She had to fight the instinct not to melt into his arms and agree that yes, she must be imagining things, and then drift into a relaxed sleep as they cuddled in bed. She loved him and she loved his body – he was always there to protect her, to soothe her, to say just the right thing. But she was feeling anything but soothed now as she removed the last of her eye make-up. She brushed her teeth and then joined Adrian in bed. She noticed that he'd pulled his T-shirt back on. And he was lying facing away from her.

'I love that you're the last thing I see before I fall asleep,' he'd once said. Tonight, though, it seemed he'd rather stare at the wall.

'Are you going to answer my question? What's going on?'

Adrian heaved himself onto his back, rocking the bed. 'For God's sake, nothing, Kate. What on earth makes you think we're hiding something?'

'It's... it's the way you look at her. Touch her. Always try to sit close to her.' Even as she was saying these words, Kate knew they made her sound irrational and jealous. It was so hard to verbalise what she'd witnessed – they were just *feelings* resulting from her observations, after all. Nothing particularly rational or concrete. She'd not caught them in bed together, for instance, and not even kissing. She hadn't checked his phone yet – they knew each other's passcodes – but if she didn't get answers, then it might come to that.

'You think I'm having an affair with Darby?' Adrian sprayed out an indignant laugh and shook his head.

'Shh,' Kate hissed. 'You'll wake the others.'

'Rather than accuse me of ridiculous things and getting jealous of your own sister, you might want to focus on why Fraser was acting so hostile towards Mum tonight.' She loved that he sometimes referred to Connie that way. His own mother had passed away several years ago, but he'd often called Connie 'Mum' after they'd got married.

'There's no point changing the subject because—'

Adrian hauled himself up onto one elbow, looming over Kate. She kept her eyes fixed firmly on the ceiling. 'Look, Darby and I are not having an affair. You know I wouldn't do that.' Kate felt him stroke her cheek. 'The last thing I want is to hurt you.'

'Do you promise?' Kate said, turning to look at him. The moonlight seeped in through the curtains, highlighting his face. 'Hand on heart?'

'Hand on heart,' he replied.

Kate sighed out, not quite satisfied, but not as suspicious either. She lay there, unable to sleep, listening to Adrian's breathing getting slower and steadier as he drifted off. It had always annoyed her – that he could sleep like a baby even if he had something on his mind. She certainly still had something on hers. The way he'd not quite looked at her as he'd spoken, and he hadn't actually said the words *I promise*.

If you're lying to me, she thought, still wide awake as the anger inside her grew, *then I'll bloody well kill you. I'll kill* both *of you*.

The morning sun filtered in through a gap in the curtains. Adrian was snoring softly. Kate looked across at him. She knew the signs of a deep sleep, and he was in one. His lips were slightly parted, and one arm was draped across the pillow. He was dead to the world, whereas she'd barely slept at all.

Kate eased herself out of bed, reaching for her dressing gown. Slowly, she slipped it on and knotted the belt at her waist. Then, not taking her eyes off Adrian, she crept around to his side, where his phone was charging on the nightstand.

She paused. The only audible sounds were her breath and the thump of her heart as it sped up. Her hand reached out and she picked up his phone, detaching the charger. Slowly, she placed the cable down again and waited, hardly daring to breathe. She was about to turn and creep out of the bedroom, head downstairs, when Adrian suddenly moved, one arm reaching around where she'd been lying. He made a throaty, sleepy sound then kicked the duvet off him, one leg now outside of the covers. Then the soft snore again as he fell back into a deeper sleep.

Kate breathed out, turning and creeping from the room, silently closing the door behind her. She went down the creaky staircase and into the living area, which smelt of woodsmoke and whisky from last night. She and her mum had cleared up before they'd gone to bed, but there were still a few items littering the dining table from the gathering – a half-finished bottle of her father's claret, several napkins and a woollen scarf draped over the back of a chair.

In the kitchen, Kate closed the sliding door and tapped in Adrian's passcode. Then she tapped it in again, thinking she must have mistyped it. But no, the phone was still locked. She tried twice more, each time the screen jumping in error. Why would he change his passcode if he didn't have something to hide?

Kate put the phone down on the counter, tapping her fingernail on the screen as she stared at it, not knowing what to do or think. Then she put the kettle on to boil. It was just as she was getting a mug down from the cupboard that she heard the vibration. At first, she thought it was the kettle making a noise, but the glow of the phone screen caught her eye. She picked it up and saw a text message.

Let's talk

That's all it said – and the sender's name couldn't have been in Adrian's contacts list because no name showed up, just the number. Then the phone screen went dark again.

At least it's not from Darby, Kate thought – though it left her wondering who had sent the message at such an early hour, and what they wanted to talk about. Or, what if Darby had a second phone, a burner phone stashed away somewhere in case Travis grew suspicious? She'd heard about people in affairs doing similar, read about it in magazines and online, though never for one minute did she think that she'd be suspecting her husband was involved in something like that.

The kettle clicked off as it came to the boil, but Kate had forgotten all about making tea. She looked around the kitchen for a pen and paper to jot down the sender's number, but there was nothing to hand. Her own phone was still upstairs, and she didn't dare risk fetching it and waking Adrian so she could take a photograph of the message. Instead, she went into the living area to her mother's little bureau in the corner. There must be something to write with in there.

'Oh, hi, Theo,' Kate said, startled by the boy when she opened the sliding door. He was just standing there, facing the frosted glass, his hands down by his sides. His nose must have almost been touching the glass. The thought of him spying on her gave her the chills. 'You're up early.'

'So are you,' he said blankly, tracking her as she went to her mother's desk.

'Just looking for a pen and paper,' she said, opening the flap of the desk. There was no need to arouse any suspicion in the boy, she thought as she searched for a scrap of paper, and she certainly didn't want him spouting anything off to the others if he thought she was up to something.

'Tea?' she asked as she strode back to the kitchen, having found what she wanted. She flicked the kettle on to boil again and grabbed another mug from the cupboard. Then she turned to get Adrian's phone so she could jot down the number.

'Oh!' Kate said, choking back her shock. 'Can I have the phone?' She held out her hand, waiting for Theo to pass it over. But he just stood there, his thumb poised over the screen as he stared at it, that annoying bit of greasy side fringe covering one eye.

'*Please...*' he taunted, without looking up.

'It's my phone, Theo. *Please* hand it back.' Kate hated that her voice shook. He was just a kid, yet... he oozed menace without even doing anything. She had to face some difficult people at work – angry patients who'd been kept waiting, many of them in pain, overworked GPs, nurses who were rushed off their feet – but this boy's mere presence somehow trumped all of that. She didn't know how Darby could stand to live in the same house as him. And then a thought struck her. What if her sister was unhappy in her marriage? What if she was looking for a way out in the form of an affair – in the form of her *husband?*

'It's not your phone, though, is it?' Theo said, looking up. Kate wanted to knock the smirk off his face, but, instead, as she always did at work, she took a breath. 'Your phone has a pink cover. I saw you with it yesterday.'

'It's my husband's. He said I could use it. I'm taking it up to him now, so please give it back.'

Finally, the boy handed it over and Kate swiped it from him, astonished by his gall.

'Who *wants to talk?*' Theo asked, leaning back against the

countertop. He folded his arms, a smirk on his face. 'Are you spying? Is that why you're upset?'

To prevent herself from blowing up at him, Kate tucked the phone in her dressing gown pocket along with the pen and paper and made two cups of tea. She'd jot down the number while on the landing before she went back into their bedroom. She picked up the two mugs and headed for the door without looking at him.

'Oi, where's my tea?' he called out after her.

'You know where the kettle is,' Kate replied, hating that she felt close to tears.

TWENTY

THEO

Theo had always had a good memory. No, not just good. More photographic, he reckoned. Not that it had been much use to him over the years. He couldn't be bothered with school, so memorising all the shit that was drummed into them in class seemed pointless, spewing it out in exams. For what? All the stupid tests gave him were a sore hand from writing so much for hours on end, or a clip round the ear from his dad when he bunked them.

But, as he left the kitchen, feeling a bit bad for having rankled Kate so much, he was immensely grateful for his good memory, given that one quick look at Adrian's phone screen had engraved the number of that text message into his mind.

Theo went outside and sat on the top step of the veranda, entering the digits into his contacts list and putting a question mark where the name should go. Then he lit up a cigarette before opening WhatsApp to see if the person had a profile photograph.

'Bingo,' he whispered, the cigarette bobbing between his lips. He narrowed his eyes from the smoke as he tapped the picture and enlarged it to get a better look. It was a dark and moody headshot of a woman, though her face was all but impossible to see. She was wearing a wide-brimmed hat, one of those big felt things with a band around it and a long feather stuck in one side. Her head was angled down with an almost black shadow cast over it, and he could only just make out her jawline, the side of her neck. From the little he saw, he reckoned she could be anything from twenty to fifty years old.

He zoomed in even further on the screen. What if Adrian was having an affair with this woman? The thought made him snort. Was that why Kate had snuck downstairs with his phone, because she was suspicious? She'd seemed very agitated when he'd found her in the kitchen. *God*, he thought, *I could have some fun with this.*

And then he had an idea. Before everyone got up, he went back inside to the cloakroom where he knew Connie had put that suitcase of photographs. She hadn't bothered taking them upstairs again in case the family had wanted to look at them during their stay.

He opened the case and rooted around in various envelopes, until he found the most recent batch of family shots. They looked several years old but that didn't matter. He just had to find a decent one of Adrian. Quickly, he flipped through them all – some pictures of the twins – his eyes lingering on a picture of Finn for a few seconds until he shoved it back in the envelope. There were some of his stepmother, Darby, though in most of them it appeared that she was trying to avoid the camera, and several of Connie and Ray. Theo stared at a picture of the old man, wondering if he had any inkling that before too long, he'd be dead.

And there it was – a shot of Adrian, fishing rod in hand as he looked back over his shoulder at whoever was taking the picture, grinning and looking happy, the sun glinting off the water behind him.

Theo put the photo on the floor, taking a close-up photograph of Adrian's face, making certain there were no light reflections or shadows on it. He wanted it to look like the real thing. He slipped the original picture back in its envelope, then closed the suitcase, stashing it back against the wall.

Back outside – he didn't want distractions as the others were getting up – he replaced his own WhatsApp photo with the new one he'd taken of Adrian. Then he changed his privacy settings so that only his new contact, the mysterious woman in the hat, could see his profile picture. It took a few moments to go through and tick the check boxes to block everyone else from seeing it, but then again, he didn't have many friends, so it wasn't a lengthy task.

Then he opened a new message window, tapping on the '?' in his contacts list as the recipient. For a second, he hesitated. What should he say? He needed to cover the fact that he was using a different number to the original one she'd messaged. Perhaps that would be enough to get the conversation rolling.

Use this number from now on. Safer.

He stared at the message. The one he'd seen on Adrian's phone had been brief and to the point, and he wanted to match the style. And mystery-hat-woman hadn't put any kisses, so neither would he. Then Theo hit send, waiting to see the two grey ticks.

There. Delivered, he thought, a small smile creeping across his face. He could hardly wait for her reply.

Word was, over breakfast, that the boys were going fishing. *News to me,* Theo thought as he shovelled scrambled egg into his mouth. But he didn't really mind. They had him at 'boys', which he took to mean no girls allowed.

Nope, fishing was fine by him. Men killing things. What could be better?

'Ever tried it before, Theo?' Adrian asked. 'Fishing?'

Theo shook his head. 'Not much sea in south London,' he said, squirting on more ketchup. And then it occurred to him: what if Adrian had replied to the original text from Mystery Woman on *his* phone already? That would throw a spanner in the works. She would suspect something was up and most likely alert Adrian on his real phone, checking that the other number really belonged to him. Under the table, he got out his phone and looked at the message he'd sent half an hour ago. Two blue ticks. She'd read it but hadn't replied. He decided to send another message, to be on the safe side.

And yes, we need to talk

'Can't you stay off your phone even for one meal?' Darby said. She was sitting right next to him, making Theo quickly switch back to his home screen and put his phone down on his legs, but the heat was suddenly taken off him when Kate came rushing downstairs, a concerned look on her face.

'Has anyone seen Mia this morning?' she asked, her eyes scanning between them all.

'No, sorry, I haven't,' Darby said, looking up at Kate. 'Isn't she in her room? I called her down for breakfast but assumed she must have been in the shower.'

Kate was shaking her head frantically. 'She's not upstairs... and her bed's unmade.'

'Have you tried calling her?' Adrian said, already on his phone as he went over to the window to look outside.

'It's most unlike Mia,' Connie said, putting down her knife and fork. 'Just to disappear without telling anyone.'

'I know, that's what's worrying me,' Kate said. 'Finn, have you seen her?'

Finn shook his head. He was already up from the table and shoving his feet into his trainers. 'Nope, but if she's not inside, then she must have gone out. I'll go look for her.'

'I'll come with you,' Adrian said, hanging up when the line didn't connect.

'Theo,' Kate said, eyeing him suspiciously. He'd remained silent so far. 'Have *you* seen Mia this morning?'

He stared back at her, feeling uncomfortable now that all eyes were on him. 'No, sorry,' he replied, realising he was already acting out of character. He never apologised. Then he felt his phone vibrate on his legs, so he quickly glanced down at it, hoping it was a message from Mystery Woman. But it wasn't.

Instead, 'One new notification: HELP BRUHS! HOW TO GET RID OF A GIRL?' lit up his screen.

TWENTY-ONE

DARBY

'Did you think there was something *off* about Fraser last night, Mum?'

'That's a strange thing to ask,' Connie said, glancing over to the passenger seat as she drove the Land Rover. 'Why?'

'Darby's right, Mum,' Kate said from the back. 'He was quite... *abrupt* all evening, especially given he'd only just met us. Cameron seems pleasant, though I'd never have guessed he was a vicar.'

'Did he say which parish he's from?' Connie asked, her eyes fixed on the road ahead as she steered the Land Rover along the bumpy lane.

'He told me he's in the process of transferring,' Kate replied. 'Though I think he's been preoccupied with looking after his father since they moved back.'

'That'll be a full-time job in itself, I would imagine,' Darby said, watching the beautiful scenery as they passed. 'And I doubt he'll get any thanks for it. He was a bit of a cantankerous old bugger.'

'You can't say that without knowing him,' Connie said, slowing the vehicle as they approached a junction. She turned right onto the main road when it was clear. 'Everyone has a story. We shouldn't judge.'

'Finally, a smoother ride,' Kate said. 'I always feel nauseous sitting back here.'

'Me too,' Mia piped up, retrieving the little book that Charlie had dropped into the footwell yet again. She'd barely said a word since Adrian and Finn had found her earlier, sitting on a tree stump in the forest, sobbing silently to herself.

'Oh my God, Mia... what *happened*?' Kate had said as Adrian carried their daughter inside, with Finn following behind. Darby had covered her over with a blanket when Adrian put her down on the sofa. The poor girl was only wearing flimsy pyjamas and was shivering. Kate cradled her daughter, trying to warm her up and, while she wasn't crying now, Mia's eyes were puffy and red.

'You'll think I'm stupid,' Darby had heard her whisper to Kate. 'But... but I got lost in the forest.'

'Lost?' Kate had queried, frowning up at Adrian. 'What were you doing out in the forest alone and so early? And without proper clothes or shoes.'

Mia fell silent as if she wasn't sure herself. Darby had to admit, it was strange behaviour, and, for a moment, she wondered if her niece had been sleepwalking.

'I... I was following *you*, Mum,' she'd finally whispered, though Kate and Darby were still puzzled.

'Following me?' Kate replied. 'But I've been inside all morning.'

'Here, darling, drink this,' Connie said, appearing with a cup of tea. 'It'll warm you up.' Then she sat down at the end of the sofa, rubbing her granddaughter's feet.

Mia frowned, hitching the blanket up under her chin. 'I know... I know that now, Mum, but...' She trailed off, staring into space for a moment. 'I guess I was mistaken.'

'Mistaken by what?' Kate said impatiently as she knelt beside her daughter.

'I heard crying,' Mia admitted. 'It woke me up. Like, this really mournful sobbing outside. So I looked out of my window and I saw...' She trailed off again, blowing her nose on a tissue. '...I saw a woman.'

'Did you hear anything, Bea?' Darby had asked, turning to her sister, who'd just joined them. She and Mia were sharing a room after all.

Bea shrugged. 'Dead to the world, I'm afraid. I didn't even hear Mia get up.'

'I must have been half-asleep still because I mistook the woman for you, Mum,' Mia continued. 'I thought you were upset and so I crept down to find you, but when I got outside, whoever it was had gone.'

'How strange,' Kate said, giving Adrian a look. Darby shuddered, hating the thought that someone had been prowling about in the early hours.

'I was about to come back inside again when I heard another noise coming from the forest,' Mia had continued. 'Twigs cracking underfoot and more crying, so I decided to follow whoever it was. I called out, still thinking it was you, Mum, and ran as fast as I could to catch up, but before I knew it, I was completely lost. It was so dark and every way I turned, it all looked the same.' Mia stifled a sob and took a sip of her tea. 'I couldn't even see the sky, the trees were so dense.'

'Oh, you poor thing,' Kate said, giving her another hug. 'You're safe now and whoever it was has gone.'

Mia nodded and sniffed. 'I know, you're right. I was just so convinced it was you. Especially as I'd found your blue sweatshirt on the ground near to where Dad rescued me.'

. . .

Darby hadn't really wanted to go on the shopping trip today, but at least town wouldn't be too busy on a Monday morning. The alternative was sitting at the lodge alone and stewing over Adrian. He'd been distant with her all morning, and since he'd found Mia, she noticed he'd been constantly checking his phone. She had no idea why as she hadn't sent him any messages.

'Let's hope the boys catch something decent for dinner tonight,' Connie said, her tone cheerful. But Darby noticed her white knuckles, how tightly she was gripping the steering wheel. 'Did Bea say what time she'll be joining us later?'

'It shouldn't take too long for her and Cameron to fetch her lost luggage, so probably in time to meet us for lunch.' Darby had noticed the way her little sister had been fawning over Cameron last night, literally trying to attach herself to him at any opportunity, laughing at everything he said.

Darby worried for Bea, she really did, and she wasn't certain she was ready for the responsibility a child would bring. She still hadn't found the right moment to ask her about Louis, what had gone on between the pair of them, but clearly something was up. Bea had barely mentioned him since she'd arrived, apart from revealing that she hadn't even told him about their baby yet. She couldn't stand all the secrets that were percolating in the family. It made her miss her father even more, feeling certain that he'd have had everything out in the open now in that no-nonsense way of his.

'Right,' she remembered him saying one evening after she and Kate had come home from primary school and Connie was cooking supper. Her father had traipsed in from the farm in his overalls, smelling of fresh air and sheep. It was lambing season, and he probably wouldn't even get to finish his dinner before he was called back out to supervise another ewe delivering. 'Who's got a secret to tell?' he'd continued as they all settled down at the table. Bea was in her highchair, too young to understand what was going on. Their father's weekly question was a kind of family amnesty – *confession time*, he'd called it – and they'd all grown used to the weekly ritual, saving up anything that was bothering them for Friday nights.

'I have!' Darby had always wanted to be the first, even if she had to make something up just to feel she'd been able to join in. She'd discovered that even lies had a strangely cathartic effect. 'I once saw Mummy kissing a man,' Darby had said, swinging her legs beneath the table. She'd giggled then, not realising the gravity of what she'd said.

'For goodness' sake, Darbs,' her mother had replied, passing down the ketchup to her father. 'Don't you have a *real* secret to tell?'

'Yes, truth only tonight, please,' her father had said. 'If you want to make stuff up, then tell it to the horses.'

'But it's *not* made-up,' Darby went on, annoyed that they didn't believe her when, for once, she was telling the truth. 'I saw them in the village when we were at the lodge last time. I promise. *Pinky* promise.' She felt her cheeks burn scarlet when her father muttered something about her nose growing long or her tongue falling out, and that he'd have the man's guts if it were true, so she'd kept quiet after that, instead listening to Kate recounting how she felt ashamed for not partnering up with her best friend in PE because the new girl had asked her instead.

Now, as they finally drove into Ayr, Darby couldn't help wondering what her confession would be if her father were here to ask the same question. Would she be brave enough to admit to what was going on between her and Adrian? Would she tell everyone how unhappy she felt with Travis, and that she still missed Chris terribly, that she had an ache in her heart so raw and tender, she didn't think any man would ever be able to soothe her pain?

As Connie parked the car and they all got out, Darby thought: *no... no, I couldn't admit to any of that.* Just like when her father hadn't believed her about her mother and that man in the village – or rather, he hadn't *wanted* to believe her – no one would want to believe her now. She learnt long ago that telling the truth gets you nowhere.

'Over here, Bea,' Darby called out a couple of hours later as she spotted her sister coming into the steamy café. Cameron tagged along behind her as they wove between the tables. The women had spent several hours wandering around Ayr, browsing shops they'd never usually go into, until Charlie got bored and had started grizzling. They'd each bought a few treats, with Connie finding a pack of linen tea cloths from a kitchenware shop – one of those fancy places with overpriced items no one really needed in their kitchen.

'Your father would have insisted I get them,' Connie had said, paying for the pheasant-decorated towels.

Bea sauntered over to their table, dragging her battered suitcase behind her. 'I got it back!' she announced, parking it by the table as she squeezed in next to Connie and Mia, leaving a place for Cameron at the end. 'And miraculously, everything is still inside.'

'Thank you for taking her to Glasgow, Cameron,' Connie said. 'It's a fair way from the lodge.'

Darby's eyes flicked between her mother and him, wondering if Cameron realised just how much babying Bea required from the people in her life. Darby was able to read the intentions written all over her sister's face, but doubted Cameron had the same insight. He barely knew her. Then she wondered why he'd offered to drive her such a long way if he wasn't interested in her, though she wasn't sure if vicars were allowed to have those sorts of feelings.

All Darby knew was that Bea was very taken by him and, with the possibility that things between her and Louis might be over, she knew Bea wouldn't want to be without a man for long. It was the way her sister worked. She *needed* to be needed. Either way, Darby mentally prepared herself for picking up the pieces of broken Bea in a few days and, somehow, sticking her back together. Of course, her hurt wouldn't stem from the non-existent fantasy relationship she'd concocted around some random man. No, if her relationship with Louis had indeed ended, it would be Bea finally realising that he didn't want her and that she was pregnant and quite alone.

TWENTY-TWO

BEA

Bea had already decided that Cameron could be 'the one'. That Louis breaking up with her was fate, allowing her to be free and single, and therefore causing her and Cameron's paths to cross. She felt he was the kind of man who would be good in a crisis – gentle and patient – which was serendipitous given that she usually had one or more crises on the go. Never more so than now.

'What are you thinking about?' she'd heard him ask after they'd retrieved her suitcase from the station's lost property. The noise and bustle of the concourse had put her into a kind of trance, but Cameron's voice pulled her back round again. As she focused on his face, the shops and cafés and people rushing for their trains seemed to blur in the background.

'I was just thinking about my little boy,' Bea said, which although not strictly true, it would have been her next thought.

'I didn't know you already had a son,' Cameron said, taking the handle of the suitcase from her. 'Come on, we'd better hurry. I left the car in a temporary zone.'

'I don't,' Bea said, trotting behind him as he dragged her bag along. She spotted the sticker on the side – Amsterdam – with the second A in the shape of a heart. She'd bought the memento last spring when Louis had surprised her with a visit there, back when she was oblivious to what lay ahead.

Cameron turned to her and laughed. 'Don't tell me – your son is at lost property too? Should we go back?' The wink he gave her melted something inside Bea, made her believe she could trust him, that he was on her side.

'Silly,' Bea said, linking her arm through his. She felt him tense up. 'I mean my pregnancy. I think it's a boy.' The more people she spoke to about it, she figured, the less shocking being pregnant would feel to her. At least that's what she was hoping.

'Congratulations, by the way. I don't think I got a chance to say last night. When's your due date?'

'Thank you,' Bea said quietly, struggling to keep up with his pace once they were out on the street. 'But I really don't feel like celebrating.'

Cameron beeped his car unlocked – a black Rav 4 – and, when they were both inside and the doors closed, he turned to her, a serious look on his face. 'I'm sorry to hear that.'

And that was that. Nothing else was mentioned about it – just general chit-chat during the drive as Bea stared out of the window watching the scenery pass – until they pulled into the car park when they arrived in Ayr to meet the others for lunch forty-five minutes later.

'So why don't you feel like celebrating?'

Bea was taken aback by Cameron's forthright question, but almost felt relieved that someone had bothered to ask. While she'd been bombarded with the usual pregnancy questions from her family, she wasn't surprised that her sisters and mother hadn't taken her aside to figure out how she *actually* felt about the prospect of a baby – and she suspected it was because they didn't want to know the truth. As if they'd *already* guessed that she didn't want it, just by knowing what she was like. That she'd never cope and the whole thing was entirely unplanned and hare-brained. Typical Bea.

'I was raped,' she said, staring straight ahead. If she didn't look him in the eye, perhaps it would feel as though she hadn't said the three words that had been burning like acid in her throat since it had happened.

Cameron sucked in a breath and turned off the engine. He swung around in the driver's seat to face her. 'I'm so sorry, Bea,' he said softly. 'What an unimaginable thing for you to have gone through.'

Bea managed a little nod.

'Have you told anyone else?'

Bea shook her head this time. The fingers of her left hand toyed with the seatbelt strap. 'No.'

'OK,' Cameron said in a kind way, but also a way that indicated he was taking control, that he would handle things – because God only knew that's what she wanted *someone* to do. 'How can I help you?'

Bea looked at him. His eyes were so blue, so intense, she just wanted to fall into the depths of them and be cleansed. 'I don't know,' she whispered. 'I don't know what to do.'

'When did it happen?' Cameron asked. He didn't reach out to touch her or comfort her in any way, for which Bea was grateful. The thought of a man laying a finger on her was abhorrent, even though that's all another part of her wanted. To *be* wanted. She felt disgusted and ashamed. Apart from that, she felt nothing.

'It was my fault.'

'No... rape is never the victim's fault,' Cameron said gently. 'Will you believe me on that?'

Bea shrugged. 'It must have been. I keep going over and over it,' she said. 'And the only conclusion I ever reach is that I brought it on myself, that I somehow *made* him do it. That I gave him the opportunity.'

'Did you tell him to stop, that you didn't want to?'

Bea shook her head. 'Not in so many words. See? It's my fault. I didn't even scream. It was... it was as though I was dead inside. The moment I realised what was happening, that I couldn't fight him off and I was actually going to have to experience it, to go through it...' She took a breath. 'The moment I realised, I kind of shut down. I let it happen.'

'That's a very common reaction to such a horrific trauma,' Cameron said. Bea thought his voice sounded so kind, so out of reach for someone like her. 'Over the years, back at my old church, I listened to several women who'd had similar experiences, and many victims feel this way, Bea. It's your brain trying to protect you. It doesn't mean you wanted it to happen, or that you brought it upon yourself. I promise.'

Bea nodded. She didn't feel very protected by her brain. She felt wide open, raw and vulnerable.

'Have you reported it to the police?'

'No. No one knows except you – and... and the person who did it. I'm sorry to burden you; I don't even know why I told you. I think it's because you don't know me, don't know what I'm like, how broken I am... you have no measure of me, so I knew I'd get your full sympathy without judgement. That's all I wanted, just another soul to know. Please forget I even mentioned it.' She looked him in the eye. 'Promise you won't tell anyone?'

Cameron sighed. His face was a blend of calm and kindness and understanding. That was the moment Bea imagined herself falling in love with him. If someone could sit here like this, listening to her horror, her mistakes, her failings, and still look at her that way, then he was the man for her. She knew she'd never have him, of course – besides, she was pregnant by a rapist, for Christ's sake, and was certain he would never feel the same about her. But from that moment on, she would be content being alone forever, holding on to this kind and unconditional moment, knowing that she'd been truly heard. It would keep her going.

'By reporting it to the police it... it might give you back some feeling of control,' Cameron continued. 'They'll investigate, get justice for you. How will you feel in a year's time, ten, twenty years' time if you keep this to yourself? That's the uncomfortable truth you must face.'

'I don't know,' Bea replied. 'I don't think I'll ever feel any different. Numb and broken forever.'

'I understand, I really do. And there's no pressure.' He paused and they watched people returning to their cars, buying tickets from the machine, loading shopping bags and prams into boots. 'Do you know the person who did this to you?'

Bea nodded, staring at her lap. She'd opened the lid of a box she'd never wanted to look inside. 'Yes.'

'OK, Bea,' Cameron said softly. 'Is he aware you're pregnant?'

Bea nodded then screwed up her eyes. 'Yes.'

'I'm so sorry—'

'Can we not talk about this any more? Can we just go and meet Mum and the others at the shops and pretend everything's OK?' Bea forced her expression to be light and bright, her eyebrows raised, her mouth slightly open.

'OK,' Cameron said. 'I understand. For now, let's put on our normal faces and go get some lunch.'

Our normal faces, Bea thought, unbuckling her seatbelt and getting out of the car. Like there's a chance, just a tiny, thin, slim, barely-there chance that we could possibly be a *we*.

TWENTY-THREE

CONNIE

Later that evening, Connie knelt down at the makeshift grave in a longed-for snatched moment alone, sweeping away pine needles and other debris that had come down in the storm. Then she placed the single lily stem that she'd taken from the bouquet on the dining room table down on the soft earth. Only she knew it was a grave – and Ray, of course, but he'd taken that secret to his own. Part of her wished they could have been buried side by side, but then the other part of her was thankful that they weren't.

'I'm so sorry,' she whispered. 'I'll never stop saying that to you, and I'll never stop loving you.' She'd become adept over the years at blocking it all out, while at the same time, not a day had gone by when she hadn't thought of what had happened and everything that had led up to that tragic night. Life had been busy, focusing on the living, for a start, and caring for her family over the decades had taken every ounce of resolve and energy she'd ever had, as well as loving and protecting them. *My daughters...*

She heard their voices in the distance as she knelt on the earth – Kate's distinctive laugh, Darby's lower voice, more reserved and cautious, and Bea's shrill tones as she joined in. After their shopping trip, they'd come back to the lodge (Bea squeezing into the Land Rover with them) and they were chilling out before preparing the evening meal, hearing all about the fishing trip from the others.

Connie's heart felt warm and frozen at the same time. She cherished these quiet moments alone, reflecting and praying. No amount of begging and pleading with God would change the past, of course, but she could at least ask for forgiveness. She wasn't sure it had been granted yet. Or that it ever would be.

'Mum?' she heard someone call out. The living room window was open, and the sound travelled through the still forest. The grave was only fifty feet or so from the back door, a short climb up the bank – just far enough so that when she was standing at the kitchen sink and looked up, she could think of her, safe and warm tucked up here in the earth. Away from prying eyes. Away from people who wouldn't understand.

There were no obvious markers at the grave – no headstone to indicate that there had once been a burial. It was a private place that soothed Connie's pain by the minutest amount when she visited, located exactly midway between two trees that had been only saplings that rainy day of the ritual they'd performed in lieu of a funeral service – prayers, tears, remorse – and at the exact spot where a clump of daffodils sprouted each spring, planted by her many years ago. The only other way to know there was a body here would be to dig up the bones.

'Mum, are you out here?'

Connie stood up. 'I'll see you tomorrow,' she whispered, kissing her fingers then touching the earth. She straightened out her stiff back and turned to walk back down the slope to the lodge but saw that Darby had already spotted her and was walking up the incline.

'There you are,' her daughter said, almost sounding

annoyed. 'I've been looking for you. What are you doing up here?'

'Nothing,' Connie said, brushing debris off her trousers. 'Just checking around, making sure no trees came down in the storm last night.'

Darby hesitated, giving a quick nod as though it didn't really matter what she was doing because there was something far more important on her mind. 'I need to speak with you.'

'Of course, darling,' Connie replied. 'Shall we go and get a drink?'

———

'Now what's this all about?' Connie said as she and Darby sat out on the veranda with a glass of wine each. 'You seem so serious.'

Darby glanced behind her to the front door of the lodge, a slight frown on her face as she swiped away a couple of midges. Then she stood up to make sure the door was properly closed before sitting down again and knocking back half of her drink in one go.

'This isn't going to be easy, Mum. I don't know *what* to do, but I know I can't keep it a secret any more.' Darby rested her forehead in her hand, which Connie noticed was visibly shaking. Her shoulders were hunched and tense.

'OK, love,' Connie replied, noticing how her heart skipped a couple of beats. 'I'm listening.' She took a long sip of wine herself. She'd always prided herself on being there for her daughters whenever they needed to confide in her – when they were children and now, as adults.

Briefly, she recalled Ray's clumsy attempts to get them to share their worries when they were growing up... what was it he'd called it? The *family confessional* or something silly. All it did as far as she was concerned was make the girls anxious if they didn't actually have something to confess – like it was expected of them to have secrets. Connie had felt bad for her girls, but had been powerless to do anything, because really, she knew that Ray was only doing it so *she* would confess.

'It concerns Adrian...' Darby began. 'And me, too.'

Connie was silent for a moment, listening to the sounds of the forest as her daughter spoke. The setting sun glinted through the trees, making her squint when the glare caught her eye. She gave Darby a small smile, not wanting her to clam up now she'd come this far.

'Well, I can't say that I didn't already know,' she replied as kindly as she could manage, despite what she was thinking.

'You *know*?'

'Darling, you're my daughter. Of *course* I know. I know you even better than you know yourself.' Connie reached out a hand and brushed it over Darby's. 'I'm glad you've got it out in the open, to be honest. If you hadn't said something, it was getting to the point I was going to have to bring it up anyway. And frankly, it needs to stop immediately. I don't know what you're thinking, but *please*, consider your poor sister. Kate isn't as strong as she makes out.' She paused, taking a breath, aware of the shocked expression that swept over Darby's face. 'If you want the truth, I'm actually bloody angry about all of it. What you're doing is beyond low.'

Darby took in a heavy breath and sighed it out. 'I thought we'd been so careful... I had no idea. I mean, how did you find out? Why didn't you say anything before, Mum? This is *huge* news. It changes *everything.*'

'It does indeed, but you need to think what happens now, how you handle the situation. And what Adrian is going to do, too.'

Darby pulled a face – one that told Connie she thought she was off her rocker. And maybe she was. But she understood the delicate situation more than anyone – not that the others knew that.

'Handle it?' Darby said, before blowing out incredulously and taking another sip of wine. 'This isn't about an unruly colt, Mum, or a leaky roof. This affects the whole family, not just Kate. It's shocking... utterly – well, devastating, if I'm perfectly honest. It's been weighing me down since Dad's funeral.'

'Oh, Darby...' Connie shook her head, staring out into the trees – trees that she'd watched grow through countless seasons during their stays up here.

'It's not just up to me and Adrian to decide what to do, though, is it? It affects everyone. Mostly you, Mum.'

Connie looked across at Darby, the first nip of a frown on her brow. 'What are you talking about?' She was confused. 'You two need to take a step back from each other and end it immediately.'

'What are *you* talking about, Mum? I can't believe you're being so calm about all of this.'

The small frown on Connie's face turned into a full-blown one as she put down her drink on the cane table between them. She leant forward on her elbows. 'Darby, you're a grown woman and God knows, you've been through a lot. Losing Chris in that way was horrific. Please don't hate me, but you did get involved with Travis very soon afterwards. It—'

'Mum, what the hell has Travis got to do with any of this?'

'Travis has *everything* to do with it, Darby!' Connie stood up and paced up and down the veranda, hands on her hips. 'I think finding out your partner is having an affair with her brother-in-law makes him very much a part of it!' Connie loomed over her daughter, hating herself for sounding so harsh, but wanting to shake some sense into her too. *Like someone should have done to me...*

'Affair?' Darby said, standing up so she was face to face with her mother.

'Shh, keep your voice down,' Connie said, glancing through the window. The others were all laughing and talking in the living area, with Adrian and Kate sitting next to each other – Kate's arm around her husband's shoulders. But there was no mistaking that Adrian looked tense, had a distracted expression. 'Look, there's a way for you to get out of this mess and save face, but not if you go shouting it out to all and sundry.' Another glance through the window and Connie saw that Adrian's seat was empty.

'Mum, really, you've totally got the wrong end of the—'

'All OK out here?' came a voice. Connie jumped as Adrian stepped out of the front door, closing it behind him. His eyes flicked between Darby and Connie. 'What's going on?' he said, looping his arm around Darby's shoulder.

'Darby's trying to deny the affair you two are having, and I'm trying to do some damage limitation. It's a good job you joined us, Adrian, as I'm not best pleased with either of you. But you both need to cooperate if this mess—'

'Connie,' Adrian said in a deep and soothing voice. 'Listen, Darby and I aren't having an affair, for heaven's sake. The idea is preposterous!' He pulled away from her. 'Has she told you what happened, Connie?'

Connie stared at them both, starting to feel light-headed. She didn't understand. She took hold of the veranda balustrade to support herself. 'No, no... I mean, I thought you two were...' She stared between each of them.

'That's what I've been trying to tell you, Mum. Forget anything about an affair. I'd never do anything like that to Kate. Surely you know that?'

Connie nodded, feeling dizzy. 'Yes, of course. I'm so sorry.'

Adrian sighed, looking at Darby and raising his eyebrows. She gave a small nod in return, hanging her head when he started to speak.

And that's when Connie's head really began to swim, as

though she wasn't sure if what she was hearing was real or not. What came out of Adrian's mouth suddenly made anything seem possible.

'Darby and I were approached by a woman at Ray's funeral. I'd noticed her hovering around before the service, and then she sat at the back of the chapel with a hat pulled down low and a dark veil over her face. Do you remember her?'

Connie found herself shaking her head. She didn't remember that. The entire time, she'd been focused on Ray's coffin and the well-wishers paying their respects. She'd tried to get through it with dignity and resolve, but her heart had been shattered into a million pieces – as though a part of her had died too.

'This woman... she followed us back to the wake and, being dressed in black, no one challenged her. She was wearing a hat and veil, plus a face mask, and we all thought she was a family friend, I suppose. And when Darby and I went outside to get some air, she came up to us,' Adrian continued.

'What did she want?'

Voices from the past flooded Connie's mind, her conscience tapping her on the shoulder – no, *shoving* hard against her back... whispering, then shouting in her ear.

'It all happened so quickly,' Adrian continued, 'but the woman told us that you once had another daughter, Connie. A daughter who died. A daughter who was *killed*.'

And that was the last thing Connie remembered of that evening as her head hit the decking and everything went black.

PART II

TWENTY-FOUR

CONNIE

Forty years earlier

Connie had never seen anything so beautiful and perfect in her life. She thought she was seeing double as she stared down at their faces – two perfect little girls. The bedsheets were soaked – from sweat, a spilled glass of water, and the mess from having just given birth – but she didn't care because mostly they were soaked in love. Drenched in the stuff.

'And ye had no idea it was twins, Con?'

Connie shook her head. It was the truth. She knew she'd been enormous these last few months but had nothing to gauge it by. She'd never been pregnant before, had no idea what to expect. And midwives or doctors... well, they'd not been in the picture. But no one knew that, of course. And no one ever could. *Ray's way.*

'Well, we'd best get these two wee mites cleaned up and dressed, aye?'

'Just a few more minutes,' Connie whispered, gazing down at her daughters as they snuggled at her breast. One twin was slightly bigger than the other and was staring up at her inquisitively, her tiny rosebud mouth squirming and pouting as her huge dark eyes searched out those of her mother. The other baby was smaller and unmoving, her eyes closed, with her fists clasped under her little chin. But Connie knew she was fine, had heard her cry when she'd first come out.

Margie had told her it was just the afterbirth and not to make such a fuss as it would slide out on its own, but Connie was writhing in agony again, screaming the house down. And when Margie had taken a look down there to see what was going on, she'd crossed herself and put her hands together in prayer.

'Sweet Jesus, another one's coming,' she'd said. 'Con, I can see another head. You've got two!'

Connie hadn't taken in the words properly. She was simply going along with what her body was compelling her to do – push. And push damned hard. She screamed and bit and pulled out her hair and wrung out the sheets with white knuckles. After another fifteen minutes, the second baby was born while the first one still lay on the bed between her ankles.

Margie had then scooped them both up and wrapped them in towels she'd fetched from the linen cupboard on the landing. 'This'll have to do until we can get them to hospital,' she'd said, though Connie knew there would be no hospital or midwife or doctors, not if Ray had anything to do with it.

'They're so tiny,' Margie said, sitting on the edge of the bed as Connie stared down at her babies. 'I hope when I have a bairn, they'll be half as beautiful as your girls, Con.'

Connie looked up at her friend, knowing how hard this must be for her. She'd been trying to get pregnant for months, if not years, but her and Jim had had no luck.

'It'll happen for you,' Connie whispered, kissing each of her babies on the head. *But please don't let it be the same way it happened for me...*

. . .

A week later, Ray was back in Scotland. He'd kept Connie at the lodge for most of her pregnancy, certainly for the last six months as soon as she'd started to show. *Lock and key... can't be trusted... no wife of mine... punishment... shame... whore...* these were some of the comments he'd hurled at her to justify her isolated existence. And Connie completely agreed with him. In fact, she'd agreed with him before he even found out. She *was* a whore and *had* brought shame upon their family, and now she was getting everything she deserved.

Connie didn't put up a fight. Not at first, anyway. Throughout her pregnancy, she'd had enough food, she had warmth and shelter – they'd recently finished the renovations on the lodge after Ray had inherited it a few years before, so it was comfortable and had everything she needed. And she had no desire to set foot in the outside world again. But after a couple of months of being cooped up, it seemed she'd earnt Ray's trust as he gave her a key to the back door of the lodge so she could walk down to the loch and watch the sun set.

'Ray, if I'd wanted to leave, I would have smashed a window by now. I'm here, aren't I? I'm doing things your way.'

But nonetheless, Ray was still twitchy every time he left to make the journey back to Foxhills, always had that look in his eye that told Connie he'd never trust her fully again. Besides, his unplanned visits at any hour of the day or night kept her in her place. She wouldn't be running away. And even if she did, she had no money and nowhere to go.

'Jesus Christ,' was all Ray said when he saw the twins for the first time. He smelt of manure and alcohol, and Connie noticed the crescents of dirt underneath his fingernails as he reached out to touch one of the babies. Then he recoiled as if it might bite.

'Did you think I'd be pregnant forever, Ray?' she replied, staring up at him from her place on the sofa.

'But *two* of them,' Ray said, sitting down in the chair oppo-site. He dropped his head into his hands. 'What are they?'

'Girls,' Connie replied softly, each baby latched on to a breast. 'I like the names Kate and Lily. Shall we call them that? You can tell them apart by Lily's birthmark, see?' Connie pointed to the little strawberry-shaped mark at the nape of the baby's neck, desperate for Ray to show an interest in the babies.

But Ray didn't care about names or birthmarks or feeding times or nappies. He roared. He whipped back his head, staring up at the ceiling, and let out a guttural cry that turned his face purple and made the veins on his temples bulge like worms. His fists banged against his thighs and tears streamed down his cheeks.

'Why, Con, *why?*'

You sound like a baby yourself, Connie thought, but kept quiet. And she both loved and hated him for that. She could cope with twins, just about, but not triplets – not if one of them was a grown man. But she also loved him for loving her so fiercely, for not giving up on her, for protecting her and keeping her safe in the lodge during her most vulnerable time. It was when he punched a hole in the door a few days later that she knew it would never work out between them, that his trust would never come back, that she'd have to live under lock and key for the rest of her life.

She knew she had to get out.

It had been a different matter when the babies were tucked up safe inside her, when Ray's visits to Kirk View Lodge had been once every couple of weeks – the disgust dripping off his face when he saw her getting bigger and bigger each time – and she'd just about held herself together. But now they were here, helpless in her arms, the beauty and innocence shining from her babies' eyes, there was no way she was giving them up like they'd previously agreed. Not for anyone. Not even for Ray.

'I don't know why,' Connie said, finally answering his question, though it wasn't the truth. 'I've said I'm sorry, Ray. Heart-breakingly sorry. I love you... Is that not enough?'

Ray stared at her and then went to pour a drink. His answer for everything.

'I made a mistake.'

'A mistake?' He shook his head. 'And *I'm* paying for it,' he growled. Another drink knocked back. 'We made an agreement, Con. I'm taking the babies away. You will stick to that and then everything will be fine again. *We'll* be fine.'

But Connie knew they wouldn't be.

TWENTY-FIVE

RAY

It was about a year before Connie spawned the twins that it all started, with Ray unwittingly inviting the cause of it all into their lives. Hindsight was an asset that no one got the benefit of until it was too late, he came to realise.

'Hello, neighbour,' the voice said.

Ray looked down from the top of the ladder, wiping the sweat off his forehead with the back of his hand. There was a man standing beneath him, a similar age to him in his late twenties, wearing a check shirt, jeans and black boots. A shock of reddy-brown hair hung around his face, the bottom half of which was covered by a thick beard. 'Thought I'd stop by and say welcome.' He was holding a bag, and Ray climbed down the ladder and set down the paint can.

'Hello, there,' Ray said, wiping his hands down his overalls. 'I could use a break,' he said, reaching out to shake the man's hand. 'I'm Ray.'

'Fraser,' the other man said. 'Good to meet you. I thought I finally saw signs of life here. The lights were on when I drove by the other night.'

'We're renovating the old place. I inherited it from my

parents recently, and my wife, Connie, and I figured it was about time it got some use. She's inside. Making curtains.' Ray turned towards the front door on the veranda. '*Con*,' he called out. 'Con, we have a visitor. Come out a while.'

'Will you be living here full time?' Fraser asked. 'It's good to know which properties are gonnae be empty to keep an eye on them. We're a tight community around here.'

Ray tried his best to tune into the man's heavy Scottish accent.

'One day we might,' he told Fraser. 'When we retire in God knows how many decades. But for now, it'll be a holiday home. We'll be up often, though. We're planning on starting a family soon.'

Fraser nodded thoughtfully.

'Hello,' Connie said, joining her husband as she came out. 'Nice to meet you,' she added when introductions were made. Ray put his arm around Connie's slim waist and pulled her close. It was something he'd always done, just as his father had to his mother.

'Oh... I brought you a welcome gift,' Fraser said, holding out the bag in Connie's direction. But Ray swooped in and grabbed it before his wife had a chance to take it.

'Very decent of you,' Ray said, peering inside. Two large trout shimmered up at him, their scaly skin covered in slime, beady eyes fixed open.

'Caught the wee buggers this morning,' Fraser said. 'And I thought this might help wash them down.' He produced a bottle of Scotch from behind his back, again directing it at Connie and, again, Ray took it from Fraser.

'Thanks so much,' Connie said. 'We'll cook them tonight. Would you like a cup of tea?' she asked. 'Kettle's on.'

They all sat on the veranda on the rickety wooden chairs they'd brought up in the Land Rover from Foxhills, discussing various walks and pubs and fishing and hunting until Ray felt warm inside. *This is what life is all about.*

'I knew keeping and renovating this place was the right thing to do,' he said once Fraser had left. 'We're making friends already.'

'Yes,' Connie replied, staring out of the window at the thick forest surrounding them. 'He seemed nice.'

Ray stared at her, filing it away. He couldn't help wondering what, exactly, was going on in her head. What did *nice* mean? Such a bland word, but the potential it contained simmered inside Ray for the rest of the evening.

'I'm going to the pub in Glengalloch, Con. Fraser said he would be in there tonight. It'll give me a chance to meet more of the locals.'

'I'll come too,' Connie replied, smiling as she looked up from her sewing machine. She held a pin between her lips. She'd not long finished clearing up from dinner and the lodge smelt of fish.

'No need,' Ray replied. 'I'll go alone.' He stood up and fetched his jacket, grabbing the Land Rover keys. 'Don't wait up,' he said, giving her a kiss on the lips. *No point in flaunting her,* he thought.

The ceiling was low, and Ray had to duck his head as he went into the Stag and Pheasant. A yeasty smell filled the air, as well as the usual reek of cigarettes. A shroud of smoke hung beneath the beams and Ray fished around in his jacket pocket for his Bensons as he approached the bar. A woman was serving alone, and he had to wait about ten minutes to get his drink.

'A pint of that, love,' he said to her, pointing to the beer tap. She nodded up at him through long, clumpy lashes. Her black T-shirt – tight-fitting with a low-cut neckline – had stains down the front, and her big fan-shaped earrings bobbed within her wavy black perm.

'Forty-eight pence, duck,' she said, placing the glass on a drip mat.

Ray counted out some coins from his pocket and handed them over. Then he pulled out a few more. 'Get yourself a drink while you're at it,' he said with a wink.

'Aye, don't mind if I do.' She grinned back. 'You new around here?' She busied about serving a couple of other customers, pulling a packet of peanuts from the display, and then went to chat to Ray again, taking a sip from the lager shandy she'd just made for herself.

'Kind of. I've recently inherited Kirk View Lodge near the loch. I came up here a few times as a kid, but my parents didn't use it very often.'

'Aye, I know it. Near Fraser's place.' Her eyes scanned around the pub seating area, lingering when she caught sight of a group of men over by the dartboard. 'He's over there, look. Usually in here on a Sunday night.'

'He stopped by ours earlier with fish.'

'That's Fraser.' She laughed. 'Generous as they come.' Her eyes settled on Fraser again, and Ray noticed the way she adjusted her top.

'Is there a Mrs Fraser?' Ray asked.

'Not that I know of.' This time, the barmaid fiddled with her hair. 'I'm Margaret, by the way,' she said, reaching across the bar to shake Ray's hand. 'But everyone calls me Margie.' He returned the gesture and then lit up a cigarette, offering her one.

'Not allowed while I'm working. Boss'll kill me.' She laughed again.

'Well, we don't want that, do we?' Ray said, staring at her as he blew out smoke.

'I only do two shifts at the weekend,' she continued. 'Mum and Dad own the shop in the village. That's where you'll find me mostly, pricing up stuff, ordering stock, serving customers. I'm a general dogsbody.'

Ray laughed. He didn't think she had a dog's body at all, though he didn't say it. 'We have a working farm in Lancashire. The lodge is our holiday home.'

'Our?' Margie replied, pouring another pint for a customer.

'My wife and I. I inherited the farm from my parents, too. I have a manager to run it, but it still keeps me busy.'

'So where's the farmer's wife tonight, then? You keeping her locked up indoors?'

Ray laughed again. Louder this time. He took a long draw on his pint. 'No. She didn't want to come.'

'Glad to hear it,' Margie said. 'About her not being locked up, I mean.' Her cheeks reddened. 'Maybe I'll meet her soon.'

'Maybe,' Ray said, raising his pint at her as he slid off the stool and walked over towards the dartboard. When he looked back at the bar, Margie was still staring at him. Or perhaps it was Fraser she was staring at. He couldn't tell.

TWENTY-SIX

CONNIE

'Ray, *no...*' Connie begged, cradling her babies. '*Please* don't take them. Can't we talk about it?'

'Have you seen him since... since *it* happened?' He loomed over her.

'*Nooo...*' She let out a sob, holding her babies closer. 'I haven't, I swear on my life.'

One of the babies started crying. Lily. It was always her. Even though they were barely three days old, they'd already developed their own little characters and foibles. Kate was a regular feeder and, between times, she'd either sleep or happily watch her mother as she dangled home-made toys above her – an empty cotton reel hanging on string, pieces of tin foil fluttering above her, a hair ribbon with a pinecone from the forest attached to the end. However, Lily, the smaller twin, was harder to settle. She'd cry and grizzle even when she was fed and changed, and it took hours of pacing up and down to get her to nap, even for twenty minutes. Connie had no proper toys for her baby girls, and she barely had any clothes either. There'd been a jumble sale in the village hall a few months back and she'd picked up a few towelling sleepsuits, as well as half a dozen cloth nappies.

'Are you expecting, Con?' someone from the village had asked her when they'd seen her handing over some coins for the items – a woman she'd vaguely got to know from before everything went bad.

'No, no, these aren't for me.' She'd laughed with a fake grin, hoping her baggy top gave nothing away. 'These are for my sister. She's due in a couple of months.'

'Didn't know you had a sister, Con...' Then she went on her way.

I don't, Connie had thought, breathlessly trudging the long walk back to the lodge with her haul.

'There's nothing else to talk about,' Ray said now. 'We made a deal, and I kept my part of it. I stuck by you. Now it's your turn.'

She and Ray wanted a family of their own – God knows how they'd wanted that when they'd first got married – and for a while, they'd been trying. But with Ray always busy on the farm, spending the evenings in the local pub, drunk and exhausted when he finally returned home, their attempts had dwindled. Ray was shapeshifting into a man far different to the one she'd married. He'd become distracted and distant, and that had only caused more tension between them – more anger from Ray when Connie complained, and more resentment from Connie when he didn't attempt to change. No sex meant no family.

Then *this* had happened – the unspeakable and unexpected thing, and a family was indeed on the way (a ready-made one, as it turned out). But the family in question didn't belong to Ray. And neither did he want it.

'Just look at them, Ray,' Connie had pleaded, praying that he'd see something in the little girls' eyes that he could connect with, make him change his mind. As yet, he'd not held them –

he refused – but if he were to take them away from her, give
them up for adoption as he swore he would (though in reality,
she knew he was going to abandon them somewhere – perhaps
at a hospital or a police station), then he'd have to touch them.
She couldn't stand the thought of not having her babies. She
wouldn't – *couldn't* – let it happen.

'All I see in them is your betrayal,' Ray said, pacing about,
briefly stopping to glare at the babies in her arms. 'I'm taking
them away in the morning like we agreed. Everything will be
fine again, Connie. We'll put this incident behind us. Then
everything can go back to normal.'

Connie sat and thought about this. What *was* normal? And
did she even want it any more? Ray working all hours on the
farm, forcing her to give up her office job when they'd married
to take care of the home, promising her a family that never
happened, him drinking too much when things didn't go his
way and the farm lost money, him down at the pub all hours,
going back to some woman's house, staying out until the early
hours and slinking in reeking of booze and sex. He thought she
didn't know, but Connie sensed it, trusted her instincts. And it
wasn't what she'd signed up for when, aged twenty-five, she'd
walked down the aisle as a shy but happy bride, supposedly
marrying the man of her dreams.

'A farmer,' her mother had crowed. 'Fancy that!'

'I'll report you to the police if you take them,' Connie spat
up at him, not knowing if she meant it. Could she turn her
husband in, have him arrested, perhaps sent to prison? How
would she even prove it? It was her fault all this had happened
after all, and the aftermath would mean she'd end up quite
alone. Her mother had always said that whatever bed she made
for herself in life, she must put up with lying in it. Any bed was
better than no bed, she'd drummed into her. Lily squirmed and
squawked in her arms, while Kate had dozed off.

'You won't do that,' Ray replied, but it was the first time

Connie noticed the flicker of doubt written on his face, the first time he looked at the babies for more than a glancing second.

'You can learn to love them as your own, Ray, you'll see. And we can have more children, *your* children. I'll be a good wife, Ray, I promise, and I'll look after you. Just let me keep my babies safe.'

'No one else knows about the babies, Connie, and they never will. This is our secret. And after they're gone, it will remain our secret. We will get through this, just like we always have done. For better, for worse, remember?'

Ray had only ever hit her the once, not long after they'd married, but he'd come close to it several times since, the rage simmering in his eyes as his hand had slipped from her throat. She wondered if he was about to do it again as he loomed over her.

Connie nodded, reciting her marriage vows over and over in her head as she did when she doubted herself. She'd always attended church, and it had been where she'd met Ray that rainy morning as he'd stood at the back of the congregation all alone. Afterwards, when everyone was sipping tea, she'd approached him, eyeing up his oil-stained denim flares and his battered leather jacket.

'Are you new to St Andrews?' she'd asked, standing there in her pristine skirt and slingback kitten heels – a fresh-faced and naive twenty-three-year-old. She'd wanted him to feel welcome at the church.

He'd smiled at her, balancing his cup and saucer in one hand. 'I am,' he'd said and, really, that was that. Their first date was a walk through the village with a flask of tea. Their second was a dance in the church hall – except Ray hadn't danced. She later learnt he didn't do things like that. Instead, he'd sat and watched as Connie had twirled about with a girlfriend, and then he'd walked her home to her parents' house. She discovered that he owned Foxhills Farm, had taken it over after his parents had died. She'd vaguely known of them through her mother and father. During their next date – fish and chips at the pub – she found out he was a kind man with good morals. He paid for their food, complimented her dress, and drove her the short distance home, leaving behind only the tingle of a kiss on her cheek.

'I will never love those babies, Connie. Not like I love you. We will stick to our deal.' His voice was robotic and devoid of emotion. Once Ray had a plan, he always followed through.

'But you're talking as though they're disposable possessions,' Connie pleaded. 'Rubbish to be thrown out. They're humans, little girls with their whole lives ahead of them. Don't you want to be a part of that? Let's go to the hospital, get them checked over and we can say it was a blessed surprise that they came, that I had no idea that I was pregnant until they arrived. It happens, you know. There's no shame in that.'

But Connie didn't dare tell Ray that Margie had called round when she was a few hours into her labour, that someone else *knew*. She'd been resigned to getting through it alone, resigned to whatever fate the birth brought – whether that was her own death or the death of her baby. Bab*ies* as she'd found out shortly after. They'd come several weeks early.

'Coo-eee, Con, it's only me!' she'd heard at the back door. Connie was on all fours in the living area, grunting and sweating, wondering how much worse the pain could get, the embers from last night's fire twinkling in the grate. Ray had no idea their friendship had grown over the months, how Margie had persisted in calling round, with Connie eventually having to pretend that she wasn't home, telling her that she was going back to the farm in Lancashire in case she'd noticed her expanding belly. Ray would kill her if he knew Margie was there at the birth.

When Connie had heard Margie's voice at the door, all she'd been able to do was wail as the next contraction powered through her. The gut-wrenching sound was enough for Margie to kick in the door – she was as strong as an ox and the door only flimsy – and from that moment, Margie took control. What Connie remembered most from those few hours was how kind she was, how she didn't ask a single question – *Where the hell is Ray? Why are you all alone? Why didn't you tell me you were pregnant?* She'd sat with Connie afterwards, helping her get the babies to feed, making sure they were all comfortable. The next day, Margie had brought home-made soup and disposable nappies, as well as a small carrycot that a friend was giving away. And she'd arranged for the door to be repaired.

'They'll have to top-to-tail for now,' she said and, for some reason, both women looked at each other and burst out laughing. Deep, hysterical laughter until the tears rolled down their cheeks. It was what Connie had needed.

Then, a week later, Ray had come back.

'You're certain no one else knows?' Ray spat out, as though he'd taken Connie's silence as questionable. She shook her head and then he grabbed her by the shoulders, rocking her back and forth until both girls wailed in her arms.

'No, no, *nooo*,' she wept.

'Good. Keep it that way.' And then he went outside to chop wood, locking the door behind him, leaving Connie to figure out a plan because, if she didn't, she knew that very soon she'd never see her twins again.

TWENTY-SEVEN

RAY

It was a week after Connie had given birth and there was still no doubt in Ray's mind that he felt less of a man because of it, as if the whole world was laughing at him, pointing and whispering behind his back.

But Ray had been through worse. Living under the stern hand of his father, it felt as though he'd been preparing for this eventuality his entire childhood. Thank God the man wasn't around to witness it.

The axe came down over and over on the wood, splitting the logs into shards of dry kindling as he remembered his father's hand coming down hard on him when he was a boy. Over and over until he'd begged for his life.

But all he saw now was the devastating aftermath of two nights ago – the wreckage of their lives left for him to clean up. And that's what he'd done, sticking to his side of the deal, though none of it had gone to plan, and that was bothering him greatly as he piled the wood into the store.

Now someone else knows…

The rage came out as a loud roar as he hurled the logs onto the pile, cleansing himself as the pain of his past and present echoed through the silent forest surrounding the lodge.

'I made you this,' Connie said when he went back inside, sweat running down his back. She handed him a mug of tea and a plate of sandwiches. He took them, casting his eyes up and down his wife. She looked different – and not just because the huge belly he'd grown used to seeing these last few visits had deflated. She was empty in body now, of course (though the residual sag at her middle would forever remind him of what had happened), but Connie was also empty in her soul. Her eyes were dead.

It wasn't what he'd signed up for when he'd taken her as his wife. He was a Hunter man from a long line of strong men who didn't give up on what they'd started. All he could do now was move forward like the man he'd been trained to be. There was no way he was giving up on his marriage.

He thought of the advice his father would have given him if he were still alive.

'You didn't play it right, son,' he imagined him saying. The conversation would perhaps have taken place in the shadow of a combine harvester that needed repairing, or maybe in the farm office as his father pored over bills and land management plans. 'Controlling a wife is not dissimilar to planning crops or livestock. You hope for the best but prepare for the worst.'

Fleetingly, Ray thought of his mother – compliant, obedient, smiling, a worker, and she always smelt of... what was it now? Disinfectant. Yes, that was it – the pine-scented tang of cleaning fluid, as though it flowed through her veins. His ideal woman, if he thought about it.

'Contingencies, son. That's what it's all about. You can only forecast bad weather to a certain degree, and likewise, if you breed from duff stock then be it on your own head. You won't make the same mistake again.'

Duff stock, Ray pondered as he bit into the sandwich that

Connie had made for him. He could view it that way, he supposed, as he chewed the white bread and ham, washing it down with a glug of tea. His ewe had strayed, and the product had been low-quality offspring that hadn't been wanted in the first place. Lambs die all the time, after all. It was God's way of separating out the weaklings. And God's way was Ray's way, just as it had been his father's.

'I'm going out,' Ray announced. 'And tomorrow, we're returning to Foxhills.'

'You mean I can come home now, too?' Connie asked, putting away the last of the dishes she'd washed. He knew she'd been fighting back the tears, the rage, the devastation at what he'd done, holding herself together for fear of the consequences. It was good. She was learning.

Ray nodded and slipped on his jacket, buttoning it up. 'Get everything ready while I'm gone,' he said. 'And don't leave here meantime. Understand?'

'Yes, yes, I understand.' Connie nodded and Ray noticed the first glimmer of gratefulness in her eyes as she scooped up the whimpering baby. He made sure not to look at it.

'Good girl,' he replied, closing the door behind him.

After he'd left the lodge, Ray stopped off at the small wooden barn at the edge of the property and checked inside, opening one of the two creaky double doors. The Land Rover was still in there, covered in dust sheets as he'd recently left it, surrounded by spare parts, old tyres and tools that he'd brought up from home for some projects he'd planned to work on in his free time. That all seemed a lost cause now, under the circumstances. But he would get back to that, all in good time.

He checked the doors of the Land Rover, making sure they

were locked, deciding it was best to leave the vehicle where it was for now, perhaps keep it up here permanently and use it when they visited. He'd not long bought it, and it would need a bit of fixing up and a good clean after what had happened two nights ago, and the front bumper would have to be replaced, but meantime it was safe here. They'd be taking his Jeep back to Lancashire tomorrow, and Connie wouldn't need any transport when they were back home. She'd waived that privilege.

Ray walked into the Stag and Pheasant, greeted as usual by a wave of cigarette smoke and chatter as he went in. He slipped off his jacket and headed for the bar, lowering himself onto his usual stool at the end. He glanced around to see if anyone was staring at him or whispering behind his back. News travelled fast around here, he knew that, but he didn't want *his* news travelling anywhere. He took a breath as he lit a cigarette, knowing he had to act normally, as though nothing had happened, convincing himself that no one knew a thing.

Margie was behind the bar as she usually was on a Saturday night, and for the briefest of moments, her smile made him forget, as did the beer she poured for him. Though this time, he saw through her smile, noticed how it snagged on something at the corners of her mouth, almost as if it was forced. As if she was afraid of him. He hoped it was that, because she damn well should be.

'Fraser in tonight?' Ray said to her, his eyes casting around as he sipped the head off his pint. It's what he would usually ask. He had to keep things normal.

Margie frowned, then the realisation dawned on her as her face relaxed. 'He's not been in for a while,' Margie replied. She went on to serve another customer. *She's doing what I told her to*, Ray thought with a smile.

Last time he'd seen her – the time *before* last, to be precise – he'd run his fingers down the gentle curve of her hip, admiring the landscape of her slim body. Her bed was a small single, the same one she'd slept in as a child, she'd told him, but lying on their sides they both just about fitted as long as no one moved. Until that moment, he'd been on top of her anyway – a snatched half an hour while her parents were out. She'd closed up the shop and led him upstairs to their living quarters, as she'd done many times before. Margie provided the comfort he needed, the warm safe space where he could unleash his heart and just *be*.

'Maybe he'll be in for a pint later,' Ray said, sliding some coins across the sticky bar for another pint. *Though I doubt he'll ever come in again*, he thought, lighting up another cigarette.

'Maybe,' Margie replied, giving him a knowing look.

TWENTY-EIGHT

CONNIE

She owed everything to Margie. And she missed her dreadfully since she'd returned home to Foxhills Farm. Connie had never had a true friend before, not a close one. Margie had been her real-life angel who'd been at her side during the toughest time of her life. There'd been no judgement – just kindness and soothing words as she'd helped her through those gruelling hours of childbirth.

'If she could see you now, little one,' she crooned down at her baby, who'd grown so much these last few weeks. The window was open, and, in the distance, she heard the lambs bleating as they gambolled around the fields. The baby's little mouth was pressed against her breast, oblivious to everything that had happened since she'd been born.

Ray had kept himself busy on farm the after they'd come home from Scotland, but there'd also been a shift in him, too. The anger he wore like a shroud had slipped a little at the shoulders, the hem of it dragging in the dirt, as though he didn't want to be wearing it at all, but because of what had happened, he felt duty bound to.

Connie longed for the man that she'd first met to return to

her, and she spent her days over-analysing where things had gone wrong, what *she'd* done wrong, how she'd let him down and allowed her head to be turned by another man. She'd never forgive herself, of course, but consoled herself by taking care of Kate as best she could. Whenever the image of that terrible night several months ago entered her mind, she said a silent prayer to make it go away. Though nothing would ever erase it completely and she was resigned to living with the guilt for the rest of her life. And, against all the odds, she still had Kate.

'I don't care what you call it,' Ray had said as they'd driven back home from Scotland, when Connie had again asked if he liked the name she'd chosen. 'It's still the spawn of the devil.'

Connie hoped that, in time, her husband would grow to love their remaining baby, even though she wasn't his. And that was the problem, of course.

She'd never expected to feel the way she had about another man. Up until that moment, Ray had occupied the softest, most secret part of her heart and she'd always believed there wasn't room for anyone else. But since they'd married, Ray had changed, as though his edges had become sharper, their love for each other turning to mutual resentment.

But he... oh, *he* was different. He listened – *really* listened – to her, and when he looked at her, he *saw* her. In his eyes, she wasn't just as an empty shell of a woman designed to cook, clean and have sex on demand, but rather he saw her as a whole person with feelings and emotions that waxed and waned like the moon, and an ability to laugh from the inside out when in his company. *Yes*, Connie thought. *That was it. He made my soul smile.*

And now, she had no idea what had happened to him or where he was, if he was dead or alive.

The only thing she knew for sure was that it was all entirely her fault.

Connie stroked Kate's head, her soft curls caressing the

creamy nape of her neck as she fed. Her heart bled for her identical twin sister, and she knew she'd never forgive herself for what had happened to Lily. But if she hadn't at least tried to escape that night, then she wouldn't have either of her babies, and that thought was unbearable. It was a miracle Kate hadn't been taken away from her too.

'Your sister died for you,' she whispered down at the baby, kissing the top of her head.

It had all started down at the loch a year and a half ago. Ray was in one of his moods and Connie could do nothing right by him. She was twenty-six and her hair was long and her waist tiny and she had a sparkle in her eyes. The beginnings of a fire were stirring within her, but it seemed that Ray was intent on extinguishing it. His moods, the way he went days without speaking to her for no reason despite her cooking his favourite meals, washing his clothes, running him a bath – none of it made a difference. Not until he was ready to snap out of whatever had caused the dark cloud to hang over him – and then he'd grab her and take her to bed and have his way. But even that hadn't happened in at least three months, them sleeping together, and probably longer than that. She couldn't remember. Connie would stand in front of the mirror, sometimes naked, wondering what was wrong with her. Even when they went up to the lodge for a holiday or a change of scene, it was the same. He chopped wood and he fished, and he hunted and he drank at the pub. She didn't feature in his life. She may as well not have been there. It was the first time she'd considered there might be another woman. Women, even.

'Hello,' Connie had said, picking her way down the shore of the loch to where the man was standing. She'd often seen him out fishing but hadn't spoken to him since the day he'd brought the trout up to the lodge and introduced himself. 'Caught anything?' It was early morning, and the sun was still low, just peeking over the crest of the hill. She didn't know him properly yet – but enough to warrant a chat while she was out on her walk.

Fraser turned with a smile already on his face and pointed down into the bucket at his feet. 'Aye, three big ones so far. You can take a couple, if you like.'

Connie squatted down and stared at the fish. The tail of one of them was still twitching every few seconds as it lost its hold on life, drowning in the air. She understood how it felt.

'Ray's got some venison hanging for tonight,' she replied. 'But thanks.'

'A meat man,' he said, turning back to his rod as the line twitched and danced.

'Maybe.' Connie stepped closer to him – close enough to catch the scent of something. Sandalwood, perhaps, or berg-amot. 'I don't really know.'

'You dinnae know what your husband likes?' Fraser turned, eyebrows raised, his accent thick.

'I don't think I do, no.' She sighed, sitting down on the folding stool he'd brought along. 'We've been married three years and it's true, I don't know my husband.' Her voice was flat, as though she were talking to herself rather than a virtual stranger. 'How can that be?'

'Couples bumble through life together for decades without really delving into the other's soul, not truly knowing what sparks joy. It's because they don't know themselves.'

Connie thought about this, wondering if Ray knew what made him tick, what kept the beat of his heart steady each day in order that he could understand her. 'Maybe you're right,' she said, staring out across the loch. The water was calm, the weather unremarkable – everything shaded in a muted grey. Rain neither imminent nor impossible, the wind little more than a breeze, and the sun's rays making an occasional lazy appearance.

'Maybe Ray never looks inside himself to see what I see, because if he did, I reckon he'd catch sight of someone...' Connie trailed off, suddenly feeling like a traitor, discussing her innermost thoughts with a virtual stranger. '...of someone deeply unhappy.'

Over the next couple of hours, Fraser taught Connie how to thread bait onto the line and cast it out into the loch. As they waited patiently for a bite, they chatted about the area and where Fraser had gone to school, how he'd studied art at Glasgow but had never truly made it as an artist.

'I sell a few paintings here and there. Keeps me ticking along. I'm not in it for the money.'

Connie liked his laugh – it conjured up warm autumnal images in her mind, a cosy, safe feeling – and she wondered if his pictures were the same. Perhaps muted scenes of the Scottish landscape, misty mountains and washes of purple heather, the ever-changing greys, blues and green of the lochs, an occasional stag painted in the distance. She'd seen similar in local galleries.

But when he invited her back to his home and led her into his studio, she couldn't have been more wrong.

'You painted these?' Connie asked. A silly question, she realised, but she was taken aback by the contorted limbs and disfigured faces overlying dark and swirling backgrounds.

'Shocked?' Fraser asked, tightening the cap on a tube of oil paint. His studio was untidy and located in a small wooden building at the end of a path leading from his house – which was also a made of wood. It didn't appear as well kept as Kirk View and looked as though he hadn't kept up with repairs. In the muddy yard surrounding Fraser's home, there were old bikes and generators and piles of logs and all manner of stuff that perhaps once had a use but now only made the place seem like a scrapyard. Inside, the studio wasn't much different with large canvases stacked against the walls, several easels with works-in-progress on them (at least, Connie assumed they were in progress), and a trestle table that sagged in the middle from the piles of paint and brushes and other artists' materials weighing it down. The floor was dusty and spattered in reds and blacks and the colour of flesh.

'I'd never have guessed...' Connie said, staring squarely at a canvas about five feet square. 'It's a woman,' she said, squinting. 'She's pregnant?'

'Giving birth,' Fraser corrected as Connie tilted her head. Limbs and long matted hair and puddles of burgundy gave way to a tiny face on what she assumed was the floor. But there was no right way up for this painting, and no single interpretation. And that was its beauty. Each person viewing it would see something different.

'I have so many questions,' Connie said, her eyes not knowing where to look next. 'Is this... a dead body?' she asked, tentatively walking up to another painting, unframed, propped against the end wall of the small studio.

'What do you see?' Fraser said, standing beside her.

And that's when she felt his hand slip around hers. The warmth of it against her skin.

'I see... I *feel*,' she corrected, 'that the person is alive but also dead.' *Like me*, she thought but kept to herself. 'Their heart is still beating but only just, and the position they're in...' Connie gazed at the person's legs (she wasn't sure if it was male or female) were splayed at a painful-looking angle, yet there was no anguish on the plain facial features. One eye was open, the other closed. 'It's like they're restoring themselves. Like a kind of rebirth.'

Fraser let out a laugh. 'That's what the piece is called,' he said. '*Rebirth*.'

Connie swallowed as she felt Fraser's fingers intertwine with hers.

'Would you like to have tea with me in the house?'

'I would like that very much,' Connie said, looking up at him. And so they tramped across the muddy, messy yard and Fraser made tea and then they talked and laughed and Fraser looked at Connie in a way that made her feel reborn, just like in the painting. And, somehow, a few months later she fell pregnant, and it hadn't even felt wrong, even though she knew it was. So very, very wrong.

TWENTY-NINE

RAY

Three years after Connie had given birth to the twins, Ray stared down at the baby. *His* baby. He could tell by the way she stared up at him – the searching flick of her gaze and the silent opening and closing of her mouth as though she wanted to cry but had thought better of it – that she was made from his genes. He also knew she was one hundred per cent his because he'd not allowed Connie to go anywhere unless he was by her side.

'A little stoic,' Ray said, peering into the cot. 'Aren't you, Darby?' He noticed how Connie flinched at the sound of his high-pitched voice, although when he smiled across at her, she smiled back. It wasn't in her interests not to. He'd named the new baby after his mother – her maiden name, to be precise. He wanted his daughter to be strong but not petulant, to have good start in life but not be spoilt, to have initiative but not be headstrong. She'd be thoughtful, kind and obedient. The kind of woman he admired.

'She's such a happy baby,' Connie said, wiping snot off the toddler clutching at her leg. 'Kate loves having a little sister, don't you, darling?' The little girl nodded and joined Ray beside the cot, not yet tall enough to see inside.

'Lift up,' she squeaked. 'Me see...'

Ray stared down at Kate's frail body, knowing it was crushable in an instant – with her caramel curls bobbing around her face, her rosy cheeks. But these days, he didn't feel the urge to want her gone so much. He'd almost, if he was perfectly honest, grown to find several endearing qualities about her. She was becoming helpful – fetching things for him if he couldn't be bothered to move, soothing the new baby if she grizzled and Connie was busy. And occasionally Kate provided entertainment with her incessant chattering and undeniably sweet temperament. Not to mention the attention she attracted when they were all out together. *What a beautiful little girl! Isn't she the image of you both?* But the moment Ray remembered where she'd come from, his feelings towards her melted away and he could hardly stand to look at her. And, after things had gone so horribly wrong that night three years ago, he'd had no choice but to keep her.

'You've brought joy to this family, little one,' Ray said into the cot, surprising himself by lifting Kate up under her armpits so she could see the baby. 'This is what a *real* daughter looks like,' he told her, hoping she'd take note.

'Ray, *don't...*' Connie trailed off, knowing better than to harp on at him.

They'd not been up to the lodge in the last few months of Connie's pregnancy. She'd been bed-bound for a time – doctor's orders – and Ray hadn't wanted anything to put his baby at risk. Of course, he'd hoped it would turn out to be a boy, someone to take over the farm from him one day, but at least the girl he'd ended up with was his own flesh and blood this time round, unlike Kate. And he would still teach her how to drive a tractor, even if she didn't do it quite as well as a boy would have done.

But now it was time to return to Kirk View, the place where his heart lay – albeit smeared in blood. As a boy, he remembered so many adventures up there, whiling away the days with his father, fishing or hunting or chopping wood in the forest. And his mother would reward them at the end of the day with one of her home-made venison casseroles. The holidays had seemed endless and happy, as long as he obeyed his father. And here he was, having stepped up the family ladder a rung, taking his own daughter to visit. They would be happy again. He would make damn sure of it.

The journey north was a smooth one and Darby was content for most of it, needing to stop only once at a service station to suckle on Connie's breast. Ray took Kate's small hand and wandered along a grassy verge at the edge of the car park while the baby fed, listening to the child's constant stream of chattering. Some of it made sense and some of it didn't, but every time she called him Daddy – which had become more frequent since the baby had been born – a piece of him loosened inside. Was this finally him accepting the situation? he wondered, as Kate bent down to pick up a shiny flintstone. Fraser was long since gone from Glengalloch, leaving him unconcerned about any encounters. He'd got what was coming to him in the most perfect of ways. Ray smiled to himself.

'Need wee, Daddy,' Kate bleated up at him.

Ray glanced around the car park. How easy it would be to usher her out into the steady stream of traffic. He sighed. No one was nearby so he took her behind a tree and got her to pull down her pants and squat. When she was finished, they sauntered back to the Jeep and got underway again with Ray driving and Connie barely saying a word for the rest of the journey. He wondered what was wrong with his wife, how she'd changed from the girl he met that Sunday morning in church all those years ago – because there was no doubt she *had* changed – to the almost silent and empty person sitting beside him. The innocent shine she'd once had about her, the warmth in her smile also reflected in her eyes, and the care she took of herself – it had all gone, as though she'd been left outside to rust. And she wasn't quite thirty yet. He supposed, looking back, his parents had been the same. It was just the way things went.

He still had Margie to look forward to, though, and the thought of her brought a smile to his face as he turned off the motorway for the final leg of the journey. Connie and the girls were asleep when they reached the lodge, leaving him plenty of time to think about her, wondering if she'd be working tonight when he went to the pub. A man had needs, after all, and he knew there was little chance of Connie meeting them any time soon.

'I'm off out,' Ray said once the fire was lit, and the bones of the lodge warmed up. Connie had whizzed around with the vacuum cleaner and the duster soon after they'd arrived, sprucing up the place after it had been locked up for many months, and the three of them had sat around the wooden table, Ray at the head, and eaten the meal his wife had prepared. It wasn't her best effort, but she'd been interrupted several times by Darby, who'd also wanted a feed.

'OK,' Connie said, glancing up from the sofa. She was reading a book by the fire – the baby asleep in her arms, and Kate was already in bed. He noticed the questioning look in her eyes.

'To the pub,' Ray said for an easy life. He couldn't face a grilling. But instead of heading straight there, he went down the hill towards the loch.

There were no lights on in Fraser's old house and he wasn't even sure if he still owned the place any more. Perhaps it had been sold, or a family member had taken it over, though he didn't really care as long as *he* wasn't there himself. With Fraser out of the picture, life could get back on track.

He banged on the door and waited. Nothing. The forest

surrounding him was dark, even though the sun hadn't fully set. He smelt woodsmoke coming from a nearby property – perhaps his own further up the hill – and heard occasional sounds from the forest as the wildlife settled down for the night.

He thumped on the door again then peered in through the window, cupping his hands against the grimy glass. It took a moment for his eyes to adjust but when they did, all he saw in the darkness were the ghosts of dustsheets draped over furniture.

He'd been inside Fraser's house several times before – for dinner with Connie once or twice, and another time he'd staggered home from the pub with Fraser, after which they'd sat on the deck and sampled several Scotch whiskies until the sun rose above the loch. How the pair of them must have been laughing at him behind his back during that period, their dirty little secret sitting invisibly between them. Ray had always believed Fraser to be a decent and honourable man, someone to have a chat with down the pub or go fishing with. A good neighbour to have at their holiday home. He'd always struggled to make friends, and he should have realised that the man was after only one thing: his wife.

Ray kicked the door with his boot and let out a deep growl. *Goddammit*, Fraser had even looked after Kirk View for them while they were back home at the farm. He thought back to the first time they'd met, when Fraser had called round. He'd been nothing but charming and friendly. Since the discovery of their affair, when Connie had hung her head and told him about her pregnancy, he'd driven himself mad wondering if there'd been something between his wife and Fraser brewing that day, how he'd missed the spark or whatever it was that had grown between them.

People are never who they seem, he thought, marching around the back of Fraser's house, towards the studio in the garden. *Including me*, screamed the voice in his head.

Again, the small building was in darkness and this time Ray
didn't bother knocking. He turned the handle on the door and,
when he found it was locked, he kicked it in. It only took two
good wallops with his booted foot and then he was inside, met
by the stench of linseed oil, turpentine and paint. He'd never
been in the studio before, but he knew Connie had. She'd
confessed as much when he'd had his hand around her throat,
choking the words from her. It was only when her eyes had
bulged, the veins on her temples standing out and her lips
turning purple, that he'd loosened his grip. How easy it would
have been to finish the job, he'd thought. One extra squeeze to
snuff her out.

'Did you do it in there?' he'd yelled at her. 'Fuck him?'

She'd nodded, holding a hand against the red marks on her
neck. 'Yes, we did it in his studio. But it's not what you're thinking, Ray. It wasn't like that...'

If she'd not tried to excuse what she'd done, if she'd just
stuck to what he'd asked her, then he wouldn't have had to hit
her again. He didn't like doing it – it didn't make him feel big or
powerful. It was simply because she deserved it. She needed to
learn her lesson. It had been his father's way, and now it was
his. He was a Hunter man to the core.

Ray paced around the studio, turning up his nose at the
stacks of canvases against the walls, and other detritus
belonging to a failed artist. He smirked, knowing that the man
would never make anything of himself now.

Tubes of paint and dried-up palettes were littered everywhere, as well as old rags and a couple of chairs, easels, a big
mirror hanging above a deep metal sink, and a rusty fridge in
the corner with cobwebs stringing it to the ceiling. Ray's hand
came up and, in one swift swipe, he had most of the paints on
the floor. He kicked at the crumpled tubes, before putting his
foot through a canvas propped against the wall. He had no idea

what the picture was – just some grotesque splodges of colour on a black background.

He went to up to an easel and turned his head sideways, trying to work out what the painting might be... what kind of twisted mind the image came from. Because it would take a twisted mind to create something so vile. Then he held his breath as he saw a naked woman and what seemed to be a forest in the background. Her limbs were all over the place and her naked belly was huge and swollen, and at her neck was an ornate gold cross on a chain – Connie's necklace. The one he'd bought her as a wedding gift.

'Sick bastard,' he said as he recognised his wife, her red pouting lips and wavy blond hair. Then he grabbed a palette knife that had ended up on the floor and slashed it over and over against the canvas until it was nothing but torn shards of fabric hanging from the wooden frame.

In the pub, his fists still clenched as he went up to the bar, he ordered a pint of bitter and sat down at his usual stool. Margie smiled at him as she pulled back the pump handle, a twinkle in her eye as she took his coins.

'You're back again,' she whispered, fiddling with her hair, and Ray unclenched his hands, sipped his pint, and allowed the tension to flow from his body. 'I get off at ten,' she added with a wink.

Margie would make everything alright; Margie would make him feel like a man again. Margie, he knew, would do absolutely anything for him now. And indeed, she already had.

THIRTY

CONNIE

Beatrice Amy Hunter was an unexpected surprise. At first –
and Connie completely understood why – Ray was suspicious
of her announcement when she emerged from the bathroom,
her face aglow with hormones and delight, the testing wand still
sitting on the edge of the basin. Her hand rested lightly on her
belly as she told Ray the news.

'I'm pregnant.'

Kate and Darby, now aged eight and nearly five, were
playing quietly, and the long summer holiday spent by the loch
lay ahead for all of them. Ray had taken even more of a step
back from the farm these days, handing over much of the day-to-
day running to his management team. It had been the right
decision and while he was still involved and liked to be out on
the land when he could, it had given them more time together as
a family – and Connie's good news was proof of this.

'Ray, love...'

Ray had glanced up from his newspaper, looking at her in
that way she liked where his features softened at the sight of
her, as if he really appreciated her. Time had been a good
healer. Over the last few years as the girls had grown, his harder

edges had been worn away by their innocence and delight in the simple things. Darby loved nature and animals and the outdoors – a chip off her dad's block, for sure – while Kate was content with a puzzle or a doll or simply trailing Ray around. She'd tried to learn to fish, but hadn't quite got it, and she could ride a horse, but she wasn't as good as Darby. And when it came to joining in with the story Ray always read Darby at bedtime, Kate was allowed to sit beside them, but not actually on him like Darby was. She didn't think he'd ever allow that. But his tolerance of her first daughter was enough for her, and hopefully enough for Kate, to see her through to the time when she'd leave home and either head off to university or start a family of her own. She knew nothing about her past or her biological father, and Connie intended to keep it that way for the rest of her life.

Ray stared at her, and Connie could almost hear the thoughts racing through his mind. 'The baby is yours. Of *course* it's yours, Ray,' she said, hating that she still had to appease him. It was all she'd ever done, and she had no idea how things would have worked out between them if she hadn't. Appeasing was her middle name, she'd joked with Margie on one of their walks, not long after she'd found out about the new baby.

'I'm just scared what will happen if I don't go along with him, if I tell him what I really think or want or like. He still grills me about where I've been when I go out, who I've spoken to, checking the mileage on the car. I can't have an opinion. Everything has to be done Ray's way, you know?'

Margie had linked her arm through Connie's as they'd headed down to the loch. Kate and Darby were scampering ahead, still unaware they had a sibling on the way.

'Men, eh?' Margie replied, nudging herself against Connie. 'You've got a good one, though, Con. He's a hard worker. And look how he's supported you since...' She trailed off and they walked the remainder of the way in silence. Some things were never spoken of.

'It had better be a boy,' was the only thing Ray had said when he'd learnt the news.

The next nine months were some of the happiest of Connie's life. She had no sickness or high blood pressure and her back remained strong and her mood stayed even. In fact, she was directing the grain truck in the farmyard when her waters broke, calmly calling to Ray to take her to the hospital. Twenty-four hours later and she was back home at Foxhills with another baby girl in her arms. Ray tagged along behind her, bringing her bag in from the car. Connie set to cleaning up the kitchen and made a special meal for Kate and Darby when they arrived home from primary school to meet their new baby sister.

'Hello, Beatrice,' Kate said, sitting cross-legged on the floor next to the baby carrier. Darby sat the other side, wiping her nose on her sleeve. 'We're your sisters and we'll love you forever,' she added, reaching out to take Darby's hand as they each held on to the baby's tiny fists, joining them in a circle. 'No one will ever come between us Hunter girls, will they, Darbs?'

Darby shook her head, sucking hard on her lollipop. 'No. And if they try, we'll kill them dead,' she said, leaning down to kiss the baby's soft head.

PART III

THIRTY-ONE

KATE

Now

'*Mum?* Mum, please wake up...' Kate was kneeling beside her mother on the veranda, having rushed outside as soon as she'd heard the loud thud accompanied by Darby's screams. She cradled Connie's head in her hands, gently stroking her cheek. Her skin was cool and clammy, despite the mild evening.

'She just went down,' Darby said with a waver in her voice as she knelt beside Kate. 'One minute we were talking to her and the next moment she was on the deck.'

'Shall I call an ambulance?' Adrian said, standing above them. The others had trooped outside, crowding around to see what was going on. Mia let out a sob when she saw her grand-mother passed out.

'Yes, yes of *course*,' Kate wailed as she peeled back one of her mother's eyelids. Not a flicker.

'Everything OK?' came a voice from across the yard. When Kate looked up, she saw Cameron approaching, a bunch of flowers by his side. He strode up to them.

'Mum's collapsed,' Kate told him. 'Do you know any first aid?'

Cameron rushed over, chucking the flowers down and dropping to his knees. He gently moved Connie into the recovery position. 'Connie, can you hear me?' he said clearly. 'Any history of heart problems or other illnesses?' he asked, looking up at Kate. He lifted Connie's limp wrist to check her pulse, nodding as he felt one. Then he put his ear to her nose to check her breathing.

Kate shook her head frantically then looked over at Darby, who was also shaking her head. 'No, not that we know of,' she said. 'Mum's always been...' She trailed off, suddenly realising how much they'd all taken Connie's seemingly good health for granted. Their father had literally dropped dead only a few months ago, so what made them believe the same couldn't happen to their mother? 'She's always been really healthy.'

'Ambulance is on its way,' Adrian said. 'Though God knows how long it'll take.'

'I think we need to elevate her feet,' Cameron said, dragging over a wooden footstool from in front of one of the wooden steamer chairs. 'Get the blood back into her head. She's probably fainted. Has she been overdoing it lately? Not been eating, or had a shock, maybe?'

Kate noticed the way Darby looked up at Adrian, how her cheeks reddened. How he stared at her for a beat longer than was necessary, his eyes wide and panicked.

'What were you talking about before she passed out?' Kate demanded. Did her mum collapsing have anything to do with whatever was going on between Adrian and Darby? She'd be incandescent with rage if they were the cause of this.

'Just chatting... you know. Nothing that would have made her pass out,' Darby replied.

Kate heard Adrian clear his throat and saw him take a few steps away, while Darby covered her face with her hands. But she was more preoccupied with the groan she heard coming from her mother.

'*Ohh...*' Connie slurred. 'My head...' Her arm twitched as she attempted to touch her forehead.

'Mum, it's me, Kate. Are you OK?'

Connie opened her eyes and stared up at her, a small smile – or perhaps it was a grimace – forming on her lips. 'Where's... where's my baby...?' she whispered, attempting to sit up as she searched around.

'What baby, Mum?' Kate asked, but Connie didn't reply or say anything else as, between them, Adrian and Cameron helped her sit up before carrying her inside to make her more comfortable.

———————

'Are you going to tell me what the hell was going on before Mum fainted?' Kate snapped at Darby several hours later, after the paramedics had given Connie the all-clear. No concussion, no heart issues evident on the ECG trace, and all her stats were normal. They'd offered to take her to be checked out at the hospital, but Connie had flatly refused, insisting she'd simply stood up too fast and fainted.

'A plaster will do the trick, if you have one,' she'd said to the young, uniformed man, as she touched the graze on her forehead. 'Your kindness has made me feel much better.'

'Like I said, we were just chatting,' Darby replied to Kate.

'I don't believe you.' Kate folded her arms. 'Why did Mum mention a baby when she came round? *Her* baby? And why were you and Adrian giving each other... *glances*?'

Darby shook her head far too vigorously and far too long for it not to appear suspicious. It reminded Kate of when, aged fifteen, her sister had been frogmarched all the way back to the lodge by Margie, a packet of crushed cigarettes in the older woman's hand and a furious expression on her face.

'What have you got to say for yourself?' Margie had demanded of Darby as they stood in front of the girls' father, who was on the veranda reading his newspaper.

Darby had kicked and screamed and spat and done everything she could to wriggle out of Margie's grip, but Margie was as strong as an ox. All the kids in the village called her She-Hulk behind her back.

'Nothing! Get off me!'

'What's going on?' their father had said calmly. Kate was doing a sketch in her art book, sitting as close to her dad as she knew he'd tolerate. The picture was of him – a portrait in profile, though it wasn't very good. She'd never been any good at art, despite her mother's encouragement. 'You've got artistic genes, Katie,' she'd say to her when they were alone, but Kate didn't think she had. She planned on giving the picture to her father to put on the wall in his study back at Foxhills, though she figured he probably wouldn't. It would go in the drawer with all the other pictures she'd done for him.

'Your minx of a daughter nicked these from my shop while I was out the back.' Margie held up the cigarettes. Kate had stared at Darby wide-eyed, thinking she was very brave for attempting such an act, and she'd tried not to laugh as she imagined Darby being dragged all the way from the village.

'Did you steal the cigarettes, Darbs?' her father had said, standing up and going down the couple of wooden steps to where they were standing.

Darby had shaken her head vigorously, just as she'd done now, appearing suspicious as anything.

'How much are they, Margie?' Ray had asked, sighing as he'd dug his hand into his pocket. He'd handed over a few pound coins and taken the cigarettes in exchange, opening the packet and immediately lighting one for himself. 'I asked her to get them for me,' Ray had said, exhaling smoke. 'And for them to be put on my account.'

'Your account, Mr Hunter,' Margie said sternly, watching as Darby marched off inside, 'is *long* overdue.'

'Nothing was going on,' Darby said now, looking Kate in the eye. 'Mum was out of it. She wasn't making sense, talking about a baby.'

'Well, something made her pass out, and for what it's worth, I don't believe you. Perhaps I should ask Adrian about this baby?' she shot back. 'Perhaps I need to ask him a *lot* of things.'

Kate was awake early, and the lodge was quiet. Her sleep had been broken, her racing thoughts keeping her awake much of the night. Three times she'd got up to go and check on her mother, creeping close enough to her bed to hear her steady breaths as she slept. She imagined Connie doing the same to her when she was a baby – checking on all her daughters throughout the night when they were tiny to make sure their little chests were rising and falling. And now it was the reverse – Kate the concerned one, her mother's frailty in the spotlight after her earlier scare.

She swung her legs out of bed and pulled on her old sweatpants, a T-shirt and a zip-up hoodie. Scout would appreciate an early walk and, if she was perfectly honest, so would she. The lodge seemed to be closing in around her, the walls pressing against her, leaving her nowhere to go. If she was honest, she just wanted to go home now, but it was only Tuesday, and they weren't due to leave until Sunday.

More importantly, she had to decide what she'd do if her suspicions about Darby and Adrian turned out to be true. She'd never be able to trust her husband again, let alone stay married to him. Her entire world would be turned upside down – both her sister and husband lost to her forever. The thought was unimaginable.

Everything about this holiday had turned sour – her mother passing out... this *thing* going on between her husband and Darby... the strange text to her husband from an unknown number... the mysterious babygrow that had somehow turned up in the washing... someone lurking outside the lodge in the early hours... Then there was Bea and her pregnancy announcement, not to mention whatever had happened between her and Louis and the way she was throwing herself at Cameron. Plus Cameron's father, Fraser, and the bitterness dripping off him, especially towards her mother. It was all getting too much.

As Kate tied up her trainers, she realised she'd barely spent any time with her twins since they'd arrived. While she swiftly brushed her teeth, she made up her mind that as soon as she was back from taking Scout for a walk, she'd cook them a decent breakfast and take them to the sailing club to hire a couple of kayaks for the morning. They'd enjoy that.

'You're up early,' Adrian said when she went back into the bedroom, making her jump. He was already dressed – cargo shorts and a T-shirt, the same as he'd had on yesterday. His hair was ruffled from sleep as he pulled on his trainers.

'I thought I'd take Scout down to the loch. Clear my head.'

'I'll come with you,' he replied, and Kate found herself nodding, despite wanting the time alone.

When they reached the shoreline, with Scout bounding ahead, Kate pulled her hand from her husband's grip and folded her arms. She didn't think what she was about to ask warranted physical contact.

'If you're not having an affair with Darby, then who is it?' she said. 'Has Darby found out about it, and now she's keeping your secret, is that it?' Kate zipped up her hoodie as though it might offer some protection against the sharp response she was expecting.

'Love, I'm not having an affair—'

'Then who was that woman texting you so early in the morning the other day?' She took a chance that the sender was female, hoping to catch him out. All she'd done so far was add the number to her contacts. She'd desperately wanted to call it but hadn't been brave enough. 'What did she mean by "Let's talk"?'

'It's no one,' he said, turning to stare out across the loch. Then he bent down and picked up a small piece of driftwood, hurling it along the shore. Scout chased after it.

'Does Mum also know about your sordid little secret now? Is that why she passed out? Jesus, Adrian, it's like I don't even know you any more.'

'Kate, you need to stop this. You're sounding unhinged. There's nothing—'

'Is she someone from work? I took down her number, you know, and I'm not afraid to call her.' Kate's head pounded in the bright morning sun as the rays crested over the hill. She'd just wanted a quiet walk alone with Scout, to think things through. But equally, she knew she wouldn't rest until she'd got the truth out of her husband.

'No, there's no one at work.' Adrian's long sigh made him sound flat and broken, and Kate was stung by pang of guilt. She wasn't normally like this – so irrational and jealous. She was always the calm one and, if she was honest, a little bit broken inside, too. Ground down by the routine of life – working, caring for the twins, cleaning, sleeping, repeat. She couldn't remember the last time she and Adrian had gone out for an evening together, and as for hobbies or interests of her own, she simply didn't have the time or the inclination. But wasn't that how things had always been in her life, she thought, as they ambled along the shore – doing whatever it took to keep her father happy, occasionally slipping between the pages of his good books if she was lucky?

'Since Dad's funeral, you've changed so much, Ade. You've been drinking way more than usual, then there's all this secrecy with Darby. And you've been glued to your phone lately.' Kate dug her nails into her palms. She couldn't let it go.

Suddenly, Adrian swung around and grabbed her by the arms. 'Fine,' he said. 'Look, Kate, this is going to sound mad and I'm so sorry I've been keeping it from you, but it was only to protect you until we were able to find out the truth.'

'*We?*' Kate said, not having a clue what he was talking about. But something in his eyes told her that he was finally being honest.

'Kate,' Adrian sighed heavily, pulling her close, 'I think you had a sister. A *twin* sister, and she was killed soon after you were born.'

THIRTY-TWO

THEO

Theo stared at his phone. Seeing the text on his screen when he woke made him forget his thin, lumpy mattress. It even made him forget that Finn was in the bunk below him, as well as ignore the photo of his stupid girlfriend on the chest of drawers.

Is it safe to talk?

That's all the message said. Not much to go on. He desperately wanted the sender's name but wasn't sure how to get it without giving away that he wasn't really Adrian, as Mystery Woman believed.

He tapped out a reply.

Not right now. Wife here. Text me instead?

Theo didn't have to wait long for a reply. Finn was stirring on the bunk below and, a moment later, he got up and went to the bathroom. Theo swung his legs over the edge of the bunk and jumped down onto the floor.

We need to talk. You know why...

came the reply, but of course, Theo didn't know why at all. He was taking stabs in the dark.

Of course...

he replied vaguely, hoping she might reveal her intentions. Equally, he didn't want to scare her away.

Why are you being so cryptic? Do you want me to go through with it or not?

Theo stared at the screen, his heart racing. This was gold – *more* than gold. Adrian clearly had a secret, a big one by the sound of it, and it was proving just what he needed to make this dreary holiday more exciting and take his mind off other things – things that he didn't want his mind to be on in the first place. *Dangerous* things.

Yes I do...

he sent back immediately, not having a clue what 'it' was.

'Y'alright,' Finn said as he came back into the bedroom, adjusting the boxers he'd slept in. Theo stared at his broad chest, wondering if he shaved it. His skin was completely hairless. Perhaps it was for swimming, he thought, to make him go faster. He didn't think the few downy hairs he had on his own chest would cause much drag if he was any good at swimming, which he wasn't.

'Alright,' Theo replied, staring at his phone again. He was leaning against the windowsill, aware that Finn was pulling on a pair of shorts, adding a spray of deodorant under each arm. From the corner of his eye, he saw the muscles on Finn's back and shoulders standing proud. Then he caught sight of him in the mirror, their eyes locking for a couple of seconds, so he turned back to his phone, feeling the redness rising in his cheeks.

'I don't mind, you know,' Finn said, turning and coming up to Theo. 'You having a look.'

What did he mean by *that*?

Theo just muttered something in reply, keeping his eyes firmly fixed on his screen, pretending to scroll through Instagram.

'If you work out a bit, you'd get well buff, too.' Finn reached out and touched Theo's bicep, making him recoil. 'And eat more protein and stuff.'

'Whatever,' Theo replied, feeling hemmed in. The sweet scent of Finn's deodorant filled his nostrils as he slid sideways and headed for the door. He needed to get out.

There was no dog to greet him with a thumping tail and a wet nose as he went downstairs and headed outside. Someone must already be up. The morning was fresh and the sky blue and clear, and he sat on the veranda for a few moments with a can of Coke he'd grabbed from the fridge, making sure his phone still picked up the Wi-Fi signal as he waited to see if Mystery Woman replied. He stared at her profile picture again, wondering who she was, but it was impossible to tell from the silhouette of her photo. Then she came online so he quickly clicked off the screen, not wanting to appear too keen – rather, not wanting *Adrian* to appear too keen.

It reminded him of that time at school a year ago when a girl had given him her number on a slip of paper. No one had ever done that before, and he was instantly suspicious – though also secretly pleased. He'd seen her staring at him numerous times in physics and the canteen, so he'd plucked up the courage to message her. He'd just said a brief hi, asking how she was, and in return she'd repeatedly asked him for naked photos along with a string of suggestive emojis. He'd not sent any, of course, but instead he'd attached a head and body shot of him smiling into the camera, one from last summer when he happened to have his shirt off. He reckoned he looked OK – a bit skinny and pale, but it was a decent enough photo. After that, it was radio silence. Nothing back from the girl at all, even though he'd watched for hours to see if she'd come online, ducking off the screen every time he saw her live in case she replied. But she didn't.

The next day, everyone was staring and laughing at him – clusters of pupils sniggering as he passed them in the corridors, boys and girls alike, things thrown at him in class. In his next physics lesson, as he slumped down in his usual spot before the teacher came in, he looked up and saw that his selfie was four feet tall on the whiteboard, glaring out of the overhead projector, his skinny body almost as pale as the board itself. It only took a couple of seconds for him to leap up and smash the phone that was attached to the projector, crushing it under his foot as the rest of the class watched on, howling with laughter. Then the teacher walked in.

'Fuck 'em all,' he whispered to himself on the veranda, swigging his Coke. That was the least of his worries now. There were more important things to take care of.

His phone suddenly vibrated on the deck. Theo opened the message.

Where are you?

While Mystery Woman was still online, he tapped out his reply.

At the lodge in Scotland.

Two blue ticks instantly appeared showing she'd read it, but Mystery Woman didn't reply. Then she went offline.

'Fancy going kayaking with Finn and Mia this morning?' Darby asked. Theo hadn't heard her come outside. He quickly shoved his phone in the top pocket of his denim jacket and stood up.

'Nah,' he said. 'Think I'll just hang around here today.'

'What, and stare at your phone?' She laughed, giving him a gentle prod.

'Nope, I just don't want to listen to Mia prattling on about horses and books while trapped in a boat with her.' He didn't want to let on that the thought of being out on the water filled him with dread – not to mention the shame of having to be rescued by Finn again if they capsized and he got into difficulties.

'You'd have Finn to talk to,' Darby said.

'I said *no*, right?' Theo knew he'd get a dressing down from his dad for snapping at Darby, but he wasn't here so it was open season as far as he was concerned. The woman was always meddling.

'I can tell Finn really likes you,' Darby said. 'And there's no need to feel so...' On and on she droned.

You haven't got a clue how I feel, Theo wanted to scream at her, but stopped short because his dad came out with Charlie clamped around his neck, the toddler grizzling about something or other.

'Can you take him?' Travis asked.

'I was just going to help with breakfast,' Darby replied. 'Theo, you'll mind Charlie for a bit, won't you? He just wants some attention.'

'Fine,' Theo said, holding out his arms. His little brother grinned as he was passed over. 'Come on then, Charlie, let's go exploring,' he said, standing up and carrying him down the veranda steps and over to where the driveway met the edge of the forest.

'*Det down...*' Charlie wailed, squirming in Theo's arms. He let him slide down his hip and took hold of his hand. The kid was always falling over.

'Let's go and see what's in here,' Theo said, leading the way over to the wooden building, which appeared to be an old garage – its greying timbers rotten in places, and the corrugated tin roof covered in fallen pine needles and a thick layer of moss. As they approached, Theo saw that the rickety double doors at the front were padlocked, but he gave them a wiggle anyway.

'Shut!' Charlie exclaimed, clapping his hands together. Then he lifted his foot, clad in a soft little trainer, and gave it a kick. Theo laughed.

'C'mon, bro. Let's see what's round the back.' He led Charlie around the side of the old garage to where it faced the forest beyond. There was a narrow track leading behind the building, with another pathway heading round behind the lodge where it rose up a bank behind the kitchen window. Several times he'd seen Connie sitting up there, talking to herself, laying flowers down on the ground. Probably a dog's grave or something, he reckoned, though he planned on investigating that too once he'd seen what was inside the garage.

'Go in, go in!' Charlie shrieked, his shrill voice sending a couple of birds flapping out of the surrounding trees. The little boy gazed upwards, his face a picture as he watched them fly off. 'Big bird,' he squealed.

'Yeah, big birdies,' Theo replied, going up to the window in the back wall, cupping his hands to the glass, but it was dusty and covered in a layer of lichen. He pulled down the sleeve of his jacket over his hand and rubbed hard, clearing a patch and peering in again. It was dark inside, but he could see enough to make out a whole load of stuff in there, including what looked like the shell of an old car. Then he noticed the small door on the other side wall and led Charlie around to it.

'Bingo,' Theo whispered, pressing down on the old latch. With a couple of sharp tugs, the door wobbled and gave way, the rotten wood splintering around an old bolt on the inside.

'Bingo!' Charlie mimicked.

The two boys stepped inside, Charlie's little hand gripped tightly inside Theo's.

'It's treasure,' Theo said as he took in the engine parts and the rusted shell of a small vehicle, its bonnet open but no engine inside. 'Must have been the old boy's workshop.'

Theo led the way around the garage, his eyes growing accustomed to the dim light. If nothing else, he'd found a quiet spot to come and have a fag. He might even get a chance to smoke some of that weed he'd been waiting to try.

Over in one corner, beside an old leather car seat that was on the floor, he saw something propped against the wall and covered in a tarpaulin. He pulled the sheet off, exposing what looked like the front panel of a much larger vehicle than the old Ford parked in the centre of the garage. It had clearly been removed from another vehicle and was square and boxy, a greeny-grey in colour. Theo heaved it forward from its resting place against the wall.

'Looks like someone had an accident,' he said with a smirk, spotting the Land Rover marque above the radiator grille. He squatted down to get a closer look, studying the crumpled metal on the lower half of the panel. 'Ouch,' he added, running his hand over the deep dent.

'Ouchie!' Charlie repeated back, also squatting down. He pointed at the bottom corner, near where the headlight would have been. 'Bad ouch!'

Then Theo saw the dark rust-coloured patch of metal, just where Charlie was pointing. He grabbed his little brother's hand to stop him from touching it, unsure what it was. He pulled his phone from his pocket and switched on the torch to get a better look, but before he could investigate further or get a better look, it vibrated in his hand. Incoming call from '?' flashed up on his screen.

Mystery Woman.

Theo just stared at it for several rings, wondering what the hell to do. With curiosity burning inside him, he tapped the green button, covering the microphone with his hand as he answered the call. He didn't say a word – rather he just waited and listened, with Charlie babbling in the background. After a few seconds, the caller spoke.

'Hello?' she said. 'Hello, are you there?'

And then Theo hung up, staring at the old Land Rover panel, his mouth falling open as he heard her voice.

THIRTY-THREE

DARBY

'You *idiot*,' Darby said, her arms flapping by her sides. It was just her and Adrian alone on the veranda – she'd come outside for some air but had found Adrian sipping a coffee and staring out into the forest. The others were busy getting ready for the day.

A part of her wanted to wallop him, while another part of her wanted to run away and never come back. Things should never have got this far. 'Not only did you shock Mum so much that she passed out, but now you've gone and told Kate what that crazy woman said! I thought we were going to sort this out ourselves before upsetting my family. What's wrong with you?'

'I either had to tell her the truth or have my marriage fall apart right in front of my eyes. Kate's convinced herself that I'm having an affair.' Adrian recoiled from Darby's anger.

'You could have made something up. And you certainly didn't need to blurt everything out to Mum. Don't you understand, I'm trying to *protect* her.' Darby groaned, pacing back and forth. 'The more I think about it, the more I'm sure this whole thing is just a scam, and this woman looks up obituaries and preys on vulnerable people. We've had no proof of anything. She'll be demanding money next, you'll see.'

'Is it really our place to keep this a secret, though, Darbs? I've been thinking about it, too. Consider, for a moment, if what this woman said *is* true – that Kate had a twin sister who died – or was *killed*, to use her words. Surely you all have a right to know what happened, don't you – Kate most of all? Anyway, I didn't ask to be involved in this.'

'Me neither!' she spat back. 'And I don't know. I don't know anything any more...'

'When that woman approached us at the funeral... it was all so fleeting. Neither of us had time to take in what she said or ask her questions. She disappeared as fast as she showed up. And we'd both had a fair bit to drink, remember?'

Darby indeed remembered how she'd tried to block out her grief of her father's passing with wine. Seeing the curtains close around his coffin was still etched on her mind – the realisation sinking in that she'd never hear his voice again, never rest her head on his shoulder or hear his throaty laugh. And then this woman... her wide-brimmed hat, her black veil, her gloved hands, the cotton mask she was wearing over her mouth and nose as many at the funeral were wearing. She'd seemed so plausible, but she could have been anyone.

'Maybe we should go to the police,' Adrian suggested.

Darby clutched her head in her hands. 'Some random woman telling us that Kate had a twin sister who died is hardly a crime, though, is it? Then Mum and Kate and Bea... they'll all be dragged into it. Mum's had enough to deal with as it is, and now with her fainting last night – I can't do it to her.'

'It *is* a crime when you're harassing people.'

'Harassing?' Darby was confused. 'A few words from a stranger at a wake isn't classed as harassment, Ade.'

Adrian hung his head. 'I received a WhatsApp message.' Then he looked away, clearing his throat.

'What the *hell*?' Darby flung her arms wide in exasperation. 'What did it say?'

'Messa*ges*, actually,' he corrected. 'The latest one said that she wants to talk.' He hung his head, looking uncomfortable as he shifted about. 'Kate saw that one on my screen and immediately assumed the worst – an affair.'

'This woman wants to talk with *you*?' Darby was confused. He was an in-law, after all, not a blood relative.

'Yeah, but I'll handle it. Forget I ever mentioned it. I just don't want Kate getting...' He trailed off, seeming uncomfortable again.

'Jesus, Adrian, you didn't think to tell me any of this? How did she even get your number?'

Adrian shrugged. 'Maybe she found out where I work, googled my name. I don't know. I'm trying to protect Kate. Just like you want to protect your mum.' He stumbled over his words.

'This is ridiculous,' Darby said. 'I'm not putting up with this nonsense any more. Give me her number and I'll warn her to back off or come clean with what she knows. She didn't even have the guts to show her face or tell us who she is.'

'That's not a good idea, Darby, and you know it. Anyway, she's not replying now, so I'm hoping she's given up. I think we should just leave it be. And try to enjoy what's left of this holiday.'

A stiff westerly breeze swept across the loch, and the ripples on the water sparkled in the sun. Kate sat beside her, restless and agitated. 'I feel so guilty leaving Mum back at the lodge.'

'If you were a sponge and I wrung you out, you'd fill a bucket with guilt,' Darby replied. 'Mum's been checked out.

The others are with her. She'll be fine.' She wrapped the big black zip-up fleece she was wearing around her, the long sleeves covering her hands. She'd decided to join Kate down at the loch on a whim, following on in their car when Travis said he wouldn't need it. And it was his jacket and she'd grabbed it on the way out – the nearest warm garment to hand.

The two sisters looked over at the nearby jetty as Finn and Mia slipped on their orange life jackets. They'd been kayaking since they were eight and were both competent on the water. She and Kate had decided to grab a coffee at the sailing club's café and sit on the terrace, watching on.

'I got the boats for the remainder of our stay,' Kate said. 'It was more economical than hiring several times over, and I thought the others might want to have a go at some point. Mum might even want a paddle, if she's feeling up to it.'

'Do you really think that's a good idea, Kate? After what's happened?'

'Mum's always loved being out on the water, and I'll do the paddling. Anyway, I want some time alone with her. I want to talk...' Kate trailed off.

'About?' Darby felt a shiver sweep through her.

'I think you, of all people, know exactly what about, Darby.'

Darby watched as Finn and Mia launched their kayaks and climbed in, each of them helping the other and hooting with laughter as Finn nearly toppled his boat. He managed to regain his balance and get the oar in position, waiting for Mia to do the same.

'It's lovely they're so close,' Darby said, flicking a look at Kate. 'Your *twins*.' She hardly dared to admit what it might mean. 'I said *twins*, Kate.'

'I know what you said. And I know what you're getting at. And you're wrong, actually. Identical twins don't run in families.' Kate shifted round in her chair. 'Look, I don't believe a word of what some random person said to you and Adrian at the funeral. If something so huge as me having had a twin at birth was even a remote possibility, then don't you think either Mum or Dad would have said something to at least one of us over the years?' Her voice was clipped and fast. 'And one would hope that someone would have been *me*.'

'Yes, I know, you're right. And I know that about twins, too. Believe me, I investigated the chances of it happening to me when I found out I was pregnant with Charlie, given that you had Finn and Mia. But that doesn't mean that you *don't* have a twin, Kate. And you may not have been identical, anyway.'

Kate was shaking her head, a half-smile forming. 'You're really not going to let this go, are you? Has it occurred to you that, even if it were true, I may not *want* to know? And if Mum lost a baby at birth, perhaps she doesn't want to talk about it. You have no idea how it was for me as a child, growing up with a father who despised me. I really don't want to drag up the past.'

'*What?*' Darby accidentally spilt coffee on herself. 'Dad didn't despise you. He loved us all the same.'

'That's simply not true.' Kate swung around to face her, her hands banging down on the table. 'You and Bea were always the favoured ones. I was the nuisance child and to this day, I have no idea why. Mum did her best to smooth things over, to give me more of her attention to make up for it, but all that did was drive a wedge between me and you and Bea. You seemed to... resent her for it, while I felt left out and sad most of the time.'

'No, no, no, Kate. You've got amnesia or—'

'If you got a new bike for Christmas and Bea a pony, I'd get a jigsaw puzzle. If you went to a party, I'd have to stay home and help Mum with chores. If Dad took us out on one of his stupid adventures, he virtually ignored me the whole time. He only ever hugged me for show if we were in company, and then it was fleeting, and he'd never let me sit on his knee or give me a piggyback like he did you two. You and Bea always got away with things – remember the cigarettes you nicked? I never dared put a foot wrong because I knew I'd get properly punished. The list of examples is endless, Darbs. It doesn't take long to damage a child. I'm left with zero ability to believe in myself, and my people-pleasing skills are top notch.' She huffed out a massive sigh.

'Kate...' Darby trailed off, thinking back. 'Memories play tricks on us. Dad wasn't a bad person. He loved you so much.'

The sisters sat in silence, each contemplating their different versions of the same childhoods. Was it possible that Kate had experienced a vastly different relationship with their father? Had he despised her? Darby sipped her coffee, now lukewarm, and thought back. She remembered Kate looking crestfallen a few times at Christmas when all she had to open were a few presents, compared to hers and Bea's huge stockings full of gifts. But she'd always put that down to Kate being the older one – too grown-up for silly presents.

'I was so jealous of that velvet dress Mum made you one Christmas, remember?' Darby admitted.

'I remember the dress,' Kate replied. 'I bloody hated the thing. I couldn't breathe in it, and it made me look like a frumpy spinster. Mum insisted I wear it to church. God.' Kate laughed, but Darby noticed the sadness in her eyes. 'Wasn't that the year you got the tree house at Foxhills?'

Darby shrugged. 'It was a creaky old thing.'

'But Dad *made* it for you. And Bea got that pink electric car she whizzed around the farmyard in.'

'You tried to squeeze into it, remember? Your knees were up around your ears.'

They both laughed, but inside, Darby felt the tide of guilt rising. 'I'm sorry, Katie,' she whispered. 'That we didn't see it, me and Bea. I'm sure Dad loved you... in his own way.' Darby reached for her bag as she heard her phone ping with a message.

Kate shrugged. 'I adored him, you know. Absolutely worshipped him. I realise now, though, that it was a survival instinct. A child needs security and will do anything to get it, even if that means fawning up to an abuser.'

'An *abuser?*' Darby took a breath. 'Is that how you saw him?' She opened up her phone and quickly read the message, tucking it in her bag again.

'Not as a child, no. But as I got older, had a family of my own then... yes. The way he treated Mum sometimes, it wasn't right, Darbs.' Kate took a sip of her coffee, eyeing Darby's bag. 'Everything OK?'

'It was Theo asking if I've got Travis's fleece. His work phone is in it apparently, and he needs it about a job.' Darby stood up, patting herself down, feeling the big inside pockets. She didn't relate to Kate's version of events, not fully. 'Anyway, I don't think Mum was an angel, Kate. Remember when we were kids and I said I saw her kissing a man in one of Dad's "confessionals"?' She used her fingers as quote marks. 'It was true, you know. I saw them in Glengalloch on the path by the memorial. Margie was giving me a lift home when Mum hadn't turned up to fetch me from Brownies, and... there they were. Margie didn't spot them, and I didn't say anything at the time.'

Darby pulled out a phone from one of the jacket's side pockets. 'Found it. It's his new work phone from the haulage company. I'll have to take it back. Off on another trip to Poland, probably.' She rolled her eyes, sitting down again and draining the last of her coffee.

'Do you remember who the man was?' Kate asked, frowning. 'The one you saw Mum kissing? And don't worry about taking the phone back. I want to check on Mum, so I'll take it for you. Would you mind staying here for a bit and bringing the twins up to the lodge later?'

Darby pushed back her fringe, lowering her sunglasses over her eyes. She didn't really feel like going back yet, so it suited her. 'Thanks, Kate,' she said, handing over the phone. Then she drew in a big breath, deciding she might as well just say it. 'I remember that...' she said slowly, staring out across the loch, '...I remember that the man Mum was kissing was in a wheelchair.'

THIRTY-FOUR

BEA

'You did all this for *me*?' Bea looked around her, hands clasped under her chin. She felt like a little girl again, stirring feelings of when her father surprised her with one of his adventures.

'I thought you could use some cheering up,' Cameron said. 'I mean... I know it won't make your problems go away, but I figured a couple of hours of distraction might help clear your head a bit.'

'You have no idea,' Bea said, laughing as she tapped the side of her head, 'just how much clearing out it would take in there.' But still, she couldn't help wondering what the gesture meant – if he was simply being kind or if there was more to it.

'Have a seat, Miss Hunter,' Cameron said, pointing at a fold-up chair. Bea sat down, feeling the warmth of the campfire on her legs.

'Very posh.' Bea giggled as Cameron opened a wicker picnic basket and took out a flask, unwrapping two floral china cups that he'd tucked inside napkins. 'No sugar in mine,' she added as he poured them tea.

'I have brownies, too,' Cameron said, opening a plastic container. 'Made them myself.'

'A man who loves to bake,' she said, taking one from the tub. 'Don't tell my family. In their eyes, I'm this perfect vegan health-addict who practises yoga three times day and meditates under a full moon while sipping on green smoothies.'

'Now that would be boring,' Cameron replied. He bit into a brownie. 'Mmm, damned fine, if I do say so myself.'

'In reality, I'm a pregnant car crash of a person with nowhere to live, a boyfriend who dumped me and absolutely no money. I lost my last job and just found out I didn't get the position I really wanted at the gallery.' Bea stuffed the remainder of her brownie into her mouth, leaning back in the camping chair.

'I'm so sorry to hear all that, but you're not a car crash, Bea. What happened to you was horrific, and it's left you with some tough choices to make. Firstly, whether you're keeping the baby or not, and secondly, if you want to report the crime. I can't help you with the first, but I will give you a hand-hold if you go to the police. Maybe you should look for a counsellor when you're home, too.'

'Why are you doing this?' Bea said, resting the cup between her hands on her lap. She'd put on a floral dress when Cameron said he was taking her out. She had no idea he'd prepared an afternoon tea in the forest for her. It was perfect.

Cameron smiled, leaning forward on his arms. 'Because I like you. And I don't know many people around here yet who are anywhere near my age. Everyone down at the Stag seems to own a bus pass.'

'Shame I'm not from around here, then,' Bea laughed in reply. 'My life, or what's left of it, is back in London.'

'I'm just happy to spend time with you while you're up here. It gets pretty lonely looking after my dad. And he's not the easiest person to get along with.'

'Do you mind me asking what happened to him?'

Cameron nodded, as if he was used to the question. 'An

accident. A hit and run. It happened a very long time ago, before I was even born.'

'God, that's awful. I'm so sorry.'

'He hasn't always been in a wheelchair, though. He had many operations and, for a few years afterwards, he was semi-mobile. It left him with one leg shorter than the other and both hips and knees are full of metal. He's suffered with terrible arthritis and increasing mobility issues over the years. My mum was one of the physiotherapists treating him. It's how they met. She was on a placement in Glasgow but originally from Manchester. They married and moved further south for Mum's work. Dad used to be an artist but hasn't painted a single thing in years. It's like he's just given up on life lately, especially when he had no option but to use a wheelchair full-time.'

'Did they ever catch who did this to him?'

Cameron shook his head. 'Nope. And to make it even harder, Dad's memory of the time is completely wiped out. There was no lasting brain injury, thank God, but all he remembers is leaving home one night to walk to up the pub in Glengalloch – then bam! Nothing after that until he woke in hospital a few days later.'

Bea sat silently for a few minutes, imagining the scene in her mind. An innocent man taken down in an instant, the rest of his life changed forever.

'I'm terrified of dying,' Bea suddenly found herself saying. 'I mean, I know everyone probably thinks the same but... but if anything happened to me, like an accident or a terminal illness, I would just feel such...' She stared up into the trees to stop the tears she felt welling from spilling over. 'I'd just feel such a *failure*. All my life I've relied on other people, mainly my dad or various boyfriends, and now I've got someone who's going to be relying on *me* and I simply have no idea how I'm going to do it.'

'I think you'll surprise yourself and find strengths you never knew you had.'

Bea laughed. 'I'm not some bad-ass woman in a movie, you know. I'm just a common-or-garden hot mess who doesn't know what she's doing from one day to the next.'

Cameron reached for the flask and poured out more tea. 'Get your mouth round another one of these,' he said, handing over the brownies. 'You're very hard on yourself, aren't you? Where did that come from?'

Bea's mind scampered about trying to come up with an answer – flitting from one childhood memory to another. But all she remembered was how happy she'd been as a kid, how utterly content and secure she'd felt knowing that her parents adored her and that she had two sisters who doted on her.

'I don't feel as if I deserve to be happy,' she finally admitted. 'Like, I had everything I ever needed handed to me on a plate when I was growing up, and then suddenly I was out in the big wide world, blinking in the glare of real life, and I knew, I just *knew* that I was going to bugger things up. Some stupid part of me thought that by being a loser before it was all whipped away from me would give me control over it. Does that make sense?'

Cameron tipped his head to one side and opened his mouth, but Bea continued.

'I figured that you can't fall off the floor, so I put myself down there before life gave me a shove.'

'In that case, Miss Hunter,' Cameron said, leaning forward, 'I suggest you take my hand and allow me to help you stand up again.' He took a slow bite of his brownie, staring at her. 'Metaphorically, I mean.'

Slowly, Bea reached her hand out to him, and Cameron took her fingers in his. She noticed the warmth of his skin, the way the birds seemed to sing a little louder as they touched, how the sun shone its dappled light more brightly through the trees. She noticed the flutter deep in her belly. 'I want to keep my baby,' she whispered.

THIRTY-FIVE

CONNIE

'I saw your father,' Connie whispered, hugging her knees up under her chin as she sat on the soft earth beside the grave. She finally had a moment to herself. 'Your sister, Kate – she met him, too. She doesn't know he's her dad, though. And Fraser doesn't know who she is, either. It was... surreal, Lily. Like a dangerous dream or... or being in one of your father's paintings. But...' Connie sighed, leaning back on her hands. 'But on the other hand, it also seemed so utterly beautiful and serendipitous, as though, after all this time, it was meant to happen.'

Connie tipped back her head and stared up between the trees. She was used to being up here, talking to herself. It was a kind of meditation for her, being alone with Lily. She caught the tang of woodsmoke in the air, wondering if someone had lit a fire nearby.

'He seemed so different to how I remember him from all those years ago,' she said wistfully, with only the birds to hear her. Her hand went onto the soft earth, the white lily she'd put on the grave the other day now wilted. 'So angry, too, though who can blame him after everything that happened?'

She sank her fingers into the dirt, trying to get that little bit closer to her lost daughter.

'But he was still Fraser,' she said, smiling. 'And seeing him reminded me of why I fell in love with him all those years ago. We filled a void in each other at just the right moment – both lonely, but for different reasons. I've often asked myself what would have happened if I'd met him when I was much younger. Would I have fallen for him still, or was it just because I was so unhappy with Ray? No one knew what went on behind closed doors in our marriage.'

Connie felt sick as her stomach churned, and it wasn't from the after-effects of fainting. She'd felt sick for the last forty or so years – pretending to herself that none of it had happened. That she hadn't kept secrets from those she loved most in the world – her daughters.

And now she was keeping another secret from them – the one contained in Ray's will. Once she told her daughters what he'd done, there would be so many questions to answer and there'd be no holding back the truth any more. The floodgates would be open. Yet she didn't want her girls to hear it from the executors either – a couple of stuffy old solicitors who knew nothing about her life and what she'd been through. She knew the official letters would be waiting for her daughters when they got home, and there was nothing she could do to stop that.

'Once they know the truth, Lily, they'll never forgive me. I'll lose them *all*.'

Connie stood up, brushing the dirt off her trousers and blowing a silent kiss down at the grave. *Not much of a grave*, she thought, but then no one else except her and Ray had known Lily even existed.

Apart from Margie...

Ray had taken control that night, insisting they would not be going to the police, that the mess was being taken care of, cleaned up. That it was better this way.

Connie had had no choice but to agree with him, especially when, from that moment on, Ray promised he would look after Kate as if she was his own. A huge turnaround, for which Connie was grateful – a small mercy in the dark shadow of what had happened. And even when she'd plucked up the courage and finally confessed that Margie had been present at the twins' birth, that *someone else knew,* instead of the red-hot anger she'd expected from Ray, she was met with a strange calmness.

'Don't worry about Margie. I've dealt with her,' was all he'd said.

And sure enough, Margie had never mentioned Lily again.

When they'd finally travelled back to Foxhills with Kate, her unexpected arrival had caused a brief stir among their small circle of friends. Connie had explained to her mother that she'd had no idea she'd been expecting, how she'd been so small throughout, and the baby had come as a complete surprise and a blessing. While incredulous at first, her mother was delighted, believing that God had indeed blessed her daughter.

Between them, she and Ray fielded the occasional inquisitive comments, but eventually there were other things to gossip about and Connie and Ray's new daughter became old news. People were happy for them, came to the christening, brought gifts. To the outside world, they were the perfect family.

But no one knew that she and Ray had buried Kate's twin in the forest.

Connie headed down the slope, away from the grave and back towards the lodge. Kate and Darby had taken the twins kayaking and Bea was off somewhere with Cameron for the afternoon. 'Hi, boys,' she said, finding Travis, Theo and Charlie playing French cricket in the driveway. Theo looked up from his phone and gave her a nod.

'You want to join in, Connie?' Travis asked, ready to throw the tennis ball her way. 'What did Darby say, Theo?' he then said to his son. 'Did she find my phone?'

For a moment, Connie hesitated but then she held out her hands, ready to catch the ball. Charlie was waving a tennis racket about that was almost as big as him, and he squealed in delight when he saw his grandmother with the ball.

'Oh, go on, then,' Connie said, smiling.

'Nana play!' her little grandson said, jumping up and down.

'You ready, Charlie?' she said, gently tossing the ball his way. Miraculously, it connected with the bat and bounced over to where Theo was standing, but he ignored the ball, engrossed in his phone instead.

'Yeah, she found it,' Theo said, looking up at his dad. 'She just replied. Kate's going to bring it back.'

'Right,' Travis replied with a frown, pacing back and forth, kicking the dirt with his trainer.

Theo half-heartedly picked up the ball and bowled it at Charlie, but his little brother wasn't even looking, and it bounced off his head, making him burst into tears.

Connie scooped him up. 'Come on, you,' she said, giving him a kiss where the ball had hit him. 'Nanny make it better.' And there she was, back with Kate when she was little, teaching her how to catch a ball, ride her tricycle, keep her balance as she walked along the trunk of a fallen tree. Swim... roller-skate... ride a pony... Connie had been there for Kate when Ray had not. God, she'd tried to make him love that girl to her bones, but the way he treated Darby and Bea so differently was stark. To her, at least. She could only pray that Kate hadn't felt unwanted, different, as if she didn't belong. Was it too late, she wondered, to make it up to her?

'Do you want an ice lolly, Charlie?' Connie said, noticing that Travis and Theo had become bored of the game and wandered off. Charlie nodded, grizzling in her arms. She took him inside and let him choose an ice lolly from the freezer, settling him down on a beanbag in the living room. 'Hi,' she said to Adrian, who was sitting stiffly on one of the sofas, a book open on his lap and his phone in his hands. 'You didn't fancy kayaking?'

Adrian shook his head without looking up. 'You need to talk to Kate,' he said gruffly.

'I know,' Connie replied, sitting down beside him. 'I need to talk to them all.'

When Connie walked up the path to Fraser's house that afternoon, she saw that someone had recently neatened up the front garden. Cutting back the overgrown hedges and weeding the herringbone bricks made the place seem slightly less neglected, as did the pots of flowers beside the door. And the scrubby lawn had been mown, she noticed, and the windows cleaned. Connie knocked on the door, glancing back at where she'd parked the Land Rover, as if she might need to make a quick escape. She'd left Charlie in Adrian's care after the toddler had fallen asleep on the beanbag.

'Hello?' she called out through the letterbox. 'Anyone home?' She went around the side of the house to see if Cameron's car was there, but it wasn't, so she continued down to the studio at the end of the garden.

As curious as she'd been all these years, she'd not set foot on the property for decades. It was taboo as far as she was concerned. If she and Ray had ever driven past, she'd turned the other way or started a conversation with him or one of the girls – anything to stop her looking to see if anyone was home. She knew that Fraser still owned the property – he'd made that clear when they'd crossed paths in the village that one time when the girls were children. An unexpected but snatched moment cancelling out all the time that had lapsed since she'd last seen him. His tender kiss had kept her going for another couple of decades.

There was a light on in the studio. Connie's heart sped up as she approached. She still felt unsafe, as though Ray was about to catch her out even from beyond the grave.

'Hello?' Connie called out again, pushing against the studio door. It swung open. 'Anyone in here?' She stepped inside, instantly transported back in time by the smell of oil paint. And then she saw him, his back to her as he sat in his wheelchair facing an easel with a blank canvas propped on it. 'Fraser?'

'I was wondering when you'd come,' he said without turning round.

'I... I wasn't sure if I should,' she replied as she went slowly up to him. She didn't know whether to reach out and touch him or keep a distance. He wasn't the man she remembered any more – no smile to light up her soul, no open arms to pull her into a safe hug like he used to. 'Are you painting again?'

Fraser laughed. 'No.' He grabbed the wheels of his chair and swung round to face her. 'Cameron put me here before he went out. He does it every so often – gets out all my stuff in the hope a masterpiece will drop out of me.' Then he grabbed a hip flask from the table beside him and swigged from it, offering it to Connie. She shook her head. 'Sit,' Fraser said, pointing to a wooden chair.

Connie did as she was told. They were facing each other, only a couple of feet separating them. 'Not much has changed in here,' she said, her eyes flicking about.

'Cam's been up every so often over the years to check on the place, get any repairs done. And a cleaner's been in once in a while.'

'I had no idea you had a son,' she said. 'He seems—'

'Aye, and I had no idea you had a daughter,' Fraser replied. 'Three of them.'

Four, Connie wanted to tell him, but kept quiet.

'The eldest, Kate... she looks much more like you than the others,' Fraser said.

He knows, Connie thought. *The way he's looking at me, he knows...*

'I'm very proud of my girls.'

'I'm sorry about your husband,' he said. 'I was married for a time, but she wasn't... she wasn't you, Con. She was a good woman, though. She put up with a lot.' He took another swig of whatever was in the flask. 'And she gave me Cameron. I wouldn't get by without him these days.'

'How have you been... since your... since your accident?' Connie looked away, catching sight of several paintings.

'I've lived most of my adult life like this,' he said. 'How do you think I've fucking been?' His voice reverberated around the studio, and, when she turned and looked into his eyes, she saw her own emotions reflected: remorse, hurt, regret at what might have been.

'I'm sorry... I'm sorry, I didn't mean it like—'

'How did ye mean it, then, Con?' He wheeled up to her, grabbing both her hands tightly. 'Or are you sorry that you didn't tell me you fell pregnant by me? I loved you so hard, did you know that? And I *still* love you.'

Connie gasped, shocked by his admission. 'No, I was—'

Fraser tightened his grip on her hands, and she tried to pull away, but he wasn't letting go. Their faces were close, and she smelt the alcohol on his breath.

'Or perhaps,' he said, the veins on his temples bulging, 'you're sorry because of what happened to me that night.'

THIRTY-SIX

KATE

'Hi, Mum,' Kate said as she arrived back at the lodge. She'd taken an unexpected detour on the way back from watching the twins kayaking at the loch, but there was no way she could tell anyone exactly where she'd been – or, indeed, what had happened when she'd got there. She was still processing every-thing and besides, there would be plenty of time for all that. Truth be known, she was still reeling from events, the way things had panned out this afternoon, and consequently mulling over what to do.

'Did you go kayaking with the twins?' Connie asked.

Kate frowned. 'I just watched them,' she said, staring at her – the woman she felt she didn't really know at all. She was tired of keeping everything bottled up, and barely had the energy to pretend any more. *Deceived*, she thought. *By my own mother.*

'Tea?'

'Is there anything stronger?' Kate said, slipping off her jacket. She looked around for somewhere to put it, then hung it up with the others by the door.

'Oh, it's like that, is it?' Connie laughed. She made a point of looking at her watch. 'Well, it's six o'clock somewhere, I suppose.' She pulled open the fridge and took out a bottle of white wine. 'This do?'

'Sure.' Kate went over to the living area and dropped down into one of the sofas. She looked around, suddenly feeling like a stranger, as if her entire life had been a lie. She wanted nothing more than to understand her mother, learn about what had happened and try to find forgiveness, but then she didn't want to know a single thing either. She simply wanted to immerse herself in her family and pretend she hadn't been half of a whole for her entire life.

'Thanks, Mum,' Kate said, smiling as she took the wine. 'Join me?' She patted the sofa beside her, and Connie sat down with a glass of wine for herself.

'Cheers!' she said, clinking her glass against Kate's.

'Yeah, cheers, Mum. Cheers for everything,' she said flatly. *Stop it*, she thought... *stop sounding so bitter*. 'What have you been up to?'

Kate didn't need to ask what her mother had been doing earlier in the day because she knew. She'd been to see Fraser in his studio, the man who, it seemed, had started all this. Things were still falling into place in her mind, and she needed to think fast – about what she was going to do, how she was going to play it.

'Just pottering about here, mainly,' Connie replied. 'Travis, Theo and Charlie have gone out for a walk. Adrian is upstairs having a nap, if you were wondering.'

'I wasn't,' Kate said, not knowing what she'd say to *him* once he came down, how she should act. He'd hung on to this secret with Darby for months, and Kate wanted to know why.

'Is... is everything OK, love?' Connie said, reaching out and touching her hand. 'You seem a bit... thoughtful. Lost, even.'

'Lost?' Kate replied. 'Ironic.' Instead of looking her mother in the eye, she stared straight ahead, noticing the family pictures on the wall, the books on the shelf, the stack of board games under the coffee table. All indicative of a happy family life at the holiday home yet revealing nothing of the secrets buried here.

'Are *you* OK, Mum?' Kate asked. 'You know, after everything.'

Connie looked puzzled for a moment, then smiled. 'I'm fine thanks, love. I'm a tough old bat.' She touched the graze on her forehead from when she'd fainted. 'You know me.'

But Kate didn't think she did know her, not at all in fact. It seemed she'd spent her entire life not knowing her mother.

'Hey...' a voice said from across the room and, before she knew it, Adrian had come over and Kate suddenly felt a warm mouth pressed against hers. She allowed him to kiss her – it felt good. But in equal measure, it didn't, and she wanted to shove him away. 'Have a good time at the loch?'

'Mmm,' she replied vaguely, nodding and smiling up at him. *He's a handsome man*, she thought. *You're a lucky woman, Kate...*

'Where are the twins?' he asked, eyeing her wine. 'Started early? That's not like you.'

Nothing much is like me at the moment, she thought, keeping the smile on her face. It was that or she'd burst into tears, not knowing how long she could keep up this pretence. Why didn't she just have it out with her mother, with Adrian, with Darby? But mostly, her mother. She'd known about this since the day she was born, after all – or rather, since *they* were born.

'Darby's bringing them back soon,' Kate replied. 'They're kayaking. They're fine.' At least she hoped they were.

'Where's Scout?' Adrian asked, looking around.

'Travis took him out for a walk,' Connie said. 'He looked quite dejected when you didn't take him with you earlier, Kate. He thought you'd gone for a walk without him.'

'That dog,' Adrian said, 'would go to work each day with

Kate if he could. He adores you.'

'Not sure that would be allow—' Kate said, but she was interrupted by someone coming through the front door.

'Talk of the devil,' Adrian said, crouching down to greet Scout as he came bounding in. 'Have a good walk?' he asked Travis, giving the Labrador a good pat and fuss.

'We did,' Travis said as he kicked off his boots. 'Theo took a detour to the village shop on the way back.' His dark hair was ruffled and messy and the hems of his combat trousers were caked with mud. 'Kate, have you got my work phone?'

Shit.

'Oh... I—'

'Theo got a text from Darby saying you were bringing it back.'

'Sure, yes, hang on...' Kate got up and went over to where she'd hung her coat. She closed her eyes for a second as she turned her back on the others, feeling around in the pockets. Then she grabbed her bag off another hook and rummaged inside that too.

'I don't seem to have it, sorry.' She hoped that would suffice as an excuse, that she didn't have to explain where it was or what had happened. Or what she'd *done*. She couldn't face that. Not yet, anyway.

'Has Darby still got it, then?' Travis asked, looking confused. 'I really need it. For an important job.'

'Yeah, yeah, I guess she must still have it,' Kate said, going to sit back down by her mother again. But Scout had launched himself into her place instead. 'Shove up, dog,' she said.

But Scout didn't move at first, rather he just stared up at her, almost as if he didn't recognise her. So Kate dropped down onto the beanbag instead. Then Scout whined and got down to join her on the floor, sniffing around her. 'Hey, boy,' she said, reaching out to give him a hug, but the dog wandered off to his water bowl instead.

THIRTY-SEVEN

THEO

Theo went into the shop, the bell on the door tinkling as he opened and closed it behind him. There were no other customers and no one behind the counter, either. He grabbed a bag of bacon-flavour crisps from the display and a bottle of bright-blue energy drink from the refrigerator, plonking them down loudly by the till in the hope that Margie would hear him. He presumed she was out the back.

'Hello?' he called out in the direction of the tatty brown curtain that separated the shop from whatever lay beyond. 'Anyone here?' He waited, but there was nothing – no sound at all. Then the door tinkled again, and another customer came in – a woman, probably in her forties, Theo reckoned, wearing khaki shorts and trainers with a windcheater on top. She grabbed a carton of milk from the fridge.

'Is she here?' she asked Theo.

'Dunno. Not seen anyone.'

The woman waited a moment, glancing out of the window several times, then she took a few coins from her purse and dropped them on the counter. 'Tell her Sally left this, would you?' she said, before dashing out to a car waiting in the street.

'Hello... Margie, are you there?' Theo called out as he approached the curtain, peeling it back at one side. It was dark behind the fabric, and Theo decided to go through to see if he could find her. He'd run out of fags, and there was nowhere else nearby he'd be able to get any.

'Anyone here?' he tried again, walking into what looked like a storeroom. The small space was dark and cool, smelling slightly of damp, and piled up with boxes – but there was no Margie. He went back into the tiny hallway and ventured through into where he assumed she lived behind the shop. He called out again, announcing himself several more times, not wanting to get a bollocking for breaking in, as he looked around the dingy living room with its velour armchairs and greying net curtains. There was no one in there, but a small television was flickering silently in the corner.

Still holding the crisps and the drink, he walked towards another door. He pushed it open and was faced with a small galley kitchen. At first, it was hard to see anything because the lights were off and the window blind was pulled down, but then he saw Margie, her broad, plump back facing him as she stood at the end of the kitchen, leaning against the worktop, her head bowed. He thought he heard a sob but couldn't be certain.

'Hello? Sorry, there was no one in the shop and—'

Margie suddenly swung round, her eyes wide and both arms thrust out. In one hand was a long cook's knife, brandished at him.

'Jesus fucking Christ!' Theo yelped, raising his hands in self-defence and taking a couple of steps back. 'Sorry, like I'm sorry, man. Just wanted to get some fags, but... but I'll go.' He walked backwards towards the door.

'No, don't go,' Margie said, lowering the knife. She laid it on the worktop behind her. 'You caught me by surprise. I'll get your cigarettes, lad.'

'Are... are you OK, Margie?' Theo asked, relaxing a little, though he thought she looked a bit deranged.

'Aye, aye, lad. Just gimme a wee moment.' She laughed, followed by a cough, then grabbed a glass off the side and drank from it. Theo smelt the whisky from where he was standing a few feet away, noticing she was swaying from side to side.

'I was getting dinner prepared while it was quiet out front.' She pointed to a pile of carrots on the worktop beside the knife, but Theo also noticed that a bottle of pills had spilled out, alongside several other boxes of medication. The whisky bottle was half empty.

'Want a wee dram, laddie?' Margie said, noticing he was staring at the bottle.

Theo shook his head. 'Nah, just the fags if that's OK. But I can get them another time.' There was something about her, something intense and unstable, that gave him the creeps.

'Nae, have a wee one, lad. I insist.' Margie grabbed an upturned glass from the draining board and wiped the rim down her front. Then she sloshed some whisky into it, as well as topping up her own. 'Come, sit down wi' me.'

'Really, I'd better be go—'

'Sit down, lad,' Margie said sternly, nudging him back through into the living room with her elbow.

'OK,' Theo said, not wanting to rile her any more than she already seemed to be. 'You sure you're alright, Margie? You seem a bit...' He wanted to say *drunk* but decided to keep quiet.

'Perceptive for a young lad, eh?' Margie laughed into her glass, easing herself down into the beige armchair. She gestured for Theo to sit in the one beside her. 'Here ye go, get this inside you.' She passed him the glass, but he just stared at it, wanting to get the hell out of this depressing house. He was quick on his feet and would no doubt outrun Margie, but she was a sturdy woman and he didn't really want to take chances. 'And you're a good 'un, I can sense that.'

'You can?'

Margie let out a throaty and dry laugh. 'Aye, you're not like the other boys,' she slurred. 'There's a gentle side to you, even if you don't show it. All dressed up with that fake, tough exterior. When you get to my age, when you've been through enough shit in life, you notice things. Jim said I was intuitive.'

'Jim?'

'My late husband, bless his dear soul. We tried and we tried for a bairn of our own, but God wasn't having any of it.' She let out a hiccup.

'I'm sorry to hear that.'

Margie swigged more of her whisky, with Theo noticing she'd poured herself a tumbler almost to the brim. Her eyes seemed to swim and roll in their sockets, and her cheeks were fiery red. 'I'd have liked a wee lad like you.'

Theo stared at her, not sure what to say. He wondered when she was going to get his fags, because he could really use a smoke now. He hadn't had one since yesterday.

'I failed him... Jim,' Margie went on. 'He were a good man, didn't deserve a woman like me.'

'I'm sorry to hear of your troubles. Any chance of getting the fags now, Margie?'

Margie's eyes seemed glazed over and she made no move to stand up. It was as though she hadn't heard him.

'But that weren't the worst thing I ever did, being a bad wife,' Margie whispered, staring at the unlit fireplace. The light from the television danced over her face. 'Oh, no.'

'No?' Theo had a strange feeling she was about to tell him, even though he really didn't want to hear it.

'Thing is, Theo, what you don't realise in life until it's too late, is that it's all about decisions. One after the other, they keep hitting you between the eyes. By the time you get to my age, you've made millions of 'em, so chances are many will be wrong.' She made a gesture with her thumb, tapping the space between her eyebrows a few times. 'Sometimes they're small enough that you don't even notice, like what colour socks to put on, or what to watch on the television, or whether you should take an umbrella out with you. You decide without too much thought, right?'

'I guess,' Theo said, bored of her drunken ramblings now. Plus, he needed a piss.

'But then there are the bigger things. Like what to do about a man you believed loved you, a man you were taken in by, a man who deceived *everyone*.'

Theo reckoned she needed psychological help for whatever it was she'd been through, and he had no idea why she'd chosen him to pour her heart out to. Wrong time, wrong place, he guessed. It could have been anyone in the shop looking for her. His bad luck.

'And then there are the ginormous things, lad. Decisions the size of which you could never imagine, not at your age.' Margie threw her arms wide, her entire body wobbling as she did so. Theo thought she looked quite grotesque, sitting there with her tree-trunk legs poking out from beneath a voluminous grey skirt, her face turning a bruise-coloured purple. 'Decisions that come so quickly, you have no time to think. They're the kind that, if you get them wrong, they never, *ever*, leave you. They haunt you for as long as you live, whether you've done the right thing or the wrong thing. And that's not even the worst bit. The worst bit is that you even had to make the decision in the first place.'

Theo wiped a drop of her spit off his cheek, hoping she didn't notice. She was well worked up. 'Sorry, Margie, that you've had to deal with all that.' He had no idea what she was talking about.

'I'll never forget the look on that wee babby's face as I held her body. Never.'

Theo suddenly looked at her again. 'Body?'

'Aye, lad. The dead babby I held in my arms, God bless her wee soul.'

It was as Margie was crossing herself repeatedly, muttering what sounded like a frantic, drunken prayer, that Theo got up and left, running back through the shop and dumping his drink and crisps on the counter before legging it, the doorbell tinkling above him, gasping as he ran out into the street for air.

THIRTY-EIGHT

DARBY

Darby pulled into the driveway of the lodge with Finn and Mia sitting in the back chatting about how they wanted to take the kayaks up the river next time they went out, hopefully tomorrow if the weather was decent.

'Thanks, Darby,' Finn said as she pulled up to park, Mia echoing him. Darby smiled, ambling up to the lodge in their wake. Kate's car was, as she expected, tucked at the end of the driveway, and Darby wondered if she'd found their mother, had managed to get her alone, to finally ask the question burning a hole inside her. Did she once have a twin sister, and what happened to her?

Darby didn't feel much like going back inside. The couple of hours sitting by the loch in the fresh air, watching Finn and Mia get smaller and smaller on the glassy water, had made her pensive about the way she and Adrian had dealt with things since the funeral. It was becoming clear as day that the answer to that was *badly*.

She tried to put herself in both Kate and Connie's positions and consider what each of them would have preferred her and

Adrian to do with the information. But of course, the resulting answers were polar opposites. If the allegations were true, that Kate did indeed have a twin who'd died at birth, then Connie had concealed this fact for a reason, and their father too, so it was likely she'd want it kept under wraps. But then if she were Kate, Darby would absolutely want to know about a deceased twin. *What a mess*, she thought, standing on the veranda, staring out into the forest.

'You're back,' came a voice. Darby turned. It was Travis, a grim expression on his face as he stood on the veranda. 'Have you got my phone?'

Darby shook her head. 'No, sorry. Kate said she'd bring it back.'

'Well, she hasn't.'

Darby swallowed, unnerved by the sour expression on his face. 'Maybe she left it in her car?'

'Already asked her to look,' he said, folding his arms. Darby made a move to go inside, to ask Kate, but Travis blocked her way. 'What's going on?'

Darby shook her head. 'What do you mean? Nothing,' she said, staring down at the decking between them. Travis lifted her chin.

'Ever since we arrived, you've been acting... strange.'

'Have I?' She might not have known Travis very long compared to the eleven years she and Chris had been together, but he was still attuned to her mood, still able to read her, even if it was in a more clumsy and less subtle way than Chris. *God, I miss him* – her late husband with his gentle ways, his encouraging words, the pair of them laughing over the most ridiculous things. 'I don't think I have.'

'Unconvincing,' Travis replied.

Darby sighed, resisting the urge to shove him out of her way, even though she wasn't strong enough to do that. 'Being with everyone up here, it's just spotlighting the fact that Dad's not with us any more. And...' She trailed off, thinking better of it.

'What, and *Chris*, you mean?'

'No, I didn't mean that,' she retorted. One of his moods would be unbearable. 'Anyway, Trav, you can't be jealous of him. He died, for God's sake.'

'But given the choice, you'd rather he was here with you instead of me, right?'

'It's not like that, and you know it.' Darby stared down at the decking again, forcing herself not to admit the truth. 'You know how happy I am that we're together,' she added. Though deep down, she was now beginning to wonder if she was happy at all. Something had fractured between them.

A second later, Travis stepped aside, but only because Connie opened the door to see who was standing there, allowing Darby to escape Travis's grilling. Truth was, she *had* been different since they'd arrived, and she *did* wish it was Chris here with her instead of Travis. She'd not wanted her husband to die, and she'd not wanted to be told some damned family secret that she had no idea what to do with, either.

Inside, Darby sat down opposite her sister who was curled up on the beanbag. Adrian was behind her on the sofa, stroking her hair. 'Trav said you don't have his phone, Kate.'

'No... no, I'm sorry, I don't.' Kate was vague and barely looked at her.

'Where is it, then? Travis needs it to confirm job details with his new boss.'

Kate glanced up at her, shaking her head. 'I'm really sorry, I don't have it.'

'Well, did you lose it or what? I gave it to you down at the loch.'

Kate was silent for a moment – presumably concocting a story about how she'd mislaid it between the sailing club and here. 'I must have,' she said. 'Hopefully it'll turn up.'

'What the hell, Kate?' Darby said, more harshly than she'd intended. It was clear by her expression that she had other things on her mind – hardly a surprise there. But she was usually so considerate and conscientious, and now she was behaving like someone else. This wasn't like her at all. 'It's his work phone, and you're acting as though you've lost a pencil you borrowed.'

'Darbs, leave it, will you?' Adrian said. He shot her a look. 'I'm not sure now's the time.'

Darby took the hint and dropped back in the sofa, spotting the almost empty wine bottle on the floor beside Kate's glass, which was also nearly empty. She gave Adrian a look, and he returned a similar one accompanied by a shrug. Something wasn't right. Kate wasn't her usual self, and it could only be about one thing – what Adrian had blurted out to her.

'Right, I've had enough of all this,' Darby said, leaning forward again. 'Kate, look at me.'

Slowly, her sister looked up. It was easy to tell she was drunk, especially for someone who only had a glass of wine once in a while. Kate's expression was full of... *malice*. Darby had never seen her like this before.

'Have you spoken to Mum yet?' Darby said. 'I'm so sorry about keeping things from you. We didn't know what to do... and I suppose... well, we just hoped it would all go away. I know Adrian is sorry too, aren't you?' She shot him a stern look.

'Absolutely,' he said, giving Kate's shoulders a rub. She flinched. 'Most definitely.'

'No, I haven't spoken to her,' Kate said, almost robotically. She hugged her legs up under her chin, sinking deeper into the beanbag. 'Not about that, anyway. I... I don't know what to say.'

'Say about what, darling?'

Darby jumped, turning at the sound of her mother's voice. She was standing across the room wearing her 'Head Chef' apron, wringing a tea towel between her hands, a concerned look on her face.

Darby closed her eyes for a second. 'Mum, come and sit down,' she said, moving up on the sofa. 'We need to talk to you. Rather, *Kate* needs to talk to you. Should we leave you two alone?'

'No, nope, you both stay. Grab some popcorn, why not?' Kate snapped. She reached for the wine bottle and emptied the remaining couple of inches into her glass. She really wasn't herself.

'Mum, look, this is difficult, and we don't want you to get upset again,' Darby began, 'but if there's any truth at all to what Adrian and I were told at Dad's funeral, then we need to know.' She took a breath. 'Is it true that Kate had a twin sister when she was born?'

For a few moments, Connie was silent. She stared down at the pheasant tea towel sitting on her lap, picking at the hem. It was as though she was choosing the exact words she wanted to get out, but none of them were good enough. Then she slipped off the sofa and dropped down onto her knees beside Kate, taking both of her hands in hers.

'Yes.'

There, it was out. That single syllable changing their entire family's history.

'Kate, you did indeed have a twin sister, my darling,' Connie continued. 'She was called Lily. I'm so *so* sorry that I kept this from you, but please believe that I had my reasons.'

Kate sat there, blank-faced, sipping on the remains of her wine as she freed one hand from her mother's grip.

Shock, Darby said to herself, watching Kate's non-reaction intently. *She's just in shock...*

'Mum...' Darby whispered, hoping to elicit a response from Kate. 'Thank you for being honest.'

Adrian cleared his throat. 'Can you tell us what happened,

Connie? What happened to Lily?' His deep voice seemed somehow soothing, and Darby was grateful for this, that he'd asked the burning question.

'She was killed,' Connie said, covering her face. 'When she was only four days old.'

THIRTY-NINE

BEA

'Hey...'

Bea looked up. The smile came easily when she saw Darby approaching her up the steep incline behind the lodge where she was sitting on the bench. Her sister was wearing dungarees over a white T-shirt, which reminded Bea of when they were little – her tomboy outfits a contrast to Bea's love of flowing skirts and pretty tops.

'Mind if I join you? I've not had my cabin fever vaccination yet. I had to get out.' Darby climbed up the remainder of the mossy bank and sat down beside her, panting.

'That bad, is it?'

'Mum's inside talking to Kate...' Darby explained the full story. 'I'm guessing that's what made her fall into a bottle of wine this afternoon. It's no wonder she's behaving strangely. Poor Kate, it's not like her at all.'

'Christ... that's pretty big as family news goes, Darbs.' Bea's brain processed the information, sending her thoughts into overdrive. 'Like, oh by the way there were actually *four* of you?'

'Like that, yeah,' Darby replied. 'I think it's more the *why* didn't you tell me I had a twin that's getting to Kate as much as anything. And I understand that. We all had another big sister, Bea. I can't help imagining what she'd have been like.'

'Er, like Kate?'

'I guess. It's hard to imagine two of them.'

'Did Mum say how they lost the other twin? It's so awful to contemplate.'

'She said she was killed, but we've not got to the details yet. She was explaining to Kate how she didn't even know she was expecting twins when I came out here. I thought it best to give them some space. Travis has skulked off upstairs and—'

'God, I hope *I'm* not having twins,' Bea suddenly said, her mind in overdrive. 'I mean, we all know I'm not going to cope with one, let alone two.'

'I thought that about Charlie,' Darby said. 'I'm not saying it was easy, with Trav being away so much, as well as taking on a stepson, but you'll get by, Bea. You'll muddle through, I promise.'

'I had a text from Louis earlier,' Bea admitted.

'That sounds like some kind of development,' Darby suggested. 'Though from what, I'm not sure. You haven't told me what's gone down between you two in the first place. But I know something has.' She tapped the side of her nose when Bea looked at her.

'Yes.'

'Is it a guessing game?'

'Promise not to tell anyone?'

Darby shifted sideways and took Bea's hands. 'Of course I won't tell.'

'Louis kicked me out.'

'What, when you're pregnant? The wanker!'

'It's not his baby, Darbs.'

Darby was silent for a moment. 'Oh, *Bea...*' She pulled her little sister in for a hug, but she resisted.

'It's not like that,' she said. 'And I don't want sympathy.'

'You're not getting any, actually. If you've been seeing someone else behind Louis's back, then you should have broken up with him first. You can hardly blame him for asking you to move—'

'He didn't ask me to move out. He *threw* me out. Literally. All my stuff went out of the window. And I wasn't seeing anyone else.'

Darby said nothing, her breathing and the rustling of the pine trees the only sounds to be heard. Bea hated the way she always did this – held the silence until she cracked and blabbed. She knew the way her mind worked, knew exactly how to milk her. It was so easy. Bea couldn't bear the void between them, had to fill it with something.

'It was... it happened... I got pregnant by... by force. It was horrible. There. Now you know.'

Bea's mind was off. She imagined herself telling Darby how the *terrible thing*, as she'd since labelled it, had happened. She imagined Darby's shocked reaction, and everyone else's horror when Darby charged down the hill, burst into the lodge and spewed out everything that Bea had confessed. Then no one would speak to her ever again, they'd all disown her, and she'd not only be homeless, but without a family too.

'You were *raped*? Who by?'

Bea gave a little nod to indicate yes, that's exactly what she meant. She couldn't bring herself to say the word *rape* out loud again, not so soon after having told Cameron. All her courage had been used up. It was only because of him, his kindness, that she'd been able to open up in the first place. He'd made her feel less ashamed, less dirty, less culpable. And he'd helped her see that she wanted this baby, despite the terrible way it had been conceived, and that she might just be capable of doing it alone.

'I don't want to talk about it any more, Darbs. I just want to get on with my life.'

'Oh no, oh no you don't, Beatrice Hunter. Don't you dare clam up on me now. You can't just pretend this didn't happen.'

'I can and I am. I'm having the baby and that's all you need to know.'

'Oh, Bea... I understand. But have you been to the police? Just know that I'm here for you, OK?'

'Thank you,' Bea said. 'But I don't want him caught. And I don't need any help. With everything else going on with Kate and Mum, just forget it, OK?'

And with that, Bea stood up and clambered down the hill. All she wanted to do was go home, if only she knew where that was.

Bea knocked on the bedroom door. After taking a quick walk down to the loch in the hope she might run into Cameron (she didn't), she'd slipped back inside the lodge unnoticed. Her mother was in the kitchen frantically chopping something, and Finn and Mia were playing chess in the living room. There was no sign of anyone else about, so she took the opportunity to head up to her room for a lie-down, but on the landing, she heard something – the sound of stifled sobs. And they were coming from Kate and Adrian's room.

'Kate?' she said, tapping the door again. 'Are you in there?'

The noise stopped for a moment, then Bea heard someone blowing their nose. She turned the knob and pushed the door open a little. 'It's me, Bea. Can I come in?'

'Sure,' she heard Kate say. 'At your own peril.'

'Oh, *Katie*...' Bea felt a tug in her heart when she saw her sister sitting cross-legged on the bed, her face red and her eyes puffy from crying. She'd never seen her look like this before. Somehow, she looked... *different*. 'Why are you all alone? Where's Adrian?'

'He's gone to the Stag in the village for a pint. Can't say I blame him. It's like a pressure cooker in this place.'

'It's all peaceful downstairs. Finn and Mia are playing chess, and Mum's cooking.'

'They're good kids, aren't they, my twins?'

'Of course,' Bea said, laughing. 'They're amazing kids. I hope my little one is half as lovely as your two.'

'And Adrian? He's good too, isn't he?' Kate blew her nose again.

Bea looked away, unsure what to say. 'Yes... yes of course he is, Katie. What's got into you?'

'So, would you say I'm lucky?'

'I'm only indulging you because you're upset. But yes, you have a wonderful family and you're very lucky.' She chucked her under the chin and clambered onto the bed beside her, kicking off her grubby white trainers.

'It's so hard to believe that I have a twin,' Kate said. '*Had*... I mean.'

'I know, I can't believe it either. Did Mum tell you how she died? It's so tragic, her and Dad losing a baby... I bet they never got over it.'

'She was finding it very hard to talk about. It was like... like I don't even know my own mother any more.' Kate fell silent for a few moments. 'You'll think I'm mad, but all my life I've felt as though a part of me has been missing, that I'm somehow *less* than everyone else. On the outside, it might appear that I've got everything sorted, but I've never felt whole. Do you think this explains it?'

'Yes, I do,' Bea said, snuggling closer. She thought Kate felt thinner, more brittle since finding out the news. 'Try to imagine what Dad would say. He was always good in situations like this. He'd sit you down and get you to confess every single thing you're feeling. As well as plying you with a stiff drink.'

'I've had most of a bottle of wine this afternoon. Not sure I need any more.'

'Blimey, Kate, that's not like you. No wonder you're emotional.'

In fact, Bea had never seen her older sister this upset about anything. Any grieving she'd done for their father had taken place privately, with Kate making sure she had her brave face on when she was with the others. But that was Kate – practical, capable, reliable. A stoic. Was this the moment she finally fell apart?

'As for what Dad would say, that's easy,' Kate said, a serious look sweeping over her. 'According to what Mum told me just now, *he'd* be the one confessing – that he's not my real father.'

FORTY

CONNIE

'I thought you weren't coming with me,' Connie said to Kate, relieved she'd changed her mind.

'Would you blame me?'

Connie's heart ached for the upset etched on her daughter's face. 'No. No, I wouldn't blame you.'

'I was upstairs washing my face and getting ready, then Bea came in and distracted me,' Kate told her, though Connie noticed that the water hadn't done much good. Her eyes were still puffy and red.

'I'd planned on telling you everything on this trip, I swear,' Connie said as they walked across the driveway, though she crossed the fingers of one hand, hating that she was still lying, that she hadn't yet found the courage to tell her daughters about Ray's will. None of it was supposed to have happened this way.

She unlocked the old Land Rover and they climbed in. The engine started on the fourth attempt, Connie knowing its life-span was limited now that Ray wasn't here to tinker with it. He'd done all the servicing and repairs himself over the years, including replacing the front bodywork panel, too wary to give the vehicle to a garage, and he'd reluctantly got its MOT each year through a local mechanic he knew from the pub. There was no way he'd ever have sold it. *Evidence*, he'd said.

'I don't understand why it took Adrian blurting it out to get the truth from you. I'm forty-two, for God's sake. You and Dad have had plenty of opportunities. I don't even know if I should be calling him Dad now, given that he's not my biological father. I've got so many questions, I don't know where to start.'

Connie gripped the steering wheel and stared straight ahead – the same way she'd got through life since that dreadful night. By clinging on tightly.

'I was young,' Connie said to break the silence that had fallen between them as she wrenched the gear stick into first, pulling out onto the narrow lane that was barely wide enough for two vehicles to pass side by side. Plus, the steep incline made anything more than second gear a struggle. 'And I was so naive. So vulnerable. Given my time again, I'd do things very differently. I just want you to know that, Kate.'

Connie braced herself for what lay up ahead – the stretch of road where *it* happened, where everything had changed in the blink of an eye.

As she dropped the Land Rover down a gear, she took the sharp bend slowly, hugging the verge as another car sped the other way. That night, there'd been no other car. It was just her and her babies out in the forest in the pitch dark, a few meagre possessions flung in the back as they'd made their escape. She'd been so close to freedom, yet so far.

'Are you coming in, love? I know Margie would love to see you,' Connie said a few minutes later as she parked outside the shop, turning off the engine. She was unnerved by the way Kate was staring at her as she slowly unclipped her seatbelt. She'd never seen her look like this before, and she had to admit, it scared her. *You must hate me*, she thought as she got out of the Land Rover.

'Does it remind you of anything?' Connie asked as she pushed open the door, closing it and opening it again, so Kate could hear the bell tinkle.

'Not really,' Kate said, her arms folded across her chest.

Be patient with her, Connie thought, realising that the last thing her daughter would want to remember right now were childhood memories – memories that she'd only just discovered were based on lies. Finding out that you had a sibling who died so young was one thing, but to learn she was a twin sister was quite another. Then the thought struck her. It was time to show her Lily's grave. It was only a matter of time before Kate asked where her sister was buried – though she'd have to be careful what she revealed, why she hadn't been laid to rest in a cemetery.

'Hello, Margie,' Connie said as they went in.

'Aye, Con,' Margie replied. Her cheeks seemed ruddier than usual and, as she approached the counter, she caught a whiff of alcohol. She knew she liked a tipple, but this was a pungent smell as though it was seeping from her pores.

'Look who's here,' Connie said as Kate approached the counter.

'Hello, Margie,' Kate said flatly.

'Kate,' Margie said with a nod. 'It's been a wee while since I've seen your bonnie face properly. Several years since, I reckon.' Connie had been sad that her oldest friend had been absent at Ray's funeral, but she'd understood her reasons. Her health hadn't been the best lately, and there was no one else these days to mind the shop.

'That long?' Connie said, overly brightly when Kate didn't reply. Really, they should just grab the few vegetables they'd need for later and get on their way. She'd only asked Kate to come with her in the hope of normalising things between them. The first step of what she knew would be a steep mountain to climb as she braced herself for telling Kate about Ray's will.

Kate leant on the counter, grabbing a packet of fresh mint chewing gum and setting it in front of Margie.

'We just came in for some potatoes and a few bits,' Connie said. 'Travis and Theo certainly have appetites.'

'Aye, Darby's new family. The lad has been in here several times for his smokes. Nice boy.'

'He has?' Connie was shocked, wondering if Darby knew what he'd been up to. 'He's only seventeen, you know, Marg.'

Margie rolled her eyes as Connie placed a bag of Maris Pipers on the counter, along with some carrots, tomatoes, a cauliflower and some onions.

'That everything, Con?'

'I'll have a packet of Marlboro, please,' Kate said, reaching into her back pocket.

Margie laughed. 'The wee lad been teaching you bad habits, eh?'

Connie raised her eyebrows. *I know what you're up to,* she thought, deciding not to comment on Kate's sudden rebellion. She'd never known her to smoke before, but she figured she was going for shock value, protesting in small ways to prove that she still had some control over her life. If it meant having a few cigarettes and drinks, then Connie wasn't going to begrudge her that. Kate wasn't the type to take up smoking permanently.

'We'll be off, then, Margie, so you can close up shop.' Connie gathered up her shopping bag. 'See you next time.'

'Aye, Con,' Margie replied, her eyes fixed on Kate. 'You look after that family of yours,' she said, making Connie hesitate before she turned to go. The two women's eyes locked, with Connie seeing the other woman as she used to be for just a second – long glossy hair, a waist that was barely there, proud cheekbones and full red lips, a low-cut top as she pulled pints in the pub. Margie had all the men turning their heads when she was younger.

'I will indeed,' Connie replied, hearing the waft of Margie's sigh as she and Kate left the shop.

FORTY-ONE

KATE

'Put the shopping in the Land Rover,' Kate said as her mother opened the door of the vehicle. 'Then follow me.'

Connie put the groceries on the front seat and closed the door again, frowning at Kate. 'Where are we going?'

'Somewhere where we can talk,' Kate replied, grabbing Connie's hand. She noticed how her mother's skin, while soft and supple, also had a slightly papery touch to it. Kate smiled inwardly, wondering what she'd look like at a similar age, if she'd be as composed and graceful, or if all her anger would have erupted by then and she'd be a seething mass of boils and blemishes.

'Follow me,' Kate said, leading her mother over to the Stag and Pheasant, a low white building with colourful hanging baskets along the frontage. Kate's head skimmed the low doorway as they went in to be greeted by the hoppy smell of beer and the comforting aroma of pub lunches.

'Good grief, I've not been in here in ages,' Connie said. Kate felt the slight reluctance in her hand, the way she pulled back just a little as they entered the bar area. Several couples were dotted about at tables, none of whom Kate recognised, and two mothers and their toddlers were seated over against the far wall, buggies draped with paraphernalia parked beside them as the women sipped on coffees.

'What'll it be, Mum?' Kate asked, leaning against the bar. 'G and T? Whisky? Bloody Mary?' She gave her a sly look.

Connie shook her head. 'Just a tomato juice, please,' she whispered as her eyes flicked about nervously.

Kate fished in her bag and pulled out her purse, pulling out a twenty-pound note. The barmaid was busy at the other end of the polished bar, chatting with two old men in flat caps, but came over when she spotted them.

'What can I get you, ladies?'

'I'll have a pint of that, please,' Kate said, touching the nearest IPA pump, 'and Mum will have a Bloody Mary. Make it a double.'

'Kate—'

'We'll walk back, if we have to,' Kate said. 'You can pick the Land Rover up tomorrow, or get Adrian to fetch it later. Anyway, I don't know why you don't get new wheels, Mum. That ancient old thing isn't safe.'

'It's perfectly fine,' Connie whispered, looking strung out as her eyes continued to flick about. 'It's never let me down.'

'Couple of bags of dry-roasted peanuts too,' Kate said to the barmaid, laying down the cash. A moment later and the pair of them were sitting at a small round table with an upholstered banquette under the front window, their drinks set on cardboard drip mats.

'Well, thanks for this, darling, even though I shouldn't,' Connie said, raising her glass.

'Why shouldn't you? Because Dad wouldn't like it? Newsflash...' she added with a roll of her eyes, chinking her glass back.

'Darling, don't. I have to drive, cook for everyone, wash up. You know.' Connie took the tiniest sip of her drink.

'Dad was good at that, wasn't he? Guilt-tripping you?' Kate drew down an inch of her pint, not that she usually drank beer, especially on top of wine. But today, she felt like it. She was sick of playing by the rules, and she was enjoying being someone else. She remembered the cigarettes in her bag, knowing she'd probably only light one or two before chucking the packet away in disgust. 'It's how he controlled you, Mum.'

'It wasn't like that.' Connie looked away briefly.

'It was a bit, Mum,' Kate replied. 'Don't think we didn't notice it as we were growing up. Kids aren't stupid, you know. And do you know what happens then? Those children turn into adults, making the same mistakes as their parents because it's what they spent their childhoods learning about relationships. It's a shit job, being a mother, right?'

'What's on *earth's* got into you, Kate?'

'I'm simply stating the truth.'

'I think you're being overly harsh on your father, and—'

Kate made a show of spraying out a mouthful of beer, grabbing a serviette to wipe her lips. 'My father?' She shook her head. 'Firstly, he isn't my father, and secondly, Darby and Bea aren't exactly shining examples when it comes to relationships. Especially Bea.'

'I understand you're hurting, but don't say things like that.' Connie sighed heavily. 'Kate, look, there's something else I need to tell—'

'Why not, Mum?' Kate interrupted, not wanting to hear more excuses. 'It seems the truth has been a little scarce around here. Darby rebounded so hard after Chris's death, it knocked all good sense out of her, and look at Bea – pregnant, alone, jobless, pretending that her life is one long cup of matcha tea, when in reality she's one declined debit card transaction away from homelessness.'

'Kate, that's a bit harsh. Anyway, Bea would have told me if she was in trouble.' Connie stared down at her lap.

'She's protecting you from the truth, Mum. And so is Darby. Anyone can see they're unhappy.'

'But you're OK, aren't you, Katie?' The desperation in her mother's voice was almost sweet, if it weren't so tragic.

'No, Mum, I'm not. You really have no idea about me at all, have you?'

'But Adrian and you... and the twins. You're all so good together. A team.'

Kate shook her head slowly, watching her mother believe her own lies.

FORTY-TWO

THEO

'Y'alright?' Theo said, glancing up when he heard someone come outside. He was up early again, sitting on the top step of the veranda, staring at his phone, wondering if he should send another text to Mystery Woman. She still hadn't replied to his last message, and her 'last seen' timestamp was hidden. She was probably annoyed he'd hung up on her.

'Morning,' Finn said, stretching out above him.

'Want a smoke?' Theo heard himself saying, knowing full well he'd refuse. He held up the pack of Bensons anyway.

'Got any weed?' Finn said, squatting down beside him.

'Weed?' Theo hated the way his voice squeaked, but he was genuinely shocked. 'Didn't have you down as the type.' He managed a smile.

'There's a lot you don't know about me,' Finn replied, returning the grin. 'So, have you?'

'Yeah, I have, as it happens,' Theo replied, lowering his voice. 'Not had a chance to try it yet.' He listened out for any sounds of the others getting up, but it was still before seven and he figured they had half an hour or so before Charlie woke

Darby and his dad. And Scout was taken care of as he'd followed him outside for his morning pee, so he wouldn't be barking to rouse Kate.

'Fancy rolling us a joint, then?'

Theo hoisted himself to his feet, standing face to face with the boy he'd been avoiding most of the holiday so far. Had he got him all wrong? He presented as this squeaky-clean jock type with a photo of his glamorous girlfriend in their room, the perfect son in every respect, but here he was asking *him* for a spliff. Theo felt something swell inside him, as though electricity was sparking all the cells in his body. The day was getting off to a better start than he'd imagined.

'Sure, let me go and get it.'

A couple of minutes later, having dashed up to their room and fished around under his mattress, Theo returned with the little plastic bag, some Rizla papers and a pouch of tobacco. He didn't see Finn at first, but then spotted him over by the edge of the forest with Scout, staring out into the trees in the direction of the loch. He turned round when he heard Theo approach.

'Shall we go into the woods?' he asked.

'Nah, follow me. I know a better place,' Theo said, leading him around the back of the old garage. He tugged at the rusty handle several times until the door gave and opened. The same musty, oily smell greeted them as they went inside.

'This was Grandad's old workshop,' Finn said, dropping down beside Theo on the battered leather car seats. 'He loved to tinker. I miss him, you know.'

'He taught me loads of stuff about engines when I visited him at the farm,' Theo told him as he balanced a Rizla paper on his lap. Finn watched as he carefully sprinkled in the tobacco followed by some of the weed. 'Hope this stuff's not past its best,' he added. 'I got it a while ago.'

'Better than nothing,' Finn said, watching as Theo lit up. He took a couple of drags, breathing in deeply, before handing it over to Finn.

Finn did the same, stifling a string of coughs as he inhaled. 'Here's to you, Grandad,' he said, raising the joint up high after he'd taken another drag. 'Not that he'd have approved of this.' His head lolled sideways towards Theo for a moment.

'I wish my dad and Darby would smoke some.' Theo laughed. 'They might loosen the fuck up a bit.'

'My folks, too,' Finn replied, resting his head back against the wall of the garage. 'They're so hung up all the time.'

'Your mum and dad?' Theo said. 'No way.'

'Yes way. Dad walks about with a face like a cat's arse, and Mum... well, she's up and down lately. Sometimes she's cool, but just lately it's like she can't even look at anyone.'

'All this perfect family crap gets on my tits. And now there's the shit going down about a dead baby.'

'You've been tuning in too?' Finn took back the joint. 'Crazy to think that I could have had another aunt. Two are enough, believe me.'

'Yeah, it's hard not to overhear what's going down.' Theo's fingers brushed against Finn's as he held the joint again. He was still for a moment, ash dropping onto the floor, wondering if he could trust him. 'I found an old blanket, you know.' Theo's head was swimming, though he wasn't sure if that was because he was having an actual conversation with Finn, alone, or from the effects of the weed. 'A baby blanket. It was in the incinerator with a manky old fox on it.'

Finn stared at him, frowning.

'Made me wonder if it... you know, belonged to that dead baby. It was well weird. But the weirdest thing is, it had blood on it.'

Finn laughed. 'Yeah, just fox blood. Mia told me about it.'

'But what if it was *baby* blood?'

'I think you're a bit stoned.' Finn reached for the spliff again. It was nearly finished, and Theo was already thinking about rolling another one.

'Can't lie, I'm feeling mellow, but seriously, who hides something like that at the back of a shed if it's not suspicious?'

'Nan was probably just using it to kneel on while she was gardening or something, and the fox just happened to choose that spot to die.'

'Doesn't seem right, though. Darby's kept Charlie's baby stuff in a box of keepsakes. Anyway, there's something else weird.' Theo hauled himself to his feet and went over to the Land Rover panel that was propped against the wall. He pulled off the sheet that he'd replaced after he first discovered it. 'Take a look at this.'

Finn stood up and went over to him, staggering for the first couple of steps. 'What's that?'

'The front panel of a Land Rover, a late-1970s model. I googled it.'

'Grandad was always doing repairs on Nan's motor. He must have replaced it for her. It's all dented, see?' Finn seemed unimpressed.

'But *why* is it dented?' Theo said, thinking he sounded like a copper off one of those shows he sometimes watched. 'Maybe something – or some*one* – was hit.'

Finn crouched down next to the crumpled panel, taking his phone from his pocket and lighting it up with his torch. He raised his eyebrows. 'Whatever happened, it was probably a long time ago.' He dropped back down onto the car seat again. 'Nana probably hit a deer or something, and Grandad fixed it for her. God, that stuff's good, man.' He closed his eyes and rested his head back against the wall.

Theo fell silent, plonking himself down next to Finn. Maybe he was making too much of all this. Perhaps nothing untoward had happened at all and Connie or Ray had indeed run into a deer – God knows there were enough of the beasts running loose around here – and maybe Ray had fixed up the vehicle for her because it was the cheaper option. And the blanket... that could be innocent too. Just fox blood. But something was nagging away inside him, telling him it wasn't innocent at all – especially in the light of Connie's big secret.

'Some random person approached your dad at Ray's funeral, you know,' Theo went on. 'Darby was there, too. I overheard them all talking about it yesterday when I was upstairs. The floorboards are very thin.'

Theo rolled another joint, his fingers working deftly, despite the pleasant woozy feeling making his head swim. Then he grabbed his phone, pulling up Mystery Woman's string of messages on WhatsApp. He tapped on the profile picture.

'Do you recognise this person?'

Finn stared at it then shook his head. 'You can't see her face.' He took the phone from Theo, zooming in. 'I think Nan's got a hat like that, though. One with a feather in it. I remember playing dress-up at Foxhills years ago, and I swear Mia used to parade around in one like that.'

'Interesting,' Theo said thoughtfully, wondering if Mystery Woman could be Finn's sister. Or even Connie herself. But why? When he'd heard her voice on the phone, it had sounded familiar, but he still couldn't quite place it. 'I wonder where the baby's grave is,' he continued, handing the new joint and lighter to Finn. Theo watched as he held it between his lips, sucking in on the flame and inhaling deeply, closing his eyes.

'Reckon I might have an idea, actually,' Finn replied, blowing out smoke.

Theo's ears pricked up. 'Where?'

'I've seen Nan sitting up on the bank behind the lodge a few times. She takes flowers up there, lays down little crosses made of twigs, talks to someone as though they can hear her. I've never thought much of it before, but maybe that's the spot.'

'I've seen that too,' Theo replied, wondering why the grave wasn't in a cemetery. 'I guessed it was for a pet or something, but you could be right.' And then, without thinking, as though something had taken over his body and mind, he lunged forward and kissed Finn on the lips.

FORTY-THREE

DARBY

Darby didn't know whether she could carry the weight of what Bea had revealed to her without confiding in someone. *Raped?* Dear God, not her little sister. What had the three of them always sworn when they were children – that if anyone ever hurt a Hunter girl, they'd kill them? Or something along those lines. Pacts and sisterly bonds were all very well as kids when the biggest danger was someone stealing your sweets or copying your homework, but the stakes as an adult were far greater. And so was the punishment. Why Bea didn't want to report the crime, she had no idea, though she guessed it was because she wanted to protect him for some reason – whoever *he* was.

'Christ, my head,' Kate said as she padded into the kitchen. She was wearing cream pyjamas with her robe wrapped loosely over the top. Her honey-coloured hair was a mess of tangles at the back, and yesterday's mascara was clumped and smudged beneath her puffy eyes.

'Uh-oh...' Darby said, glancing up from the hob. She'd got several pans on the go, deciding her mum needed a break. 'Paracetamol is in the cupboard above the kettle.'

'Thanks,' Kate said, grabbing the packet and fetching a glass.

'Most un-Kate-like, you were yesterday,' Darby said, hearing the tap run. The bacon sizzled and she turned a couple of pieces with the tongs.

Kate turned and stared at her.

'Look, maybe you should spend some time with Mum today. Just the two of you.' Darby didn't want to say *to smooth things over*, but she'd noticed how quiet their mother had been last night over dinner.

Darby knew more than any of them how life took cruel turns at the most unexpected moments. And searching for answers and closure was potentially more destructive than the actual loss itself. She hated seeing her mother distressed. And she hated how the shock was affecting Kate, too. Not to mention that her hangover looked like a stonker.

'A cooked breakfast and some fresh air will do you good,' Darby said to her sister as she drew up close. She smelt of stale alcohol and cigarettes. 'And a shower,' she added, giving her a nudge. Kate prodded her in the ribs, and they shared a smile.

'Maybe, though I can only stomach a bit of toast. Where's Scout, do you know? He's not inside.'

'Theo took him out. I've never known him to get up so early. He seems to be enjoying himself, though. How are your two liking the holiday?'

Kate pulled a face. 'Yeah, they're fine.'

Is that it? Darby thought. *Fine?*

'Look, Kate, I'm truly sorry that Adrian and I kept things from you. We didn't even know if that woman at the funeral was telling the truth. But...' Darby hesitated, concentrating on the bacon instead.

'But what?'

'But... I think you should know that Adrian has been receiving texts off her, whoever she is. I don't know what they said, but you know... just thought I'd mention it.' She flicked her eyes up at Kate, who gave a slow, thoughtful nod. Then, without saying a word, Kate left the kitchen. A moment later and Darby heard her outside the window calling out for Theo.

'Right, tuck in, everyone,' Darby said. She wiped her forehead with her sleeve, wondering how her mother had managed to cater for everyone virtually single-handedly since they'd arrived. In fact, she was wondering a lot of things about her mother this last day or so, seeing her in a completely different light.

'Who wants more coffee?' She walked around the table, topping up everyone's mugs from the pot, feeling as though she was back at work in the café. She missed the bustle and busyness of it. The constant stream of traffic and people outside on the hectic street, the regulars coming in for their takeout coffees on the way to work, the mums and toddlers mid-morning, the lunchtime crowd queueing up for their paninis, and the usual few who'd camp out at a table most of the day with their laptops while she kept them plied with hot drinks. She loved Glengalloch and the loch, but she'd be relieved to get back home in a few more days. Just her, Travis and the boys.

'Thanks, love,' Connie said, resting her hand on Darby's arm. Darby smiled down at her, noticing that she seemed to have aged almost overnight. The fine lines around her eyes and mouth were more visible, and her hair seemed a paler shade of silver than before. But it was her frailty that she noticed the most – how vulnerable she suddenly seemed.

'So, what do we all think about a group hike today?' Darby volunteered. 'Then we can have an afternoon's swim back at the loch. Kate, you've still got the kayaks on hire, haven't you?'

Kate looked up, a piece of dry toast between her fingers. 'Um... yeah, I think so.'

'No more wine ever again for you, love,' Adrian said, giving her a brief hug.

Kate smiled, staring down at her plate. Instead of eating, she took a long sip of black coffee.

'I'll give the walk a miss,' Bea said from where she was sitting next to Mia. 'I'm feeling quite sick this morning.' Darby noticed she hadn't touched any of her scrambled eggs and looked deathly pale.

'Want to come kayaking with me?' Finn said to Theo, who'd been staring at his phone since he'd sat down at the table. Darby watched her stepson, wondering if he and Finn were getting along, finally becoming friends, feeling relieved that one good thing might result from this holiday. *He could do with a mate*, she thought. But Theo remained silent, shrugging in reply. Darby had caught the whiff of smoke and weed on the boys when they'd come back inside, but no one else seemed to have noticed. She'd decided not to say anything for now, not wanting more upset.

'I'd like to know where my bloody phone's got to,' Travis piped up with a full mouth. He glared across at Kate, who thankfully didn't notice the look he gave her.

'I'm sure it'll turn up,' Adrian said. 'Kate doesn't even remember having it, do you, love?'

Darby stared at him, her mouth hanging open. She wanted to scream out that of *course* Kate remembered taking it from her, that she gave it to her at the loch only yesterday when she offered to bring it back here. But Darby maintained her silence. Her sister was still upset from everything that had happened, and a lost phone was no doubt the last thing on her mind. There was an undercurrent of tension around the table that she didn't like, and she saw little point in stirring things up further. She made a mental note to search in Kate's car after breakfast, perhaps find out if she'd stopped off for petrol on the way back or popped to the village shop. It could have fallen out of her pocket or the car door.

'Have you tried to locate it using the Find My app on Darby's phone?' Theo asked his dad. He had a sheepish look about him for some reason.

'Of course I have,' Travis snapped unnecessarily. 'It's not picking it up, so I guess it's either out of battery or there's no reception wherever it is, which wouldn't surprise me around here.' He clattered his cutlery onto his plate. 'And you might want to consider getting off your phone for once and eating the breakfast Darby has made you.'

Theo opened his mouth to retaliate but then fell silent, looking both hurt and thoughtful. He picked up his knife and fork.

The knock at the door prevented Darby from sticking up for Theo and telling Travis he was only trying to be helpful. She was grateful for the interruption and got up to see who was there.

'Oh, hi, Cameron,' she said when she saw him, an anxious look on his face. 'Everything OK? Come in and have a coffee.'

'Morning, sorry to disturb you all,' he said, wiping his feet then coming through to the dining area. 'I just wanted to check if Dad was here? I know it's a long way to push himself up the hill but... well, he's not at home.' He scratched his beard, looking concerned.

'Really?' Connie said, wiping her mouth on her napkin. 'When did you last see him?' She went over to Cameron.

'That's the thing,' Cameron replied, shifting from one foot to the other. 'Not since yesterday afternoon, though that's not unusual. He was in his room – he sometimes holes himself up with a book and stays in there for a day or two at a time – and he had food and water, everything he needed for bedtime. I went to help him get dressed this morning, but there was no sign of him, and his phone was still beside his bed.'

'Could he be in his studio?' Connie suggested, but Cameron was already shaking his head.

'I checked there, as well as all around the house and garden. No sign of him anywhere.'

Darby was about to ask if he wanted them all to help look for him when a shrill message alert suddenly pinged.

'Whose phone was that?' Theo demanded in a harsh voice. He suddenly stood up, glancing around everyone in turn, then tapped on his own phone briefly, before looking at everyone again as he listened out.

The shrill *ting-ting* of another text message sounded again, though it was hard to pinpoint from where.

Cameron felt in his pocket, pulling out his phone, and Darby grabbed hers from the kitchen to check. Adrian didn't move – rather he just carried on eating his food – while Connie simply shrugged, waiting to hear more from Cameron about Fraser. Travis grumbled something about *chance being a fine thing*.

'It's not me,' Mia piped up.

'Me neither,' Finn added, looking at his twin. Kate just sat at the table with a blank expression until, finally, she shook her head to confirm it wasn't her.

Darby was about to ask Theo what on earth it was all about, telling him not to interrupt Cameron, when Bea suddenly cupped her hands over her mouth as though she was about to throw up, and dashed out of the room towards the downstairs toilet.

'I knew it!' Theo said triumphantly, though no one took any notice.

FORTY-FOUR

BEA

Nothing much came up, given that she hadn't eaten any breakfast yet. Bea wiped her mouth on some toilet paper and stood up, waiting a moment to see if she was going to be sick again. She leant against the wall feeling light-headed, yet she knew the strange feeling inside was only partly to do with her pregnancy.

'Oh Christ,' she said, staring at herself in the mirror. Who was this ashen creature staring back? How had she gone from a fun-loving, happy young woman living a carefree life with the man she'd believed was the love of her life to someone she barely recognised?

Bea let out a little sob and turned to unlock the door. When she opened it, Travis was standing there, blocking her way.

'Oh!' she squealed, tensing up and looking away. She didn't want him to see inside her eyes, and she didn't want to see inside his either. 'Sorry,' she muttered, trying to slide past.

Travis grabbed on to her arm. 'What's wrong with you?' he growled.

Bea froze, unable to move, just as she had done that terrible night. She couldn't stand anyone touching her now, let alone a man. 'Nothing,' she forced herself to say as she felt his fingers digging into her arm. She desperately wanted to scream, to yell at him to get off her, but her heart kicked up into a furious gallop, choking her. She was pinned in the doorway with nowhere to run.

And there she was, back there that night at Darby's house in London... except Darby wasn't there. Only Travis.

'Oh my God, Bea, you're a lifesaver,' Darby had said on the phone earlier in the day when her sister had called to ask the favour. 'You're sure you won't forget?'

'Darbs, I know I'm a scatterbrain but it's only tonight. Even *I* won't forget that.'

Darby had blown a few kisses down the line, telling her she owed her, before hanging up. Her babysitter had cancelled at short notice, and she couldn't find another one. It would be cutting it fine time-wise for Bea to get from Islington down to Deptford by six, but if she left work on time, she'd just make it. Besides, as she'd told Darby, skidding in at the last minute was her speciality.

'Travis booked these tickets for my birthday ages ago and I daren't let him down,' Darby had said at the start of the call. 'Theo's got plans tonight, so he can't help out. And you know what Travis gets like. I don't need a moody man on my hands.' Darby had laughed then, to soften up what could otherwise have sounded like a harsh comment about her partner.

Bea didn't think she did know what Travis was like as she'd not spent much time in his company. Not because she didn't like him – she hadn't formed much of an opinion of him yet – but because she wasn't organised enough to carve out time to visit. But at least now she'd get to spend the evening with her cute little nephew.

'Look, get your ass to the theatre and I'll take care of Charlie. We'll make a blanket fort and eat sweets until we're sick,' she'd joked, hanging up a few minutes later.

But when Bea had arrived at Darby's small, terraced house, her coat hitched up over her head to shield her from the rain, her sister wasn't home. It was Travis who'd opened the door to her.

'Bea,' he'd said in that gruff voice of his. 'Come in.'

Bea had kicked off her wet shoes on the doormat and Travis had helped her slip out of her padded coat, his hand slowly trailing down one of her arms.

'Where's Darbs?' Bea asked as Charlie came toddling up to her. He hugged her legs, wiping a melting chocolate biscuit down her white jeans.

'Didn't she tell you?' Travis said, guiding her inside the little living room with his hand in the small of her back. 'She's going straight from the café and meeting me at the theatre.' He hung her coat up on the back of the door, gesturing to her to sit down. 'Fancy a drink?' he said, glancing at his watch. 'Might join you for a quickie. I've still got time before I have to leave.'

'Sure,' Bea had said, grinning up at him. She'd had a terrible day at work and needed to unwind.

A few moments later, Travis returned. He sat down beside her on the sofa – so close that their thighs were brushing, even though there was plenty of room. He handed her a drink, filled to the brim. 'Cheers,' he said, not taking his eyes off her as he swigged from his bottle of beer.

Bea raised her glass at him but was more preoccupied with the way he was touching her leg. She stared down at his hand, about to ask him what he thought he was doing, but nothing came out of her mouth. Her voice seemed to have dried up.

'Chocolate,' he said with a wink. 'On your nice jeans.'

'Doesn't matter,' she finally managed to say. 'Where's Charlie?' He'd followed his dad out to the kitchen when he'd gone to fetch the drinks.

'In his playpen amusing himself in the other room,' Travis said. 'Just while we relax.'

Bea swallowed down the lump in her throat, checking the time on her phone. 'How long does it take you to get into town?' she asked, simply for the sake of saying something. She felt uncomfortable with him sitting so close, the way his fingers were still on her thigh, even though he'd stopped rubbing at the chocolate stain. 'Shouldn't you get going? You don't want to be late. I know how excited Darby is to see the show and—'

But Bea was cut off mid-speech as what happened next changed the entire course of the evening. The entire course of her *life*.

Bea screamed, shoving her way past Travis in the toilet doorway and dashing back to join the others in the dining room. She stood perfectly still for a few seconds, everyone staring at her as they waited for her to explain what was wrong, but she couldn't. As had happened when Travis touched her leg, her voice had dried up completely.

Without thinking what she was doing or where she was going, Bea pushed past the chairs at the table, grabbed her phone from where she'd been sitting and headed for the front door of the lodge. Grappling with the latch for a moment, she ran outside, her legs not feeling like her own as she hurtled past the cars on the drive and down the track. She kept on running, stopping only when she thought she might throw up again.

Her pants turned into sobs as she leant forward, resting her hands on her thighs as her chest heaved in and out and the tears fell from her eyes.

'Oh God, oh God, *oh God*... I don't... I don't want to be me any more...'

She allowed herself to drop down into the bracken at the edge of the track, having not even made it to the lane yet. She had a grumbling pain in her lower belly, which she put down to cramps from being sick, her legs felt unstable and weak, and her lungs burned from running. As she sat on the muddy verge, she drew up her knees, wrapping her arms tightly around them, and rested her forehead on them. Perhaps if she stayed like this forever, this whole terrible thing would go away. She felt as though she were living someone else's life – a nightmare not of her own making.

And that's when she heard a voice.

'Bea!' he called out, running towards her. 'What's wrong? What's happened?'

Bea looked up, her eyes blurry from tears, though she was still able to make out that it was Cameron approaching. He crouched down beside her, panting, and put a hand on her shoulder. She couldn't help the flinch as more tears came.

'I... I can't do this,' she sobbed. 'That night... it all just flooded back to me – being trapped, hemmed in by Travis, no way out. Oh God, Cam, what am I going to do?'

Cameron cradled her gently in his arms, rocking her back and forth, and Bea allowed it. 'Is it time?' he eventually asked. 'To report this to the police?'

Bea forced herself to stop crying and looked up at him, wiping her nose on the back of her hand. Then she gave the tiniest of nods.

FORTY-FIVE

CONNIE

Adrian took charge of the search, for which Connie was grateful. He, Travis, Darby and the two boys had all gone out to look for Fraser in the local area, with Mia and Charlie ambling along behind as she babysat and entertained the toddler. Apart from that, there wasn't much else they could do at this point, aside from calling the police, which Connie had urged Cameron to do.

'Mum,' Adrian had said to her before he'd left, walking boots on and a hand planted firmly on her shoulder as he looked her in the eye. 'I want you to stay here with Kate and relax in the living room, OK? And no washing up, either.' He glanced at Kate, and she nodded in return.

Odd, Connie had thought after they'd left, that Kate hadn't tackled the breakfast dishes as she usually would have – but then again, nothing was normal any more. She made them each a mug of tea, and now they were sitting on opposite sofas with Kate looking like death and neither of them knowing what to say.

'Sorry, Mum,' Kate said, avoiding eye contact. 'Stonking hangover, or I'd have helped you in the kitchen.'

Connie wanted to ask what had got into her, why she was acting so out of character, but held off. It was hardly a question that needed answering. She *knew* what was wrong – and she hated that she was about to make things even worse.

'Will you come with me?' Connie said when the silence between them had become too heavy to bear. She put down her tea on the mat and stood up. 'I can't make this feel any better for you, Kate, and I know you'll probably never trust me again. But I can at least try to help you see things from my point of view, give you an idea of what things were like back then, why I... why your dad and I kept things secret all this time.'

She held out her hand towards Kate.

At first, Kate just stared at Connie's fingers, but then she stood up and allowed herself to be led outside.

'This way,' Connie said, leading the way up the steep bank behind the lodge. The path was worn and crumbling, with the steps having eroded over the years. 'I come and sit up here sometimes,' she said breathlessly when they reached the spot where the earth flattened out. The forest skirted around them, shielding them from the sun, though as Connie peered over the roof of the lodge, she saw the tell-tale dark clouds gathering in the direction of the loch, heralding another storm.

'Why?' Kate asked, staring around.

Connie knew that all Kate would see was a patch of scrubby earth with a few wilted flowers left lying about. Given how distracted her daughter was, she doubted she'd even notice the home-made crosses she'd tied from twigs and ribbons that were propped against the base of a pine tree, let alone the little notes that she'd left, semi-buried, over the years. Most had rotted away.

'Just there,' Connie said, pointing at a particular spot. 'That's Lily's grave.'

Kate was silent, while Connie was suddenly preoccupied by something else that had caught her eye. Something poking up from beneath the soil and pine needles that hadn't been there last time she'd visited.

'She's buried *here*?' Kate asked, staring down.

Connie could almost hear all the questions surging through her mind – *How could you keep this a secret? Why did she die? How old was she?* She'd tried to answer them already, but the right words kept evading her.

'Yes, she is. It's a private place for us to grieve.' *For me to grieve*, Connie thought, knowing Ray hadn't grieved at all. At least not for the same reasons as her.

'But you made it so only *two* of you were allowed to be sad, Mum,' Kate shot back. 'As far as anyone else was concerned, this poor little girl might as well have not existed. That's a lot of mourning for me to catch up on.'

'I know and I'm so deeply sorry. None of this has been fair on you, Kate...' Connie trailed off, her eyes snagging on the bit of what seemed to be fabric hidden in the dirt. 'Your father and I... we were so young and...' She stopped, still finding it hard to accept how badly Ray had treated her over the years, and in turn, Kate. At the time, she hadn't known it was wrong, how she'd been bullied and shamed and controlled by him. It was all she'd known, how he'd always been. *Ray's way.*

And even though he was dead and buried, his actions were about to cause yet more pain.

'Look, love,' Connie continued, reaching out to take her daughter's hands. 'This isn't going to be an easy thing to hear, and I wanted to sit all of you down together but... but it's about your dad's will. I saw the executors recently and—'

'He's not my dad,' Kate said quietly, pulling her hands away.

Connie sighed, knowing if she didn't get this out now, she never would. 'And I'm afraid that's how Ray saw things, too,' she continued. 'I'm so sorry, darling, but he didn't leave anything or make any provision for you in his will. That doesn't mean to say he didn't love you. I didn't want you to find out through a cold solicitor's letter, and... and I'm going to give you my share of the farm proceeds as well as making sure that...'

She trailed off, seeing the shocked and hurt expression sweep over Kate's face. Unable to bear witnessing her daughter feel yet another blow, she lowered her eyes to the grave, hugging her arms around her body as she waited for the news to sink in.

What *was* that poking out of the ground?

Connie suddenly dropped to her knees. She was aware of Kate saying something as her fingers pushed through the dirt – her daughter's voice getting louder and angrier above her – but for now, she was more focused on was whatever was buried right on top of her baby's grave.

Panting, Connie tugged at the fabric – the *crocheted* fabric. As she pulled hard, the soil on top dislodged, falling from the weave of the cream and green wool – the wool she remembered threading between her fingers on those long, lonely nights.

As her heart raced, she was vaguely aware of Kate going back down the steps to the lodge, leaving a trail of disbelief as she absorbed the news. Connie knelt, staring at the blanket she'd made for Lily all those years ago. It was partly burnt and charred, and covered in mud and blood, but she still pressed it against her face. Still sobbed for everything that had happened.

Someone must have put it there recently. Someone who *knew*.

She got to her feet, still clutching the blanket. 'Kate, *wait!* Come back!' she called out, but Kate didn't even turn around as she ran down the bank. 'Please... let me explain. I want to talk...' Connie watched as her daughter disappeared around the side of the lodge towards the drive and out of sight.

For a while, she stood quite still, her laboured breathing the only sound, and her hands hanging limply by her sides. Then she placed the blanket on the bench near the grave – the bench that Ray had built for her to sit on and contemplate.

To think about what you've done... he'd said to her when he'd banged in the last nail. He might as well have been nailing her to a cross.

As she stood staring out across the treetops, Connie lifted her chin towards the sky and hugged herself again, standing on the edge of the bank. Above the trees, she saw birds and wispy clouds moving fast against the azure backdrop. She felt the whip of the breeze against her face, cooling her cheeks where her tears were streaming.

Then she let out a roar... the sound she'd been holding on to for what seemed like her entire life. All the anger and frustration and regret spewing out of her as she screamed until her throat burnt. Her voice echoed through the forest, and it seemed as though all the wildlife in the area scampered and flapped and scurried away from the dreadful noise as she wailed out her pain.

And then, when she had nothing left inside, she dropped to her knees again, frantically pushing her fingers into the dirt... scooping out handfuls of earth, feeling it work up her fingernails as she dug out fistful after fistful of soil, her vision blurry from the tears as they fell onto her baby's grave.

Visions of that night flashed through her mind – the gash on her cheek, the pain in her forearm from the broken bone, her mind drifting in and out of consciousness from the blow to her head, the baby crying... Ray's anger echoing around her. Then later, back at the lodge, him breaking the terrible news to her about Lily, how they must never say a word to anyone, *ever*, about what had happened, that he was protecting *her* because she'd spend the rest of her life in prison if they so much as told a soul about what had happened. Together, he promised, they would keep their secret safe for as long as they both lived.

But she knew now that Ray was only protecting himself.

Connie's phone pinged. She felt it vibrate in the back pocket of her trousers. For a moment, the spell was broken – her frantic breathing the only sound she could hear as she knelt over the small grave. Then another text pinged onto her phone.

Stopping what she was doing, she pulled it from her pocket.

I've found Fraser down at the loch

the first text from Kate read.

Rather, I've found his empty wheelchair

read the second.

FORTY-SIX

KATE

The loch was deserted. And that was a good thing as far as Kate was concerned, because there was no one around to get caught up in the shrapnel that would result from the explosion brewing within her. It had been building for years. *Decades.*

'Happy fucking families,' she said to herself, kicking the shingle on the pebbly shore. After texting her mother, she slipped her phone back into her pocket, picturing the Hunter family enjoying themselves here over the years, holidaying in the tranquillity and scenery of Glengalloch.

She stared out across the glassy surface of Loch Muir. A small dinghy cut across the loch in the distance, heading away from where she was standing. It was almost out of sight – just an orange dot, a widening ripple left in its wake.

Kate bent down and picked up a flat piece of shale, turning it over in her hands, marvelling at how it had formed over millions of years in the water. Each layer told a story – similar to the layers of her family and the secrets hidden within.

She now realised that she'd grown up with a very different life story to the others – as a *half*-sister – having been spun a web of lies about her past. She drew back her arm and hurled the stone at the water, skimming it across the loch's surface. It bounced four times, once for each of the Hunter girls, before disappearing beneath the depths. She'd lived her life not knowing who she was or where she'd come from. And it hurt like hell.

She walked further around the inlet, away from where she'd left the car in the parking area, mulling everything over in her mind. No, not mulling over – *wrestling with*. There had to be a way to release the pressure inside her. What had happened simply wasn't fair. Her childhood had been so very *very* different to that of her sisters that she didn't know where to begin with the feelings burning inside her. And unless her mother was true to her word, she hadn't even been left a penny in the will, had nothing to show for the damage caused, the lies told. For now, she lit a cigarette, pulling the packet from her jacket pocket. That had shocked them all, she thought with a smirk. Her smoking.

It had only taken a few minutes to drive down here from the lodge, and she expected her mother to arrive at any moment, fuelled by the contents of the message she'd just sent to her, the thought of Fraser's empty wheelchair by the edge of the water spurring her on.

That in itself conjured up story enough – a frail and bitter old man, sick of relying on others to get by. Perhaps he'd managed to crawl into the water, paddling out until he was exhausted and couldn't make it back to shore. Or maybe he'd dosed up on his medication, crunching his way through a bottle of sleeping tablets before taking a swim. Or it could be that the icy cold water had done for him, a heart attack with no one around to save him.

But it was none of those things.

The others had gone out looking for him, for her father – her *biological* father. Because she now knew that's who he was – her dad. *Fraser*. Not that Connie had any inkling she knew

this, though the way she'd found out yesterday was still smart-
ing, compounded by the shock that she'd been excluded from
Ray's will.

'Fuck them all,' she said, a smile twisting her lips as she
sucked on her cigarette.

She wondered about her sisters – her *half*-sisters, Darby
and Bea. They suddenly felt like strangers. If she was forced
to re-evaluate herself and who she was, then they were caught
up in that net too. And Cameron, therefore, was her half-
brother. Funny how life worked, she thought, taking another
drag.

Then Adrian was on her mind – a once fit, fun and adoring
husband. There was no doubt he was a good dad, a provider,
competent and capable. But she'd noticed other things about
him – as though he didn't quite fit inside himself any more.
That aside, his belly was starting to hang over the top of his
jeans and there was that thinning patch of hair on the crown of
his head, plus his breath had smelt sour this morning from too
much beer last night. She didn't think he was much fun at all, if
she was perfectly honest.

'You could do better, Kate,' she said out loud as she reached
a craggy jut of land, the rocks rising high above the water.

She stopped for a moment, contemplating the climb up.
She'd got trainers on, at least. Would easily manage it. But she
wanted to finish her cigarette first. Enjoy the calm before the
inevitable storm.

Sitting down on a rock, she looked through the contacts list
on her phone. One name in particular made her cough as she
inhaled. *Other woman?* was the name assigned to the phone
number. A bitter smile crept across her face as she decided to
call whoever it was, but there was no signal down here, so she
clambered higher up the rocks.

Eventually, balanced precariously on a high ledge that
allowed her to see down into the next inlet along, one bar of

signal appeared on her phone. She jabbed the screen and it rang several times before a woman answered.

'Hello... who is this? Hello... *hello?*' a breathless voice said.

Kate hung up, staring at her phone in shock. She knew exactly who the person on the other end of the line had been and hearing it made her want another cigarette. She lit up, the smoke from her first drag billowing above her as it was carried away on the squally breeze. Another storm was approaching.

She felt like Queen of the Loch, standing so high up, her face tilted towards the sky, her feet planted firmly on the precarious patch of loose shale beneath her. She spread her arms wide and screamed until her lungs hurt, just as she'd heard her mother do when she'd left the lodge to come down here, her cries echoing through the forest.

'Kate!' she heard someone call out in the distance. She turned, squinting into the wind, catching sight of a figure far below, heading from the car park and across the uneven shore.

Connie.

Her mother's hand went up to her brow as she glanced one way along the shore then the other, scanning around. 'Kate!' she cried out again. 'Where are you?'

From up high, Kate watched her for a few more moments as she walked closer to the water, presumably looking for Fraser's empty wheelchair.

She wondered how they'd met, her parents. If they'd truly loved each other. Knowing her mother as she did, she wouldn't have put her down as the type to have an affair. But it had happened, clearly, because here she was – one of a pair of twins, who'd each been dealt very different fates.

'Up here, Mum!' she called back. At first, she wasn't sure if her mother had heard her because she didn't look round. 'I'm up on the rocks,' Kate yelled again, her voice carried away by the wind. The weather changed so quickly here. Suddenly, the shale loosened beneath her feet and she stumbled, her arms waving about as she teetered then regained her balance. Her heart pounded for a few seconds. Falling off the ledge wasn't in her plan.

'Kate... what are you doing up there?' Connie stopped and peered up the steep cliff where her daughter was perched, her jacket billowing in the wind. She jogged towards her and Kate felt the first few raindrops on her face. In the distance, at the other end of Loch Muir, the rain was already falling heavily – the misty sheet of drizzle heading their way like the folds of a net curtain.

'It's Fraser,' Kate called out, pointing down the other side of the rocky cliff. 'His wheelchair is down there,' she added as her mother stared up the dangerous route.

'Can you see him, Kate? Is he there too?'

'No, I can't see him.' She tucked strands of her hair back behind her ears as they whipped in front of her face, but the wind immediately set them loose again. 'His wheelchair, it's tipped on its side.'

'Oh heavens,' Connie said, looking distraught. 'Call for help, Kate. We need an ambulance. Something bad must have happened to him.'

'I don't have my phone,' Kate said, her hand resting on it in her jacket pocket. 'Do you have yours?'

Connie shook her head, patting herself down just to make sure. 'No, I left it in the car.'

'Can you climb up here, Mum? It's easy to get down the other side once you're up.' Kate peered down the sheer drop – an almost vertical cliff with the choppy waters below lapping at the semi-hidden rocks. 'We need to find him quickly. I see a house further along the inlet where we can phone for help.'

'Are you certain?' Connie called up. 'I... I swear I remember it being really dangerous the other side.'

Kate saw the unsure look on her mother's face. 'No, you're

mistaken. It's a little bay with a car park and a house and benches. Please... come up.'

Connie hesitated, looking puzzled. 'But I thought—'

'Mum, you're *wrong*. Fraser must have gone a different way to reach the bay. But we don't have time to argue about it or go around the other way! Please, *hurry*...'

Connie stared at the steep rocks, not knowing where to begin her climb. But she was lean and fit for her age, determined too, and once she got high enough, Kate would be able to reach her hand and help her to the small ledge where she stood.

'That's it, Mum, just keep hold of the rocks with both hands. Watch out for the loose bits.'

Connie leant forward and grabbed hold of the first jut of shale. The climb was easy to start with and had only taken Kate a couple of minutes, but then her joints were several decades younger. Her mother let out a few grunts and puffs as she slowly climbed, her slim fingers clawing onto the lichen-covered rocks.

'You're doing great, Mum,' Kate said. 'Not far and I'll be able to grab you. Then it's easy to get down to where Fraser's wheelchair is.' Kate made sure that Connie didn't see the smirk on her face as she stood watching, hands squarely on her hips as she waited for her mother to reach her.

'Oh!' Connie suddenly exclaimed, her left foot slipping on loose shale. Her knuckles were white, but she soon righted herself. 'God, I'm... I'm not sure this is a great idea, Kate... I'm a bit nervous. Maybe I should go back down and get my phone from the car. I'm just a liability up here.'

'No,' Kate barked, louder than she'd intended. 'No, keep going, Mum. There's no time to go back now, and you're nearly up.' As her mother drew closer, Kate thought how easy it would be to stamp on her fingers as she neared the top, catch sight of her horrified expression as she dropped back down – her eyes wide with fear, her mouth agape.

But chances were, she'd just slide to the bottom unscathed if she fell from this side.

No, she wanted her mother to come all the way up.

'Almost there,' Kate told her, squatting down so she could reach out to her. 'Just a bit further... that's it.'

'Grab my hand,' Connie huffed as she neared Kate, reaching out. Their fingertips brushed, just missing each other as Connie wobbled and slipped again, but then she righted herself and pushed on, locking hands with Kate. Finally, her mother was standing breathless beside her on the little ledge barely big enough for them both.

'Made it!' she said, her face earnest. Then her eyes darted behind Kate, and she looked at what lay beyond – a sheer drop onto the rocks and the water fifty feet below. 'I thought you said—'

But Connie's words were drowned out by a loud clap of thunder overhead as the rain began to pelt down.

FORTY-SEVEN

THEO

Theo was grateful the lodge wasn't locked, though he knew Connie always left a key under a pot of flowers by the door. He was tired of walking around, yelling out Fraser's name in the hope they'd find him. Anyway, it gave him time alone, which was what he needed. It felt as though the forest was closing in around him, the walls of the lodge trapping him. Everyone was acting weird, not to mention the way Kate was behaving. He just wanted to get out of this goddamn place and go back to London.

Up in his room, he opened his laptop and logged into the chat forum. He'd not checked it for a while, and since he'd been brave enough to kiss Finn in the garage, his emotions had been all over the place. Neither of them had said much to each other since – with Kate yelling out his name as she hunted for Scout spoiling the moment. Who knew where things might have gone if she'd not interrupted? As it played out, he and Finn had pulled apart when they'd heard her voice, bursting out laughing at Kate's screeching.

Theo! Theo, where are you? Where's Scout?

And since then, neither of them had had much of a chance

to talk about their encounter. Theo had liked it that Finn had invited him kayaking, but that had been scuppered by Fraser going missing. Now he was wondering if Finn was regretting it, or maybe he hadn't wanted to kiss him back in the first place, or, as his mind now convinced him, it hadn't even happened at all and he'd imagined the whole thing. He'd replayed it over and over so many times, he'd pretty much worn out the memory.

He tapped in his password and clicked on the notifications for his thread *How to get rid of a girl?* One new message.

> *weasler365*: U considered u might be gay, bruv? *laughing emoji* *shrugging emoji* just sayin. If so u in wrong place here *devil emoji*

Theo stared at the reply, his cheeks heating up. His eyes prickled with tears as the anger and shame welled inside him.

'What are you up to?' came the voice.

Theo whipped up his head, wiping his fist under his eyes when he saw Finn standing in the doorway. 'Not much.'

'All this fuss about Fraser, it's a panic about nothing, if you ask me.' Finn came into the room, taking off his baseball cap. 'He'll turn up.'

'Yeah,' Theo replied, trying to sound normal. Finn sat down beside him on the lower bunk, peering at his laptop. Theo tried to close the lid, but Finn put his hand on it and stopped him.

'Let's see,' he said. 'What are you into?'

'It's nothing, really.' Theo angled it away it so he couldn't see, but Finn was quick, and his face was already in front of it, his eyes flicking across the screen.

'What girl?' he asked. 'Is that you posting?'

Theo shook his head, but Finn had a grip on the computer now.

'*Th3ology* – that certainly looks like your username,' Finn said, giving him a nudge. 'What forum is this?'

'Why all the questions?' Theo asked, shrugging. 'It's nothing.'

'Because...' Finn hesitated, his cheeks colouring up.

At close range, Theo saw the smattering of blond hair on his jaw where he'd shaved it. More stubble than he had, which was nothing, and bristlier too.

'Because, you know, I like you.' Finn shrugged.

'You do?'

'Yeah, of course.' He appeared embarrassed, but not as much as Theo was squirming inside. 'I wouldn't have let you kiss me otherwise.'

So it *was* real.

Theo swallowed, almost choking on his tongue.

'Yeah, look. I'm sorry about that. You have a girlfriend. I shouldn't have done it.'

Finn let out a little snort – something between a laugh and a scoff. 'So tell me, who is this girl you've posted about?' He pointed at Theo's laptop. 'The one you want to get rid of.'

Jesus, Theo thought. He couldn't possibly tell anyone what he'd been posting about, let alone Finn. It was all just a stupid fantasy, and he should never have done it.

'She's no one. I've never even met her.' Theo couldn't help it, but his eyes flicked over to the photo of Finn's girlfriend on the chest of drawers. He stared at her. There was no doubt she was pretty and the sort of girl he imagined Finn would go for – slim, blonde, straight white teeth. But he'd resented her from the moment he'd first set eyes on her.

'*Her?*' Finn said, his tone incredulous, also looking over at the photograph.

Theo nodded.

'Wow.'

Theo stiffened when he felt Finn's arm slide around his back.

'You've got it all wrong, you know,' Finn said.

'She's your girlfriend, right?'

Finn laughed. 'I don't *have* a girlfriend. Never have. She's all for show, whoever "she" is. It's just a random photo I found online and printed out.'

'Really?' Theo's mind was all over the place. 'But why?'

'She's for my dad's benefit mainly. He's... how shall I put it? Old school. He'd never understand about me being gay, or who I really am.'

Theo laughed. 'Mine too.' He tapped the laptop. 'That's why I went on this forum. It's embarrassing but... but it's true I wanted advice about getting rid of a girl.' Theo glanced at the photo again and cleared his throat. 'I figured she was standing between me and my crush, and I wanted to know how I could get rid of her, to give me a better chance with... with you.' He gave Finn a smile. 'It seems silly now, and I guess I didn't word it very well. Though I seem to have stumbled on a forum filled with... I dunno what.'

'They look like a bunch of incels to me. You don't want to get caught up in all of that. Want me to delete your account for you?'

Theo frowned. Surely this was a trick to catch him out, to ridicule him, mock him and make fun of him like most people his age did. Get him to admit his feelings then plaster them all over Insta and Snapchat. But what if it wasn't – what if Finn was genuine and was actually into him? His emotions were all over the place.

'Look, I like you, Theo. Is that so hard to accept? The kids at my school – let's just say if you're not into sport, girls and getting into a Russell Group university to study law or medicine, then you're virtually an outcast. I only do all my activities to please Dad. Given the choice, I'd take up drums, join a band and maybe even think about art college or music school. You're cool, Theo. Not like the other lads I know. When we first met several years ago, I saw decent qualities in you. You're sensitive and creative, not afraid to do your own thing.'

Theo laughed and looked away, feeling his cheeks colour up again.

'Like when you kissed me.' Finn took hold of Theo's hand and gave it a squeeze. 'That was brave. You took a chance.'

Theo was still unsure if it was all a hoax. He wondered if Mia was outside the door recording the conversation, or worse, his dad.

'So there's no girlfriend to get rid of because she doesn't exist.' He reached over to the chest of drawers and turned the photo frame face down.

Theo related to that at least – he'd done similar to make the kids at school think he was straight, pretending to be interested in girls so they'd leave him alone. But that had only ever backfired.

Finn took hold of Theo's laptop and in a few clicks, his thread was erased and the account deleted. 'There, done. You don't need that shit in your life.'

'There's enough shit in it already.' Theo laughed and stood up, a lopsided grin on his face as he paced about the room, hands stuffed in his jeans pockets. 'Weird stuff's going down around here, you know. It's freaking me out a bit, if I'm honest.'

'I know what you mean,' Finn said. 'The adults... they're all acting super odd right now. Especially my mum.'

'Come with me,' Theo said, beckoning to Finn. 'There's something we should take a look at.'

The boys made easy work of clambering up the bank behind the lodge. No one else was back from the search yet, and Theo wanted to check it out while they had the chance.

'Oh crap,' he said when they reached the top, staring down at the muddy hole.

'What do you think happened?'

'You know we suspected there might be a grave up here?' Theo stood squarely, hands on hips, assessing things. 'Well, I think we were right.'

'Grim,' Finn said, looking down at the spot. 'Do you really think it's... you know, where the baby is buried?' He lowered his voice.

'Could be,' Theo said, feeling a bit queasy. 'It looks as though someone's been digging recently. But who and why?'

'What's that over there?' Finn asked, pointing to a nearby bench. The boys went over and found a muddy cream and green blanket draped over the wooden seat.

'I don't understand.' Theo picked it up. 'I hid this behind a loose slat under the veranda the other day. What the hell is it doing up here?'

'Looks like it's been buried,' Finn said, eyeing all the mud on it. 'Perhaps that's what was dug up here.' He scuffed at the dirt with his foot. 'Do you think it's to do with the baby who died?'

Theo shrugged. 'Maybe,' he said, remembering what Margie had said to him when she was drunk. He looked around the area, the skin on the back of his neck prickling as he thought back to when he'd hidden the blanket under the veranda. He recalled Cameron coming up the drive with the whisky, then Bea coming out to greet him. He'd not seen anyone else nearby, though he remembered hearing sounds in the forest just before Cameron arrived – twigs cracking underfoot, a stifled cough. Had someone been watching him? He shuddered at the thought.

'Well, I don't like it,' Finn said. 'We should probably put the blanket back on the bench and leave well alone. I don't want to upset Nan.'

'What about if we dig down a bit deeper, to see what's there?' Theo suggested, staring at the grave.

'What, you mean dig up a body? Is that even legal?' Finn shifted uncomfortably from one foot to the other.

'I'm not sure burying a baby in your back garden is very legal either.' Theo dropped to his knees and pushed his fingers into the dirt, wondering how deep he'd have to go. But then he stopped, glancing up at Finn. 'It's just that with finding that blanket up here, Margie's drunken ramblings about a dead baby and... and everything else, I just thought—'

'Hey, slow down,' Finn said, gripping Theo's shoulder.

'Sorry,' Theo said, brushing the mud off his hands. He shook his head. 'I'm being paranoid. I'm not making sense.'

'Too much weed?' Finn laughed. He glanced around to make sure they were alone. 'But I agree with you.' He crouched down, talking in a whisper. 'Things aren't right around here, especially with my mum. I can't explain it, but she doesn't seem like *Mum* this last day or so.'

Finn hesitated, looking back down to the lodge and the driveway beyond. Then, suddenly, he leant forward and started to dig. Theo joined in again and, after ten minutes, each of their hands grimy and muddy, their fingernails embedded with dirt, they stopped.

'Listen,' Finn said, tapping the earth. 'Does that sound like metal to you?'

Theo nodded. 'Though I thought coffins were made from wood.' After more scraping, the boys revealed the top of a metal box with handles on the side. 'What if we get cursed?'

'Exactly what I was thinking,' Finn said, wiping his brow with his forearm. 'This could be my aunt in here. It's so sad, but then the truth needs to come out.'

They looked at each other solemnly for a moment and, between them, the boys managed to grab a handle each and pull the metal box from the earth.

'It's galvanised steel,' Theo said, brushing the soil off its lid. 'Looks like an old toolbox.'

After gouging out the packed-in soil from around the hinges, they finally managed to prise open the lid. It creaked as they lifted it up, holding it at arm's length, not knowing what state the remains would be in or if they would smell or even be recognisable after all this time.

They were both silent for a few moments, staring inside the box. 'Oh my *God*,' Theo whispered eventually, just as the first big spots of rain began to fall.

FORTY-EIGHT

DARBY

'Theo,' Darby said as she came through the front door of the lodge with Scout plodding in behind her. 'There you are.' She was breathless and her hair was wet and mussed up from the rain. She wiped her shoes and slipped off her damp jacket.

Theo glanced up from the sofa. He gave her a small nod and a semi-smile.

'No sign of Fraser yet. Cameron is really worried now.' Darby went and sat down next to Theo and Scout followed her, dropping down on the rug in front of the fireplace. 'Is anyone else here?'

'Finn,' Theo replied. 'He's upstairs.'

That figured. Mia was looking after Charlie and they'd both gone off with Adrian and Travis, while Kate and Connie were together somewhere, she supposed, though she hadn't seen either of them for at least an hour or so. 'Cameron's calling the police,' she said. 'That's what your dad told me when I bumped into them on the way back. Given Fraser's vulnerabilities, I reckon that's wise. Bea's with him.'

Theo nodded. 'When are we going home, Darbs?'

Something tugged at Darby deep inside her chest. *Darbs...*

he'd never called her that before. She smiled. 'You fed up already?'

Theo shrugged. 'Just feel like going back to London, that's all. Things are weird around here now.'

'You're right... and I'm so sorry about that,' Darby said. 'I'm worried about Mum. And Kate. And Bea.' They both smiled, their eyes meeting for a second in a moment of mutual understanding. 'I'm just one big ball of worry.' She laughed nervously.

'But who worries about you?'

Had those words really come out of Theo's mouth? What she wanted to say was *Your dad... Travis worries about me*, but she wasn't certain that he did, not any more. When they'd met, things had happened so quickly – the attraction was fierce and intense. Soon after, she'd fallen pregnant with Charlie – much wanted now that he was here, but a baby hadn't been in her sights at the time. She remembered how she and Chris discussed having a family, what their children would look like, who they'd take after. She'd never imagined that her first child would be with someone else.

'God, I miss him...' Darby clapped a hand over her mouth.

Theo stared at her for a moment, his eyes narrowing in thought. 'You mean Chris?'

She bowed her head, shocked by his perception. 'Yes.' She felt ashamed for admitting it to Theo of all people, but the grief inside her was still gaping and raw. She'd not allowed herself time to heal, and that wasn't fair on Travis or Theo.

'I'm sorry about what happened to him. It must have been awful.'

'One minute I was with him, everything was normal and we were happy. The next minute he was gone. The last time I saw him was just before I left for work. We were making a shopping list for the weekend trip to the supermarket. It's crazy the things that stick with you. Chris wanted us to make sushi. He was jotting down all the ingredients we'd need. I've still got the list. We never got to make the sushi.'

'I'll make it with you,' Theo said, his fingers reaching out and curling around Darby's hand. 'I've never had it before.'

Darby stared at him, allowing her fingers to squeeze his back. For the first time since she'd known him, she wanted to hug him. Really squeeze him hard for being so kind. But she knew he'd be embarrassed, so she didn't.

'Thanks, I'd like that,' was all she said. Then she lifted up his hands. 'Muddy fingernails?' she laughed, nudging him.

'You didn't answer my question, though,' Theo continued. 'Who worries about you?'

'That's easy,' Darby replied. 'No one.' And that's when Theo reached over and wrapped his arms around her.

Darby carried three mugs back into the living room. 'Here you go, Finn,' she said, handing him his tea. 'And Theo, one sugar in yours.' She sat down again, still feeling the impression of Theo's arms around her. She'd appreciated his gesture more than he'd ever know. That hard, bad-boy exterior he put up was just a front – though for what, she wasn't yet sure.

'When will the others be back?' Finn asked.

'I don't know, but I expect they'll hang about at Fraser's place until the police come or there's news. Travis and Adrian were heading over to his when I came back.' She sipped her tea. 'Oh *Christ*...'

'What?' Theo asked.

'Your dad wanted me to have another look for his phone. It's why I came back in the first place. He asked me to... well...' She flicked a glance at Finn, knowing he wouldn't approve. 'He wondered if maybe I could have a look through Kate's stuff in case she'd forgotten that she had it.' Darby didn't want to say *stolen*, though it's what Travis had said. 'Maybe she tucked it away somewhere... by mistake, of course. Would you be able to have a quick scout around Kate's room, Finn?'

'If you want,' he said. 'But if she said she doesn't have it, then she doesn't have it. Mum never loses or forgets things like that.'

'I know, right? That's what's puzzling me. I'm certain I gave it to her when we were down at the loch. I swear on my life. And now she's claiming I didn't. It's not like her.'

'She's got a lot on her mind, I guess,' Finn said, standing up. 'But I'll go and have a look upstairs.'

'I can try to locate it, if you like,' Theo said quietly once Finn had left the room. He was turning his own phone over and over in his hand.

'You can do that?'

'Maybe. I know Dad's password for the tracking app,' he admitted. 'It's OK, he gave me his Apple ID once to get some apps for him on his regular phone. I'm assuming his work phone will be logged into the same account, but if it's not, we're stuffed.'

'Yes, do it,' Darby said. 'Though won't it just be offline like when your dad tried before?'

'Depends if it's still got battery or reception,' he said. 'Worth another shot, though.'

He tapped on his phone and entered the password. 'We're in!' he said, showing Darby the screen. 'Though nothing's coming up on the map yet,' he said, watching the app. 'It's still trying to locate it.'

They heard Finn's footsteps upstairs thumping about in the room Kate and Adrian were using, followed by the sound of him coming back down the stairs.

'Nah, nothing,' Theo said. 'I'll keep refreshing, though, in case.'

Darby nodded. 'Thanks for trying.'

'Couldn't find it,' Finn said, joining them again.

'Thanks for looking anyway,' Darby said. She was as baffled as Travis about what had happened to it.

'Wait!' Theo exclaimed, sitting bolt upright on the sofa. 'I think the app's picking something up, look!'

Darby and Finn huddled round Theo, watching as a blue dot resolved on an expanse of green on the map.

'Where is it?' Darby asked. 'Can you zoom out to give some context?'

They soon spotted a couple of familiar landmarks – Glengalloch village, Loch Muir, the main road leading to Ayr.

'It's not that far away, by the looks of it,' Darby said excitedly. 'Thank God for that. I bet Kate lost it on her way back from the loch and didn't want to admit it.'

'Mum wouldn't have done it on purpose,' Finn said, though Darby didn't press the matter about Kate denying having the phone in the first place.

'I'll take a few screenshots,' Theo said. 'In case it loses signal again.'

'Is it moving?' Finn asked. 'Like, has anyone got it or is it just static.'

'Looks like it's static,' Theo confirmed. 'It's about three or four miles away from here, I reckon. Though... it's not on the way back from the loch, look. It's *north* of the water.'

Indeed, Darby saw that the blue dot was located in a totally different direction to the route Kate would have taken to get back to the lodge. 'That's odd,' she said. 'But I don't care. We've found it! Send me a few screenshots of it close-up as well, Theo, and I'll take the car and go and fetch it back.'

'Wait, it's not that easy,' he said. 'It only gives an approximate location. If it's lost in the forest, you could be hunting for hours.'

'Great,' Darby said. 'That's my night sorted, then.'

Theo tapped on the screen a couple more times and suddenly the map changed to a satellite view of the actual physical geography. 'Wait... it's down a track in the forest, look.' He tweaked his fingers to zoom in. 'And there's some kind of a building there.'

'Could just be one of those derelict cottages,' Finn said.

'Plenty of those around here,' Darby replied. She was just relieved that Travis would be able to relax now his phone was found. Though that didn't explain how it had got to such a remote location. 'I bet someone found it and either took it home or dumped it when they realised it was locked, the cheeky buggers. Well, at least we know where to find it now. Right, I'm heading off.'

'I'll come with you,' Theo said.

'And me, too,' Finn added, following them both out with Scout trailing behind.

FORTY-NINE

BEA

'It was meant to be me helping you, not the other way around,' Cameron said, pacing about Fraser's furnished living room.

Since they'd got back from searching, Bea had opened all the downstairs curtains and was about to clear up the kitchen as a distraction, but Cameron had told her not to touch anything, just in case the police needed to look for evidence – though of what, she wasn't sure. 'They said an officer would be here soon,' he added with yet another glance out of the window.

'Let's hope so.'

'Dad can be difficult sometimes,' Cameron continued, sitting down on the old brown sofa. 'And who can blame him after what he's been through. But it's not as if he can get very far without help. He doesn't drive, and as for getting the wheel-chair over anything other than fairly even ground by himself – it's impossible. Either he's had an accident, or he's gone off with someone else, though I've no idea who.' He fell back in the sofa, letting out a frustrated sound as he covered his face. 'I've failed him, haven't I?' He looked at Bea.

'No... no, not at all. Look, he's probably got a friend to give him a lift somewhere or called a taxi. Or perhaps he's gone fishing or fancied a trip to town.'

'Dad doesn't have any friends,' Cameron replied. 'That's half the problem. He spends his days alone, while I do everything for him. Before she left him, that all fell to Mum. He's been through a string of carers who came in several times a day, but he hated strangers in the house, so that's when I stepped in. It's not a healthy way for him to live. I've suggested he get involved with groups and activities, but he won't hear of it. And as for painting again, he told me he'd be happy if his studio and everything in it burnt down.'

'It sounds like he might be really depressed.'

'You could be right. Dad's had a hard life, and things have got steadily worse over the years. I just want him to be happy.'

'Do you think he might... have hurt himself?' Bea didn't want to use the word *suicide*. It sounded too final, too shocking, too unbelievable.

Cameron shrugged. 'I don't know.'

'Does he have financial worries?' Bea asked, thinking that was enough to drive someone to end things. The thought of supporting herself and her baby was something she couldn't contemplate without spiralling into a pit of fear and gloom.

'I don't think so,' Cameron replied. 'He's not rich but he's always been comfortable, and he has a small pension and a couple of rental properties managed by an agent, so I don't think it's that. He gets by.'

'God, I hope the police hurry,' Bea said. She couldn't help fidgeting – her legs restless, her fingers tapping the arm of the sofa. She didn't want to reveal to Cameron just how concerned she felt for his father, or tell him that someone had been hanging around the lodge – with Mia having followed a stranger into the forest. This whole trip had taken a sinister turn.

She checked the time on her phone, a shudder pulsing

through her as she saw the two unread message notifications on her phone, reminded of what had happened at breakfast.

The two messages that Theo had sent, demanding to know who had received them.

There was no way she could possibly say it was her, put her hand up and confess everything... No *way*.

Half an hour later and there was still no sign of the police. Cameron peered out of the window again, the rain now lashing down the small panes. 'This weather's not going to help things.'

While they were waiting, Bea glanced at her messages again, her finger hovering over the two notifications on her screen. She didn't want to open them, confirming that she'd been conned, though she had no idea why. All she knew was that Theo had sent the texts earlier, and it somehow appeared as though they'd come from Adrian's new number. What the hell was he playing at and, more importantly, what did he know?

'Oww,' she suddenly said, leaning forward and gripping her stomach.

'Bea, are you OK?'

'It's... it's just a cramp. I think that can happen in early pregnancy...' She trailed off, wincing at another wave of pain.

'You've gone really pale,' Cameron said, sitting down beside her.

Bea suddenly felt light-headed, and the room swam around her. Her heart began to thump and another surge of nausea swept through her.

'I... I think I need to lie down,' she said, easing herself back on the sofa. Cameron shifted along and put a cushion under her feet. 'I'm sorry to cause a fuss,' she said. 'I'll be OK in a moment.'

Cameron fetched her a glass of water then went back to the

window, watching out for the police, the others, or even Fraser in case he came back. But as time wore on, the situation was becoming more and more worrying.

As the pain gradually eased, Bea dozed off, but she was woken by the sound of her phone ringing. Startled awake, she stared at the screen – Louis's name was displayed. He was one of only a few people she'd sent her new number to after she'd got another phone.

Cameron whipped around. 'Is it about Dad?'

'No,' Bea said, dropping the phone onto her legs until it rang out. 'It's my ex.'

When it rang again, Bea sat up, clutching her head as another wave of dizziness hit. Against her better judgement, she answered the call.

'Hello, Bea?' Louis said. 'Are you there?'

It was noisy in the background, and he sounded as if he was on speaker.

'Yes, I'm here.'

'I'm in the car. Can you hear me OK?'

'Yes.'

Bea was aware of Cameron pacing about still, checking his phone for messages.

'I'm coming up to Scotland,' Louis said.

'What?' Bea stiffened.

'I'm coming to see you. We need to talk. I... I miss you, Bea.'

'No! No, please don't do that!' Bea leapt up off the sofa. That was the last thing she wanted, to face the man she still loved, the man she'd lost, the man who she was trying her hardest to get over. It would set her right back to the beginning. And then there was *him* – all of them together, here with her. It would be her worst nightmare playing out in front of her eyes.

'Please, Louis, I'm begging you don't come,' she said, cupping her hand over the speaker so Cameron didn't hear. 'I... I don't want you to. You don't understand. I was...' She was on the verge of telling him what had happened to her, how she'd become pregnant, why she was damaged and dirty and not worthy of anyone, let alone him, but, as had happened before, the words simply wouldn't come out. Of all the people in the world, she couldn't bear for Louis to think less of her, that she'd brought on the *terrible thing* herself.

And then she was back there, in Darby's house, Travis squashed beside her on the sofa, his hand on her thigh, Charlie babbling in the playpen in the next room...

She let out a sob, pressing the phone to her ear.

'Don't come, Louis, *please* don't come here.'

She was aware of him saying something down the line, insisting he was coming up, that he wanted to see her, but she couldn't take in his words. Her mind was a tangle of images from *that* night.

There'd been a knock at Travis and Darby's front door, for which she'd been grateful as it meant that Travis had had to get up to answer it. She'd taken the opportunity to get up too, go and check on Charlie, pick him up and use him as a human shield. What was she supposed to tell Darby – your partner was hitting on me?

'Hey, Adrian, this is a surprise, mate,' she'd heard Travis say. 'Come in out of the rain.'

She'd taken Charlie through into the little living room, balancing him on her hip. 'Adrian, hi, what are you doing here?' Kate hadn't mentioned anything to her about him being in London, though she knew he was sometimes down for work. It was an easy train ride from the Midlands. She'd never been so pleased to see him.

'Finished work early so thought I'd pop by on the off-chance and see my favourite nephew. Sorry I didn't call ahead.' Adrian had taken hold of Charlie's hand, making silly baby noises at him. Bea noticed his long black coat, his suit beneath, the purple-flecked tie, his battered leather briefcase. The rain highlighted the grey in his hair. 'Well, and you guys too, of course.' He laughed. 'I had a client near London Bridge and it's not far to get here.'

'Ah, mate,' Travis had said, looking pained. 'Darby's not here. I'm meeting her in town shortly. Bea's here to babysit.'

'Oh, shame,' Adrian had said. 'But don't let me keep you. I'll head back to Euston, then.'

'Don't be silly,' Bea had chipped in, grateful for his presence. 'Stay a while and keep me company. Charlie would love a play with Uncle Adrian.'

Don't be silly... words that had changed her life.

Bea didn't remember much else about the evening after Travis had left, or what happened after Adrian took off his coat, grabbed himself a glass of wine, started telling her about his day. As for recalling the *terrible thing* itself, she knew it began with his wet mouth on her neck, his fingers digging into her upper arms as she struggled. The stale smell of his breath. The roughness of his day-old stubble. The hair low down on his belly.

After he'd gone, as she tried to wash herself with a flannel in Darby's bathroom, sobbing over the basin, she remembered thinking, *I didn't say no... I didn't tell him to stop.* And her struggles and thrashing and crying had lessened once she'd realised it was futile. All she'd been able to do was screw up her eyes and wait until it was over.

'Bea, are you there?' came Louis's voice down the line. 'Bea... what did you say? The line broke up.'

'Yes... I'm still here,' she replied weakly. 'Oh, *Louis...*' she said, breaking down in tears.

'I'm not far, honey, hang on in there,' Louis told her. 'I'm so sorry about everything that happened between us... I love you and I just want us to be OK again. I'm driving like a madman. I'll be there in a couple of hours, I promise, and we can talk.'

After the line cut off, Bea sat perfectly still, staring at the two notifications from the earlier messages. She took a breath and tapped on them, knowing that she had to see what they said.

I know who you are...

I know what you've done...

The words sat beneath the equally cryptic conversation she believed she'd been having with Adrian, when he'd told her she had to use a different number to contact him. But, despite it being his profile picture, she now realised it *hadn't* been Adrian messaging her at all.

She'd only contacted him in the first place in the hope of sorting out this horrid mess. After what had happened that night, there was no way she could talk to Adrian about it face to face – she was too ashamed – and it had taken all her strength and resolve to even come on this trip in the first place, knowing *he'd* be here. And when she'd asked him in one of her previous messages if she should *do it*, what they'd been talking about before he apparently switched phones, he'd then replied that yes, she should. That she should go ahead with an abortion. She hated that she felt so unsure of herself that she'd even needed to consult him in the first place, but she'd felt so helpless. So *alone*.

But now she knew it wasn't Adrian at all. It had been Theo.

'I've been so *stupid*,' Bea whispered to Cameron, resting her head on his shoulder as a tear dribbled down her cheek, just at the same moment as a police car pulled onto the drive.

FIFTY

CONNIE

'I... I thought you said... that Fraser's wheelchair was down there?' Connie panted, pulling up the hood of her anorak as the rain pelted down, she and Kate huddling on the rocky ledge. Another clap of thunder rumbled over the loch, its accompanying flash lighting up the landscape only a second later.

'There's no way we can climb down there,' she continued, pointing at the dangerous descent. 'It's a fifty-foot sheer drop at least!' She hugged her free arm around her body as the wind whipped around them, the water churning beneath them as the gusts increased. 'It's far too dangerous to be up here,' she called out above the noise of the wind.

'I lied to you,' Kate said, her rain-soaked face blank and stern. 'And I don't care about Fraser, either.'

She pressed up close to Connie, the pair of them balanced precariously. Connie remembered many times telling her children not to climb up here, and she'd *known* it was dangerous the other side. Why had Kate insisted otherwise? Why hadn't she listened to her instincts, knowing it wasn't safe? She'd only been drawn up here by the promise of finding Fraser. The man didn't deserve to have anything bad happen to him. He'd been through enough. *And it's all my fault.*

'Why on earth lie to me? What's got into you, Kate? You made me climb all the way up here... for what?' Connie wiped the rain from her face with her sleeve.

A small smile crept across Kate's mouth. 'For no reason,' she admitted, pulling a packet of cigarettes from her pocket. It took a few goes to light one, the lighter blowing out the flame every time she clicked it. She cupped both her hands around her face and eventually took a deep drag. 'I guess sometimes people lie.'

'And what the hell's got into you with this smoking rubbish?'

'So many questions, Mum. Shouldn't *you* be the one doing the answering?'

Connie sighed, though there was no chance of it being heard above the howling of the wind. Her legs wobbled beneath her. 'I know, I *know*. And yes, I will. Ask me anything you want, darling, but do we have to do it up here? It's so exposed. I don't like it.' She suddenly shifted her left foot sideways to keep her balance. She'd never been good with heights, let alone ones where one wrong move could be fatal.

She turned cautiously, looking down at her feet to make sure she didn't step onto the loose bits of shale at the dangerous edge of the rocks, shuffling her way slowly back towards the route she'd taken to get up. She'd have to climb down backwards. 'I'm going to find the others. Come with me, Kate, before you have an accident. This is madness!' Her hair whipped in front of her face, strands of it having blown loose from her hood. She swiped it out of the way, unable to see properly.

'No,' Kate snapped, grabbing hold of Connie's arm and yanking her back. 'You're not going anywhere.'

Connie tried to get free from her daughter's grip, but didn't dare pull too hard in case she suddenly let go and she fell.

'*Please*, get off me, Kate. I want to go back.' Her voice wavered and her legs felt like jelly.

'Are you scared yet?'

'Of *course* I'm scared,' Connie said loudly to be heard above the wind and rain. 'And so should you be!'

'Mum!' Connie suddenly heard from below. 'What on earth are you two doing up there?'

Slowly, so she didn't overbalance, Connie twisted round to see Bea running down to the shore, coming from the direction of the parking area.

'*Bea...*' Connie called back, relief flooding through her. Perhaps she'd be able to talk some sense into Kate.

'The police are with Cameron now, so I thought I'd have one last look down here for Fraser before I head back to the lodge...' She stopped, panting and breathless, her hair flat against her head from the rain.

'It's OK, love, we're coming down,' Connie yelled back. She gave another tug on her arm, but Kate was holding on tight.

'Be careful,' Bea called up. 'It's so dangerous up there!' She shook her head, hands on hips, and Connie could just make out the worried scowl on her face.

'Let me go, Kate, please,' Connie said as calmly as she could muster. 'Let's go back to the lodge and you can ask me anything. *Please.*'

For a moment, Connie thought that Kate was going to release her – the look on her face softening for a second. Was she having some kind of breakdown? A psychotic episode? This behaviour was so far removed from the Kate she knew. But then her grip tightened around Connie's arm again and she chucked her cigarette butt into the choppy water beneath them, taking hold of both her arms now.

'You really want to sit me down, make me a cup of tea, and tell me another bunch of lies? You honestly think that you can erase how you've conned me – your entire family – for four decades and believe that everything will just go back to normal? You, Ray, Fraser... Do you know the damage and hurt you've all caused?'

'No, it's not like that—'

'Tell me what happened the night Lily died,' Kate spat through the rain. 'Tell me everything!' She gave her a sharp shove, making Connie stagger backwards, closer to the sheer drop below. Inky black water swirled over the jagged rocks jutting from the loch. No one would survive that fall.

'OK, OK,' Connie said, knowing she'd have to play this carefully. Something was wrong with Kate; it wasn't her fault... whatever it was, she'd get her the help she needed. She just had to get them both down safely first.

'Mum!' came another cry from Bea. 'Mum, if you don't come down, I'm coming up to get you.'

Connie raised a hand to halt Bea. The last thing she needed was another daughter up here. A *pregnant* daughter.

'Let's at least sit down, Kate,' Connie suggested. 'Then I'll tell you the exact events of that night.'

'No. Stay standing,' Kate barked at her.

'OK, *OK*... we'll do it your way.' Connie prayed that Bea had already sensed something was very wrong up here, that she'd have the good sense to call the police. Perhaps Adrian or Travis or one of the boys would appear soon, or maybe the police would follow Bea down here to search for Fraser.

'I was trying to escape from Ray,' Connie said in as soothing a voice as she could manage, though her heart was thumping beneath her anorak. 'I was fleeing with you and your sister, Lily. You were only a few days old, and I was trying to protect you both. Lily was younger than you by about fifteen minutes.'

Connie smiled in the hope it would soften Kate's hard expression. It didn't.

'We weren't good together, Ray and I. Things had gone so badly wrong. I don't know when it started, exactly, or how, but life had... it had soured. It was insidious, creeping up on us. We desperately wanted a family, but it wasn't happening.' Connie didn't feel it necessary to explain how Ray could hardly stand to look at her, how she'd known he'd been seeing someone else in Glengalloch, choosing to spend time in another woman's arms rather than hers. She wasn't stupid, though to this day, she had no idea who it was.

You've made your bed... she heard her mother's voice echoing in her head.

'Then, by chance, I met a man. A kind man. He was so talented. So funny. So thoughtful. And he saw me, Kate. Do you understand that? The few times we met up, Fraser really *saw* me as a whole woman, rather than just being invisible, a convenience.'

Kate let out a bitter laugh. 'I've been invisible my entire life,' she whispered through the rain. 'I get it.'

Good, I'm getting through to her.

'Then I fell pregnant by Fraser.' Connie winced at the choice of words – *fell*. Her eyes flicked down to the rocks below. She explained Ray's fury, how he'd kept her locked up in the lodge, refusing to let her see anyone or get medical help. How she thought she'd have to give birth alone. 'If it weren't for Margie finding me when she did, I doubt any of us would be here.'

She told Kate how Ray had always planned on taking the baby from her, abandoning it at a hospital or police station. *Punishment.*

'Bab*ies*, as it turned out,' Connie added. 'But I couldn't let him do that, Kate. I adored you both, you were my world, my reason for living. So one night at the lodge, when Ray was out getting drunk...' She missed out the part about him being with another woman. '... I packed up a few essentials in the Land Rover and carried you both out. Like now, it was sheeting down with rain, a terrible storm that night. I didn't have any car seats or any of that paraphernalia, but I knew I had to get away – just get us all in the Land Rover and drive. He was going to take you both away the next day.'

Connie felt Kate's grip loosen a little as her daughter absorbed what she was saying.

'I put you both on the back seat of the Land Rover. I thought it was the safest place. I remember the smell inside – it's funny the details you recall. This earthy, mossy, damp smell from the logs stacked up in the back. Ray had loaded them in earlier, and I didn't have time to get them out. He was planning on selling them to someone in the village, but he'd gone to the pub instead.'

'Mum!' came the screech from down below. 'Kate! Will you both come down!' Then she heard Bea's sob.

'Wait,' Connie called back. 'We'll be down soon. It's OK, Bea.'

She just needed to stall her while she gave Kate what she wanted. What she *deserved*.

'I wedged you both on the back seat with blankets as best I could, knowing I had to get out before he came back. You must understand, Kate, that I couldn't go to the police. I couldn't face the shame, the humiliation of what I'd done, and Ray would have either left me or made my life hell. *More* hell. I had no money, no job, nothing to my name. I didn't care if I had to sleep in the car with you both, or if I starved, but there was no way I was letting him take you from me.'

Kate made a sound at the back of her throat as she processed what her mother was telling her.

'I was driving too fast, but I was shaking so much. I could hardly see a thing out of the windscreen, it was raining so hard. I was only a couple of minutes from the lodge when it happened. Coming up the steep hill with the sharp bend on the way to Glengalloch. I took the corner too fast – *way* too fast to brake when I spotted someone walking along the side of the road. His face was a picture of horror, lit up by my headlights. It all happened so quickly, though seemed to be in slow motion, too. The image of him has never left me.'

Connie bowed her head, and she would have covered her face too had her hands been free. But Kate had a tight grip on them still.

'I tried to swerve, but it was too late. I hit Fraser hard, skittling him onto the verge. I smashed my head on the steering wheel as I ploughed into a tree, and it knocked me unconscious for a while. When I came round, I remember steam hissing out of the engine, everything still and quiet apart from the ringing sound in my ears. Then there was a small cry from the back of the Land Rover. I dragged myself out of the vehicle and limped around to the front, holding on to my arm. I didn't know it was broken at that point. Fraser was lying on the ground, his legs trapped under a wheel and part of his body crushed between my front bumper and the tree I'd hit.'

Tears were streaming down Connie's face, making the drop below not seem so terrifying now it was blurry beneath her. Perhaps a fitting punishment if she fell to her death.

'I... I dragged myself to the back of the Land Rover where I'd heard you crying, Kate. You'd dropped into the footwell, but you were OK. You were wriggling and screaming, so I scooped you up. Then...' The tears came hot and fast, and Connie was hardly able to talk between her sobs. 'Then I went around to the other side of the car to get Lily, but...' More sobs. 'But I couldn't get to her. She was buried under a pile of logs that had fallen through from the back on impact. The... the last thing I remember was dropping to the ground beside the vehicle. That's where Ray said he found me later, unconscious with you still in my arms.'

Another clap of thunder reverberated around them, seeming to make even the rocks shake. The rain and wind buffeted them, lashing in from the west.

'Mum, *Mum*... hang on, I'm coming up...' A panting, breathless voice shouting from below as Connie was vaguely aware of Bea getting closer. Then her hands appeared at the top of the climb, her fingers latching on to handholds, distracting Kate for a second, making her loosen her grip. Connie took her chance and pulled her arms sharply, twisting them free from Kate.

Almost.

'No!' Kate yelled, reaching out for her mother again. Instinctively, Connie stepped backwards so she wouldn't be caught, one foot slipping in the loose shingle near the sheer drop. Connie yelped and made a grab for Kate to steady herself, but all that did was overbalance them both as they struggled together at the edge of the rocks.

Everything happened in slow motion – just as when she'd ploughed into Fraser, Connie thought as she saw the panicked look on Kate's face.

It's OK, it's OK, I've got you... she wanted to say, but didn't. Because she knew she hadn't.

More scrambling as Bea hauled herself up on her hands and knees, breathless and screaming as she lunged at the pair of them.

Stop it! Stop it now!

Words floating around them. Screams, too. Ethereal. The rain... the slick rocks beneath her feet. Hands everywhere as they both thrashed and grabbed for one another, Kate yelling, their faces close.

It seemed to take forever, the fall.

Yet it can only have been a couple of seconds before she hit the rocks below.

When the world turned black.

'Oh my God, oh my *God*...' Bea screamed. She crawled across to the edge, peering over. Another scream as her fingers interlinked with those of the hand beside her, the pair of them perched precariously, shaking in the rain, as they stared down at the body.

Unable to believe their eyes.

She looked so peaceful. Her hair splayed out. Her legs bent sideways and one arm across her chest as though she was hugging herself. The water sloshing and swirling up to her waist as she lay on the semi-submerged rocks. Only a small amount of blood trickling from her mouth, her nose, the side of her head. Her mouth was slightly open.

'Oh my God, *Kate!*' Bea shrieked, frantically looking for a way down. Then she fumbled in her pocket, pulling out her phone with shaking hands as she dialled the emergency services.

Connie didn't move, still lying where she'd reached out, trying to save her daughter. It had all happened so quickly. Yet so painfully slowly, too, that she could recall every detail – each line on Kate's face visible, the scent of her fear as she realised what was happening, the earrings she was wearing, the hood of her coat billowing in the wind, her pale-pink nail polish. That last look she'd given her seeming to go on forever. Both of her twins taken from her.

FIFTY-ONE

DARBY

Darby drove to the loch as fast as she could. Bea had sounded frantic when she'd called just now, her words garbled and choked with tears, not to mention the line cutting in and out with the poor reception where she'd been at the derelict cottage. She'd tried to phone her back but couldn't get through. Theo was now trying to reach her as he sat in the back seat of her car, gripping on to the door with one hand as they lurched around the corners in the rain.

'Bea said something about Kate, about the police, about Mum...' Darby muttered for the twentieth time as she drove as fast as she dared on these roads. Travis's phone rattled about in the compartment by the gear stick, where she'd tucked it after they'd found it.

It had only taken Cameron a few minutes to arrive at the place where they'd located the phone from the tracking app – a derelict shack in the forest as they'd predicted – after Darby had finally got through to him, informing him what else, or rather *who* else, they'd found there. The only spot where she could get reception to call him was by a smashed window – the same spot where they'd found Travis's phone.

Darby's mind was reeling as she tried to piece together everything that had happened. She was still in shock from who and what they'd discovered when they'd reached the old cottage, and when Cameron had sped down the track, following her directions, he'd told her that his thoughts had been spinning as well. A derelict cottage in the forest certainly wasn't where he'd expected to find his father.

Now, Darby skidded to a stop in the car park at Loch Muir where Bea had begged her to come, noticing her mother's car was also parked there. Finn was following on behind with Cameron and, a moment later, they pulled up alongside.

'Wait here,' Darby directed at the passenger seat, before getting out and running off with the others. 'Bea said they were down by the water,' she called out. 'Something about rocks and… and a fall.' *Dear God, don't let Mum have hurt herself.* 'I couldn't hear her properly, but she was screaming something about a terrible accident.' She glanced at Theo as they ran, their feet crunching over the loose shingle as they approached the water.

'Help! *Help!*' she heard someone screaming. *Bea…*

'Oh my God,' Darby said breathlessly as she saw her younger sister and another figure perched fifty feet or so up on a ledge.

'Stay calm, Bea,' Cameron called up to them as they reached base of the rocks. 'We'll get you down.'

'It's Kate!' Bea screamed hysterically. 'She's… she's fallen onto the rocks… I can't get to her!' More wailing. 'I think she's… Oh *God*… Is the ambulance coming?' Even from down on the ground, Darby saw that her sister was deathly pale, her face contorted with worry.

'I can get up there,' Theo said, launching himself at the rocks.

'Me too,' Finn said, following closely behind. The boys were scaling up in no time.

Then Connie's face appeared over the ledge as she crawled closer to see who was down there.

'Mum, are you OK?' Darby called up, watching as Theo and Finn shinned easily up the rocks. 'What's going on?'

But her mother remained silent, staring down at them, her face also deathly pale, her eyes wide, paralysed by shock and fear.

Darby hugged herself as she watched Theo and Finn help Connie and then Bea slowly climb backwards down the rocks, not leaving their sides. Their gentle words and kind coaxing, the pair of them working as a team to make sure neither of them slipped or fell, gave Connie the confidence to make the descent, with Bea following close behind her. Cameron was halfway up the rocks, helping them down the last part, holding their hands as they reached the ground.

Both women stood side by side, hugging each other as they shook, their expressions shock and disbelief.

'*Mum, Bea*, thank God you're OK,' Darby said, wrapping her arms around them.

But Connie and Bea said nothing.

'Mum?' Darby held them at arm's length. 'What's happened? What's the matter?'

Connie staggered a couple of steps and Cameron grabbed her, supporting her as her legs buckled and she sat down on the wet shingle. She stared up at Darby, rain running down her face. A second later, Bea dropped down too.

'It's Kate... She... Oh my *God*...' Bea finally whispered. Then she broke down in tears, curling up as if she was in physical pain. 'She slipped and fell onto the rocks... She's... I think she might be... I can't bear it, but I think she's... I think she's dead.'

'*What?* But—'

'They're in shock and not making sense,' Cameron said quietly, halting Darby by shaking his head in a way that told her not to press it. 'We need to get them back to the car and warm them up.'

'Oh, *Kate*,' Connie whispered. 'Not my dear Katie... no, no, *no*...' She drew up her knees, burying her face as she sobbed.

'Mum, it's OK, don't worry, it's all going to be fine,' Darby said, crouching down and rubbing her back.

'*No*, you... you don't understand. You're not hearing me...' Connie protested, shaking her head, her breathing fast and shallow. The expression in her eyes was vacant as she stared out across the loch.

'Come on, Nan, let me help you up,' Finn said, scooping her up from behind. 'Can you walk a little?' He helped his grandmother to stand, and Bea followed suit, each of them unsteady.

'But *Kate*... there's no way she survived that fall, not without terrible injuries,' Bea cried, not taking her eyes off Darby as they trudged back to the car. 'Where's the ambulance? Oh *God*, it was so awful...' Bea stopped and turned, heading towards the rocks again. 'We need to go back, there might be some way that we can get to her and help—'

'Bea, I... I don't understand. I think you're in shock, not thinking straight,' Darby said, taking her arm and guiding her towards the car park again. She glanced at Cameron, concerned that her sister was getting too stressed. It wasn't healthy for her baby. 'Let's get you and Mum back home for some sweet tea and we can talk about everything,' Darby said, huddling close to warm her up. She was confused by what Bea was saying, but didn't want to upset her further, so thought humouring her was best for now.

'No!' Bea yelled, squirming from Darby's grip. 'You're not listening to me!' She started off, stumbling over the shingle as she ran back towards the rocks. Cameron went after her.

'I tried to save her, I swear I did,' Connie said, barely audible through her sobs. 'But... but I lost my grip on her and... *oh God*...' she wailed before breaking down in tears.

Cameron rejoined them, supporting Bea as she walked reluctantly beside him. Finn did his best to help Connie as they headed back towards the car park, the two women with their heads bent down, hardly able to hold up their own weight.

'You're safe, Mum, no one fell,' Darby said, trying to make sense of what they were both saying. She was about to tell them what had happened after Theo had found Travis's lost phone, how it had led them to finding a lot more than they'd expected, and that everything really *was* going to be OK, but a shrill voice called out from the edge of the car park, interrupting her.

'Mum! Bea!'

A figure trudged slowly towards them through the rain, a grey hoodie wrapped around her bedraggled and frail form.

Connie and Bea looked up, their pace slowing to a stop as they took in what they were seeing. Instinctively, they reached out for each other, clinging on as they stood there, soaking and shivering, their faces slick with rain and tears. For a few moments, they were completely frozen – unable to speak or move.

'Kate...?' Connie finally managed to whisper.

'Smash it in!' Darby had yelled at the boys earlier in the afternoon when they'd finally found the old shack. As soon as she'd seen Kate through the grimy glass, she knew time wasn't on their side.

Finn and Theo had made short work of shouldering the rickety old door until it gave, the pair of them hurling their bodies against it. The roof of the low building looked as though it could fall in at any moment, and the single, dingy room downstairs was thick with ivy and other plants that had invaded the wreck. The whole place was dark and musty and clearly hadn't been lived in for decades.

'Jesus Christ, Kate, what *happened* to you?' Darby dashed

over to her sister, who was sitting in wooden chair – her head flopped sideways and her hands bound behind her back. One ankle was taped to the chair leg, while it looked as though she'd worked the other foot free. Her mouth was sealed shut with tape and her hair was matted and sweaty, her eyes rolling in their sockets.

Carefully, Darby peeled away the tape, and Kate gasped, writhing and wriggling as Darby untied her hands. 'It's Fraser... he's over there...' Kate managed to say, indicating a dark corner. When Darby turned, she saw the old man sitting in his wheelchair, his head slumped forward, and his limbs also bound up.

'Who *did* this?' Darby asked, dropping to her knees to release Kate's ankle.

Once free, Kate stood up, but then wobbled and had to sit back down again. The smell of stale urine wafted up. 'If I told you...' she whispered, her voice barely audible, 'you'd never believe me.'

First things first, Darby thought, shaking and incredulous as she took in the gruesome scene. She gently untied Fraser's hands where they'd been taped to the arms of his wheelchair and eased off the tape stuck across his mouth. He seemed to be asleep or unconscious... at least that's all Darby hoped it was.

'Fraser, can you hear me?' she said, feeling his wrist for a pulse. It took a moment, but she found it – the weak, slow beat of his heart. 'How long has he been here, Kate?' she asked, turning to her sister, who was trying to stand again.

'I don't know exactly.' Kate rasped out a cough. 'I've lost track. Less time than me. She brought me here first.'

'She?' Theo asked. He'd already found his father's phone, lying beneath the broken window.

Finn was hugging his mum, burying his face in her shoulder. 'I thought you were out looking for Fraser with the others. I can't believe this has happened to you, Mum.'

Kate shook her head. 'You'll all think I'm crazy. Maybe I *am* crazy... but it was *me* who did this.' Her voice sounded hoarse and dry. 'I mean, it wasn't me, but it *was* me. She was identical. Looked just like me in every way. I think it was...' She shook her head, as if she was unable to trust her own mind.

'We need to call the police. And Cameron,' Darby said, unable to take in whatever Kate was saying. Perhaps she was delirious from dehydration or low blood sugar, but she wasn't making sense.

'I was driving back from the loch yesterday, taking Travis's phone back to him,' Kate continued. 'Then this car in front of me – it had pulled out of the sailing club before me – just stopped after a short way, blocking the entire road. And...' Kate trailed off, as though she couldn't believe her own words, let alone expect anyone else to. 'And then a woman got out and approached my car. It was *me*. Apart from her clothes, she was identical to me in every way. Even the same hair.'

'Jesus, Mum...' Finn said, glancing at Theo. 'That's crazy.'

'Cam, hi, it's Darby,' she'd said into her phone, leaning as close to the broken window as she could get to pick up the only patch of reception. 'I've found Fraser. Yes... yes, he's going to be OK, don't worry, but you need to get here as fast as you can.' She quickly gave him directions. 'And call for the police and an ambulance, too, in case I can't get through. Reception is bad here. I'll drop you a pin where we are. Hurry!'

Fraser stirred and moaned in his wheelchair, lifting his head and looking around.

'It's OK, help is on the way, Fraser,' Darby said, glancing between him and Kate. 'Boys, let's get them outside. I don't like being under this roof in the storm.'

Finn and Theo leapt into action, and, between them, they'd got Fraser and Kate in the car where it was warm and dry. Darby had some water in a bottle and offered it between them as they waited for the ambulance. Ten minutes later, Cameron's car had bumped down the track through the forest, pulling up beside Darby's. She felt a rush of cool, wet air as he pulled open the driver's door where she was sitting, her head resting on the steering wheel, exhausted and drained.

'Cam...' she said, getting out and reciprocating the brief squeeze he gave her. 'Your dad's in the back. I think he's going to be OK. He's confused and scared, but he's been talking. I've given him water.'

'You're an angel,' he said, opening the rear door and bending down to speak to his father, while Darby checked on Kate again.

The next few minutes had been a blur as the ambulance and a police car arrived, two uniformed officers getting out. They'd fired questions at her, which she answered as best she could, and they'd called for backup, sealing off the cottage with police tape. The paramedics had carefully removed Fraser from the back of Darby's car and got him into the ambulance on a stretcher, while another paramedic had crouched at the open car door to talk to Kate. And still the rain continued to fall, pelting down through the forest canopy above, the thunder rumbling in the distance.

'I need to get down to the loch,' Darby said to Cameron after she'd hung up from Bea's frantic call. 'Something's happened. It doesn't sound good.' Darby paced about, not knowing what to do.

'You can't go alone, Darby. I'll come too,' Cameron insisted. 'Then I'll head on to the hospital to see Dad. He's in safe hands for now.'

'What's going on?' Kate had asked her as she'd got back in the car. She'd refused to get checked out at the hospital, insisting she was fine.

'I don't know, Kate,' Darby had said, reaching across and taking hold of her sister's hands. 'I think there's been some kind of accident. Bea was hysterical on the phone just now. I need to get down to the loch.'

'What are we waiting for, then?' Kate had replied, giving her a concerned look. 'I don't like the sound of this one bit.'

'It really *is* me, Mum,' Kate said now as she embraced Connie and then Bea. 'I *promise*.'

'Oh, *darling*,' Connie said, sobbing with relief as she clung on to her daughter. 'I thought... I just don't get it... the fall, the rocks. But God, I'm just *so* glad to see you, that you're OK.'

'I... I don't understand either, but thank God you're here,' Bea said, hugging her sister hard. Then she winced, clutching her stomach as if she was in pain.

'Are you OK?' Darby asked Bea quietly, just as the emergency vehicles, their sirens blaring, arrived at the loch.

Bea shook her head. 'No, no I don't think I am.' She clung on to her sister, glancing down at her legs.

'Oh, Bea, you're bleeding.' At first, Darby thought she must have suffered an injury from her ordeal up on the rocks, but then she realised where the blood was coming from as it soaked down her pale jeans.

'I... I think I'm losing the baby,' she whimpered, allowing herself to drop down onto the shingle as she pawed at her thighs.

'It's OK, little Bea, the ambulance is here now...' Darby said, comforting her as best she could. Never had she felt so torn between who she should help first – her mother, who was sobbing in disbelief while clutching on to Kate as she tried to explain what had happened, or Bea, who was clearly losing her baby and needed urgent medical attention. Or, indeed, Kate, who had been through a terrible ordeal that no one yet quite understood.

As the news got back to Adrian and Travis, they rushed

down to the loch to help, with Mia and Charlie joining them soon after.

The whole group watched in virtual silence as the rescue operation unfurled in front of them – flashes of blue light from the emergency vehicles pulsing through the rain, first responders in brightly coloured protective gear swooping down to the loch as they conducted a breathtaking manoeuvre that involved ropes and climbing equipment.

The Hunter family stood together in the rain, witnessing the body being hauled up and over the rocky outcrop – proof that Connie and Bea hadn't imagined it, that someone had indeed fallen. Travis put his arm around Darby, pulling her close, while Theo and Finn comforted Connie. Mia made sure to keep Charlie safe and away from the scene, while Adrian, Darby noticed, kept glancing over at Bea as a paramedic led her to an ambulance, the blood still seeping through her clothing. Cameron, on Darby's insistence, had just left for the hospital to be with his father, while Darby held tightly on to Kate, never wanting to let go of her again.

Finally, the stretcher with its scarlet body bag strapped onto it was carried past them and up to the awaiting ambulance. The police officer in charge approached the group, a solemn look on her face. 'I'm so sorry about your loss,' she said, glancing between them all. Her eyes lingered on Kate, a frown joining the dots in her mind. 'Your twin sister?' she said, bowing her head briefly. 'I'm afraid she didn't survive the fall.'

FIFTY-TWO

KATE

The fire blazed in the hearth as Travis chucked in more logs. He and Theo had just brought in another basket from the wood store, trying to help the family in practical ways after the day's ordeal.

'This is the worst storm I've seen in a long while,' Connie said, making everyone fall silent as they thought about the deeper meaning behind her words.

'It'll pass,' Darby said, going around closing all the curtains. She rearranged the blanket over her mother, having just made another round of tea for everyone, while Mia took Charlie upstairs for a bath and story-time before putting him to bed. 'Just like everything passes in time.'

Kate was also wrapped up in a blanket on the sofa beside her mother, the rest of the family sitting around them. It was getting late and while no one felt in the mood for food particularly, Adrian had promised to pick something up on the way back from the hospital. For some reason, Bea had seemed reluctant for him to fetch her, but when she'd phoned Darby earlier saying she wasn't being kept in overnight, Adrian was already getting his coat on, insisting he'd give her a lift.

Kate rested her head back on a cushion. The exhaustion and trauma from her ordeal were only just hitting her. She'd been running on adrenaline since it had all happened, and only now felt safe enough to gradually let down her guard, surrounded by her family at last.

The two police detectives who had come up to the lodge earlier had been sympathetic but also incredulous about what she'd told them, and Kate had worried they'd think she'd made the entire story up. They'd admitted to never having heard a case like it before.

'So you're saying that the person who abducted and falsely imprisoned you was... *you?*' DC Wilkins had said – an officer with a kind face, late-thirties and the beginnings of a doughy beer paunch.

'It might as well have been me, yes,' Kate had replied, incredulous herself. 'She was my identical twin.'

She recounted to the officers how she'd left the sailing club to come back to the lodge, bringing Travis's phone with her, how she'd allowed another car to exit the car park first, which had then come to an abrupt stop a mile or so along the road, blocking her path. She took her time telling the story, to make sure she got it right.

'The woman driving got out and came up to my car and... when I saw her, it was like all my common sense left me. Imagine how you'd feel if your exact double approached you. I'd only recently learnt that I had a twin, but Mum told me that she'd died as a baby.' Kate shook her head as if she couldn't quite believe her own words.

'And what did this person say to you?' the other officer asked – DC Ross, a keen woman younger than Wilkins, dressed in a black Puffa jacket and dark sports trousers. Despite her age, she looked like she meant business – her sharp features, neatly cropped hair, the way she studied Kate's every move, however small. Her default setting seemed to be disbelief.

Kate touched her forehead as she thought. 'She said that there was no time to explain, but that I must come with her. That there'd been a family emergency and I was needed. I was cautious, especially when she wanted me to get in her car. But she was *me*... my exact double. It was just mad, but with the revelation about a twin sister this week, my mind was in overdrive. It didn't seem possible that she was still alive, but there she was, right in front of me. So, stupidly I now realise, I got in her car. I wanted to hear her story and... well, to be honest, I was terrified I'd never see her again if I didn't go with her. She took my keys and moved my car off the road and into a gateway, so it was out of sight, I now realise.'

'But there was no family emergency?' Wilkins asked.

'No. Not at that point anyway.' Kate shook her head. 'Little did I know, *I* was about to become one of the family emergencies that happened today. Anyway, we drove off, and of course there were so many questions – if she was my twin, how come I'd been told that she was dead, where had she been all this time, what had happened to her, who'd brought her up, where did she live? I was in total shock.'

'And what did she say?'

'She didn't answer at first. She was mainly silent, just telling me not to worry. Then we got to this derelict cottage in the forest. She said there was someone inside who urgently needed my help. She was so believable and insistent and... and while she was quite agitated, she also seemed *kind*. I wanted to help her. I wanted to get to know her.'

DC Ross made notes on her tablet, while DC Wilkins jotted a few things down. 'Of course, you'll all have to make official statements at the police station tomorrow, but while things are fresh, we need some basic information to kick-start the investigation.'

They all nodded, Kate's fingers entwined with her mother's

as they sat on the sofa. Travis had just got the fire going, and while the police spoke to Kate, Darby and Connie, the others had retreated upstairs at the officers' request.

'I think she'd been planning this whole thing for a while,' Kate revealed. 'She told me that she was called Sarah, though Mum said she'd called her Lily when she was born. Apparently, she'd been watching me. Watching *all* of us for ages. She knew everything about our family. She only told me this after she'd pulled out the knife and threatened to kill me.' Kate shuddered at the memory.

'God, that must have been absolutely terrifying for you,' Darby said, gripping Kate's hand tighter. 'And so creepy to think she'd been spying on us all for all that time.'

'I know,' Kate replied, glancing at her sister. 'She'd been lurking around here too, waiting to make her move. When she told me all this, I was so scared I could hardly breathe.' Kate stared into the fire as she replayed events in her mind.

'Get inside!' Sarah had screamed when they'd arrived at the derelict cottage, brandishing a hunting knife that she'd pulled from the front pocket of her hoodie.

'OK, *OK*,' Kate had said, raising her hands in surrender and backing towards the cottage from the car. 'Please... let's just stay calm, shall we?' she'd said, tripping on the step as she was forced inside. Her mind had been all over the place as her heart pummelled her ribcage.

'Sit down!' Sarah had yelled, pointing the knife at an old wooden chair.

'Please don't hurt me...' Kate had begged. 'What do you want? I thought you said someone needed my help?'

'Shut up with all the questions,' Sarah had barked, jabbing the knife in her direction.

Kate had done as she was told and sat down, taking in her surroundings in the dingy shack.

'No one will get hurt if you do what I say. But try anything on and I'll be after your family, too. Including your kids.'

Kate had nodded frantically.

'Take off your hoodie and shoes,' Sarah had barked at her, the knife only a foot or so away from her face. 'We're swapping clothes. It's time I stepped into your shoes, Kate Hunter. Literally.'

Kate had known that she meant business, and for those few seconds, she didn't think they looked anything alike. Her eyes were filled with bitterness and... and *sadness*.

'I said take them off!' Another jab from the knife and this time it poked Kate in the shoulder.

Slowly, Kate had done as she was told. It was as she'd been unzipping her fleece that the moment of opportunity came her way. Sarah had pulled her own top off then, dragging it up over her head, holding the knife between her knees for just a few seconds as she undressed.

Kate took a breath, shuddering at the memory.

'You're doing great,' DC Ross said. 'Are you able to continue?'

Kate nodded at the police. 'It all happened so fast,' she explained, watching as they made notes.

Then came the struggle, the fight between them as she'd fought back – punches, kicks, biting and shoving. The two of them had ended up on the floor, entwined in the dirt. *Foetal*, almost, she thought as she recalled how tightly bound together their bodies had been in the fight.

'I never expected it to turn out how it did,' Kate admitted. 'That she'd overcome me. She was strong, I'll give her that.'

But against the odds, despite her ordeal being tied up, she'd survived. It could have been *her* on up on those rocks, *her* who'd fallen into the loch – though of course she'd never have lured her mother up there in the first place. Her twin had got what was coming to her.

'After the struggle, she tied me up, taping my ankles and wrists to the chair. But what she didn't notice during the fight was that a phone had fallen out of a pocket – *Travis's* phone, it turned out. I managed to kick it away, hiding it under a pile of rubbish on the floor so she wouldn't spot it. I figured it was my only hope.

'It was an hour or two later when she came back to the cottage with Fraser, having lured him from his house with a fake family emergency, just like she did to me. The poor man, he was totally helpless as she dragged his wheelchair inside. Then she was demanding answers from him, wanting to know every detail about what had happened in her past, forcing him to admit he was our father. Even though he'd tried to put up a fight, she threatened him with the knife too. She tied him to his chair, blocking the wheels with old bricks so he couldn't move. The rage, it was seeping out of her as she yelled at him, blaming him for everything, for ruining her life. She was ranting about everyone lying to her, how she was sick of being left out, that she wanted what was rightly hers. I think she meant the inheritance. She was out for revenge.'

Kate paused for another breath, taking a sip of her tea. She wanted to make sure she got all the details straight for the police.

'After Sarah had left the cottage again, I promised Fraser that somehow, I'd get us out of there. The poor man wasn't in a good state. Finally, I managed to work one of my ankles free and tried to reach Travis's phone with my foot, but all I did was end up pushing it further away, closer to the window. Which, as it happens, was a good thing because there was a small patch of signal there that it must have connected to. That's how Theo located it. I didn't know what else to do. I was stuck in that chair.' Kate screwed up her eyes at the thought of it all.

'You're going great, Kate,' DC Ross said. 'In terms of backstory, what did Sarah reveal about herself? Where had she been living? And, importantly, how did she find your family?'

Kate turned to look at Darby, a pained expression on her face. 'Sarah told me it all started with Chris, Darby's late husband.'

FIFTY-THREE

KATE

'*What?*' Darby's eyes grew wide as she braced herself for a shock. 'Sarah knew *Chris*?'

'That's what she told me,' Kate replied, trying to find a way to break the news gently. She'd gone on to explain to the police how Chris's hobby had been researching his family history. He'd been building up Darby's side of the family tree, too, and had bought them both DNA testing kits to see if they could discover any living relatives they didn't know about. They found a few distant ones, but it also revealed a woman who showed up as Darby's first cousin. Curious, Chris had contacted her through the website.

'I didn't know about this particular match,' Darby told the officers. 'It's true my late husband was obsessed with family trees, but to be honest, it left me cold. And I was so busy with running the café that I never had time to show much of an interest. It was Chris who had access to the website, and I just provided the saliva for the test when he asked. I even joked that he need only bother telling me results if I was related to royalty or something equally as flippant.' Darby shook her head in disbelief. 'Sarah told you all this?'

Kate nodded. 'She did... almost relishing the details.' She paused, watching Darby's reaction. 'Anyway, this DNA match intrigued Chris because he knew neither of Darby's parents, Ray and Connie, had siblings. So there couldn't be any first cousins.'

Connie had let out a small whimper at this point, listening as the story unfolded.

'I wish he'd told me about it, or that I'd shown more of an interest,' Darby said.

'The upshot is,' Kate continued, 'that Chris agreed to meet up with Sarah. He was drawn in because she said she had some interesting information about relatives, as well as some old family photos to show him. She'd got Chris's attention. And so...' Kate trailed off.

'And so he drove a hundred miles to see her, right?' Darby said quietly.

'Yes, exactly,' Kate replied. 'Sarah told me she knew that Chris wasn't going to let it drop about her being such a close DNA match to you, Darby. But first cousins can also show up as half-siblings. The results overlap. And that was what had intrigued Chris. She said he'd been shocked when he first set eyes on her, not believing that she wasn't actually *me* because we looked so alike. He'd wondered if I was playing a practical joke on him. Of course, at that point, Sarah didn't want anyone else to find out about her. She had plans, after all.'

'But Chris died four years ago,' Darby said. 'Sarah knew about us for *that* long?'

Kate nodded. 'She said she registered on the DNA site a few years back to see if she could find her biological parents. Apparently, she'd had a terrible childhood growing up in the care system, had been mostly unemployed as an adult due to poor mental health, and had even...' Kate hung her head. '...even spent several stints in prison for theft and drug dealing. She'd been told that her mother had abandoned her on a park bench at birth. From the way she was talking, that was what had messed her up the most – that she was dumped like a piece of garbage. She was out for revenge.'

'I... don't believe this,' Connie interrupted, imploring the officers. '*None* of this is true. That's not what happened at all. Please, you've got to believe me.'

'It's OK, Mrs Hunter,' DC Wilkins reassured her. 'We'll take your statement shortly.' He gave her a weak smile, turning back to Kate.

'Darby, I'm so sorry...' Kate continued, 'but Sarah told me that, initially, she had no plans to hurt Chris.'

Darby gasped, letting out a sob as she covered her mouth.

'In fact,' Kate went on, 'she told me how she'd tried to get him onside, begged him not to tell anyone else about their meeting. She thought she could silence him by the promise of a share of the inheritance she believed would one day be due to her. She'd done her homework, after all, and knew what the family farm was worth.

'But when she realised that Chris's loyalty lay with the Hunter family, she suggested a walk along a river. "A chance to get to know each other" was what she told me. It was so scary listening to her. She was just blurting it all out, spewing out venom, waving the knife in my face.

'She and Chris ended up at a remote stretch of the river, with her pretending that she was excited to meet her long-lost family. She told me that she'd acted on impulse, but it was her *eyes* as she was telling me...'

Kate stared directly at the officers then, almost as if to mimic what she was describing.

'There was *nothing* inside them, just pure evil. She'd been so convincing, luring me into her car – I can easily believe how Chris fell for her charms. And she must have done the same to Mum, tempting her up onto those rocks. I can't explain it... she was this convincing actress, conning us both, but equally, she was dead inside, too.'

'Chris never told me about the DNA match,' Darby whispered, a tear rolling down her cheek. 'I just can't believe it. My *poor* husband. Maybe... maybe if I'd paid him more attention, got involved with his hobby, I'd have somehow seen through Sarah's scheming.' She reached for a tissue and blew her nose. 'He never even told me he was going to meet her. I remember it was a teacher training day at school, but the police later discovered that he didn't show up. They'd not thought much of it at school at the time, as it wasn't compulsory for his department.'

Kate kept quiet about what had happened next, not wanting to upset Darby any more than she already was – how Sarah had dropped back behind Chris and, when he was standing on the edge of the river, she'd hit him on the head with a rock. When he'd fallen into the river, unconscious, she'd stood and watched as he'd drowned, lying face down in the water.

'I never intended actually killing him,' Sarah had told Kate in the derelict cottage, her face showing no emotion. 'But he'd pissed me off with all this family tree stuff, going on and on about how he was going to tell the entire family. I was sick of hearing about your perfect lives when I had nothing.'

No, Kate decided that she'd reveal the gruesome details when she was alone with the detectives.

'There's more shocking news, I'm afraid,' Kate said, turning to her mother. 'It's about Dad.'

'Oh, God, *no*...' Connie said, bracing herself.

'I know he died from a heart attack, Mum, but did the cardiologist ask you about any unusual stress or shocks that Dad might have had before he passed away?' She knew how hard this was to hear.

'No... no, they didn't ask me anything like that.'

'As I've explained,' Kate continued, 'Sarah told me how she'd been watching the family for a long while, "getting to know us without us knowing her", was what she'd said. Once she had our names from Chris, we were all easy enough to locate online, to follow, to watch. She came snooping around your bungalow, Mum. It was when you were in the garden, apparently, that she crept inside.'

'*What?*' Connie's frown deepened in disbelief.

'I had plenty of time to think about all this while I was tied up in the cottage. Sarah told me the exact day that she'd been sniffing about your place. It was May bank holiday, and I was off work. The timings suggest that Dad had not long hung up from a video call with me and the kids when he saw her in your bungalow. So he *knew* for certain that I was at home a hundred and fifty miles away.'

'Oh dear God,' Connie whispered.

'Sarah told me that it wasn't long after she confronted him that he collapsed, clutching at his chest. She was telling me all this with a kind of twisted grin on her face, as though she was enjoying it. I'm so sorry, Mum.'

Connie covered her face with her hands as she processed the information. 'But Kate, we *buried* her. Ray and I, we buried your twin sister, Lily, here, in the forest. I've sat up there for countless hours over the times we've visited, saying prayers for her, talking to her, laying down flowers.'

Both the officers' attention turned swiftly to Connie.

'And... and I'll face whatever charges or punishments come my way for that,' she said solemnly. 'But I swear on my life, I had no idea about any of this. I truly believed that my darling daughter was killed in the car accident when she was a baby. It was Ray who'd insisted I had to keep quiet about it, that I mustn't breathe a word. He told me that I'd have Kate taken away from me, too.'

'Actually,' came a voice from the doorway leading to the stairs, 'you didn't bury anyone.'

They all swung around to see Theo and Finn standing

there, their cheeks burning scarlet, indicating that they'd been eavesdropping.

'I don't want to see you get into trouble, Nan,' Finn said, approaching the officers. 'But that grave...' He glanced at Theo, who gave him a nod, encouraging him to continue. 'There was nothing in it. It was just an empty metal box. There *is* no grave or dead baby, Nan.'

Connie gasped. 'Oh my God...' She took a moment to process what it meant. 'It's true that... I never actually saw Lily again after the accident. Ray and I buried the casket together, but *he* was the one who rescued her from the aftermath of the accident, lowered her makeshift coffin into the ground. I wanted to remember her the way she was. Perfect and beautiful.'

'It's OK, Mum,' Darby said, edging closer and giving her a hug. 'You're not to blame for any of this.' Then she turned to the boys. 'Get Mum a shot of something strong from the kitchen, would you? I think she needs something to take the edge off.'

And that was when Kate noticed Darby's gaze drop down to Theo and Finn's hands – their fingers interlinked as they headed off to the kitchen to fetch a drink.

FIFTY-FOUR

CONNIE

'Bea's back,' Connie said an hour after the police had left. 'I just heard a car pull up.' She'd dozed off on the sofa for twenty minutes, the whisky having calmed her nerves a little, feeling exhausted after all the questions. The officers had asked the family to come to the station tomorrow to make formal statements, but for now, they'd agreed them to let them have the night to rest and recuperate after a traumatic day. Travis was stoking the fire, while Darby had opened a much-needed bottle of wine.

Sure enough, the door opened, and Bea came in, followed by Adrian. She was holding a paper prescription bag containing medication and she looked pale, an empty expression on her face.

'Oh, *Bea*, darling,' Darby said, going over to hug her. 'I'm so sorry you lost the baby.'

Connie held open her arms, hugging her daughter when she came over to the sofa. What they'd all been through today was... *unthinkable*. Yet, that's all she could do, play out Sarah's – *Lily's* – final moments over and over in her mind as she'd plummeted to her death. The daughter she'd believed had died at birth –

and now she'd lost her twice. She hadn't ever got over the first loss, so how was she supposed to grieve all over again, having only known Lily was still alive for such a short time?

Had Ray *lied* to her? Had he known that her baby had survived the accident and abandoned her somewhere, like he'd originally threatened? But the more she went back over past events in her mind, the more she realised how implausible that would have been. There was no way he'd have had enough time that night – he'd barely left her side after the accident, making sure she didn't try to escape again. He was cursing and angry as hell as he'd paced drunkenly up and down the lodge, deciding what to do.

But *maybe*, Connie thought, taking another sip of her whisky, someone else had done it for him. And if so, who?

'It's OK, I'm fine,' Bea said in a voice that indicated she wasn't fine at all. She turned and glared at Adrian, who swiftly looked away, taking the two takeaway food bags he was holding into the kitchen. Travis went to help him unpack it. The smell of curry soon permeated the lodge.

The group sat around the table – with Connie and Kate managing to eat a little, but they soon retired back to the sofa, lying close to each other. 'I'm exhausted but I don't think I'll be able to sleep tonight,' Connie said to Kate.

'Me neither,' Kate replied, taking her mother's hand. 'It's all so... *awful* about Sarah, her pretending to be me, conning you all while Fraser and I were tied up. She got away with it for twenty-four hours before Darby found me. I just can't process it – but I'm so happy to finally be with my family. I honestly never thought I'd see you again.'

Connie squeezed her fingers, knowing exactly what she meant. She'd felt the same as she'd teetered on the rocks in the lashing rain, knowing it would either be her or her daughter who fell to their death.

'I tried to save her, I swear,' Connie whispered, feeling

Kate's grip on her hand tighten. 'And I want you to know, darling...' She lowered her voice to a whisper so the others couldn't hear. 'There's no way you're being written out of Ray's will. I'm giving you my share. The farm sold for an awful lot of money, and you're equally as entitled to it as the others.' *If not more entitled, after how things were for you as a child*, she thought.

'Oh... *Mu-um*,' Kate replied, seeming to relish saying her name, the way she drew it out. 'I appreciate that more than you'll ever know. Thank you.'

Connie noticed the corner of her daughter's mouth curl up by a flicker as she glanced over at her sisters, praying it would go some way to making her feel more wanted, more a valued part of the Hunter clan.

Suddenly, a shrill ringtone got everyone's attention.

'Hello...' Bea said, quickly answering her phone. '*Louis...*' she said, talking in a low voice. 'Yes... I'm doing alright, thanks. Yes, I'm back at Kirk View now... OK, please drive carefully on these narrow roads, it's a horrid night out.'

'Everything OK?' Darby asked once she'd hung up.

Bea nodded. 'It was Louis. I called him from the hospital to... to tell him what had happened.' Again, she glanced over at Adrian, placing a hand on her stomach. 'He phoned me earlier to say he was driving up from London. He's nearly here now.' She stared down at her phone, turning it over and over in her hands, something else clearly playing on her mind.

She looked over to where Adrian was still sitting at the table. Then, slowly, she walked over, looming right above him as she dialled a number on her phone. He frowned up at her, uncomfortable from her proximity.

'Hello, yes, please put me through to the police. I... I want to report a rape.' Bea almost choked on the words, but she stood her ground, her head held high as she spoke.

Several gasps echoed around the lodge, then the sudden loud scrape of chair legs as Adrian quickly leapt up.

'Yes, it happened to me,' Bea said down the line, steadying her wavering voice. 'Several months ago... I... I was raped by a family member, my sister's husband.' She shot a sad look in Kate's direction. 'His name is Adrian Hunter, and I want to make an official report.' She then proceeded to give more details, but Connie was unable to hear what was said because of the commotion.

Adrian darted towards the front door, swearing loudly as he went, but Travis bolted in front of him, spreading his arms and blocking his exit.

'Not so quickly, mate,' Travis said, squaring up to him. 'I think you and I should go and sit down again, have a little chat while we wait for the police to arrive, don't you?'

'She's lying, for God's sake!' Adrian spat, glaring over at Bea as he tried to pull away from Travis's grip.

'Sit down!' Travis barked, grabbing him roughly. 'You might have been a part of this family a lot longer than me, but I've got more decency than you in my little toe. Scum like you make me sick.' Travis manhandled Adrian back to his seat, standing over him so he couldn't try anything on.

'Tell them, Kate! Tell them that I'd never do anything like that,' Adrian said, sounding as though he was on the brink of tears. 'You believe me, don't you? She's lying. It's all made up.'

Adrian looked over at his wife, his face pale, his expression one of desperation, but Kate said nothing. She remained on the sofa, turning to stroke Bea's hair, and Connie noticed that she had the flicker of a smile on her lips again.

During the evening, Connie drifted in and out of a broken sleep on the sofa, wanting to go up to bed, but too terrified to commit to a deeper sleep, knowing that she'd be tormented by nightmares. Finn, Mia and Theo had since taken themselves off to bed, the teens sticking together and providing the comfort they needed between them. She had no idea how they'd all get over what had happened and, until she unravelled everything in her own mind, Connie knew there was little chance of her helping anyone else come to terms with events.

Apart from the obvious – Lily's tragic fall – Connie couldn't stop thinking about how they'd all been taken in by her pretence, how none of them had realised that, for going on twenty-four hours, Kate hadn't been *Kate*.

Now she knew the truth, there'd been signs, of course. The smoking, the excessive drinking, the way Scout had ignored Lily... *Sarah*... she wasn't sure what to call her now.

But then again, with the upset of finding out that Ray, the man Kate had believed was her father for forty-two years, the man who had written her out of his will, was not actually her father, not to mention the discovery that she had a twin sister she'd known nothing about, Connie could equally believe it was enough to turn Kate's usually calm behaviour on its head.

They'd all been taken in by Sarah, including Adrian – the one person she'd have thought would have noticed his wife was an imposter. Though it transpired he'd been preoccupied with secrets of his own. Connie had already promised Bea the best legal representation available to help get him put away for a long time.

'I can't believe you didn't notice *something*...' Connie had overheard Kate say to Adrian earlier, before he'd gone to fetch Bea from hospital, and before the police had come to arrest him. 'You're telling me that you didn't realise that *I* wasn't *me*. For twenty-four hours! Shows how much attention you pay me.' She'd folded her arms tightly, scowling at him.

'It wasn't like that, Katie,' he'd replied, looking embarrassed, not realising Connie could hear their conversation. 'You believe what you want to see. If I'm honest, I sensed there'd been a

sudden change in you, that you were acting a bit out of character, but I figured it was because of what you'd found out about
your past. I honestly had no idea it wasn't you. Sarah was identical to you in every way, especially dressed in your clothes. I
truly had no clue.'

'Did you... did you sleep with her?'

'No! I mean, we shared a bed last night, but nothing
happened. I swear.' Kate had seemed satisfied enough, Connie
thought. Though something was still niggling at her. Something
she couldn't quite put her finger on.

'Darby,' Connie said now, propping herself up with cushions. Scout lumbered over, pacing about, restless and unsettled.
She reached out a hand to stroke him, but he whined, hanging
his head. 'Who do you think the woman at the funeral was – the
one who approached you and Adrian?' It was a piece of the
puzzle she didn't understand, though she now had her
suspicions.

But before Darby had a chance to reply, Kate interjected.
'It's obvious it was her. *Sarah*. She wanted to stir things up as
much as she could, turn us all against each other. The woman
had her eyes set on Dad's inheritance and was prepared to do
anything to get a piece of it.'

'I'm inclined to agree,' Darby said. 'Looking back, she was
the same height and build as you, Kate. With her dark suit, her
hat and veil, plus the face mask, she could have been anyone.'

'I agree,' Connie said quietly. It took all her effort to hold
back the tears. She had to stay strong for the family. 'Sarah was
a very troubled woman, and I only wish I'd known about her
long ago so that I could have got her the help she needed.'

The others chimed in, agreeing with the theory.

'The police dealing with Chris's death in London will need
to know about everything,' Darby said. 'I might finally get some
answers, some kind of closure.'

She pressed herself closer to Travis, who had his arm firmly around her, and for the first time since he'd come into her daughter's life, Connie saw what Darby valued in him. He was a protector, a pillar in a life that had been far from stable when they'd met. While he was the opposite in every way to Chris, Connie was familiar with the need for someone to lean on who was the antithesis of what had caused the pain in the first place. She didn't begrudge her daughter this.

She watched as they linked fingers, certain that, when he was out of hospital, Connie would give Fraser the support he needed, too, if he'd allow it. Nothing could heal the past or make his injuries better, but going forward, she hoped that perhaps, between them, they could regain something of what they'd shared all those years ago. She'd already decided that she was going to sell the bungalow, move up to Kirk View permanently.

Hunters' Castle, she thought to herself, giving a slow, imperceptible nod. It was where she needed to be.

Connie looked at each of her daughters in turn – Kate, Darby and Bea. Her precious girls. How proud she was of them all and, despite the burdens they each carried, she knew they were survivors, that in time, they'd be just fine. An invincible trio, just as they'd always been.

She smiled, even though it hurt inside. A part of her wished that Ray was still here to see how brave and perfect they were, how they'd dealt with the aftermath of their parents' joint wrongdoings, but another part was quietly content that he was gone, that he'd finally got what he'd deserved.

Kate leant forward to reach her glass of wine on the coffee table, the collar of her baggy sweater stretching open, exposing the soft hair at the nape of her neck with just a few loose tendrils floating free from her clip. Scout stared up at her, his lip curling slightly as he let out a growl.

Connie frowned, her body tensing as she sat up to get a better view.

There.

Something red on Kate's neck, just above her hairline.

Barely visible. Unless you knew what to look for.

Was *that* what had been bothering her all evening, niggling away – a mother's instinct?

A little strawberry birthmark, seeming so much smaller now she was an adult.

Exactly the same shape as the birthmark on the nape of Lily's neck.

Connie sat perfectly still, her eyes wide with disbelief as she watched her daughter... as she watched *all* of them discussing everything that had happened, an occasional smile here and there as they processed events. There was even talk of future plans, her daughters so happy to be safe and all together. Her heart pounded in her chest as Kate... *Lily*... raised her glass up high. Connie's mouth dropped open to speak, but nothing came out.

'To the Hunter clan!' Kate said, and the others echoed back the toast.

But Connie kept quiet, knowing that sometimes, it was best to say nothing at all.

EPILOGUE

MARGIE

News travelled fast in Glengalloch, especially after the emergency vehicles had sped through the village earlier, their blue lights flashing through the murky weather as they'd headed down to the loch. Margie had grilled various customers about what had happened, but everyone seemed to have a different story.

A young couple got into trouble on a boat... a suicide... a diving accident... a car went into the water... a body in the woods... a kidnapping...

It seemed the entire village was speculating.

Margie closed the shop and sat in her living room with a bottle of Klintoch whisky, knocking back an entire tumblerful in several glugs. She poured herself another measure before picking up the telephone. She knew Connie's phone number off by heart – surely *she'd* know what had happened, being nearer to the loch. From what she'd heard, it was where all the police activity had taken place.

But Connie wasn't picking up.

Margie knocked back her second drink then bundled herself up in her coat and boots, curiosity driving her on. There was only one way to find out what had happened, and that was to head down to Kirk View Lodge herself and see if anyone knew anything. Or to Hunters' Castle as Ray had called it, she thought, tying her headscarf under her chin. It was dark and blowing a gale outside, and the rain was still coming down hard. But Margie didn't care. She'd seen worse storms.

She missed him. Ray.

But she also hated how he'd manipulated her, how they'd both betrayed Connie. She'd been a good friend over the years and hadn't deserved to lose a child. And, despite what people thought about Margie – being a gossip, a telltale, a meddler – her lips had been tightly sealed ever since that awful night.

Almost.

She'd not been able to help herself when Fraser had wheeled himself into her shop all those years ago. She'd already spotted him with Connie by the memorial on the green, witnessed their secret kiss as she'd driven little Darby home from Brownies. And God, how she'd hated herself ever since, for blurting out to Fraser how Connie had given birth to twins a few years before, that one of them had died. She'd only wanted to find out if he *knew*, to gauge his reaction. Margie had seen the shock on Fraser's face plain as day, the realisation dawning on him, which had told her all she'd needed to know.

Those babies were his, and he'd had no idea about them.

Margie buttoned up her coat, preparing to face the storm. Finding out about the police presence earlier wasn't her only reason for visiting Connie at the lodge now.

No. The time had finally come to be honest with her. Now that Ray had gone, she needed to release the guilt that she'd lugged about for the last four decades. It was too heavy to bear any longer.

'It's nae wonder God hasn't blessed me with any bairns,' she muttered to herself as she stepped out into the storm. 'His punishment.'

Margie knew the roads around the village like the back of her hand – she'd been walking them her entire life. And similarly, these dark lanes leading down to the loch, knowing every inch of them as she tramped through the rain.

Though it never got any easier, the place where *it* had happened. The accident.

She'd have done anything he told her to back then. Ray. As a young, naive girl, she'd idolised him in a way she'd never thought possible to feel about a man. Sure, boys had come and gone in her life, mainly those she'd met working in the bar. But Ray had had a hold over her mind and body and, even though she knew it was wrong to sleep with her friend's husband, she couldn't help herself. She was reckless and stupid, and it had been a compulsion. A drug, but not an excuse, and she'd betrayed her friend in the most despicable way. But he'd had this way with her – just like she knew he'd had with Connie. What was it he'd called it? *Ray's way.*

But now it was time for Connie to know the truth – about *everything*. She deserved that much, however late in the day, after what she'd suffered.

Margie walked on, her boots making a splashing noise on the slick tarmac of the road. There was no footpath this far out of the village, and no street lighting either. Just the dark forest as she walked down the hill through the night.

And then came the bend. How many times had she passed it since it had happened? Hundreds, if not thousands of times over the years. But every time, she said a prayer for the little soul who'd lost her life here. Lily, Connie's youngest twin.

'Though she didn't lose her life, did she?' Margie muttered to herself as she passed the tree that Connie had ploughed into. *Don't look... Keep on walking...*

Margie had been with Ray that night – him leaving her in bed when he'd got up to go, warm and satisfied. But shortly after, he'd called her in a panic, begging her for help.

She'd have done anything for Ray. And indeed, she had.

'You need to get rid of the body for me. The baby... She didn't survive the crash. I can't deal with it. I have the Land Rover to clean up, to get hidden, Connie to look after. She's hit her head badly and she's in and out of consciousness,' he'd gabbled in a panic outside the lodge when she'd arrived. She'd never seen him so distraught, so *scared*. He wouldn't let her inside to see Connie.

He'd handed her a bundle of blankets. Lily limp inside.

Wide-eyed and willing to do anything for him, Margie had nodded solemnly.

She'd driven through the night with the wee mite on the passenger seat to a town south of the border. There was no plan, no cleverly thought-out way of disposing of the little thing's body. She could have thrown her in a river, or dumped her at the refuse site, but she figured that would lead to a more serious investigation if she was discovered. There'd be a murder investigation, for sure. No, an abandoned baby was far less suspicious. As though the mother, perhaps young and vulnerable, had at least tried to help it by leaving it to be found. They'd assume the poor baby hadn't survived the night.

Yes, that was what she would do.

The bench wasn't exactly in a park – more a green space located opposite a police station in a small town. She thought it was the kind of spot a young mother might choose. She peeked inside the blankets one last time, noticing how remarkably unscathed the baby appeared, as well as the strawberry birthmark on her neck, knowing then it was the younger of the twins. She was hit by a wave of sadness, remembering their birth, how she'd found Connie terrified and alone as she battled her labour pains. She'd tried to be a good friend. And she'd failed.

The area was deserted when Margie laid the bundle down on the wooden slats, not far from a street light. Someone would find her in the morning and alert the police. There'd be a couple of appeals in the local paper reporting the tragedy, urging the mother to come forward. But, of course, no one would.

Margie turned to go, giving one last look back at the bench from behind the cover of a hedge, crossing herself as she mumbled a prayer for the child's soul.

But wait... someone had stopped already – passers-by. A couple, bending down, unwrapping the baby.

Oh my God... she'd heard the woman gasp.

It's a baby... the man had exclaimed.

And then, as she was about to creep away, she heard a cry. The unmistakable squawk of a newborn. For a moment, Margie just stared at them, terrified and not knowing what to do.

She was *alive* – Lily, by some miracle, had survived the accident.

Had the baby been unconscious all this time? Or had Margie's prayer worked? She had no idea, but she crossed herself again, thanking God the mite had been spared as she watched the couple scoop up the baby and hurry over to the police station. She vowed, as she'd already promised, that she wouldn't tell a soul – including Connie and Ray. *Couldn't* tell a soul now that she was involved in a crime. For once, her lips would remain sealed.

Margie walked on down the lane, tightening her scarf around her head to shield herself from the rain. Her intentions were clear in her mind. She would confess everything to Connie – about her lengthy affair with Ray over the years, and, worse, how she'd colluded with him to dispose of poor little Lily. It wasn't to ease the guilt that she'd carried ever since that terrible night over forty years ago – how she'd known all this time that the twin with the birthmark had survived.

No. This was purely for Connie and would be delivered with the good intention that a full confession might go some way to helping her heal, to allow her to find peace. Perhaps even help locate her long-lost daughter.

As she marched on with the sound of the rain pelting around her, the huffing of her heavy breath, the rumbling of thunder in the distance, Margie didn't hear the car that sped around the corner behind her.

Didn't turn to see the cones of its headlights until it was too late.

Didn't even have time to react to the squeal of its brakes, the roar of the engine.

And she never knew that the driver of the vehicle was racing, as fast as he could, to get to Kirk View Lodge to make everything better, to take his beautiful girl in his arms and never let her go.

Because suddenly everything went black.

A LETTER FROM SAMANTHA

Dear Reader,

Thank you so much for reading *The Inheritance* – I sincerely hope you loved every page and enjoyed meeting the Hunter family and following their story. As ever, I'm working away on my next book (if you enjoy tense, family-based psychological thrillers, then this one's definitely for you!) and you can be kept up to date about my new releases and offers by clicking on the link below (don't worry – you can unsubscribe at any time).

www.bookouture.com/samantha-hayes

The death of a loved one stirs up many emotions and feelings in a family, with everyone experiencing their grief differently. The seed for this book began when I decided to examine the sorrow and heartache that naturally follows a bereavement, but also the legacy of what the deceased person left behind in the form of their inheritance.

Aside from the deep sadness surrounding their loss, the Hunter family are faced with practical considerations – and no one is more shocked than Connie when, seemingly from beyond the grave, her husband is still able exert power over her. I felt that exploring this in depth, having a dark secret from the past that refused to stay buried, would wreak havoc in the present. It seemed the perfect opportunity to turn up the heat on my characters.

Many thanks again for choosing *The Inheritance*. If you loved my book and have a moment to spare, it would be amazing if you could leave a quick review on Amazon. It makes such a difference for authors and is the perfect way to let other readers know what books you enjoyed. As I mentioned at the start of this letter, I'm busy penning my next psychological thriller, which I can't wait to share with you. Meantime, you can also follow me on my social media.

With warm wishes,

Sam x

facebook.com/samanthahayesauthor

twitter.com/samhayes

instagram.com/samanthahayes.author

ACKNOWLEDGEMENTS

This time, I'd like to say a huge thank you to Lucy Frederick, my clever and lovely editor. It's been an absolute pleasure working with you on this book during Jessie's leave. I can't tell you how much I appreciate your enthusiasm and brilliant input! And of course, a big wave to Jessie! Also, my sincere thanks and appreciation go to Sarah Hardy, Kim Nash, Noelle Holten and Jess Readett – the ace publicity team at Bookouture, who all do such an amazing job letting readers know about my books.

Big thanks and respect to Seán Costello (who I admire and fear equally!!) for his astute copy-editing, and thank you too, Becca Allen, for your proofreading and patience. The wonderful cover design is by the very talented Lisa Horton – thank you so much. And, as ever, a huge thank you to the entire team at Bookouture for everything you do.

Of course, sincere thanks are due to Oli Munson, my lovely agent, who, along with the team at A. M. Heath, looks after me so well.

And no acknowledgements would be complete without a HUGE thank you to you, the reader, as well as all the bloggers, reviewers and book lovers around the world who take the time to turn the pages and share their love of books. Thank you, thank you.

And with much love to my dear family, Ben, Polly and Lucy, Avril and Paul, Graham and Marina and Joe.

Sam xx

Printed in Great Britain
by Amazon